ISMAT CHUGHTAI was born in Badayun, India, in 1915. She was the first Muslim woman in India to gain both a BA and a degree in teaching.

In 1941 she wrote and published 'The Quilt' *('Lihaf')*, a story about a neglected housewife's erotic relationship with her maid. Charged with writing pornography, she underwent a trial in Lahore which lasted two years until the case was finally dropped. 'The Quilt' has been published in one of her several collections of short stories. Ismat Chughtai also wrote novellas, novels, plays and essays. With her husband, Shahid Latif, a film director, whom she married against her family's wishes in 1942, she produced and co-directed six films, and produced a further six independently after her husband's death.

The Crooked Line is her magnum opus, written in the 1940s; it remains one of the most important novels to date by a subcontinental woman writer.

She received a number of literary awards, the last being the prestigious Iqbal Award for Literature in 1989.

Ismat Chughtai died in Bombay in 1991.

TAHIRA NAQVI obtained an MA in psychology from Punjab University and an MA in English education from Western Connecticut State University, where she has been Adjunct Instructor of English since 1983.

She has translated a substantial body of work from the Urdu, including Ismat Chughtai's 'The Quilt' and many of her other stories. As well as writing her own fiction, Tahira Naqvi has contributed academic papers on socio-cultural themes, and on the challenges of translation.

S0-BFA-577

ISMAT CHUGHTAI

THE CROOKED LINE

(TERHI LAKIR)

Translated from the Urdu by
Tahira Naqvi

Heinemann

Translator's acknowledgements

I would like to thank Ritu Menon for making this project possible, and Seema Sawhney for allowing me to be with Ismat Apa again. Thanks also to Christine King, whose support, understanding and immense patience during the editing process meant much to me. I am grateful also to Professor Umar Memon for his timely and useful suggestions regarding the introduction to *The Crooked Line*. And special thanks to my husband Zafar, who, when all Urdu dictionaries failed me, came to my help.

Heinemann Educational Publishers
A Division of Heinemann Publishers (Oxford) Ltd
Halley Court, Jordan Hill, Oxford OX2 8EJ

Heinemann: A Division of Reed Publishing (USA) Inc.
361 Hanover Street, Portsmouth, NH 03801–3912, USA

Heinemann Educational Books (Nigeria) Ltd
PMB 5205, Ibadan
Heinemann Educational Boleswa
PO Box 10103, Village Post Office, Gaborone, Botswana

FLORENCE   PRAGUE   PARIS   MADRID
ATHENS   CHICAGO   MELBOURNE   JOHANNESBURG
AUCKLAND   SINGAPORE   TOKYO   SAO PAULO

First published in Urdu as *Terhi Lakir* in 1944
This translation © Tahira Naqvi 1995
First published by Heinemann Educational Publishers in 1995

Series Editor: Ranjana Sidhanta Ash

British Library Cataloguing in Publication Data
A catalogue record for this book in available from the British Library

Cover design by Touchpaper
Cover illustration by Gurminder Sikand

ISBN 0435 950 894

Phototypeset by CentraCet Limited, Cambridge
Printed and bound in Great Britain
by Cox & Wyman Ltd, Reading, Berkshire

95   96   97   98   99   10   9   8   7   6   5   4   3   2   1

*To those orphaned children whose parents
are imprisoned by life*

Introduction to *The Crooked Line*

In *The Crooked Line (Terhi Lakir)*, Ismat Chughtai, one of Urdu's boldest and most outspoken writers, cuts to the core of the female psyche, exposing it layer by layer in her searing, candid style as no other writer of the Indian subcontinent, male or female, has done before or since. She leaves out very little. Relationships of women with each other within the sphere of the extended family, the dynamics of a nascent female identity as it reveals itself in relationships between young girls grappling with sexual urges in an environment dominated by a female presence, relationships between women and men, the connection between women and their social and political milieu – there is hardly any aspect of female experience that Chughtai does not examine in *The Crooked Line*. The narrative, drawing heavily on Ismat Chughtai's own experiences, as does most of her other fiction, revolves around the experiences of Shamman, beginning with her birth as the tenth and youngest child in a middle-class Muslim family, where traditional mores and cultural constraints maintain an oppressive hold on the lives and behaviour of all its members. But the narrative functions only as a vehicle whereby Ismat Chughtai exposes the social–cultural conflicts and the psychosexual determinants that govern the development of female consciousness.

It is important to note that the subject of women's lives had often been taken up by Indian writers before Ismat Chughtai appeared on the scene. An example is Mirza Ruswa's *Umrao Jan Ada*, a classical Urdu work of the late 1800s in which the narrator/protagonist is a beautiful courtesan who is a gifted poet with a mind of her own. One of Urdu's earliest novels, *Nashtar (The Surgical Knife)*, written by Hasan Shah in 1790, centres on the life of Khanum Jan, a dancing girl who also appears to be well versed in the traditions of classical literature. Another massive, three-part novel, *Goodar ka Lal (A Jewel Among Rags)*, written in the 1920s by a woman who merely called herself Walida Afzal Ali (Mother of Afzal Ali), focuses on the value of education for women by drawing parallels between the lives of Mukhtar Dulhan who has little education and is doomed to failure until she breaks out of her conservative mould, and Mehr Jabin, who is well educated, sophisticated and progressive. In addition, there was the work by such women writers as Hijab Imtiaz Ali, who created romantic, melodramatic storylines and larger-than-life characters, but who did attempt to approach the subject of women's lives in a new and innovative manner. However, it was Ismat Chughtai who, fearlessly and without reserve, initiated the practice of looking at women's lives from a psychological standpoint. This brings me to the interesting parallels that one can see between 'The First Phase' in *The Crooked Line* and the section entitled 'The Formative Years: Childhood' in *The Second Sex*[1], Simone de Beauvoir's pioneering work on female sexuality which appeared in 1949, five years after Chughtai's novel. As a matter of fact, there are certain portions in Chughtai's novel that seem to be fictionalised prefigurations of de Beauvoir's description and analysis of childhood play-acting and fantasy; it seems as if Chughtai and de Beauvoir were drawing on a common source. In both works, feminine experience is explored from childhood through puberty and adolescence to womanhood, these being the stages in the development of a sense of self that finally results in an acceptance of sexual impulses and subsequently leads to the awareness of a sexual identity. In the first chapters of *The Crooked Line* the baby Shamman forms a strong attachment to her wet-nurse Unna; she fondles and caresses Unna and, later, after Unna is wrenched away from her she develops a dependence on her older sister Manjhu and feels intense jealousy when she has to share her with another child, in much the same way that de Beauvoir observes that the girl 'kisses, handles, and caresses ... in an aggressive way ... feels the same jealousy ... in similar behaviour patterns: rage, sulkiness ... and they resort to the same coquettish tricks to gain ... love ...' (de Beauvoir, p. 268). While playing with her doll, Shamman pretends to be the mother and, like de Beauvoir's girl, takes to 'dressing her up as she dreams of being coddled and dressed up herself ... [and] by means of compliments, and scoldings, through images and words, she learns the meaning of the terms pretty and homely ...' (de Beauvoir, p. 279). With unselfconscious ease and never losing her grip on the narrative technique, Chughtai actually reveals, bit by bit, the process that determines a woman's role in society, thereby bringing credence to de Beauvoir's claim that a woman 'is not born, but rather becomes, a woman' (de Beauvoir, p. 267).

In the early chapters of *The Crooked Line* we see how women, unempowered in a man's world and unable to govern their own destinies, develop a flawed and second-class mode of empowerment within the confines of their limitations and begin to oppress other women; it becomes apparent how some women, quite unselfconsciously, often naively, participate in the

oppression of women w/ the nature of muslim culture

Shamman sees culture as oppressing women, cutting down their capabilities, and re-establishing this oppression when the next generation.

perpetuation of the tradition of oppression, how they can cruelly cut down another female just as society cruelly cuts them down. One example is Shamman's oldest sister Bari Apa, who, widowed a few years after her marriage and having returned to her parents' house with two young children, has relinquished the joys of living in keeping with the demands of convention, 'had annihilated her femininity for the sake of her father's honour', even though she is still young. Frustrated sexually and emotionally, lacking proper status in society, weakened in her traditional role as wife and mother, she now seeks a scapegoat and finds it in the person of her youngest sister Shamman who, unlike her, seems to have no regard for any kind of convention.

However, Shamman's rebelliousness is not without cause. Taking us through some of the most brilliantly written pieces about childhood fixations and fantasies, Chughtai focuses on Shamman's emotional deprivation in a house filled with siblings, nannies, servants and a mother and father. These feelings, induced by her mother's aloofness and later heightened by her traumatic separation first from her wet-nurse Unna and then her older sister Manjhu, and the rejection she experiences at the hands of her oldest sister Bari Apa, convinces her that she is fated to remain unloved. Shamman's rebellion against all that is considered proper and 'nice' further complicates the situation. As a matter of fact, her birth is 'ill-timed'; with her early arrival she surprises and disappoints her mother whose 'longstanding desire to send for the English midwife came to naught'. And the 'howl' with which she makes her appearance puts fear into the hearts of her older sisters and others who happen to be around, and marks the first sign of mutinous behaviour. Bari Apa finds it easy to make Shamman the target of her own discontentment and sense of defeat in the face of unrelenting social standards. She badgers and torments her young sister, attempting at every step to draw comparisons between Shamman's ineptness and her own daughter Noori's superiority, continuing with Shamman's belittlement in mean and nasty ways until Shamman comes to hate her and, totally unsympathetic to Bari Apa's 'stifling of her own desires', she begins to think of her as a 'snake' and 'would not have minded at all if Bari Apa decided to sell herself'. Bari Apa in turn has been treated badly by her mother-in-law, who, when her son was living, used every opportunity to make her daughter-in-law as unhappy as she could, her efforts largely aimed at keeping her out of her son's bedroom. And so the cycle of oppression feeds on itself among all the females in this household.

In her effort to seek and define connections between culture and female experience, especially in the middle-class Muslim societies she often writes about, Chughtai incises and dissects custom and ritual with a keenly discerning eye, and for this reason her fiction can also be read as ethnography. Every ritual and every custom is decoded, in a wonderfully clever and seemingly artless manner, to reveal its psycho-social content: connotation is laid bare along with denotation. Wedding rituals are one example of the manner in which repressed female sexuality expresses itself vicariously. As young girls playing wedding games with their dolls, Shamman and Noori happen to be spectators at a wedding in the neighbourhood in which they come face to face with rituals and customs in an environment dominated by women. The only male present in this instance is the bridegroom. The shy bride is covered in *dupattas* and the groom, reticent and bashful, 'happily' licks *kheer* from her palm while 'the women tittered merrily at every lively ceremony imbued with innuendo' and 'Shamman too found herself in the grip of a strange longing' while 'Noori insisted that they go to the storage room and play the wedding game right away'. Later, young, unmarried girls are shooed away while 'like flies, women were glued to the windows and the chinks in the doors' during another ceremony in which 'a few, fun-loving females were taking active part'. Interestingly enough, all this time 'husbands and children waited impatiently at home'. Here, in this world, women undoubtedly reign supreme.

In another powerful scene which dramatically illustrates the rites of passage, Shamman and Noori, quite unselfconsciously and altogether by accident, wander into the realm of gender awareness. The rag doll on which the girls have been practising wedding rituals is threadbare and worn. At their request Bari Apa cuts out a nose from a cotton swatch to put on its face, makes fingers from a length of cord and attaches them to the doll's arm stumps, and further embellishes the doll by adding a long braid intertwined with a colourful ribbon. But something is missing. In the course of a game later the two girls secretly stuff the doll's vest with tiny cotton balls and they 'felt such shame, they couldn't even look at her'. The breasts turn the doll into 'a woman real and alive'. Unfortunately their secret is exposed, Bari Apa tears out the breasts and the vest and, in a gesture that graphically sums up the repression endured by young girls, stitches up the doll's shirt at the waist. But a lesson had been learnt. 'From that day on, they lost interest in the doll. To them it now looked like a bundle of rags with a triangular piece of cloth on its face instead of a nose, and cords dangling from the palms instead of fingers.' These lines mark the beginning of a new phase in Shamman's life.

Moving along in a narrative pattern somewhat akin to a *Jane Eyre* format, a novel which Shamman confesses 'affects her the most', the action shifts from Shamman's home to the school hostel where, like Jane, Shamman experiences deep friendships for the first time. But here the resemblance between Brontë's romance and Chughtai's novel grows dim. Chughtai's account of Shamman's life in school is a thorough, extremely frank and often blunt exploration of the different levels of friendship that exist between the girls; Rasul Fatima's endless and pitiful fawning and her secretive, nightly physical advances repel and sicken Shamman, but only a short time later Shamman herself experiences similar feelings for the beautiful Najma only to be rebuffed because Najma and Saadat, who happens to be Shamman's room-mate, are already bound in a jealously guarded relationship. Although bewildering and unfathomable, the strong sexual desires that govern these relationships cannot be disregarded either by the characters in the novel or by the reader. However, one must remember that Ismat Chughtai was not out to shock or titillate. As with her story 'Lihaf' ('The Quilt') she undertakes an intricate exposition of certain aspects of female sexual experience as an essential part of her narrative. She is not interested in polemics or in presenting weighty solutions; rather, she is interested in telling a story and telling it effectively, and it is essential to her story and the development of her character that she provide the reader with an account of Shamman's relationships as she matures and journeys towards womanhood, which she does without resorting to innuendo or awkward insinuation.

We next meet Shamman in college. Here, she comes face to face with feelings, both sexual and emotional in nature, that determine her new relationships in ways she had never imagined before. Motivated unconsciously by her intense need for a strong father figure, she develops powerful feelings for her friend Prema's father, a charismatic man who showers affection on Shamman, and mistaking these feelings for love Shamman suffers a terrible jolt. A year later she meets Iftikhar, the careless young freedom fighter who is worldlywise and cynical, and driven again by similar feelings heightened this time by a new sexual awareness, she is swept up by a maelstrom of deep and stirring emotions she cannot fully understand or accept. Clearly a sexual attraction exists between them but, conditioned to deny the force of such feelings, Shamman sublimates the emotions Iftikhar arouses in her, relegating her relationship with him to the realm of the platonic, the nonsexual. Next, overwhelmed by the physical attraction she experiences for her classmate Satil, she tries to justify it by attributing her sentiments to Satil's overpowering sensual overtures, going so far as to suggest that he is like a male prostitute who calmly waits for 'fruit to fall off a tree'. Unlike Alma, Shamman's rebellious, daring friend who finds herself embroiled in a relationship she later regrets deeply, Shamman refuses to succumb to her strong, passionate feelings for Iftikhar, nor does she allow her feelings for Satil to become apparent. In a society where women are not rewarded for craving independence, both Alma and Shamman are tragically doomed, and worse still, Shamman cannot feel loved. But, although her emotional machinery is rusty, making it nearly impossible for her to sustain a loving, physical relationship with a man, at college she does succeed in emerging from the shell of self-deprecation as she becomes aware of the 'hidden embers of rebellion and self-reliance' and is dazzled by the 'radiance' of this 'new Shamshad'. — people depending on her

Unfortunately, by the time she meets and marries Ronnie Taylor, an Irish army captain who is a friend of Alma's, the passionate side of her nature has been corroded by years of denial and disappointment. She has begun to feel she is a rock on which nothing will take root. Set against the turbulent times of India's struggle for independence from the British Raj, the romance between Ronnie and Shamman assumes larger meanings, not only for them but also for the reader. Breaking with tradition once more but lacking meaningful direction, Shamman finds herself struggling to stabilise a pitching boat that has been cast on uneven waters. She and Ronnie fight constantly. Their inability to come to terms with the differences in the 'colour of their skins' eventually shatters whatever hope there might have been for the relationship to develop and mature; like the British and their colonised subjects, who can no longer see eye to eye on anything and must end their relationship, Shamman and Ronnie too struggle to be free of each other. Analogous to the political tussle plaguing India, their struggle also suffers from doubts, confusion and despair and, like India, Shamman must grapple with the pain of rebirth and impending independence. She finally does achieve peace and independence, but, much like her nation in the throes of labour, not without a cost.

Stylistically, *The Crooked Line* provides a sampling of the many qualities that characterise Chughtai's short stories: an energetic and robust diction laced with unique examples of the *begumati zuban* (the speech patterns used specifically by the ladies of the house); picturesque, vibrant imagery; fast-paced narrative; plausible, lifelike characters; a sharp piercing wit; an unselfconscious cynicism; an uncommon courage to speak one's mind – it's all there. In addition, one cannot fail to notice that many of Ismat Chughtai's short stories seem to be germinating in *The Crooked Line*. The character of Bari Apa and her circumstances are reminiscent of the young Qudsia Bano in the novella *Dil ki Duniya (Realm of the Heart)*, whose husband has abandoned her in favour of an English wife and who is waiting out the days of her youth at her parents' house. The young boy Ajju, called Aziz in the novel after his amazing transformation and whom Shamman so despises, is with only slight variations unmistakably Kallu in the story of the same name, while the visit of Chacha and Chachi accompanied by their eligible son Abbas Mian, all of whom are elaborately entertained by the family's calculating, conspiring older women obsessed with matchmaking, brings to mind *Chauthi ka Jora (The Wedding Suit)*. The autobiographical content in *The Crooked Line* appears to have a direct connection with *Kaghazi Hai Perahan² (The Papery Raiment)*, an early autobiography by Ismat Chughtai. Here we see Alma, her friend at the college in Aligarh, also Manager Sahib at the school in Aligarh where she was headmistress and who assumes a similar role in *The Crooked Line*, and there's Razia Begum too, complete with her antics, and a host of other colourful characters and happenings that have also found their way into *The Crooked Line*. In fact, the autobiography reads like detailed notes for *The Crooked Line*. This is a phenomenon linked closely with another aspect of Chughtai's writing; most of her work is openly autobiographical in nature, sometimes to such an extent that it is difficult to know where autobiography ends and fiction begins. Perhaps Ismat Chughtai's work is one of the best examples of an imaginative blending of fact and fiction and perhaps that is why we find everything she says so believable.

Chughtai also mentions in *Kaghazi Hai Perahan* that she modelled many of her 'heroines' after Rashid Jahan³ and that when she thinks about her own fiction she realises that she 'grasped her [Rashid Jahan's] frankness and her forthrightness', but she couldn't grasp 'all of her personality'. All the same, her debt to Rashid Jahan is indisputable. Chughtai hated 'the type of femininity that was characterised by weeping and complaints, that only produced children and forever mourned'. Rashid Jahan, on the other hand, symbolised for her the woman who had broken ties with the suffocating aspects of tradition and who was fearless and undauntedly bold, much like Ismat was to become. In the ultimate analysis, however, Ismat Chughtai was her own 'heroines', *she* was Shamman, *she* was a crooked line herself, someone who was, in the words of de Beauvoir, 'taking charge herself of her own existence', a rebel who refused to yield to society's stereotypes about women, but who never wished to be anyone but a woman.

TAHIRA NAQVI, 1995

1 Simone de Beauvoir, *The Second Sex* (New York, Knopf, 1978), pp 279–82.

2 Ismat Chughtai, *Kaghazi Hai Perahan* (Lahore, Chaudhry Academy, 1980), pp 386–7.

3 Rashid Jahan, a gynaecologist by profession, was one of the most important members of the early phase of the Progressive Writers' Movement which originated in 1932, soon after the publication by its members of a very controversial collection of short stories entitled *Angare (The Embers)*. She had also written for the collection and came to be known as Rashid Jahan of the *'Angare* Group'. The collection caused a furore, just as Chughtai's own story *'Lihaf'* ('The Quilt') did several years later, being banned by the United Provinces state government. Ismat Chughtai considered Rashid Jahan to be her mentor.

Translator's note

Kinship titles in Urdu afford a certain variety which may sometimes confuse the reader. For example, aunts and uncles are specified in terms of their exact relationship to the mother or father, while, on the other hand, the titles 'aunt' and 'uncle' may also be used for family friends. Spouses of aunts, uncles, brothers and sisters are also variously titled and therefore need to be identified. The following list of kinship titles should be helpful to the reader in clarifying ambiguities that may otherwise result from references to particular family members. In addition, Urdu words italicised in the text can be found in the Glossary starting on page 332.

Kinship titles

Abba father
Amma/Amma bi mother
Bi a suffix somewhat similar to 'ma'am', 'miss' or 'dear girl' attached to women's names or titles; short for *bibi*
Baji older sister
Bare Bhayya older brother
Bari Apa older sister
Begum literally lady, appended to women's names to denote respect
Chacha/Chacha jaan uncle; father's brother

Chachi jaan   father's brother's wife; *jaan* or *ji* used to denote affection
Dulhan   bride; form of address used for daughters-in-law
Khala   mother's sister
Mamun jaan   mother's brother
Mumani jaan   mother's brother's wife
Mian   literally gentleman/sir; somewhat formal
Nani   maternal grandmother

THE FIRST PHASE

1

To begin with, her birth was ill-timed. Bari Apa, whose friend Salma was to be married soon, was working briskly on a crêpe *dupatta*, stitching gold lace to its borders. Amma, who regarded herself as a youthful maiden despite the fact that she had given birth to so many children, was scrubbing off dead skin from her heels with a pumice stone. Suddenly, dark clouds rolled in, and in the ensuing commotion the longstanding desire to send for an English midwife came to naught, and 'she' appeared. The minute she arrived into the world she let out such a thunderous howl . . . God help us!

Another addition after nine children – why, it was as if the hands on the clock had moved to ten. Who had time for weddings now? Orders were to heat water for the baby sister's bath, and, shedding tears that were steamier than boiling water, and cursing at the same time, Bari Apa put water on the stove to boil. As if to mock her, some of the scalding water spilled over from the pot and seared her hand.

'May God curse this baby sister! Why won't Amma's womb close up now?'

This was the limit! A sister, a brother, then another sister and brother – it seemed that beggars had found a way to their house and now there was no keeping them out. Were there not enough mouths already? Why all these newcomers? Coming in like cats and dogs, ever hungry, they had depleted the grain reserves, milk had become scarce even though there were two cows in the house, and still the bellies of these newcomers remained empty.

This was all Abba's fault. Amma was never given the opportunity to breast-feed her children. As soon as a baby arrived, the wet-nurse from Agra was sent for to nurse the infant and sit next to Amma's bed all day.

The house was more like an animal shed than a house. Why, food was always prepared in excessively large quantities, and as for drink, gallons of that too, and if you wanted to sleep, you would find every corner of the house deluged with life, ready to teem over!

And this last baby, with her diminutive nose, eyes tiny like tamarind seeds but keener than those of an eagle, when this little creature who had the face of a mouse smiled, Bari Apa and Manjhu both felt she was sneering at them. Surely she knew that the two sisters would wait on her like slaves. Amma must be worried too. All these girls – will fortune smile on them? True, the family had money, but it wasn't fashionable to parade the girls before people; how long could they be kept under lock and key? What was going to happen?

Shamman's navel didn't get infected, nor was she ever sick, and with each passing day she became healthier and plumper. The first two or three babies had been pampered and coddled, but now even Bari Apa had had her fill and was exhausted. However, the wet-nurse was still around, so Shamman was well taken care of.

Unna, the wet-nurse, was very young, sixteen or seventeen perhaps. Sometimes at night Unna continued to sleep while Shamman lay wrapped in soiled nappies. It wasn't easy to awaken Unna, but she certainly had plenty of milk to offer, and when Unna's lover hitched Shamman on his shoulders and ran around pretending to be a horse, Shamman, forgetting all her sorrows, chortled and giggled. Unknown to other members of the household, the three of them often retreated to the barn where the hay for the cows was stored. Here Unna rolled on the hay and her lover tumbled after her while Shamman crawled around the two of them, mirthfully clapping her hands. But seeing him fight with Unna distressed her and she began whimpering. She hated quarrels. Whenever she saw two dogs tangled in a ferocious tussle, her whole body trembled fearfully and she screamed and screamed until the dogs, alarmed by her shrieks, abandoned their scuffle and made off. No one could touch Unna while Shamman was awake. If Unna's lover tried to tease her by holding Unna's hand and saying, 'She's mine,' Shamman immediately let out a sharp cry of protestation.

But she was soon punished for her brazenness. One day, while the three of them rolled around in the hay as usual, she fell asleep and was

2

soon lost in a world of innocent dreams. In front of her, behind her, all around her she saw Unnas and more Unnas; mad with joy, she leapt eagerly from one lap to the next. Then, suddenly, all the Unnas disappeared. Her spirits drooped and, sniffing around like a hungry bitch, she began looking for Unna. Finally she found her. On a pile of thatching grass, fleshy and ripe like a mango, was her soft, warm Unna. She cooed and burrowed herself into the rounded softness, her lips moving, the veins in her throat throbbing as if she were gulping down great quantities of milk. She gagged. And when she reached out her chubby hands a monster pushed her away and, grabbing Unna, wrestled her down. She screeched fiercely as though she had been bitten by snakes, her childish eyes dazed by the revolting scene before her. Hearing her scream and howl, the water-carrier, the sweeper and the cook made a hurried dash to the shed, and the offenders were apprehended.

Shamman stared at Unna's face in consternation, her eyes questioning, 'You're not hurt, are you? I saved you, didn't I?' But Unna didn't seem to be in a good mood and, instead of displaying amusement at her pranks, she kept pushing her away roughly. Shamman used all the innocent and feeble tricks she knew to charm her, but she couldn't make her laugh. If only there was some way she could ask Unna why she was annoyed with her, but today Unna refused to comprehend what was in her eyes.

That same night Unna was sent back to Agra by train. Shamman felt as if she had been orphaned. For many days and nights she gazed about her with a wide-eyed, fixed stare, sobbing and moaning. Everyone gathered at her bedside, but she would not be pacified. How was she going to find the Unna whose soft, warm bosom provided the comfort she had experienced in her mother's womb? She went into a fit as soon as she was given the bottle. How could this horrible, glass bottle compare to the soft-complexioned, cuddly Unna? But the burning intensity of her hunger eventually forced her to accept the worst and, when Manjhu took her in her lap, gave her the bottle and a few drops of milk slunk down her throat, she became calm. But every now and then she would suddenly reject the bottle and cling to Manjhu, snuggling in her clothes like a puppy, looking for her Unna. Alarmed by her behaviour, Manjhu would put her down on the bed, and complain to Bari Apa that Shamman had taken to tickling her in a most unbecoming manner.

Experience proved to be an effective teacher and, just as cows and buffaloes mechanically chew cud, Shamman too gulped milk down, but

3

her hands continued to wander. Gripping the smooth, slippery surface of the bottle with her hands, she often clasped it to her breast and sometimes, while she was drinking from the bottle, she thought she saw Unna's eyes, her nose, her tiny nose-ring, her ear-bobs; her heart welled up and, taking her mouth away from the teat, she would begin to cry in a mournful voice. But within minutes, compelled to vigilance by hunger, she would stop crying.

Manjhu took charge of her after Unna's departure. Who knows why she felt affection for her? Perhaps she first took pity on her when she burrowed her face in her clothes looking for Unna. When she finished drinking from the bottle, Manjhu clasped her to her breast and stretched out in bed with her. If Manjhu wasn't beside her she couldn't sleep; lying next to her, she felt the same warmth she had known in Unna's lap, and with her small fingers she stroked Manjhu's neck and her cheeks, something Manjhu didn't seem to mind at all.

Then one day, while Manjhu was bathing, Shamman walked in without any warning. 'Apa, do you hear me, get her out of here!' Manjhu screamed.

'I say, what does she understand, she's just a little thing.'

But Shamman stared at Manjhu so strangely she made her blush. As if in a daze, she continued staring at her. 'Get out, do you hear!' Manjhu scolded her, picking up a ladle-jug to cover herself.

But she seemed to be drawn to Manjhu as if led by a magnetic force. Panicking, Manjhu chided her again and, when she continued to advance, her eyes twinkling and lit with a meaningful expression as she smiled, Manjhu doused her with a handful of water.

Being smacked with water proved to be unnerving; Shamman began to whimper and quickly crawled out of the bathroom. That day she didn't drink her milk properly, nor did she smile or chatter; she stared at Manjhu with a wounded expression in her eyes, as if Manjhu had done her great harm, and again and again she broke into tears.

When Manjhu got into bed with her that night and pulled the quilt over them, she gazed at Manjhu silently.

'What is it?' Manjhu asked lovingly, and Shamman smiled sadly. Slowly she raised her hand and touched Manjhu's neck, her eyes fixed on the small mole glistening on Manjhu's left cheek.

'Now don't be naughty.' Manjhu took her wandering hand and patted it down. Shamman started sobbing and gave Manjhu such a pleading look that her heart softened and, placing her hand back on her neck, she held her close and fell asleep.

4

Manjhu stitched beautiful frocks and hats for Shamman. She bathed her frequently, applied *missi* to her teeth and kohl to her eyes, and Shamman submitted to everything without a word of protest. But woe to anyone else who dared touch her; if Manjhu accidentally got some soap in her eyes she reacted with only a whimper. Manjhu was Manjhu, after all.

But as Shamman grew older she began to find Manjhu's cleaning routine tiresome. Manjhu dressed her up, gave strict orders that she was not to allow one hair to get out of place or else she'd be dead, but she was powerless; she had no control over her restless legs which longed to run about. For a little while she remained still. Then, as soon as Manjhu's back was turned, she slipped out of the house, and reappeared in the evening looking like a mad bitch who had just finished tossing about in an earthen platter filled with sludge. The once billowing frock resembled a dead rat's skin, its surface decorated with a shower of fine dust; her hair, eyes and face would be blanketed with a thick layer of dust, her nostrils so densely packed with snot and muck they reminded one of doors walled in with cement. Plastered over everything was a covering comprised of secretions and seeds from mangoes, guavas, berries, or whatever fruit happened to be in season. To crown it all, she emitted an odour that one could only associate with a plague-ridden rat.

The first thing Manjhu did was to brush off as much dust as she could with smacks, pummels and punches while Shamman continued to bray like a calf. The sand caught between her eyelashes was washed out with her tears, while the salt in the tears helped unclog her nose with the swiftness of a blocked drain being unplugged with acid. Then, to the accompaniment of thunderous thwacks and slaps, she was given a bath. Dressed again in a clean frock, she became acutely aware of her mistake and, begging forgiveness for her past sins, she repented and made a promise to stay on the straight and narrow path, avowing never to go near mud and sludge, promising she would never again roll in the dirt. At that moment her face shone with the mystical light that radiates on the face of an ascetic who has renounced the material world and his own body with it. Her eyes, ordinarily sharp as an eagle's, suddenly became timid like a pigeon's eyes and drooped sleepily.

But times were bad. The next day, exactly at the same moment, in the same deplorable condition, glimmering in a cloud of starry dust, she walked in like an inebriated drunkard. Those who saw her were

5

confounded and, when the dust was shaken from her, the earth and the sky shuddered.

Once again she repented, took an oath . . . but only to forget it all. Satan tempted her. No sooner did she appear all dressed up and clean than everything around her seemed poised to attack her spotless clothes. The red mud in the fields and the whispering sand on the edge of the pond tantalised her, the moist, fragrant grass in the stables pursued her with open arms, the dirty, foul-smelling chicken coop drew her to itself as if it were a bride's flowery bed. She forgot everything. The pledge she had made repeatedly with her conscience, her promise to Manjhu and, most importantly, her pride which was being crushed by these daily blows. Her struggle to turn away from these evil splendours left her exhausted. They continued to beckon her and finally, like a kite cut off from its cord, she fell into the pit of sin, an act for which she paid with daily suffering and pain.

In a short while she was covered with spittle and blood again. Round silky balls of mud, tiny mounds of sand, brown like fried farina, a small broom constructed from the hay in the stables, feathers that had fallen off from a hen's tail, all this and Peena – this was her world. Peena, her closest friend, the sweeper's daughter: next to Manjhu, Peena was everything to her. The two girls went behind the cow's stall and strolled with their arms wrapped around each other. Sometimes they tossed about in the sand like rolling pins. Then they pitched fistfuls of sand as if it was water they were scooping up in their hands, until finally the two of them began to resemble grotesque mud statues. Sand penetrated their very beings, but still they had not had enough of sand and mud. Making spoons out of dried leaves, they scooped up sand and swallowed mouthfuls; they devoured it as if it were delicious caudle. Like pregnant women, they relished the aroma of mud. Who can say what sons were being nurtured in their swollen, melon-shaped bellies?

In time they began to resemble women who are pregnant. Their smooth, ruddy complexions grew sallow and a white mould spread over their tongues. Yellowish streaks appeared in their eyes, and Peena's waistband became so tight it finally stayed open in the front. They became lethargic, a foul taste lingered permanently in their mouths. The use of nails and teeth in the course of a fight became more frequent, and they constantly whined, as if they were a pair of witches imprisoned in a cage. That was why she was given the name 'witch'.

When everyone teased her by calling her 'witch', she rolled her eyes like a witch and growled. Like a cat she attacked her enemy, scratching and drawing blood with her nails, and, when she bit somebody, her teeth clamped together forcefully on her enemy's flesh.

Apparently the son growing in her belly was drawing her to the aroma of mud. The elders sprinkled salt on her tongue, rubbed her tongue with quinine, but no one could come up with a punishment that would end her craving for mud. 'Burn the witch's tongue!' someone suggested. 'Prick her tongue with needles, the wretch!' came more advice from another quarter. But there was no treatment that could cure what ailed her. When Manjhu caught her nibbling on clay, she slapped her until her lips bled, but she chewed on charcoal if she couldn't find any clay, or scraped lime from the walls with her nails and ingested that instead.

One day, while she and Peena squatted on the toilets busy chatting and defecating at the same time, the son she had been nourishing in her belly appeared. With a heart-rending scream she bolted from there and went straight to Manjhu.

'A snake!' She hid between Manjhu's legs. Manjhu pushed her away. After an investigation by the doctor it was revealed that she had roundworms in her stomach. But she would not believe what the doctor said. All night she was screaming, 'Snake! Snake!' She felt there were innumerable clusters of snakes looping about in her stomach, the way they do in a snake-charmer's basket, creating havoc inside her, slithering after each other, thousands of them, playing hide-and-seek.

That was the day she stopped meeting Peena to gulp down sand in spoons shaped out of dried leaves. She gazed longingly at the sand particles until suddenly they turned into tiny snakes, their eyes rotating as they leapt towards her. She would scoop up some sand in her fist and hold it lovingly against her stomach. She wished she could take all of the world's mud and collect it under her tongue, mix it with her spittle and then let the viscous curds glide down her throat. But just then the snake in her stomach began stretching and, behaving like a lunatic, she hurled fistfuls of sand in the air, rolled on the ground and rubbed her cheeks on the cool mud. Her body arched like a fishing rod and she was consumed with the desire to pierce her way into the bowels of the earth. When her frenzy subsided somewhat, she banged her head slowly on the ground.

'Open the door,' her forehead pleaded, but the earth remained stubbornly still. Why did she love the earth so much? She wanted to disappear into its bowels. Whenever someone caught her the sand was

7

immediately dusted off, but as soon as she had the opportunity she again tried to immerse herself in sand and mud.

'May you sleep in dust! No matter how many times you bathe her, she's always filthy!' Manjhu cursed and scolded her and she thought if only someone knew that to sleep in dust was not a curse as far as she was concerned, it was a benediction. This was what she desired the most.

2

Girls generally nurse a desire to get married, but of late Shamman had been experiencing a desire to hit people. Suddenly, for no apparent reason, she was beset with this urge to hit someone, to knock and crush somebody with her chubby fists. She would be sitting quietly, contemplative, her eyes fixed on the tail of the hen pecking at grain in the veranda, fixed on the minuscule bead of dropping stuck to the end of a feather and quivering with every movement of the hen's body, or she would be watching the little mouse which had peeped apprehensively from behind the trunk three times already since this morning, or she might be staring at something else, when suddenly she would be seized with a desire to strike somebody. Who was brave enough in her family to subdue her? Didn't Manjhu smack her brazenly on her back whenever she saw fit? Shamman yearned to deliver a solid blow to Manjhu's strong back and, gripped by this desire, she would soon be lost in a world of dreams in which she was slapping Manjhu, taking off her clothes, giving her a bath. At this time a vague memory of her long-lost Unna surfaced from somewhere, making her sad and then so angry that in her reverie she deposited large amounts of gram flour on Manjhu's hair and rubbed it in violently, then scrubbed Manjhu's elbows and heels vigorously with a pumice stone, and finally, taking a coarsely woven towel, rubbed her down until her skin began to peel and her nose turned red like a beet. Then she dressed Manjhu in a beautiful frock and said:

'If you move from here I'll break your legs!'

But on her return from the world of dreams, Shamman realised there was nothing there. Both her hands lay stonily in her lap, the muscles in her neck painfully stiff. Taking a long, vindictive breath, she stiffened her whole body and, as if gone mad, suddenly began punching the pillows wildly. When she had had her fill and was spent, she relaxed her body, relieved, satisfied.

One day she felt the urge to strike her doll. First she gave it a few mild, cautionary slaps, but then she lost control and began pummelling and kicking the doll with her hands and feet. Soon she was shredding it with her teeth and nails, behaving as though she were face to face with a menacing adversary.

Finally the doll was in shreds, the sawdust filling inside its body scattered everywhere, some of it stuck to Shamman's tongue. She was sated. Sighing in contentment, a little out of breath, she lay down on her bed. For a long time the taste of sawdust stayed on her tongue like stale blood.

But a little later she was overcome by fear; she felt she had actually murdered someone. Terrified, she quickly hid the fragments of the smashed doll under a trunk and ran to Manjhu for comfort. Manjhu was sewing her *kurta*. Shamman stretched out next to her and reached up a trembling hand to fondle her neck.

Manjhu didn't only know how to sew frocks; one day she also sent for the *alif-bay* Reader and stitched all the pages together with her sewing machine. Watching the teeth of the machine go '*kat, kat*' over the paper, Shamman experienced a somewhat pleasurable, tingling sensation in her teeth; she rubbed a finger over her teeth and felt a strange current streaming through her body.

Once the Reader had been put together, Manjhu took Shamman in her lap.

'Today you'll start reading, all right?'

'All right,' Shamman said excitedly. This was the second book to which she was going to be introduced. The first book had been the one Manjhu liked so much that she spanked Shamman if she happened to pester her while she was reading it. Actually, any interesting items related to reading and writing were kept out of Shamman's reach. But this book was no good for hitting or smacking. She preferred the newspaper which Abba folded into the shape of a boat and lovingly tapped her head with.

'Let me see, let me see, Manjhubi!' She snatched the book from Manjhu, rolled it into a cylinder and hurled it at Manjhu's chest.

'You fool, you've bent the book all out of shape,' Manjhu scolded, picking up the Reader. 'Look, this is *alif, alif.*'

'Where?' Shamman sounded incredulous.

'Here . . . *alif* for *anar.*'

'What? *Alif* isn't *anar, anar* is a firecracker . . . *phrr, phrrr*, right?'

'Silly! Look here, this is *alif, alif* for *anar* . . . say *alif.*'

'Say *alif.*'

'No, this is how you say it . . . *alif*!'

'I don't want to say it, first tell me what is this . . . this, this.'

'This is *jim.*'

'And this?'

'This is *suad* and this is *zuad.*'

'No, no, no . . . this isn't *suad, zuad*, these are teapots.'

'You silly girl, look, here's *alif*, say *alif* for *anar.*'

'Say.' She stared foolishly at Manjhu's face.

'Listen to me, fool, say *alif*!' Manjhu was losing her patience.

'Say *alif.*'

'You witch!' Manjhu pushed her out of her lap and walked off in the direction of the veranda.

Shamman picked up the Reader. A pig, just a pig, the book was, with crooked black pictures and the *jim* that looked like the face of the female sweeper! She didn't like anything in it, not even *suad, zuad* and Oh God! *alif* for *anar*? Hunh! How could that be? This round, pitcher-shaped *anar*, with no red shooting sparks, nothing? So useless! Well, she'll read *alif* perhaps, but she'll die before she reads *jim*. What was there to lose? She examined the book closely to distract herself and her eyes fell on the marks made by the sewing machine. Her teeth began to tingle again. She tugged at the piece of thread at one end of the seam and, like sutures on a wound, the stitches unravelled neatly all the way to the end of the seam. It felt good, as if she were hastily skipping down a staircase. Soon the pages were scattered all over the place.

Oh dear! Manjhu was sure to be angry at this, and she wouldn't be at all surprised if she also spanked her. With great speed Shamman collected all the pages and, placing them under the needle in the sewing machine, she began turning the handle. '*Kat, kat, kat, kat* . . .' This way and that she led the paper, expertly in her opinion, until the Reader resembled a piece of quilting. That was just as well. *Suad* and *zuad*, kettle-shaped and silly, were gone and *jim* too was obliterated.

But when Manjhu saw the condition the Reader was in, she spanked Shamman harder than ever before and boxed her ears. For some time

10

Shamman sat by herself sobbing tearlessly. It would not do for her to shed tears every time she was beaten; her eyes would have long been washed out, and if she had wept with every slap and blow she received, she would have been finished by now even if she had the seven seas at her disposal. For this reason she now cried only with her throat. Her mind remained unaffected and calm.

Much to her chagrin, the book became a chronic nuisance she could not get rid of. With much forbearance she read *alif*, but *jim*, and eventually *suad* and *zuad*, the wretches, she had to read those as well. However, what truly surprised her was the discovery that,

> ''Tis only the beginning of love, why cry so?
> Wait and see what next awaits you.'

Here is what happened. She asked Manjhu one day, 'Manjhubi, when the book is finished, will there be sweets for everyone?'

'Yes, and then we'll start with the next book.'

'Next? Again?'

'And then you will be able to read the kind of thick, heavy books Bare Bhaya reads,' Manjhu explained quite innocently. How naively she had introduced Shamman to the demons of tomorrow.

Quietly Shamman sat, her hands folded in her lap, feeling as if a large, monstrous book was falling periodically on her head with the force of a millstone, a book in which there were things more contemptible and wearisome than '*suad, zuad*.'

The days spent in a large, busy household, in the company of so many brothers and sisters, were soon lost in the darkness of the past, like minuscule pebbles rolled about and caught between the teeth of a winnowing fan. Like kites flying high, swishing and rustling, life raced on.

3

So what if Manjhubi [*sister*] hit her? She cuddled her too, didn't she? After a good beating she put her to sleep and warmed all her wounds with the heat of her bosom. However, Shamman's tongue had now loosened. When Manjhu spanked her she didn't hesitate to call her all the names she had picked up from the servants.

'May she die, Allah, may Manjhubi die!'

On hearing Shamman swear at her dearest daughter, Amma [*mother*] became furious. 'I'll dig a hole and bury you alive in it, you wretch, if you swear at my child!'

Of course, Shamman wasn't Amma's child; after the departure of her wicked Unna, Manjhu had taken the place of her mother.

'Here's what you say: Allah, may Manjhu get married soon, may Manjhubi get married soon.'

This form of swearing seemed to have a special effect. First, Manjhu appeared to get upset and whacked her vigorously, but then her hands would become sluggish and she would break into a bashful smile.

Who knows what the inauspicious time was when that prayer had been uttered, because it was immediately heard. There was such confusion, Shamman couldn't understand what was going on. The house was turned upside-down. Manjhu was corralled into a room and much commotion followed. Everywhere there was an abundance of all manner of exotic sweetmeats and resplendent, satiny clothes. The house was transformed into a veritable bazaar. Attired in red and green clothes, the women darted in all directions, and 'dhooan! dhoon!' sounded the trumpets and the drums. When the women scrambled to get a glimpse of Manjhu's groom, Shamman began whining; someone picked her up and tried to show her the bridegroom. But she couldn't see. 'That's a man, that's not a bridegroom,' she screamed, and threw a tantrum. No one made an attempt to show her the bridegroom after that, and shortly, tired and cranky, she nuzzled up to Manjhu, who was bathed in fragrance, and fell asleep.

At the time of the ceremonies people tried to get her to place a dab of henna on the bridegroom's hand, but she protested violently again, proclaiming that in the first place this was an ordinary man and no bridegroom, and secondly, men don't wear henna. As a result of this

12

show of behaviour she was cursed, someone called her an imbecile, and she was pushed away.

Manjhu was sitting dressed up as a bride, so Shamman rambled all over the place like an ox without a nose-string. First she took some of the sugar that had come from the groom's side and mixed it with the water in the water containers in the bathroom, leaving the ladies aghast when they washed themselves. Then she turned her attention to the kitchen and deposited salt, coals and ashes into the cooking pots. The cooks were engaged elsewhere. She began counting the plates of *kheer* which, studded with silver paper and pistachio slivers, were arranged like embroidered patterns on a carpet and looked so appealing. Suddenly, she was seized with the desire to step into the spaces between the plates. She put a foot down gingerly ... one, two ... three. Someone spotted her. As she tried to flee from there, she fell with a splash and was soon covered from top to toe in the mush of *kheer*.

Somebody ventured to give her a bath, but she was used to being bathed only by Manjhu. Irritated by the slow manner in which she was being bathed, she flew into a rage and began splashing water in all directions. Later, while the maidservant was searching for the wooden stick with which to string Shamman's waistband, she wrapped a towel around herself, came out of the bathroom and began wandering from room to room. Manjhubi's heavily embroidered clothes had been arranged for display in one of the rooms. Shamman went in, removed the coloured sequins from the shirts and, using her saliva, affixed the sequins to her forehead; pulling out gold and silver bands, she coiled them into spiralling loops; opening up the carefully folded *dupattas*, she scattered them all around her. Then her eyes fell on the gold-filigreed *cholis* with their golden strings. How she had longed to wear one of these *cholis*! But she never even got to see them. As if it were a foul word to be uttered only in secret, Amma secluded herself in the bathroom to put hers on, and the hamper containing the unwashed clothes was too deep for Shamman to reach into. She swiftly put her arms through whatever holes she could find, tightened the cords around her neck and, drawing out a weighty crêpe *dupatta*, she draped it over her head. And the sight of the brocade pyjamas made her heart convulse with longing. She was sick of wearing nothing but underpants all these years. With some effort she managed to squeeze her legs into the beautiful flowered pyjamas. Afterwards, she pulled the *dupatta* down over her face and, raising her hand to her forehead, began offering salaams to imaginary guests.

'May you live long, daughter, may you be blessed with sons and grandsons,' she heard the guests say to her. Resting her chin on the palm of her hand, she assumed the bearing of a housewife.

'*Arree*, Rasulan, O Rasulan, where have you gone off to, wretch! Go and quickly tell Ali Bukhsh not to get any provisions . . . yes, instead, tell him he should get mung *daal*, and yes, roasted peanuts, and for Shammanbi some sugar candy.' She scolded the imaginary ayah. While she was talking she thought, 'Oh, the baby is asleep in my lap!' Why, he was awake. She shook her knees pretending to rock the baby.

'No, no, my precious, my dearest . . . are you hungry? Do you want milk? Mmmmm . . .' She lifted her shirt front, but in that instant her attention was drawn to a mosquito bite and, forgetting the baby and everything else, she lowered her head to examine the bruise on her knee.

'The wretch bit me, may he die!' She slapped her knee . . . and soon she was assailed by the desire to pound something. Swiftly and without restraint, she proceeded to pummel violently with her hands the items displayed as part of the dowry. In a short time all was clutter and confusion. People came and dragged her out of the room and, since no one had the time to find her clothes and dress her, she roamed around all evening wrapped in nothing but a towel.

But she did learn a useful lesson; the towel was much more comfortable and practical than pyjamas. For one thing, you didn't have to have the waistband loosened every now and then, and in the second place, seeing her attired in this unusual fashion, the other children were consumed by the fire of envy; some waited for her towel to slip so they could see her naked, but she warded them off by throwing her shoes at them. She was thoroughly enjoying this game.

Wherever Shamman went she was greeted with reproach and castigation; her sisters slapped her and turned her away, but no one bothered to unlock the suitcase and get out her clothes. Later that night, when the time came for the bridegroom's *anchal* or some other important ceremony like that, a search began and finally she was caught playing a strange game in the veranda in the back of the house, and was punished.

The bridegroom arrived. A clamour followed. Somebody gave Shamman the bridegroom's shoe to hide. For a long time she played with the shoe and then she fell asleep. Late at night, when the bridegroom was leaving, a hue and cry rose for the missing shoe. Frightened on being suddenly awakened, she clung to the person who was shaking her and began screaming.

'My money . . . my money!'

It is said the bridegroom had to leave in his bare feet. The next morning the shoe was discovered floating in the drinking water like a swollen corpse. The in-laws had drunk water from this pitcher all evening. An effort was made to find out why she had thrown the shoe in the water pitcher, but she couldn't tell anyone anything.

'Shoe? Water pitcher?' she kept asking, but when she saw the swollen shoe, her heart tickled with amusement and she became weak with laughter.

4

When the moment of Manjhu's departure arrived, Shamman didn't cry at all; instead, she quietly sneaked into the palanquin. Manjhu kept asking to see her before she left, but she was nowhere to be found. When the bride and her female companions entered the palanquin, the stoutest of the women with Manjhu landed in Shamman's lap. Shamman would have screamed but, sensing the need for silence, she controlled herself and dug her teeth into the fat woman's buttocks. A terrible disturbance followed. The palanquin almost came apart. Shamman was caught and forcibly hauled out of it. She thrashed her legs, cursed heavily, but no one paid any attention to her.

Manjhubi left. It was as if someone in the family had died. Everyone went to sleep, but Shamman's share of sleep seemed to have disappeared. Again and again, she called out Manjhu's name and wept, her throat ached from constant sobbing, her voice weakened, but who was going to listen to her?

'Manjhubi . . . Manjhubi . . . ohhh Manjhubi!' All night she wailed. The guests and the hosts, exhausted after the day's events, slept oblivious to the world, and Shamman roamed all over the house alone.

She was in trouble after Manjhu's departure. For many days no one remembered if she was in the house or not, or that she needed to be bathed or have a change of clothing. When the stench emitting from her became unbearable, people began avoiding her as if she were a fetid gutter. Tormented by grime and itchiness, she would wake up crying at

15

night, while during the day she skulked about in the corners of the house. This was when Amma thought she should be given a bath.

Her hair had become matted, ribbons of dirt rolled off her body. The ayah was powerless. When she tried to bathe her, Shamman struck her and then, pushing, ran out into the veranda naked. The race between them continued a long time, with Shamman in the front and the ayah in pursuit of her. Finally, Shamman slipped near the gutter and fell. The ayah caught her and, bringing her back to the bathroom, proceeded to finish giving her a bath. But only Shamman knew what kind of a bath that was. Her tousled hair remained a stringy mass of dirt and filth; the grime on her skin swelled when water was poured over her, and a towel got rid of the moisture. The actual crust of dirt wasn't touched at all, and she slipped into her clothes. Well, following this, whenever she was to be bathed, Amma sat nearby with an enormous switch and she was washed as if she were a corpse; a mild beating wasn't enough to keep her down.

During the day she forgot Manjhu, but at night she cried for her. Finally, in exasperation, Amma said to the old ayah, 'Why don't you sleep with the wretch?' But when Shamman woke up in the middle of the night and saw the ayah sleeping next to her, she pulled the woman's hair and kicked her off the bed. Sleeping alone, she chewed on her palms and, when everyone was asleep, she awoke, her hands seeking Manjhu's neck. She longed to put her hands around Manjhu's neck just once and then, she told herself, she would die rather than let go. Lying in bed, Shamman would curse Manjhu's greedy, vile husband who had pounced on her like a vulture and snatched her away. And perhaps God heard the curse meant for Manjhu's ignoble husband because one day a telegram arrived and lamentation and sorrow filled the house.

'Your brother-in-law is dead, why don't you cry?' The *tehsildar*'s daughter asked her.

'Who? Manjhu's groom?' she asked with incredulous joy.

'No, Bari Apa's husband.'

Who cared about Bari Apa's husband! He was such an unpleasant man. Last time when a bundle of sugar-cane came in from the village, he sent every last bit to Amma and wouldn't let Shamman touch even one little piece. Because everyone thought she would be as upset as the others at the news, she, along with the rest of the children, was sent to the *tehsildar*'s house where she got to eat fried, sugary eggs.

'When Manjhubi's husband dies then we'll get even more delicious

16

eggs,' she thought happily, trying to retain the taste of the eggs in her mouth.

Bari Apa returned to live at her mother's house after she was widowed. Her two children also came with her. No one was allowed to touch them. Just as a female pigeon viciously attacks the hand that creeps into her nest, so did Bari Apa leap fiercely, ready for attack, if someone touched her children.

When, after a long period of waiting, Manjhu came for a visit, Shamman was beside herself with anger. She thought that just as without Manjhu she had lost her senses, Manjhu too would return weeping for her, her appearance grubby and dirty like that of a rat. But she felt extremely humiliated when she saw Manjhu looking chubbier and healthier than before. What a liar! In her letters to Amma she wrote, 'I miss my Shamman.' If she had missed Shamman, her face wouldn't be glistening. Attired from head to toe in satiny clothes she was, in her ears glittering, tinkling earrings which she deliberately tossed about as she talked, a shining gold bob in her nose which she glanced at sideways every now and then while speaking bashfully, and that transparent silken lace *kurta* under which the golden *choli* flashed occasionally like the moon hidden among clouds.

As soon as Manjhu arrived she began embracing everyone, but she didn't even look in Shamman's direction. Of course, Shamman had changed so much. All the fine dainty frocks were worn out by now and instead of panties she had taken to wearing badly fitting, unattractive pyjamas. Finally, who knows how, Manjhu thought of her.

'Where is Shamman?' she asked, piercing Shamman's heart with sorrow. Oh, so now Manjhubi couldn't even recognise her. Who is this watching her constantly for nearly an hour, standing next to the door? Who has tried, several times and unsuccessfully, to get her attention by tugging at her silken *dupatta*? And who is this standing patiently by the door? If it's not Shamman, then who is it? But only when she's had her fill of hugging her mother and older sisters will someone else's restless heart find peace. Apa's daughter, Noori, came along and Manjhu took her in her arms right away. But Shamman, was she a witch that no one could see her?

Nevertheless, when Manjhu finally clasped her to her fragrant breast, a thousand springs gushed forth in her heart and, sobbing hysterically, she clung to Manjhu.

'Lice! Lice! Careful, Manjhu, the wretch has thousands of lice crawling in her hair,' Bari Apa and Amma both screamed, and Manjhu pushed her away fearfully.

'She's dirty, a sweeper's child,' Noori murmured and, going up to Manjhu, jumped into her lap.

Manjhu was soon lost in a new surge of prattle and no one noticed that Shamman, after being pushed away, left the room. Finding a pile of dirty laundry, she hid her face in it and burst into tears. Today her heart as well as her mind was wrenched; the soiled, smelly clothes absorbed her tears. No one knows how long Shamman stayed there, crying bitterly. No one thought of her. The children were running about, chewing on the sweets Manjhu had brought with her. Noori was still installed in Manjhu's lap, playing with her necklace. Manjhu handed her a doll and, taking out another doll, she called Shamman.

'No, I want both,' Noori said, squirming. Shamman was not so low as to be tempted by Manjhu's doll, but when Noori grabbed both dolls, she could not control herself any longer. First, she turned away and fixed her gaze on the cobwebs that dangled from the ceiling with half-dead flies swaying in them. Then she had a fit. She began ripping dirty clothes with her teeth; in her anger she wanted to swallow everything, the stinking pyjamas, the grimy undershirts, the *kurtas* rank with stale odours.

Finally exhausted, she came out and sat in a corner of the veranda. It seemed to her that today she was wearing a magical cap which made her invisible. In order to test her theory she walked past everyone several times, but neither Manjhu noticed her, nor Noori, who sat on Manjhu's bed with both dolls secure in her lap.

Some faded remains of Manjhu's bridal state still lingered on her bed. The pillows were the same, red satin encased in frothy lace covers, and the same quilt with the golden edging. Jumping on the pillows was Noori. Shamman wished she could kick Noori with such force that she would fall into a blind well and then she could snatch away the two dolls.

For a long time she peered at Manjhu's feet from afar, her gaze transfixed on Manjhu's henna-red soles. Red feet and the anklets with the silvery bells! Her throat was constricted with longing. If only she could crawl under the bed and, approaching Manjhu's feet, touch the bells that struck against her henna-red heels, tinkling with every slight movement Manjhu made. Just then Noori spotted her.

'Khala, Shamman is the sweeper's daughter, Nani bought her for two paisas,' she lisped and Bari Apa tweaked her cheek affectionately.

18

Manjhu turned and saw her, but she ran from there. Then Manjhu's groom arrived and Manjhu began talking to him demurely. Perhaps the groom's vision was exceptionally sharp; he was quick to detect Shamman's presence.

'I say, why is your sister Shamman standing over there all by herself?'

'She has lice,' Noori informed him instantly.

'Oh, ohho, lice? That is not nice, poor thing.'

Who was he, the wretch, to feel sorry for her?

'Come on, come here,' he said, looking at Shamman again. 'Why doesn't anyone speak to her?'

This time Noori jumped into the groom's lap. He motioned to Manjhu with his eyes and she turned to give Shamman a startled look. Shamman realised what was going on. Stumbling, tripping, she dashed off from the room because she knew a conspiracy to be nice to her was now in progress.

Returning to the small, dark room, she called out for Manjhu again, but it was like trying to drag out a corpse from its grave by calling its name.

'Shamman.' She felt a hand on her shoulder. Shamman had to be very brave. Every fibre of her being strained to drown itself in Manjhu. 'Come here, you miserable child! What have you done to yourself in just a few days?' Manjhu whacked her hard once or twice. Shamman burst into tears, but not from pain; her heart was deeply saddened by the pleasure of these attention-laden smacks. Manjhu dragged her into the bathroom. Shamman's heart beat furiously. Her anguished tears flowed unchecked like a fever. The sweetness of Manjhu's smacks, for which she had yearned so long, melted into every corner of her being and washed away the dirt from her soul, from the corpse that had putrefied inside her. Her blood sped inside her veins, her muscles fluttered, and in a short time she was shrieking and bellowing like the Shamman of old.

Manjhu too felt as if she had quenched a burning thirst. She fell upon her with a vengeance. After the bath she struggled with Shamman's hair, untangling it, combing it, and then, taking a break from eating or drinking, she spent a whole day picking lice from her hair. Everyone tried to stop her, but she continued as though she had to repair a house which was falling apart, and that too before the monsoon rains. In the evening Shamman's step was light; her body already felt feathery and now her mind felt weightless as well, so she took to bouncing on

19

Manjhu's bed. With her fists she clobbered the pillows and, stretching the quilt over herself like a tent, she lashed her legs about underneath.

'*Hai, hai!* You'll tear the quilt!' Bari Apa screamed. 'That's it, just give her a little leeway and she's no longer fit to talk to. There's Noori too, but she doesn't behave in this insane manner.'

Shamman saw Noori sitting in Manjhu's husband's lap, twittering, and her heart burned. She would tear Noori to bits if she could help it. The wretch! Both mother and daughter jump at every chance they get to insult her. Noori is fair, *she's* dark, Noori is delicately built, *she's* ungainly, Noori is personable, shy, well-mannered, and clever at reading, *she* is bad-tempered, ill-mannered, and illiterate, shirks her studies. Noori learned the daily Koran lesson quickly and repeated it correctly in no time, whilst Shamman, on the other hand, was rebuked and chided regularly during her lessons, especially since she always forgot what she had learned earlier. Squatting on the wooden stool, Noori washed with water from a small clay pot and then stood alongside her mother for prayers and everyone praised her. But Shamman knew perfectly well that Noori didn't know even a bit of the *namaz* and she just stood there moving her lips, going '*hud, hud*'. Shamman didn't care much for *namaz*. Actually, no one really said prayers regularly in the house. Bari Apa had started offering prayers with diligence only after she was widowed. The other thing was, Shamman's clothes were nearly always soiled and dirty so no one bothered to teach her the *namaz*.

She didn't know what to do with the newly returned Manjhu. She was tired of embracing her, she was bored with touching her, although her hunger still persisted.

At night she was determined to sleep in Manjhu's bed. Silently, keeping every impulse under control, she sat on the bed afraid that Bari Apa might remove her from there on some pretext or another and make Noori sleep there instead. It was her habit to thrust her daughter everywhere. When Shamman was told to go and sleep on her own bed, she got angry. 'No, I'll sleep with Manjhu.'

'Leave her be, Apa,' Manjhu said, her eyes fixed coyly on her nose-ring. Shamman fell asleep with her hand on Manjhu's knee.

On waking up in the middle of the night, she stretched out a hand to feel Manjhu's neck and broke into tears immediately; instead of resting on Manjhu's warm neck, her hand lay helplessly on the edge of her own bed. This was her bed, which she hated more than the grave. She sat up hastily and began clamouring for Manjhu in a choked voice.

'Quiet, witch! Don't you dare make a sound,' Bari Apa growled from the bed nearby and Shamman understood what had happened. These heartless people had taken her from Manjhu's bed when she fell asleep and had thrown her down here. She quickly ran to Manjhu's room. The door was shut and the room was in darkness, but she could hear the sounds of Manjhu's soft laughter mingled with her husband's whispers.

'Manjhubi, it's me, your Shamman . . . open the door.' Manjhubi's laughter ceased abruptly. But the door remained shut.

'Manjhubi, it's Shamman . . . open the door,' Shamman pleaded.

'You witch! Why are you making her life miserable? Come on, if you get up from the bed now I'll shut you up in the little dark store-room.' Bari Apa dragged her by the arm and flung her on her bed.

Shamman's heart seemed to be bursting; her breath held, she wept silently. Everyone was asleep, but she couldn't close her eyes. After a long time the tears stopped, but her sobbing continued. Soon she felt she couldn't remain in bed any longer and she got up and came out in the courtyard. It was winter, but she didn't feel the cold at all. In the centre of the courtyard the nim tree stood like a giant with outspread wings. For a few minutes she leaned against its trunk, rubbing her palms over the rough surface. Then, her mind blank, she went and sat down on the chicken coop; here she was attacked again by tears and, sobbing heavily, she wept for hours. Except for the clucking sound made by the hens, all was silent around her. Suddenly a cat jumped off the wall, the chickens in the coop flapped their wings and clucked apprehensively, and she ran towards the veranda. Just then her eyes fell on the vegetable beds planted with coriander and spinach. In the dark the seedlings looked like whorls of tangled black yarn. Bari Apa's vegetable beds!

In an instant she had attacked the fresh, green vegetation like a hungry lioness. Using both hands, she began clawing as if extracting the intestines of an enemy, and then she took the seedlings in her hands and ground them into the dirt. She snapped and smashed the flowers and vegetables in the patch, she pounded them, crushing them into the earth with her feet. Finally, exhausted, she began laughing. Like a bitch she made dry, hacking sounds as she laughed.

'There, do you see now?' she said, speaking to an imagined victim, and then she rolled about in the dirt right there. Manjhu had given her a bath this morning, she had cleaned and combed her hair, so this was her punishment now! Scooping up fistfuls of dirt she showered her hair with it, tossed about some more in the wet soil and, muddying her hands, rubbed them over her face and neck. If she could help it she would incinerate her body so that Manjhu could see what she had done.

21

In the morning when the servants found her lying unconscious next to the vegetable patch, completely covered in mud, they screamed in fear. They thought someone had murdered her because her clothes were torn and a nosebleed had caused blood to spread to her chin and part of her neck.

For four or five days she remained unconscious due to fever. When she came to she found her chest bound tightly in plaster, and sitting next to her was a very worried-looking Manjhu. Her heart was filled with joy. Even Bari Apa looked troubled and had been at her bedside all night.

That was when Shamman felt she had been born again, now as an only child. She made stubborn demands, and Manjhu promised that when she was better she would sleep with her. Her husband had left and she now slept on the bed next to hers. Shamman was pampered during her illness, but ah, she was recovering with great speed. The fever disappeared and soon she no longer felt any weakness. Bari Apa's manner underwent change; grapes and pomegranates were withdrawn, as was sago pudding. Shamman was extremely annoyed at being healthy again. Chulla's mother who lived in the neighbourhood – how fortunate she was to be forever infirm. Did Allah have to be stingy with Shamman even when it came to bestowing an ailment upon her? She had no choice but to get well.

5

When she was returning to her in-laws, Manjhu took Shamman along with her. Noori was finally humbled. She wailed and threw a tantrum. Everyone deceived her; first she was told she would be going, but Manjhu quietly informed Shamman that was just a pretence to keep Noori happy. Shamman was overjoyed. When they were leaving, Noori went and sat in the carriage and Shamman feared that Noori might actually be coming with them. But a few minutes before the train's departure Bare Chacha said:

'Noori, come, let me get you some sweets.'

'No, no, I don't want any sweets.' Noori was accustomed to being subjected to such ploys.

'My dear, get some sweets for me, we'll take them along with us,' Manjhu suggested.

'In a basket, Khala?' Noori asked excitedly, and Shamman smiled, aware that the poor creature was in for trouble. As soon as Noori climbed into Bare Chacha's lap the train's whistle tooted. Noori was left behind bellowing. Shamman laughed until she was out of breath, but after a while she began to miss Noori; the two of them together would have had more fun.

She didn't like Manjhu's house at all. Two or three small rooms and a small courtyard. And then there was Manjhu's mother-in-law; the moment she set eyes on her she surmised this was the enemy. She didn't like the old crone from the very first. And she also cared nothing for Manjhu's mother-in-law's grandson, Kuddan. A beetroot-red complexion, blue eyes like those of a cat, and puffy cheeks!

One room was occupied by Manjhu and her husband, in the other her mother-in-law and Kuddan slept and that was where Shamman was to sleep as well. By now Shamman had come to accept she couldn't sleep with Manjhu in her room while her husband was around. But sometimes she wondered why that was so. No one had ever given her a satisfactory answer.

'No, you can't sleep with Manjhu.'

'Why?' she asked.

'Look, girl, don't talk nonsense now,' was the answer she got and she stopped talking nonsense.

She didn't have the nerve to ask Manjhu, who she thought had changed somehow. If she let Shamman lie down next to her by chance she would warn her beforehand, 'Now don't crowd me, it's so hot.'

But sometimes, for appearances' sake, she did cuddle her, but Shamman didn't feel any of the old warmth she had been accustomed to. That was why Shamman remained a little detached from her, although Manjhu seemed not to notice her aloofness.

Shamman disliked Kadir, alias Kuddan, because although he was older than her, he never failed to take a beating from her, he dreaded bickering and squabbles and cowered if Shamman mentioned wrestling even in jest. All day long he sat next to his grandmother and chewed betel-leaf; sometimes he played with the nutcracker and ran errands for his grandmother.

As for the old woman, Shamman did not make any concessions from

23

the very beginning. Despite Manjhu's threats she refused to call her Dadi, saying instead 'Manjhu's mother-in-law' when talking about her, which infuriated the old woman. When she made Manjhu scold her, Shamman became even more obstinate, beginning to use a disrespectful form of address and referring to her in the third person.

In a few days she grew tired of Manjhu's house and began to miss home. She missed Noori and her two older brothers – they didn't beat her all that much, although they did squeeze her fat cheeks – and Bari Apa, well, she was a problem. But she didn't have to have any contact with her if she didn't want to. Here, on the other hand, were Kuddan and the old woman, both of whom were of no interest to her.

In the afternoon Manjhu shut herself up in her room and went to sleep. Her mother-in-law, meanwhile, sat in the veranda sifting lentils. Shamman would walk along the flower-beds as if she were out of her mind, or run behind the hens in the courtyard. Sometimes she went to the kitchen and roasted potatoes, and if all of this left her restless and uneasy, she climbed the parapet and sat there silently, her feet dangling, watching the dry leaves scurrying after one another on the empty road. On the trees nearby, monkeys bounded from here to there, leaping from one branch to the next like rope-dancers in a circus. If, by chance, one of the monkeys lost its grip and suddenly fell with a thud on the wall, Shamman burst out laughing. If only she too were a monkey. The monkeys must have more feeling than Manjhu's mother-in-law and Kuddan. All these two ever seemed to do was clean lentils, winnow grains and, if there was any time left, collect rags of all colours to make unattractive *kotis*.

One day Kuddan took out his collection of coloured glass marbles and said, 'Come, Shamman, let's play.'

As a rule Shamman didn't allow Kuddan to be too familiar with her but, when she saw the green and red marbles, she melted. Placing a marble next to her eye, she gazed for a long time at the colours darting through its centre. It seemed as if someone had taken a rainbow broom and swept circles with it inside the marble. Another marble was like a silk tassel caged in glass, the tassel suddenly moving like a caterpillar as she watched spellbound.

'Kuddan, come, let's plant these marbles in the flower-bed.'

'In the flower-bed?'

'Yes, and when the trees grow, thousands of marbles will appear like berries, and then, indeed sir, we'll break them off and collect them, yes, we will.'

'But Dadibi will beat us, won't she?'

'Hunh! And how will Dadibi find out? Oh, but when the trees grow she'll die from happiness, you just wait and see.'

'All right, let's do it.' Today Kuddan decided to do something without his grandmother's consent. Shamman felt a surge of affection for him. After planting the marbles in the soil they poured plenty of water on it and then sat down, their elbows resting on their knees, and waited.

Shamman was very eager to see the marbles grow. Once, when she had planted coriander seeds, she went early the next morning to see if the buds had appeared and, when she saw nothing, she was alarmed; was the coriander ruined? But on the third or fourth day she saw tiny brown strands rising from the earth. Having rent the earth's bosom, the minuscule seedlings had finally sprouted. A few among them were completely bent, their backs hunched over as if someone were dragging them down. Shamman tried to straighten them by supporting them with twigs, but they immediately snapped in the middle. That day her spirits drooped and, sitting next to the vegetable patch, she spent most of her time scrutinising the struggle of the buds to emerge from the earth. Some had appeared while she was eating breakfast, and the others were still involved in a tussle. One in particular was pulling itself out just like a live worm and within minutes emerged like a baby snake slithering out of its hole. Shamman breathed a sigh of relief, as if she was the one making all the effort. Hanging from the tip of the bud was the nose-bob of the coriander seed, which, some time later, snapped off, and by late afternoon the bud was standing tall, stretching out its arms like a victorious soldier.

Today she was going to see the marble buds sprout. The slippery, multicoloured glass orbs, like rice cakes twisted into a diadem. She'd take these orbs and string them into a necklace – no, no, how will the trees grow then? Bunches of colourful marbles resembling damsons danced before her eyes.

The buds had still not sprouted by late afternoon. Shamman dozed off. When she woke up in the evening her heart broke. Manjhu's mother-in-law was washing the marbles in the mortar in which she ground spices. What? Perhaps she was going to sauté them with the meat. Shamman attacked her.

What came next was most unpleasant. Shamman bit Manjhu's mother-in-law's wrist, and Manjhu slapped Shamman until her bones rattled.

Today her heart and her mind broke down in tears together. Hunh!

You can't seed marbles. Why, if she could help it she would pick up Manjhu's mother-in-law and put her in the ground. And then she got to thinking . . . she dug a hole and planted the old woman in it . . . the next day a seedling appeared, brown, striped . . . like the cobra the snake charmers carry in their baskets . . . just like that! Shamman, mad with joy, looked at it and was beside herself with excitement. Then, when it grew taller than the nim tree, bunches and bunches of shrivelled up, foul-smelling old women dangled from its branches. Drawing a long breath, she began shaking them off, as if they were ripe tamarinds, and soon the entire courtyard was swarming with thousands of coughing, sneezing old women, some with *paan-dans*, some sitting on divans cutting up betel-nut, others crowding the kitchen, wreaking havoc with the food cooking on the stove, two or three leaping about next to the pickle jars. Terrified by the sight of so many old women, Shamman stretched out her hands and tried to push them away.

How fortunate that she quickly decided to abandon the notion of planting the old woman; what a disaster that would have been. One old woman had succeeded in making her life unbearable, and what if there were more? She was also very upset with Kuddan for running to his precious grandmother with the news. She wanted to scratch out his eyeballs, which reminded her of a kitten's blue eyes, and place them where the marbles had been.

Manjhu –
consenting to parda

6

Slowly her hatred for Manjhu grew, until finally she began to despise everything about her. For one thing, she was gradually becoming fat and indolent. The old mother-in-law followed her around like a maid, but Manjhu didn't have a kind word for anyone.

One day Shamman saw Manjhu chewing on a piece of yellow clay. Shamman's heart lurched. She remembered that when she used to eat clay a snake had been born. And now Manjhu was eating clay.

'Manjhubi eats clay,' she quietly informed Kuddan.

'Who? My *Chachi*?'

'Yes, and that's why her stomach is swollen. You'll see, a big snake, so big, will come out from her stomach.'

Kuddan went and told Dadibi.

'Dadibi, Shamman says a snake will come out of *Chachi*'s stomach.'

'Dust in her mouth! Didn't I tell you, boy, not to talk to this lunatic, but you don't pay any attention. Look at her, she's saying such vile things about her own sister.'

The old woman grumbled for hours. Shamman continued to observe secretly Manjhu's pale, dispirited face and her sluggish body. She imagined there were massive, hissing snakes coiled about in Manjhu's stomach and her hatred for Manjhu grew. But no one seemed to be worried. As a matter of fact, the old woman appeared happier than usual now that she had the run of the entire household; she deliberately cooked heavily spiced food for Shamman and ate ghee and sugar herself.

Amma came one day and Manjhubi became very sick.

'Kuddan, you'll see who is right, your grandmother or me – I can't tell you how big the snake is – that's why Manjhubi is weeping.'

'*Chacha* is away on a trip, who will kill the snake?'

'The policeman in the police station, who else, my dear?' she said with confidence.

In the middle of the night Shamman woke up to the sound of bells ringing. There was a commotion in Manjhu's room. Screaming, she bolted towards the room. One or two women tried to restrain her. She kept wailing, 'Ohhh, my Manjhu, ahhh, my Manjhu!'

'Is it dead?' she asked one of the women.

'Who?'

'The snake,' she whispered.

'I say, daughter, why are you bothering with her? She's my daughter-in-law's sister, the wretch is mad,' Manjhu's mother-in-law said before hurrying to take care of some household business. Today she seemed to be walking on air. A little later Amma appeared; she too seemed somewhat agitated.

'Amma, Manjhubi . . .' Shamman said with a sob.

'She's all right, come, come and see your baby nephew.' Amma was bursting with joy. Leading her by the hand, Amma took her in.

'Oh!' Shamman's eyes flew open in amazement. A tiny baby, resembling a Chinese doll, rested in a woman's lap and Manjhu lay quietly on her bed.

'And the snake?' Shamman asked her mother fearfully.

'Don't be foolish, girl.'

27

'Where did this baby come from?' she asked the next day.

'You know that memsahib? She brought him for Manjhu.'

'Oh. Amma, can you get one for me too? Manjhu's mother-in-law won't let me touch him.'

'Yes, I'll get one for you,' Amma said and some of the women started laughing.

'Then the policeman must have killed the snake. That's right.'

But Shamman could not understand how such a dark-complexioned memsahib could bring them such a fair-skinned baby. And Manjhubi had shrunk!

'Two and two is four,' she counted, 'but something is definitely not right.'

Bored now with her stay at Manjhubi's, she returned home with Amma.

7

On her return from Manjhu's house she felt as if she had buried her, and strangely enough she was not the least bit sorry. 'I thank the burglar who took so much from me; he left me destitute and with no fear of losing anything more.' It was just as well that the malady had been obliterated. She now understood that she could never have Manjhu, and to torture herself trying to regain her was as pointless as attempting to make a leech suck on a rock.

Widowed, Bari Apa moved back permanently and became Shamman's guardian. There was only one task in the world Amma was fit to perform, and that was giving birth. She had no idea what came after that, nor did anyone feel the need to enlighten her. As for Abba, his need for his wife came before the children.

Shamman never quite trusted Bari Apa. Although Bari Apa constantly avowed that Shamman's good was what she most desired and all she wanted to do was to ensure a proper future for her, she really used Shamman as a tool for making Noori rectify her mistakes.

'If you are not obedient everyone will curse you like they curse Shamman.'

'If you don't bathe you'll have lice like Shamman does.'

'If you don't study you'll remain illiterate like Shamman.'

'You're being stubborn like Shamman again.'

'You're telling a lie, just like Shamman does.'

And, 'It's this Shamman who has ruined you – don't you dare play with her any more!'

That was not all. Bari Apa taunted Amma as well.

'Well, I'm not Amma so . . .'

'I can't fuss like Amma,' she'd say, although she constantly kissed and licked her two children's cheeks as if they were mangoes.

This made Shamman's mother blush with embarrassment and she proceeded to wish for Shamman's death. But she felt her greatest accomplishment was that along with all the riff-raff she had produced, she had given birth, had she not, to Bari Apa, a gem of a daughter?

But this gem of a daughter had been widowed in her youth. The deceased left behind two children over whom she now sat guard like an eagle. These were not children, however, these were the two wheels of obedience and good manners. You may spin yarn for ever, but little chance that the spindle will ever bend out of shape. Salaams to everybody on first waking up in the morning, greeting guests promptly with their proper titles, reciting, swiftly and without hesitation, 'I remember the old days' and 'There is a prayer on my lips'. And then would begin a test of how well they knew their English:

'Noori, what is *nak*?'

'Nose.'

'And *kan*?'

'Ear.'

'*Dant*?'

'Cheek.'

'No, no, dear, that's *gal*, what is *dant*?'

'Teet',' Munoo would quickly volunteer with a lisp.

'Good! Well done,' the guests would applaud.

'All right, now recite "Twinkle, twinkle little star" – stand up on the chair and do it with actions.'

And then, standing on the chair, Noori recited nursery rhymes, jumping up and down like a female monkey; later Munoo continued to name different parts of the body in English, his attention actually riveted on the *ladoos* arranged on a plate before the guests.

Usually Shamman was not present when guests were being entertained and, if she wandered in by accident, unwashed, dressed in soiled clothes, no one introduced her. When some of Bari Apa's friends, mistaking her for a neighbour's child, handed her some biscuits, Bari Apa immediately admonished her: 'All right, that's enough, go and play now.'

Who else did poor Bari Apa have in life except these two little children, what else except sorrow and tears? Widowhood at this age? But she was more ill-tempered than before, as if by becoming a widow she had earned a special right to be disagreeable. Had she done anyone a favour by not wearing bangles and coloured *dupattas*? She not only mourned her dead husband, she also made life a hardship for her in-laws and her own father and mother, all of whom were very much alive. With the arrival of a holiday she began enacting her own little drama; her face covered, she would crouch in a corner and start weeping and moaning. Within minutes the henna would be tossed out, the bangle-seller would be sent away, and the preparation of sugary-sweet *see-wayan* would be postponed. One received the Eid money as if Amma had a loan to repay, her life hanging in balance.

But the sweet, fatherless girl was coddled no end. Large quantities of henna were mixed for her and designs created with it on her palms. However, Shamman found the idea of applying henna so repugnant and useless that she refused to have any on her hands.

'It's horrible, like wet mud,' she'd say hatefully.

'Why look, your hands are so pretty when it's all washed off,' Noori would say, extending her red palms towards her.

'Hunh! Red like the hands of a villager! It's like betel-leaf spittle splattered all over your hand. *My* hands are white like a mem's,' Shamman said, although she knew that the hands of white women were not at all so dark and filthy. But her remark made Noori feel belittled, something Shamman found very gratifying.

No one should think that Bari Apa never wore a coloured *dupatta* or that she had withdrawn from the world. There were such tints in her white *dupatta* that she glowed, and once even a new bride's wedding garments seemed pale in comparison. A white crêpe or chiffon *dupatta* on which the unfortunate widow had stitched some delicate Bombay lace; her *kurta* a white embroidered muslin, the neckline adorned all over with dainty needlework of flowers and trimmed with fine silken braids, a mesh devised of golden stars and tassels made of beads at every step – yes, and there was no need to impose the gloom of widowhood on the pyjamas, which were wide-bottomed and fashioned from pale green or light blue raw silk. And on her wrists were the two delicately crafted bangles Bare Chacha had given her at the time of her husband's passing away, and on her finger the emerald ring which had been her husband's gift, and yes, sometimes only at the insistence of her younger sister came the long earrings; otherwise she wore the old clove-shaped pearl studs. Black pumps went along with white, flowered socks, silken if possible, but cotton socks would do as well. As for the parting in her hair, she wasn't allowed to have one, but who would have stopped her? It was the poor woman's own heart that was dead. For this reason she fluffed up all her hair on the top and left curls on each side of her face, just long enough for her earlobes to peer from under them. Because her eyesight was ruined from constant weeping, she used gold-rimmed glasses when she went out.

But when Bari Apa went out adorned in this manner in her state of widowhood, people expressed great amazement.

'Why, she's blossoming in rags!'

Once a proposal arrived for one of the other sisters and the women, seeing Bari Apa, made a demand for her instead.

Amma said, 'What's this? This poor creature is a widow.'

It was with great pride that Bari Apa narrated this story of how she, a mother of two children, was mistaken for a virgin. Actually, her face had the youthful, naive look of an unmarried girl.

No sooner did anyone mention Bari Apa's husband, than Amma began sighing, embarking on lengthy praises of the deceased.

'Ahh, he did not have a tongue in his mouth, and what a broad chest he had, and a face like a platter.'

Amma was notorious for making up things and always embellished her stories with exaggerations and half-truths. It was nothing for her to describe a two-inch object as being three feet long.

'She's like the underside of a flat pan, and Amki like saffron mixed with dough,' she'd say, although neither was 'she' like a flat pan, nor was Amki like saffron-coloured dough. Still, people believed what she told them because she was a well-respected elder.

Mourning for her husband's death had made Bari Apa cantankerous, but what great catastrophe had befallen Munoo and Noori? Why did they act like they were the heirs of Genghis Khan? If they wanted something, they threw a tantrum and got it. Actually, the truth of the matter was, their father had died; this dead father carried more weight than a hundred living fathers. The entire household, no, the whole family, trembled in fear of the dead man's ghost, so much so that often

31

Shamman was forced to pray that she too might become a widow, or at least that her parents might die. Then she would show them all.

Her parents' honour held safely within her grasp, Bari Apa was continuing to do her family a favour. But the act of stifling her own desires was imbuing her with greater power to dominate. She had annihilated her own femininity for the sake of her father's honour, but Shamman was not the least bit grateful. She would not have minded at all if Bari Apa decided to sell herself. Bari Apa's children would still be more favoured than anyone else; ahh, the poor widow, the orphans!

8

Everything entered her life with the force of a hurricane. Without warning the idea of providing an education for her seized everyone's thoughts like the plague; everybody came after her with a whip that swished 'Study!' Bari Apa was less concerned with teaching her and more with making her look stupid and inferior in comparison to Noori. As for Maulvi Sahib and Master Sahib, they too treated her badly.

'Go to the bridge,' one of them would say, directing her attention to a word problem in her book.

'But why?' she wanted to know.

Then would come a question about someone's brother-in-law. So, what did Shamman care? He wasn't her brother-in-law, was he? She became irritated; why should she learn this lesson if she had no intention of having anything to do with someone's brother-in-law?

'Count up to ten.'

At this point her patience ran out and she felt like taking a hammer and, counting to a hundred, hitting Master Sahib on the head with it. And then, 'Six times five is thirty.' Can you imagine – why is five times six not sixteen? After this, addition, subtraction, multiplication and division. If only she knew whose flesh she was dividing, whose blood was being drained, because then she might at least feel some compassion and develop an interest in what she was studying. But not becoming interested was impossible in Master Sahib's company. Usually, glancing surreptitiously at someone else's work, she copied the answer, making sure she was the last one to present it to Master Sahib, but every now and then Master Sahib got wind of what was going on and insisted on examining her slate carefully. That was such a difficult time for her; depositing globs of saliva on her palms, she rubbed her slate fearfully, her throat dry and the muscles in her stomach contorting, making her feel sick. But Master Sahib's blows acted like magic and all her discomfort evaporated in the twinkling of an eye. Word problems had become attached to her existence like a disease and endlessly agitated her very soul.

'If you can buy two oranges for one paisa, how many oranges can you buy with a rupee-and-a-half?'

In the first place, she was not fated to have the luxury of buying two oranges with one paisa, and in the second place the oranges one would buy with two paisas would be more than enough; who would be foolish enough to buy a truckload of oranges for a rupee-and-a-half? Won't all of them rot? Last summer their aunt in Agra sent two large baskets of melons and most of the melons had to be thrown away eventually because they went bad. Just then she remembered the aunt's bearded husband; she and Noori got hold of the piece of wet clay he had set aside for ablutions and plastered it on a wall. Perhaps that was why he had stopped sending them melons. The melons were so nice, slippery and sticky as they were washed in colanders in the middle of the courtyard and . . .

'*Tarr!*' A slap landed on her and, sliding over the melon seeds, she awoke from her reverie, the corner of her slate hitting her nose with the sudden movement of her hand.

'Listen, you dimwit, if you were given a paisa, how many oranges would you buy with it?'

If, by some remote chance, fate warmed up to her and she did have a paisa in her possession, was she completely mad that she should go out and use it to get tart, tangy oranges? And why shouldn't they be tart? Any oranges bought with two paisas were sure to be tart and tangy. Master Sahib was a sour one himself; why did he want her to buy tangy oranges? She had decided a long time ago that if she ever got a paisa she would immediately go and buy *gazak* speckled with pistachio bits, making sure she also got a *rewari* to taste.

'Are you listening? How many oranges will you get?'

'Oranges . . . Umm . . .' She hadn't quite decided between the *gazak* and the oranges when Master Sahib lost all patience.

'You moron! Yes, oranges, if you can buy two for one paisa, how many will you get for one-and-a-half rupee?'

'One-and-a-half? One and-a-half rupee, just think!'

'Yes, can you convert that into paisas?'

You couldn't say no in Master Sahib's presence, so she said, 'Yes.'

'All right, go ahead then.'

And she began converting the sum into paisas. There had to be quite a few paisas in a rupee-and-a-half, a lot as a matter of fact, yes, a lot. She remembered that at Eid her *koti* pocket was weighted down with the eleven annas she had collected as *eidi*. She was so perturbed when Amma asked to borrow three annas for something or the other. Amma was so eager to spend someone else's money; no sooner did she see anyone with money than she draped herself in a mantle of impoverishment. What was taken was never returned, and who had the courage to make demands?

'Speak, girl! How many paisas in a rupee-and-a-half?'

'How many paisas in a rupee-and-a-half?'

'Yes, you wretch!'

'Sixteen,' she blurted out to save herself from the blow that was being readied for her.

'Sixteen? Sixteen paisas?' Once again Master Sahib erupted, as if someone had snatched sixteen paisas from him. After he had boxed her ears he proceeded to convert the sum into paisas himself. 'Ninety-five, you imbecile. Now tell me, how many paisas do you have?' The payment for the conversion was exacted in the form of a wallop.

'Ninety-five.'

'All right, now you go to the bazaar.'

'Yes.' As if someone would let her go to the bazaar, though she had no energy left to go anywhere after all the blows she had received. Secondly, these were all excuses to make a fool of her. However, she had no choice but to pretend she was going to the bazaar because she could see floating before her eyes the hand that was raised to strike her.

'Now you buy oranges at the rate of two for a paisa.'

Ohh! The same tart oranges again! Well, she buys them grudgingly.

'How many did you get?'

'Eh?' She made a face as if she would have the right answer shortly. 'Oranges?'

'Yes, how many oranges will you have, you wretch!' Master Sahib bellowed.

'Three,' she said hesitatingly.

34

'Three oranges for a rupee-and-a-half?'

'No, no,' she sniffled while trying to ward off Master Sahib's hand with her elbows.

'Then give me the correct answer, quickly.'

All this would continue into the evening. Exhausted, bathed in sweat, Master Sahib teetered as if someone had spun him around on a wheel. His limbs turned this way and that of their own volition, and looking at him one got the impression that instead of teaching children he had been engaged in chronicling his own fate. He was crushed when he left, but he did not leave without first avowing that he would forcibly make her buy the remainder of the oranges.

The rivers Jhehlum, Chenab, Ravi, Bias, Sutlej – Jhehlum, Chenab, Ravi – one after another, like the round beads on a *tasbih*. Jhehlum, after Jhehlum – Chenab, like children holding each others' shirt ends and going round and round in a circle, playing trains. Jhehlum, then Chenab, followed by Ravi and then –

'Did you learn the lesson?' Master Sahib attacked her suddenly.

'Yes, Jhehlum, Chenab . . .'

'Munoo, you wretch, sit properly, yes, go on . . .'

'Jhehlum, Chenab, Ra . . .'

'You won't behave, Achu? Where's your slate? Take it out of your bag. Is it laying eggs in there?'

Master Sahib continued to distribute four-fingered slaps with great expertise; there was no way any one section could become negligent.

'Yes, yes, where does Jhehlum begin from . . . yes, take out a pencil . . . yes . . . why are you sitting quietly, girl?'

'Jhehlum . . . umm . . .' She started to slip.

'Go on, you wretch, why are you stuck at one place – yes, come on.'

'Chenab,' she would stutter hesitatingly.

'Yes, yes, yes, now where does it begin? I'm watching you, Munoo, you blockhead! Yes, speak up.' It seemed as if Master Sahib was playing a game; he would bark in this direction and that and end up teaching no one.

'Speak, you wretch, where does it flow?' (a river)

'On the earth, sir.'

'What? On the earth?' Master Sahib lost his temper as if by dragging the river to earth someone had insulted him. He became exasperated.

'But tell me where it flows from and what regions it flows through.'

'Regions, sir?'

'Yes, regions, or do you think it's going to flow through your head?'

35

'Sir, it flows through . . .' she floundered, trying her best to remember.

'Yes, you've forgotten, haven't you? Well, what other rivers flow in the same region?'

'In the same region? Rivers, sir?'

'Name all the rivers. Chenab and?'

'Chenab, sir?'

'Yes, Chenab, you dimwit, and what else?'

'And . . . umm . . . and Chenab.' She pressed down hard on her memory.

'You've forgotten the names of the rivers again, haven't you, you fool!'

'Jamuna, Godavari, ji, and Krishna,' she would begin hurriedly, raising the crook of her arm over her head as she rushed through the names. But Master Sahib was already in the grip of frenzied rage. And then she broke down and wept without restraint.

How much better than these dreadful rivers was the small creek that zigzagged through the fields like a silver snake. Along its banks tiny, fly-sized frogs hopped in the grass, and when she placed these frogs as passengers in a paper skiff and set it down in the creek, how stately the little boat looked as it sped gallantly through the water. She would run along the banks, clapping, and when a twig or a piece of wood got caught in the boat's folds, making it spin and become unravelled, the little frogs jumped out into the water and swam to the embankment like daring swimmers. Sometimes fish appeared in the creek, and then hundreds of birds came to its banks to have a feast. How much fun that was!

But Jhehlum, Ravi, Bias, Sutlej – she had to memorise these too.

9

Noori was, after all, Bari Apa's daughter; the offspring of a snake is a snake. Shamman had developed a friendship with her after a great deal of thought. She and Noori were the only girls in the house. All the other children were boys and she didn't get along with them at all. And Noori also had dolls so both she and Shamman could have doll weddings every day. Perched in the window of the storage room, the two girls spent hours playing together with their rag dolls. When they got tired of their games they turned to watch the boys playing in the street. The street was more than a street, it was like a stage. There goes the old blind woman's daughter-in-law, from the window Sadiq calls out, two boys pass by, scuffling, calling each other names – 'Berries, come and get berries!' 'Kidneys, liver, lace, beads, soap' – and then there were the well-behaved female monkeys who sat on the parapet, nibbling on the lice they picked from their babies' hair. And finally Mullah *ji* from the old mosque, whose appearance quickly made the girls hide beneath the window, their hearts pounding, their noses wet with perspiration. But a little later, their curiosity aroused again, they were tempted to a peek. Slowly, like frightened mice, they lifted their heads. His nose to the wall, Mullah *ji* stood for hours engaged in behaviour that seemed strange and frightening. One day, while they were totally engrossed in watching him, he turned to look at them and said something. At first they couldn't make out what important matter it was that he wanted to convey to them, but then they leaned forward and were rooted to the ground with fear, like monkeys who become hypnotised when face to face with a cobra; holding their breath, their fists grasping the bars of the window, they were suspended at the window, staring. Then, as if jolted by an electric shock, they fell back like injured birds but, wasting no time, they scrambled to their feet and ran as though Mullah *ji* was about to jump through the window bars and grab their necks. For a long time afterwards they remained in a stupor, their throats parched, their hands and feet numb.

After a drink of water had brought them back to their senses, they regained enough strength to look at each other fearfully, as if asking, 'Are you feeling all right?'

Then they broke into laughter. Glancing at each other from the corners of their eyes, they tittered, as though there was some deep, dark secret churning around in their hearts. They said nothing to each other, acting like mature women even though question marks floated on their faces and they were visibly nervous.

For several days they didn't have the courage to look in the direction of the window, and behaved as though they had murdered somebody there with the corpse still lying where they had left it, rotting. When they went past the window they threw meaningful glances at it from a distance. Sometimes their imagination leaped across to the other side and then fled from there in terror. But with time their fears diminished and they fled from the window only when it was time for midday prayers and the street was as deserted as a cemetery. However, they became so bold finally that they would first hide themselves deliberately when they saw Mullah *ji* appearing, and then jump up to sneak a look at him. Whenever they saw him they felt nauseated, their stomachs turned, and their wounded imaginations shuddered.

Noori's girl doll and Shamman's boy doll were married every day. The bride sat in a shoebox-turned-palanquin; her wrist encased in a beaded bangle, she offered salaams to everyone, and then went to sleep on the bed. Now came the bridegroom, jumping, and stood on the chair – end of the game!

When their friend Sadika's aunt got married, not only did the two girls watch all the hustle and bustle from the parapet, they also learned many new wedding rituals. A hand mirror was placed in the bride's lap and the bridegroom saw a reflection of her face in it.

'Wife, I'm your slave, open your mouth,' the nervous bridegroom was forced to say, and then he was made to lick *kheer* from the bride's palm. He happily licked *kheer* from the bashful bride's hand and all the people gathered laughed, as if someone had been tickling them. The women tittered merrily during every lively ceremony imbued with romantic innuendo. Shamman too found herself in the grip of a strange longing, while Noori insisted that they go to the storage room and play the wedding game right away. And that was not all. After the ceremonies were over, the women began teasing the bridegroom with such gusto one would think the bridegroom was a sugary delicacy being offered to them for tasting. Then, at night, the bridegroom was submitted to further embarrassment, a plot in which a few young, fun-loving females were taking active part. The unmarried girls were scolded and shooed away from the scene. Who knows what was going on. Like flies, women were glued to the windows and the chinks in the doors, while husbands and children waited impatiently at home.

This time the dolls' wedding was celebrated with great pomp and show. Puffed rice instead of dried dates was scattered about, and the bridegroom licked *kheer* from the bride's palm. Noori, the careless girl, got the bride's *dupatta* all splattered with *kheer*, so Shamman threw her daughter-in-law across the doorway. This was followed by a wrestling match between Shamman and Noori during which they savagely pulled at each other's hair.

The doll was filthy now, with a face like a horse. So when Bari Apa made a new doll for them, they had her stitch on a nose crafted from a piece of cloth; a black sock was unravelled for the braid and a long scarf was also added. But still the girls were not satisfied, so they asked for fingers made from string. And then one day, summoning up great courage, they secretly stuffed two balls of cotton in the doll's *koti*. They felt such shame, they couldn't even look at her. Draped in a filmy crêpe *dupatta*, the doll with the cloth nose and the string fingers now looked like a woman alive and real. God forgive them! They were not interested in anything else and all day long they played wedding games with her. But one day, while searching for some swatches in the rag basket, Bari Apa stumbled upon the doll and their secret was exposed. Such a beating they received that soon they were praying for death. Bari Apa tore off the *koti* and stitched up the shirt. From that day on they lost all interest in the doll. What was she except a bundle of rags with a piece of cloth for a nose and strings hanging from her palms instead of fingers?

10

Amma was fed up with Shamman. All day long she harassed her brothers, quarrelled with the servants and interfered with their work, made life unbearable for her sisters-in-law, and was a terror to her nephews. Master Sahib had accepted defeat, and the Mullani who taught the Koran touched her ears and said, 'May God have mercy! My word, what a shame someone's offspring should turn out like this.'

And the person she was spoiling the most was Noori. What Bari Apa had feared came to be. Shamman's influence corrupted Noori completely and with each passing day she deteriorated. This was when Bari missed her dead husband more than ever, because on the one hand Noori was getting out of hand, and on the other, her own health was declining. She was rarely able to digest her food properly any more, and the quota of sleep that Allah had allotted to her was obviously depleted. One of her husband's cousins had just obtained a degree in medicine and it was he, the poor fellow, who kept his sister-in-law going. If there was one person who had the slightest bit of success in curing her seizures, which no doctor had been able to treat until now, it was Rashid.

But what can you say about seizures? They don't send out warnings before they strike. You can call it a coincidence or Allah's mercy that at the time of the seizure Rashid was always at hand. What would happen if he were not there? A thousand medicines had been consumed, but the seizures had persisted.

Some members of the family made efforts to get him to cure the middle one's acne, but he hedged, and in the end poor Sanjhu was married to a lawyer. Sanjhu, the unfortunate girl, was one of those women who come into the world gracefully, and live respectably in their parents' home until some man weds them and takes them away. Then, as long as their strength holds out they bear children, nurture and raise them, and ultimately, burdened with some chronic disease, suffer painfully until Allah puts them in their graves, and everyone can't help but say, 'How commendable! What a virtuous wife she was!'

But Sanjhu wasn't dead as yet. Her life was just beginning. No sooner did she leave than Bari was afflicted with seizures and, God forgive us, she was badly stricken. She felt lethargic and her spirits drooped. In order to distract herself she started playing the harmonium. The off-key strains of 'He may be the son of Marium' accompanied the '*peen peen*' of the harmonium for hours, but her heart grew even more agitated. Rashid came and sat down with her for long periods of time, provided instructions about her illness, and every now and then gave her an injection in her arm. Getting an injection in the arm tickled her until she became giddy, but at least the seizures stopped for three or four days following the treatment.

However, Bare Bhaya developed an inexplicable hostility towards Rashid. Actually this is what happened. His wife, who was always looking for excuses, kept asking for a prescription for diarrhoea and poor Rashid just forgot to bring it. But she insisted that he was deliberately ignoring her request at someone's bidding. Bari swore on her two children that the fault lay with Bare Bhaya's blockhead of a servant who paid no heed to Rashid's requests for a paper to write on.

'The poor man is ready to take care of everyone,' Bari said. But when Bare Bhaya also complained, she was enraged. 'He's not anyone's servant. He comes here because of me and as soon as he's here the entire household suddenly develops maladies.'

And that was indeed true. Bari was the only one who had any claims on her in-laws. So what if her husband had died, his family was still there, wasn't it? If she left today, who could hold her hand? It was she who had decided to destroy her spirit.

It is said Bare Bhaya took this to heart. How could he have thought of such a thing? Obviously it was the doing of his darling wife. So he began his pursuit. Whenever Rashid came, Bhaya appeared and sat with him, forcing the poor fellow to leave in a hurry. *Array*, has anyone known seizures to be treated in a hurry?

Matters took a really alarming turn when Bare Bhaya intercepted Rashid's letters and sent Bari a clear warning that if this exchange didn't stop, Abbajan would have to be informed. If she was so serious then she should get married honourably. Bari's mother-in-law got wind of this and the old crone arrived on the scene in a huff, cursing and protesting furiously. Such was the disturbance that followed that poor Rashid was prohibited from coming to the house any more. From that day, the seizures lost some of their intensity and why not? Whom could they rely on now? But Bari's anger grew threefold and her love for her children made her restless. For this reason she couldn't bear to see Noori's destruction at the hands of Shamman. And so there was no other recourse but to send Shamman away to school.

11

When Shamman arrived at school she first looked carefully all around her to make sure she knew exactly where the enemy might strike her from. She immediately told the matron that she should be kind enough not to pat her affectionately, nor treat her lovingly in an attempt to prevent her from getting homesick. Shamman was quite familiar with such shows of affection and, after having tested Manjhu, she was convinced that to love someone or have someone love you was a farce. She fled from love the way a young bird flees from the noise flapper. She was no longer used to such things. What a long time it had been since words of compassion and tenderness came her way. She was so accustomed to hearing a rebuke in response to everything, she did not understand what it meant to accomplish a task simply for the sake of

41

praise. As a matter of fact, she was disappointed if she didn't receive a reprimand at every step.

On entering her classroom she cast a scornful look at her classmates, as though she found their whispering and giggling extremely distasteful. All the girls rose to their feet when the teacher walked in, but, like an idiot, Shamman remained seated. This made the girls break into laughter and, elbowing each other, they whispered remarks about her rude behaviour.

'Shamshad Fatima,' the distinguished-looking Miss Mumtaz said curtly, 'you can't stand because you have a backache?'

'Eh?' Shamman squawked. She was not used to being called by her real name, Shamshad.

The girls roared with laughter and Shamman's ears turned red with shame. She thought Miss Mumtaz was hateful. Not only was her tone formal, it was also tinged with just a touch of sugary sarcasm. Miss Mumtaz didn't say anything else to her. Struggling with feelings of shame and consternation, Shamman didn't know what was taught that day or what she learned.

For a few days she did not speak in class. She had enough sense now to stand when all the girls rose to greet the teacher, and then sit down; she also went in and out of the classroom with her fellow students and, during registration, she now said 'Present, Miss,' instead of the 'What is it?' she had responded with in the beginning. But after she said 'Present, Miss,' her ears burned with the memory of the first time she had blundered and the girls became hysterical with laughter. As a matter of fact, even on Miss Mumtaz's sombre, dignified face a smile had appeared which lingered for a long time.

In a week's time Shamman was demoted to a lower class. This was nothing new for her, but the girls turned the incident into a sensation. Wherever she went she was pursued by insinuations; the girls giggled, mocking her stupidity, and it became common knowledge that she had been demoted. Miss Mumtaz had reported that she was failing and could not continue in this class.

Surrounded by younger girls in her new class, she took on the status of a leader. Being younger, the girls were somewhat intimidated by her and in a few days she discovered that she was way ahead of them in age, intelligence and knowledge, and therefore she didn't need to study. When she went home after two months, she had become several times more stubborn, more coarse in her speech and more headstrong. Also, it was no longer easy to punish her. She stared at you very rudely at first

42

and then came out with a sharp rejoinder. In addition to all this she had developed the ability of stealing food from the kitchen cupboards without getting caught. With one quick glance about her, she reached into the cupboard and in one swoop plopped something in her mouth. The rest she hid under her arm and, the morsel lodged safely in her mouth, she walked away calmly, humming, so that anyone seeing her would think there was nothing in her mouth. She was also stealing money, but no one thought of suspecting her; joining the others, she searched for the stolen items with equal zest, her performance serving to further confirm her innocence. She had learned other horrible things as well from the girls at school which she now proudly shared with Noori.

On her return to school she discovered she had to deal with a new teacher. She seemed young, so Shamman immediately took to creating trouble. For a few days her mischievous battle continued, but then she realised she was losing. Instead of punishing her for her pranks by making her stand in a corner or on a bench, the new teacher ignored her completely, seemingly indifferent to her antics. Standing in the corner, Shamman used to make faces at the girls, forcing them to laugh, causing the teachers to seethe with anger so that they ordered her to stand on the bench next. From her place on the bench she faked dizziness and fell on the girls, once again disrupting class and making her classmates break into riotous laughter.

Instead of all this, in a few days she found herself in the grip of a thousand responsibilities. She was the class monitor; she had to clean the blackboard, keep track of the chalk supply, worry if the nail holding up the map was secure, keep the girls under control when they became noisy, put Miss Charan's umbrella and books in her desk, and every now and then also transport the exam notebooks to Miss Charan's room. When she was in her room, Miss Charan didn't look like a teacher at all. Assuming a very informal manner she would ask Shamman to sit down.

'Now, will you have tea or lemonade?' she would ask and Shamman would feel embarrassed. No one had ever talked to her like this. In a short while the two would be laughing and chatting like old friends. Shamman told her everything about her life at home. Miss Charan was upset with Bari Apa, the stories about Shano and Satto's pranks left her in stitches, and she liked Noori only a little.

Soon Miss Charan was asking Shamman to come to her room and help out with housework. She did the work proudly, but she felt sad when her chores were completed. Miss Charan had also begun assigning her extra classwork and after the exams she gave her a double promotion. Shamman was happiest knowing that she was now ahead of the class Miss Mumtaz taught.

Miss Charan continued to tutor her. She was the first person after Manjhu to create a place in Shamman's heart, to have the power to influence her. At Miss Charan's behest, she accomplished the most difficult of tasks; she would not hesitate even to kill for her.

Miss Charan's name was on her lips all the time. The girls tried to tease her, but her fixation intensified, gradually becoming tinged with a romantic feeling that overwhelmed her thoughts. The moment she set eyes on Miss Charan she was drawn to her and often it didn't matter where Miss Charan was; she remained as close to Shamman as her own heartbeat. If she happened to pass by, Shamman forgot what she was doing, and if she had been talking, she would begin to stutter. If Miss Charan was coaching another class in sports, Shamman couldn't concentrate on her work; the sound of Miss Charan's laughter made her tremble from head to toe. Everyone was of the opinion that Miss Charan was extremely dark and ill-looking, but Shamman saw her differently. She couldn't imagine anyone more beautiful. Although Shamman cared a little for her relatives and was afraid of God, she had never been preoccupied with either. Miss Charan, however, meant more to her than her family, her faith. Often she created an image of Miss Charan in her mind and worshipped the image passionately and with great devotion. 'Here comes Miss Charan . . . there she goes . . . there's a corner of her sari fluttering, there's the sheen of her blouse . . .'

Shamman's heart was not in her books. She forced herself to study only to please Miss Charan. She began to feel her teacher's physical presence even when she was not there. She's standing and Miss Charan's image rushes by her side; she's sleeping and Miss Charan is petting her; she's thirsty, her throat is parched, and Miss Charan is dripping cool, fragrant juices into her mouth. Sometimes she sees herself rambling in the night, crying, then finds herself on the frosty grass, shivering with a chill, and suddenly Miss Charan picks her up and puts her on the bed, her head resting on her down-filled pillow, and there Shamman pretends to be unconscious because she's afraid if she opens her eyes the dream will be shattered.

One night she found herself in the veranda in front of Miss Charan's room, searching for something. She stood still. How did she sleepwalk all this distance? Quickly she returned to her room and cowered inside her quilt. What was happening to her? Was it she or her spirit that dragged her about at night?

Some days later she found herself in front of Miss Charan's room again, this time sobbing hysterically. Frightened, she felt she was choking and was unable to utter any sound. Why was she crying? She didn't know why. She felt terrified as she made her way back to her room. It was dark in the veranda and, because it was winter, all the doors to the rooms were shut. She wasn't a coward and she wasn't afraid of cats, but she ran as if pursued by supernatural creatures. When she approached the matron's room she saw a lantern burning dimly. Just before she turned, a shadow lunged before her and disappeared. She shrieked. Her eyes bulged with dread.

Matron awoke and came out of her room. 'Who is it?' she asked.

Rushing forward, Shamman grabbed her. Matron was taken by surprise and, not sure who or what this was, she pushed Shamman away with great force.

'It's me, Shamshad, Shamman,' she stuttered, getting up hastily from the floor. 'There was a ghost after me just now.' She was paralysed with fear.

'Ghost? What ghost? Go back to your room.' Matron propelled her towards her room. She too seemed a little frightened.

'Making trouble at night too,' Matron grumbled. Returning with her to her room, Matron turned on the light and Shamman saw the same ghost standing next to her. She screamed again: 'Ghost!'

'Where? You stupid girl, this is your own shadow.'

Overcome by mortification, Shamman slipped quietly into bed. Matron turned off the light and, muttering under her breath, left the room. For a long time Shamman lay awake, unable to go back to sleep. Her heart beat violently, her whole body was stiff with fear.

The next day Shamman did not mention the incident to anyone. If Miss Charan were to find out that Shamman turned into a ghost at night and wept outside her room, she would surely begin to hate her. She didn't even want her teacher to know that she was obsessed with thoughts of her. But this was something that could not remain hidden for long and one day the principal informed Miss Charan that her influence on the girls' morals was questionable. The fact of the matter was that the principal was Miss Mumtaz's older sister, and since Miss Charan's arrival, Miss Mumtaz's popularity had steadily declined. Shamman of course adored Miss Charan, but the other girls liked her as well.

Miss Mumtaz was the badminton coach and Miss Charan the instructor for basketball. Most of the students preferred to play basketball, and Miss Mumtaz claimed that by being too informal and free with the girls Miss Charan was encouraging the girls to be disrespectful to all their teachers. Spurred on by her, she maintained, the girls opted for basketball instead of badminton. This was a blow to Miss Mumtaz's pride and subsequently a source of irritation for the principal. Shamman hated badminton because Miss Mumtaz humiliated the girls who didn't play well. She had formed two teams, one consisting of the girls who played skilfully and another made up of girls who didn't play too well, Shamman being a member of the latter. Every day the girls who played well won while the others lost. For this reason, on the days she had badminton practice, Shamman pretended to be sick or made some other excuse and spent that period watching Miss Charan playing basketball with the girls. She wanted to imprint every move of Miss Charan's on her heart. That's how she tosses the ball, with a flick of her slim hand, and there goes the ball – the girls proclaimed that Miss Charan's hands were skinny and dark, but to Shamman they appeared to have been cast from marble.

One night when she awoke she was shocked to find the principal standing in Miss Charan's room, dressed in a long robe and holding a torch in her hand. And Miss Charan was trying to make Shamman sit up straight. She wasn't even aware that she was sobbing loudly. Suddenly she became quiet and stared wide-eyed at Miss Charan. She was sitting on Miss Charan's bed! A real bed! Not the bed of her dreams, no, there was the pillowcase with the embroidered green flowers, the brown coverlet with the reddish-gold edging.

She was dragged back to her room.

The next morning the principal asked her a hundred questions, but she sulked and kept her mouth shut. How was it possible that she tell her all the things she thought, felt and saw?

Three days after the incident Miss Charan left. She didn't even come to meet any of the girls. All at once the watchman brought out her luggage and then she appeared with her handbag and walked straight out of the gates. A commotion ensued in the school. The girls questioned each other, but no one seemed to know what was going on. Surrounding her from all sides, the girls showered Shamman with questions, but she couldn't tell them anything. When the news of Miss Charan's departure became official, all the girls who liked her began weeping, for which the principal and Miss Mumtaz reprimanded them severely.

But Shamman did not shed a single tear. She walked about guiltily without a word, but all the time her steps were measured, as if she were carrying a delicate, cracked object that would be shattered with the slightest jolt.

After Miss Charan's departure she became very hard-hearted. She knew now the fault had never been Manjhu's. The fault lay somewhere with her, and she was ready to accept that fact now. She tried not to think of Miss Charan at all because her memory jabbed at the wound in her mind and left her in spiritual agony.

• realizing her faults

That year she failed her exams so she was transferred to the local mission school which Noori also attended. Here the teachers were even darker than Miss Charan, but Shamman didn't like any of them. Noori was very smart and, with help from Bari Apa's regular and diligent tutoring, she soon made a place for herself. But as for Shamman, people seemed to harbour a strange animosity towards her. She was expected to do·better even when she did her best. She was certain that she was a complete dimwit, and there was no doubt in her mind that her memory was deplorably bad. Everyone said she forgot things very quickly. Didn't she forget Miss Charan? Even when she forced herself she couldn't remember the exact details of her physiognomy, her clothes, the way she taught students to play basketball. Sometimes when she studied in Miss Charan's room she would hear her humming softly, a sound that seemed to help Shamman when she was stuck at a difficult question in her book; the tiny waves of Miss Charan's humming stabbed at the knot in her question, unravelling it for her. But she had forgotten all this.

Shamman studied at the mission school for two years. Once she received a double promotion and was awarded some prizes as well, but she carelessly discarded all honours. The thought of becoming attached to something made old fears come to the fore, the wound associated with Miss Charan's memory seared her mind. For two years she studied the Bible and learned a great many poems in praise of Jesus Christ. But she wasn't at all happy with kneeling on the canvas cushions in the church that pricked her knees as if they contained needles.

• fear of attachment + loving someone

There were times when she decided she would quietly become one of Christ's lambs, but her fear of Amma prevented her from taking this step. She was amazed to discover that Jesus was the son of God and that people didn't let him live in peace despite that. Why is it that the world is full of sinful people? Why don't people quickly learn goodness and happily head for heaven?

47

The Sacred Mother was a virgin! Thinking of this made her smile. She too was a virgin, was she not? If, God forbid, the Holy Father caused her to have an innocent baby Jesus, what would she do? Certainly Amma would refuse to give him any milk, but yes, she would use her own old *kurtas* to make clothes for him. Then she remembered that when the washerman's daughter had had a baby boy, everyone ostracised the girl. Shamman tried her best to explain: 'So what if you're a widow? Who can interfere with the Heavenly Father's will? He can do what he wants.' But the girl kept repeating, 'No, *bibi*, I've committed a sin.' And even after hours and hours of thinking, Shamman couldn't understand what this sin was and why people committed it.

When she came home from school and recited to Amma and the others the poems she had learned in praise of Jesus, Amma hit her palms against her forehead and began scolding Shamman. Did she now intend to become a Christian? she was asked. What else was there to do except send her back to the old school, and upon her arrival here Miss Charan's memory scorched her mind again, and her hatred for Miss Mumtaz grew four-fold.

12

This time her new life at the school started with new demons which fell upon her in one stroke. The most shameful, disgusting and hateful predicaments besieged her. For many days she planned suicide because swallowing poison once was a thousand times better than dying a slow, painful death. But finding any kind of poison at home was also difficult. Unnerved and confused by the changes in her body, she shed tears in seclusion. She was reminded of her frightening first-grade teacher, an awkward lump of flesh whose hands and feet were skinny, but who had piles of meat heaped on her chest and her stomach. The girls made fun of her and strange, lewd jokes became associated with her. Shamman's hatred for her was not just hatred, it was an emotion tinged with revulsion and fear. Actually she first experienced revulsion when she walked into her bathroom by mistake one day; she always forgot to

48

latch the bathroom from the inside. This was the second person after Mullah *ji* who made Shamman so nervous she felt she was immobilised.

Shut up in the silent isolation of her room, Shamman ruminated endlessly. The future, clothed in the ever-changing attire of terrifying dreams, danced before her. If only there was some medicine she could take to shrink herself to the size of a mouse. She was growing very rapidly. Different parts of her body were developing at different speeds. First, her legs seemed to have acquired a loathing for her torso and kept getting longer and longer. At night she felt as if her legs were stretching, twirling like long lines, jumping from the bed to crawl on the walls, headed for some unknown destination. Picking herself up on her elbows, she looked at her legs only to find they had swiftly shrunk back like worms, as though apprehended in the act of escape. From the corners of her eyes she watched her legs to see what they were up to next, but like wily snakes they pretended to be still. That was not all. Every feature on her face was behaving in a similar manner. Her nose, seemingly annoyed with the rest of her face, wandered off on its own. She had read a story in which there was a prince whose nose grew to be three feet long. The poor prince! No one talked to him. Her plait had also become peculiar, like the handle of a teapot, a stiff, small tail that wouldn't rest properly on her long neck.

There was one ailment whose cure she had stumbled on. It had to do with Amma's illness, although it had been hidden from her, and she had seen the bottle that had saved Amma's life. As soon as she had a chance, she gulped down its contents. The effect was instantaneous and she became well right away. Now if she had told someone of her illness, would she have received prompt treatment? Everything she said was always ignored. Once when she had mentioned the subject to Manjhu, she had scolded her severely, calling her 'shameless'. And the worst of it was that Noori, who was now attending the same school, was always probing into her most embarrassing secrets. But she stayed away from her because she knew Noori would smile contemptuously and then go and tell everybody. Shamman dissolved in her own grief. What? Dissolved? Why, there were lumps of flesh being plastered all over her.

She no longer walked or ran. Even the slightest breeze seemed to hurt her. Her body was like a ripened sore and the muscles in her legs seemed to be stretching painfully. She had always hated the older girls, always making fun of them. '*Dhap-a-dhup!*' they went when they were skipping, and when they landed on the floor it seemed there were cats fighting under their shirts. Shamman was able to get out of sports by making some excuse or the other. She was punished for dodging sports, but she suffered gladly, so much so that one day when she couldn't come up with a good excuse she slashed her foot with a razor, smiling smugly at her success for a long time afterwards.

Suddenly she began feeling very sick. She would get dizzy, her digestive system seemed to have gone awry, and black and white spots appeared on her face, while her forehead was pocked with acne. Her whole body seemed to be in the grip of an upheaval, and she felt her blood course through her body as if it were oppressively heavy, scalding hot oil.

No one took notice of her lethargy, and her punishments continued to multiply until finally the unfavourable reports reached Amma and Abba.

When the time came for annual check-ups, she was beset with a thousand fears. She looked around for excuses. Escape becomes nearly impossible once the executioner has picked up the sword.

When Matron asked her to remove her clothes she called her an ass, at which Matron broke into tears and cried until she was hysterical. Poor old withered Matron, what did she know of Shamman's misery?

The lady doctor slapped Shamman twice, but she struggled with her as well. The doctor asked her many obscene questions all of which she answered with a 'No'. The lady doctor had decided to torment her.

The next time she was examined she caused a lot of disturbance. That contemptible lady doctor was just fond of groping with her hands; the witch wouldn't let go.

Shamman was forced to take medicine and in a few days that horrible disease erupted again. And to make matters worse, the news spread throughout the entire school. The girls, consumed with curiosity, made all kinds of conjectures. Noori came on the pretext of seeing how she was doing. But Shamman, refusing to tell her anything, only scolded her.

'Tell me the truth, Shamman,' Noori said.

'Tell you what?'

'That . . . that, well, Birjees says you've had a baby.'

She began screaming in horror. So that's what it was. But the doctor hadn't told her anything. This was the limit. What if someone told Abba? Surely that would mean certain death for her. She remembered well how poor Genda had suffered. But then she started missing her tiny little baby.

'Where is he?' She started thinking. Maybe he's been hidden. But how could she raise him? Schoolwork, and then the exams looming ahead – who can raise a child like this? But it was not fair that they did not even show her the baby. At least she'd know who the baby had taken after, whom he resembled. How small he must be. Setting other worries aside, she became preoccupied with a new problem.

Her fever came down and she returned to her room, but even then no one showed her the baby. One day she mentioned the baby in passing to Saadat who opened her eyes wide and stared at her for a few minutes.

'But you're not married,' Saadat said.

'What? If I'm not married, then Saadat . . .?' She didn't continue. The image she had formed in her head of the baby, as small as a mouse, slowly began to blur.

'But Noori said . . .'

'What does Noori know?' Saadat said with an air of authority. 'Now don't say this to anyone else, you silly thing.'

Then Saadat proceeded to tell her so many things, becoming helpless with laughter when she was finished. Shamman joined in the laughter.

When she was alone in her bed she felt a certain sadness at the loss of this imaginary child. After hearing what Noori had said she had actually begun to feel the presence nearby of a little baby, crying, squirming. Sometimes she felt as if he were sleeping right next to her so that if she moved even slightly he would wake up. This feeling made her stiffen and, holding her breath, she would remain motionless for a long time. Often, while she slept, the sound of a crying baby crept into her ears and she would wake up with a start, staring about her wide-eyed in the darkness, searching for the illusion until finally she fell asleep again. And if Saadat had not revealed the truth to her, she would have continued to play hide-and-seek like this with the little creature for who knows how long. And now? She didn't know why, but the very thought of a baby made her baulk. How shameful, she thought guiltily.

Life was slipping out of the shadows into light. Gradually her sorrows diminished, although she did still feel stifled. But now she had become accustomed to everything. Life had taught her how to make compromises.

13

The matter was finished but Noori broadcast the story so audaciously that one day Shamman grabbed her and gave her a beating. When she was home she occasionally gave Noori a few smacks behind Bari Apa's back. But woe betide Noori if she ever complained to anyone. True, Bari Apa could punish Shamman in retaliation, but afterwards Shamman could easily give Noori a taste she would never forget. Ever since her arrival at the school, Noori had presented a very civilised demeanour. She even went so far as to refer to bird droppings as 'bathroom' and used overly polite phrases affectedly in her speech. Then Shamman beat her in the presence of her friends. Like a grown woman Noori broke into tearful lamentation, hitting her breast and wailing; that evening she rolled up her bedding and, gathering all her things, she shifted into her friend Jalees's room. Later she wrote a sorrowful letter to Bari Apa. Remembering the girl's deceased father, Bari Apa cried bitterly and then penned a pleading letter to the principal, begging her to save the orphaned Noori from Shamman's clutches. Noori was only too happy to be with Jalees, and Rasul Fatima, the girl with the enormous eyes, moved into Shamman's room.

Shamman hated Rasul Fatima with a passion. Rasul Fatima's bulging eyes were unusually large and lifeless, as if someone had placed two frogs on to a flat plate. Thin, straw-like eyelashes and rough-skinned, brown eyelids. A look of helplessness, impoverishment and stupidity was reflected constantly in those eyes. Sometimes, for no reason at all, Shamman would feel anger directed towards those eyes building up inside her, an emotion that made her wish she could drive two fiery steel nails into them.

Shamman scolded Rasul Fatima at every step. If she left her soiled *dupatta* or her battered book on Shamman's bed by mistake, Shamman would be so incensed she would hurl Rasul Fatima's things across the room angrily. Shamman's loathing increased when Rasul Fatima began responding to Shamman's harshness by revealing her crooked teeth in a fawning whimper. Sometimes Shamman threw her things with such might they struck her face.

'Now now, we don't like these pranks.' Rasul Fatima thought all this was a joke, as if Shamman would stoop to joke with her. Shamman shuddered like a snake whose hood had been crushed, but Rasul Fatima would glance at her lovingly, attempting to create sweetness in her lifeless eyes.

Sleeping next to each other was explicitly forbidden. But Rasul Fatima was such a coward she pulled her sleeping cot next to Shamman's as soon as the last bell had gone off. More than once Shamman had spurned her scornfully, but she pleaded and actually started touching Shamman's feet. She said that her mother's plague-ridden body had remained in the house for two days after her death and since then she had developed a terror of corpses. As soon as darkness approached, she whimpered, she would feel as if there were ghosts all around her.

'All right, shut up now.' Shamman chided her in a hate-filled tone. Rasul Fatima became silent. Then, mumbling verses from the Koran Sharif, she blew all around her. Once when she tried to blow the benediction of these sacred verses on Shamman, she received a slap on the face from her.

'You pig, you spat on my face!' Shamman gnashed her teeth and pushed Rasul Fatima down on her bed. Rasul Fatima was small and skinny; even a slight nudge left her breathless.

One night Shamman felt as if there was a mouse bouncing on her neck. Startled, she got up and stared around her in the dark. The mouse scurried off to Rasul Fatima's bed. She lay back. Just as she was dozing off she again felt the mouse crawling over the side of the bed. On looking closely in the half-darkness Shamman came to the realisation that it was not a mouse, it was Rasul Fatima's hand that was moving while she slept. Shamman turned on her side and idled into sleep.

In her dream she saw the mouse again, crawling, and before she could push it away it vanquished her completely. All the veins in her body became taut, stretching like a wire, all her strength seemed to ebb from her, and she was sure she would never be able to move again. Rasul Fatima's bony fingers dug into her like nails, but she couldn't stop her. Just as a lion wrestles with its prey before swallowing it, just like that . . . Terrified into silence, she remained still and unmoving and the mice kept scurrying. Gradually her submerged strength began resurfacing and, with her whole body bent on revolt, she decided to shove off Rasul Fatima and run. But she remained motionless. A sense of shame and humiliation immobilised her energy. *Uff!* To suffer so and that too at the hands of Rasul Fatima! If she announces she is awake she would have no recourse but to kill Rasul Fatima. She decided she would move in a manner that might indicate that although she was still asleep, she was stirring, and, perhaps sufficiently warned, Rasul Fatima might let go of her. Finally, so exasperated she could no longer stay still, she turned from side to side with such force her elbow landed in Rasul Fatima's bulging eye. Then she announced her state of wakefulness.

'Who is it?'

'Me . . . it's me, your Rasul Fatima.'

What? *Her* Rasul Fatima? If she hadn't been so nervous she would have taught her a lesson for her insolence, but this wasn't the time for it. She got up muttering and pushed away her charpoy with such force that it hit Rasul Fatima's old battered suitcase and split it into pieces.

The next morning Shamman didn't have the courage to face Rasul Fatima, but she was seething inwardly with anger and couldn't wait for Rasul Fatima to open her mouth so she could kill her. Rasul Fatima, on the other hand, sat timidly in a corner, intently pressing crimps into Shamman's newly dyed *dupatta*. Seeing the *dupatta*, Shamman jerked it out of her hands so violently that Rasul Fatima fell down and scraped the skin on her palms. When Shamman angrily pulled at the crimps to open them, the *dupatta*, which had seen many washings, ripped. Enraged, Shamman pushed Rasul Fatima so that the unfortunate girl's new three-paisa water container was completely smashed. Rasul Fatima's large, lifeless eyes dilated like a frog's belly and bulged, and a repugnant wetness floated in them.

Although Shamman was always scolding her, Rasul Fatima continued to suffer silently, or opened her mouth and laughed in a wooden voice as if Shamman's scorn was imbued with the sweetness of persecution.

'Why, what use is this joking – you broke all our bangles, you tyrant.' She stared at Shamman with such love that Shamman was forced to flee from the room. She wanted to go to Matron and tell her everything, but her feet dragged. What will she tell her? Only last month some of the girls from the lower classes had been punished for playing dirty games. Crouched inside quilts, they were busy delivering each other's babies! May God forgive us!

The sight of Rasul Fatima inflamed her. One evening while she was studying with Saadat, a little girl came to the door and, peeping shyly from behind the door, said, 'Shamman *Baji*, come here.' These young girls in the hostel act like the older girls' slaves. Running small errands, delivering messages, stealing flowers from the garden, transporting books from here to there, and in return for this they are rewarded by having the honour of massaging the older girls' feet. The more popular a girl is the more the young girls are ready to serve her. Shamman was not too popular with these girls.

'What's the matter?' she asked brusquely, going up to the door.

'Rasul Fatima Apa gave me this for you.' Handing her a note bashfully, the girl ran off.

Who knows what inducements and payoff Rasul Fatima had employed to get this girl to act as messenger, because most girls, especially the younger ones, despised her.

Shamman's hands trembled when she took the note. Her back to Saadat, she quickly slipped the piece of paper into her sweater and returned to her books. But she was so anxious she couldn't pay attention to what she was reading. It seemed as though the letter contained a threat of abduction which placed her in real danger.

She was dying to read the letter so she got up on the pretext of going to the bathroom. Once there, she unfolded the note and began reading:

> Goddess of my heart's temple,
> Ahhh . . . why are you angry with your devotee? How long will you be vexed with me?
> If you hate me so much then strangle me with your beautiful hands — what spell have you woven? Let me fall at your feet once and beg forgiveness.
>
> *Rasul Fatima, the worshipper of your beauty.*

Shamman became numb with fear. What an obscene letter this was. What now? She was terrified at the thought of returning to her own room. She should make up some story so Saadat would give her refuge in her room. The bedtime bell went off and she still hadn't come up with an excuse. The ringing of the bell mingled with the pounding of her heart, which was so loud she feared Saadat might hear it.

She tiptoed to her room. Without changing into her night-clothes, she sat down on her bed, her feet dangling to the floor. Her mind was tormented by bizarre thoughts. A long sigh echoed in the room and Rasul Fatima turned on her side. Shamman quietly lay down. In the dark she felt Rasul Fatima's large probing eyes touching her body and she was overcome by a strange fear. Suddenly she wished she could find refuge in someone's lap, just as chicks frightened by the presence of an eagle run to hide under the hen's feathers. Finally she couldn't stand it any longer so she left the room and, coming out in the veranda, leaned against a pillar.

'Why are you standing here? You'll catch a chill.' Rasul Fatima crept after her. Shamman pushed away her hand and walked off in the direction of the toilets. When she returned she saw Rasul Fatima standing where she had left her, shivering. She wasn't wearing a shawl and her insignificant body showed through her unsightly night-clothes. Pushing her away again, Shamman went to the tap to wash her hands and watched absently as the water filtered between her fingers.

'Won't you come in, Shamman?' Rasul Fatima murmured. Shamman said nothing. Shutting off the tap, she slid her wet fingers in her throat. Her throat tickled.

'Ogh! Ogh!' She began retching. Despite her brush-off, Rasul Fatima was all over her, anxiously rubbing down her back. Shamman was vomiting now. With every spasm the veins in her neck seemed ready to burst and she thought her tongue would fall out. When she was somewhat calmer, Rasul Fatima ran weeping to fetch the matron. Grumbling about the cook, the matron gave Shamman some cardamom seeds to chew on.

'Please send me to the sick room. What if I'm sick again?'

Even though she was aware of the hostel rules, Rasul Fatima insisted she would go with Shamman. But the matron scolded her. What if it's a contagious disease?

Covered by a quilt and pretending to be sick, for a long time Shamman smiled smugly to herself. Her throat was sore and her temples ached, but she knew that she was under the hen's feathers, safe from the eagle.

The first night she wasn't given any supper, and the smelly breakfast biscuits were also discontinued, so finally Shamman had to be well by the afternoon. At lunch she didn't sit next to Rasul Fatima and, since the prayer had already been offered, Rasul Fatima couldn't get up from her place to come and get her. Shamman's glance strayed to the other end of the table while she was eating and she saw that Rasul Fatima wasn't eating anything and had set aside food for her as was her custom. Seeing the feeble expression on her face and her dilated eyes, Shamman wanted to vomit again. That day she told Matron she wanted to change her place at the dining table. There was an empty seat next to Saadat which she took.

At prayer time she couldn't speak. Rasul Fatima came and stood next to her, folded her hands and began her prayers. During the course of

56

the *namaz* Shamman kept trying to avoid touching Rasul Fatima's arm, her anxiety making her forget the verses again and again.

In a short while night loomed before her again like a calamity and she was consumed with apprehension. Today she felt truly helpless; she couldn't think of any way out. For a long while she recited special verses, then she prayed for strength a number of times. Today God invaded her thoughts. In her prayers she begged and entreated, but what was she praying for? Not a word issued from her lips, while sitting next to her Rasul Fatima was asking for benediction, her hands cupped and raised as she rocked back and forth. Shamman was even more perturbed. She felt as if innumerable prayers had collected in Rasul Fatima's cupped hands and how nice it would be to slap the hand and make all the prayers fall out and disperse like barley seeds, and then when Rasul Fatima bent down to scoop them up ... But then she thought of something else. Night had fallen and Matron had already done her rounds and retired to her room. Seeing the two girls engaged in prayer, she had said nothing. This was a religious matter. Once she had objected when the girls wanted to celebrate *Shab Qadr* out in the grounds, and a terrible disturbance ensued. The next day the headings in the local newspapers spewed poison against the Christian matron.

Shamman got up quietly, slipped out, and slowly bolted the door of the prayer room from the outside. She heard Rasul Fatima say 'Shamman!' in a startled voice, but she walked to her room in haste.

Once in her room, she felt her heart flutter like a bird freed from its cage. She lay in bed and silently cackled to herself.

The prayer room was at the far end of the veranda so that Rasul Fatima could only be heard if she screamed. Her head lowered, Shamman waited for her cries, but she couldn't hear anything except for the '*cheen, cheen*' of the grasshoppers. What if Rasul Fatima complained about her in the morning? What will happen then? What? She began considering all kinds of excuses. She felt as if she had crushed the head of a menacing serpent with a stone and now the serpent lay writhing while life ebbed from it. They say if you kill a serpent, its mate seeks vengeance. But after Rasul Fatima was gone, there was no female serpent to be afraid of. She was alone in the world, lived alone, and would depart alone. Tomorrow Shamman would change her room. But why doesn't Rasul Fatima create an uproar?

The way all the girls crowded the area in front of the prayer room the next morning, one would think the room had been broken into during the night by thieves. Shamman walked by casually. Rasul Fatima lay

57

swaddled in prayer mats. Some of the girls were trying to help her up, some others had run off to fetch Matron. Rasul Fatima was burning with a fever and her lifeless eyes were bloodied like red-hot coals.

Matron transported her to the sick room and asked her repeatedly if she knew who had locked her inside. But she kept reiterating that it was no one, she had fallen asleep while praying.

'But who locked the door from the outside?'

'No one,' she kept saying.

Shamman was so terrified of Rasul Fatima that she pleaded with Matron and had her room changed. Saadat was alone in her room, so Shamman was permitted to move in with her. Shamman's happiness knew no bounds. Now she and Saadat would both study together, live together. She got along very well with Saadat.

Rasul had become obsessed w/ Shamman

14

When Shamman arrived excitedly in Saadat's room to tell her the good news, Saadat fell silent instead of jumping with joy. Getting up suddenly, she went to Matron's office where she was heard muttering and grumbling for a long time. Matron was screaming when she left. Banging the door behind her, Saadat walked away in a huff.

Shamman's euphoria was ground into the dust. She had thought that Saadat would be overjoyed at having her as a room-mate. She felt humiliated, but she tried to console herself; perhaps because Saadat had always had the best room in the dormitory she considered Shamman's presence an infringement of her rights. When she saw her in a pensive mood, Saadat settled down to do her schoolwork and soon, embroiled in maths and geography, Shamman forgot everything.

Twice Rasul Fatima secretly sent for her, but Shamman did not go. The girls were prohibited from visiting Rasul Fatima because the doctor had said she had TB. It was also rumoured that she would not be allowed to return after the summer break.

Although Saadat seemed happier now, Shamman still occasionally felt as if she hated her. She felt that her presence created a stifling atmosphere in the room, because as soon as they had finished studying, Saadat would leave to go to a friend's room.

This friend of hers, Najma, had been with her since the beginning of high school. Then, when Saadat failed a class due to an attack of typhoid, she moved a class ahead of her. She was studying for her intermediate degree, and assumed a superior air with the high school girls. On seeing Shamman in Saadat's room, she would flare up momentarily, and then she would either remain silent or leave quickly on some pretext or the other. Sometimes Shamman walked into the room to find Saadat and Najma laughing and talking, but within minutes of her arrival they would shut their mouths and in the very next instant Najma would remember some important task that had to be undertaken and she would leave. Seeing Najma disturbed Shamman in some strange way; as long as Najma was in their room chatting with Saadat, her heart beat uncontrollably and she would try and distract herself by taking up some useless bit of work. But when Najma was gone Shamman felt sorry she hadn't looked at her properly. Her purple-flowered *shalwar* with its turbulent folds, the white embroidered cotton *kurta* with its slightly drooping neckline and the parallel pleats which were intended to tighten the *kurta* at the waist, along with the softly rounded shoulders which made her waist look slimmer, her purple crimped *dupatta* which hugged her shoulders and looped around her underarm with one end falling over her arm, swinging like a bunch of fresh flowers; and when she turned to go the tassel of her *paranda* danced on her hips, and peeping from below the ends of her *shalwar* her nut-brown heels looked almost fair, like the brown eggs of a peacock!

Najma was very delicate. It seemed as if she didn't have a solid bone in her body. Shamman felt uneasiness at the thought of touching her. Warm and soft, so that if you tried to hold her between your hands she would slip through like a boiled egg.

One day she came and sat near Shamman on her bed. Shamman became agitated and when Najma flung a corner of her *dupatta* it fell on Shamman's arm. Shamman felt as if a snake had dropped on her from the ceiling. Benumbed, she sat still. Then she inched slowly, dislodging the *dupatta* from her arm. But she immediately felt sorry, as if she had tossed out some very precious object from her lap. She was praying that Najma would fling her *dupatta* again in the same impish manner, but Najma left.

Sometimes when Najma and Saadat were talking, Shamman would

glare fiercely at Najma. She observed the slight movement of Najma's lips, the glance cast carelessly over her shoulder as if in response to someone's loving gaze, the motion of her hand as she turned the ring on her supple finger while staring innocently at the ceiling. Shamman would witness this little drama like someone not in control of her thoughts. Sensing Shamman's fixed look upon her, Najma would suddenly stop talking and purse her lips as if asking: 'What do you want? Why don't you say what you want and be done with it?'

But Shamman became flustered and a chilly perspiration began crawling down her spine, her stomach convulsed and she would feel thirsty. That was when she hastily occupied herself with some trivial chore.

Then something else started happening. Out of the blue she would be overcome with the memory of the movement of Najma's lips, her *dupatta*, and the pleats on her waist. For a few minutes she took satisfaction in these thoughts, but soon, exasperated, she would toss them away.

One day a strange incident occurred. Saadat came to class wearing Najma's *koti*. Shamman's hand brushed against her back by accident and she felt as if she had touched a hot plate. Quickly she snatched away her hand, but in the next instant she felt the urge to return her hand to Saadat's back. She felt as if there were smooth snakes slithering on her palm. Because it was quite warm in the afternoon, Saadat took off the *koti* and, hanging it over the back of her chair, she went off to have lunch. When Shamman returned from lunch and saw the *koti*, her heart began pounding. She made excuses when the bell rang for class.

'Come on, we'll be late for Miss Jarmi's class, she'll kill us if we're late.'

'You go on, I'll be there in a minute.' Picking up the washing-pot, Shamman pretended she was going to the bathroom.

After all the girls had left Shamman put down the pot apprehensively and eyed the *koti*. Still not satisfied, she went to the door of her room and locked it. Tiptoeing slowly, she advanced. Her heart beat so rapidly she thought her chest would explode. A mesmerising whiff entered her nose, making her feel dizzy. Outside someone kicked the rubbish bin and she hastily threw down the *koti* on the bed. But she returned from the door; in her haste she had left the *koti* on the bed instead of hanging it over the chair. And what if Saadat had seen it on the bed? Surely she would have guessed that the *koti* had been moved.

What Miss Jarmi said in admonition when she arrived in class,

Shamman excited about touching the koti

Shamman did not know. For a long time afterwards her fingers tingled from the touch of the *koti*, burning as if they had been rubbed with chillies.

After school she sat down on the parapet next to the flower-beds. Scratching the brick surface with the tip of her pencil, she started thinking. Today she felt as if she had committed a beautiful theft. Once at a school party she had picked up a *rasgulla* while no one was watching and quickly plopped it into her mouth when she heard footsteps. The taste of the *rasgulla* had remained on her tongue for no more than a few seconds, but even now, whenever she wanted to, with the aid of her imagination she could bring back the sweetness so that the imagined taste filled her mouth with pleasure. So too, she drew the fragrance of the *koti* into her nostrils today. It wasn't perfume, but it was surely something. She knew Saadat always smelled like a baby chick, but this fragrance had the aroma of burnt cloves, completely new, and could be easily drawn to fill the nose. *Shamman admiring Najma's clothes*

She felt bashful in Najma's presence now and couldn't keep her eyes on her for long. But the power of her feeling told her everything. She knew where Najma's glance was directed, on which side her scattered hair was thicker. Today she's wearing a sandalwood-coloured Shanghai silk *kurta* which clings to her body, making it look as if it has been polished with sandalwood varnish. Today her even, shiny teeth rimmed red from *missi* look like a string of pearls floating in a glass of wine. Shamman rubbed her tongue over her own teeth, a tingling sensation.

When Shamman approached her room she was held back by Najma's laughter. Najma and Saadat were in the box-room laughing and talking noisily. These last few days, whenever Najma came to their room, she'd ask Saadat for something for which a suitcase had to be opened, and Saadat would head for the box-room with Najma at her heels. For hours thereafter the two of them would stay in there talking in whispers. Shamman couldn't keep her mind on anything, and, holding her breath, she would strain to hear their conversation. She didn't have the courage to join them, but she started hating Saadat because she knew she was deliberately trying to keep Najma away from her.

A fancy-dress show was organised by the school to which the girls from the college were also invited. The two hostels were not far from each other and the girls were not prohibited from socialising, but usually the festivals and holidays were celebrated separately. It was Eid and there was to be a very elaborate dinner after the fancy-dress show. Every girl harboured the desire to wear male clothes, so the day scholars

61

brought whatever they could from their homes for the others. Shamman also obtained a suit for herself.

Dressed in male attire, the girls flinched bashfully, especially those who had put on beards and moustaches. Some were hiding in their rooms, covering their faces with their hands in embarrassment, while the more courageous ones were trying to drag them out. Akhtar, the wretch, had donned a Maulana Shaukat Ali beard and cap which was making the girls scream, but she sauntered about unabashedly. Another girl was dressed as an Arab youth and looked every inch a woman. Not far from Shamman was Noori, hopping about in a silk sari. Poor Noori had never worn a sari before so for her that was something novel. The Arab youth was pursuing Khursheed who resembled a Punjabi maiden despite her Egyptian costume.

Shamman, wearing her black suit, came out the door thrice and then, frightened, ran back in again. Two or three of the girls tried to drag her, but then left her alone; there were many girls in suits. Shamman was extremely agitated, feeling as if she were naked. The guests had assembled in the hall and the girls from the college were also arriving. She saw Saadat in a washerman's dress: white turban, a long moustache, and a bundle of clothes slung on her shoulder. And along with her was Najma. She was the washerwoman, but today she looked more like Padmini. A widely flared, shimmering *lehnga* and a lacy *dupatta* flecked with gold lace – and the same *koti*, the same clove-scented, satin *koti*. Her lips were tinted with *missi* along with lipstick, and she had also applied some rouge to her cheeks, and her feet? The sight of her feet took away Shamman's breath. Red paint on the peacock-egg heels – she was barefoot and a silver anklet grazed the floor as she walked. On her forehead was a *tika* which sparkled just like a diamond. Forgetting her shyness, Shamman gaped at her in awe.

'*Array*, look at Shamshad!' Najma laughed loudly and all the girls looked in her direction and cackled.

'She looks just like a boy.' Najma's face turned red.

'Why aren't you coming? Come along now.' Saadat spoke drily.

'Come on. Why, washerman, you're a clod, and this here is Sahib Bahadur – we like him more.' Najma grasped Shamman's hand in jest and Shamman felt as if she were asleep, as if this were all a dream.

Nobody was too impressed with Shamman's attire, but Najma blushed and broke into laughter every time she looked at her. Shamman was also staring. Today she sat close to her, so close that Najma's lace *dupatta* slipped down to her hand more than once.

62

Saadat, however, was glum. She was not at all happy with Najma's joviality and the easy familiarity she exhibited towards Shamman. During dinner Shamman was so excited she didn't eat a thing. Najma's anklet kept coming undone so she had to fumble with the clasp constantly, and her heavy earrings were also uncomfortable so Shamman had to help her there as well. Although Shamman didn't talk much in response to Najma's constant chatter, her innocent face with its roguish moustache, hair that slipped out again and again from under the hat, her shyness and her flustered demeanour, her quiet, disconcerted smile – these were all things that compelled Najma to be drawn to her and she started calling her Shamman.

Shamman's comments were making Najma laugh. With a grave expression on her face, Saadat carried on a conversation with a teacher about a forthcoming exam. She had pulled off her moustache and her turban was now draped over her shoulders like a *dupatta*. She looked like an old woman instead of a washerman.

When the award ceremony drew near Najma began looking frantically for Saadat, but she was in her room. Najma dashed off to get her. Shamman's heart sank. Najma obviously adored Saadat. Shamman couldn't stop herself, so she went after Najma. She saw that Saadat was stretched on her bed, weeping uncontrollably, and Najma was bent over her trying to pacify her. But Saadat's rage knew no bounds. They became quiet when they saw Shamman. In the meantime some other girls stormed in saying, 'Najma *baji*, Miss Jarmi is asking for you.' Reluctantly Najma got up to leave and Shamman followed her timidly.

All the girls in fancy dress were in the hall, marching before the audience with their partners. Whenever a pair in unusual costume went by the hall rang with applause.

'*Array*, where's the washerwoman, Najma!' Miss Jarmi was calling for her.

'Saadat isn't feeling well,' Najma said in a wooden voice.

'Oh, that's a shame. All right, find someone else, hurry up, it's your turn next.'

Without another word, Najma caught hold of Shamman's hand and advanced. Shamman foundered and stumbled. All she knew was that her hand was clasped in Najma's and she herself was in the air. There were only three prizes, but later the girls started giving prizes to each other so that in the end everyone had something.

Najma didn't speak to Shamman afterwards. Taking the prize, she went back to Saadat, and, when the girls were singing the song for the finale, Shamman felt as if her voice was stifled in her throat; Saadat was standing in line looking ecstatic and, with her arm around her waist, Najma was singing in perfect harmony with Saadat. Both were totally absorbed in each other, far away from the rest of the world.

In bed that night Shamman cried bitterly for a long time. Her fist clamped over her mouth, she muffled the sounds of her sobbing. Saadat was not in the room today. Because today was a holiday the girls were allowed to visit each other's rooms. She was with Najma! What's happening to me? Shamman agonised. She was behaving like the Rasul Fatima with the bulging eyes! Ohh! She began thinking of Rasul Fatima and felt it was she who was her killer. Wasn't it she who had locked up Rasul Fatima, leaving her in the room to become stiff with cold?

And now she, like Rasul Fatima ... *Uff!* Shame and revulsion made her break out in a sweat. Her chest burned with an icy cold fire. 'Najma, Najma,' her soul cried.

Rasul Fatima, her bony wrists and mousy hands, her bad health and her disproportionate build – all the images swam before her eyes one by one. Ohh! She was her killer ... Her last pleading gasps, her stifled moans – Shamman felt they were crawling all over her like spiders.

But she wasn't dead. Matron said if she went to the hill station she would be all right. If only, oh, if only she would go to the hill station! Shamman started praying.

But Najma? The feelings of guilt she had just experienced with regard to Rasul Fatima seemed to give her the right to think about Najma again.

Sleep evaded her. She tossed and turned restlessly, but Najma had filled her mind like a dense, terrifying dream. When she had got rid of Rasul Fatima she had thought that she had crushed a snake. But concealed in her heart was the fear that if you kill a serpent, its mate seeks revenge. The female serpent sees the picture of her enemy in the serpent's dead eyes and sets out to sting the killer. So, was Najma seeking vengeance for Rasul Fatima's injuries? Shamman snapped from fear and anguish. All night she heard the rustle of snakes hissing around her bed, the sounds leaving her spent and lifeless.

15

The next morning Shamman didn't speak to Saadat, who was somewhat distant herself. Sitting quietly in the library, Shamman did her best to study. The three days of break were like a mountain crushing her lonely, wounded spirit. Saadat disappeared every night and for Shamman the dormitory echoed with the silence of a graveyard. She stared with vacant eyes at the massive dictionaries before her. Not one book there contained a cure for what ailed her. She was weak with the fearful anticipation of some dreaded outcome. When was it going to find release, this smoke that smouldered in her heart?

It seemed as though someone had heard the footfall of her silent prayers. Her heart swelled like a balloon and she felt that if Najma continued to stand in the doorway any longer, the balloon would explode. But Najma advanced slowly and began looking through the books on the shelves. She was standing behind Shamman, who felt there was a fire burning at her back – tiny sparks seemed to be jumping all over her body. Her breath held, she kept her eyes on the page before her and the balloon began to deflate, slowly.

'*Array*, so you have this book. I was wondering who had taken it.' Najma pulled out a chair and sat down next to her. Shamman hurriedly turned some pages.

For a few minutes Najma talked of this and that, mostly a lot of nonsense. Shamman stole glances at her satin *koti* which had two buttons missing, and her white *dupatta*, one end of which was draped over her arm. Najma was shaking her leg restlessly. Her shimmering, pale green satin *shalwar* rippled. Suddenly she stopped talking and stared intently at Shamman's face which at that moment glowed with fear and elation.

'Shami,' Najma whispered, her voice like the vibration of two gossamer-thin filaments rubbing together. Shamman's tremulous eyes were raised and then instantly lowered. Najma placed her fingers lingeringly on Shamman's palm. At once a convulsion spurted in her palm and it began to devour Najma's fingers. In the doorway stood Saadat, smiling. Najma snatched away her fingers. A strange, weary smile appeared on her lips.

'Saadat,' she said bravely, 'come on, where were you? I was

looking . . .' But Saadat dismissed her with a scornful movement of her head and busied herself with some books.

Najma went after her. Shamman saw that they stopped at the end of the gallery to resolve some important matter. Najma was trying to say what was on her mind and Saadat seemed intent on hedging, but Najma clasped her hand firmly.

Soon the news that Saadat and Najma had fought spread like fire in the hostel. Not only that, Shamman too came under suspicion. Although no one thought there was direct complicity on her part, yet those with a discerning eye knew she had a role in what was going on. Saadat's headache returned while Najma felt nauseated from the smell of meat, so neither of them came for lunch. The girls prattled and snickered. Saadat's sickness was prolonged, but Najma came to the dining room as usual after the first day of absence. She was suddenly very sociable, bantering and laughing with the girls she had never talked to before. But her eyes would cloud over without warning, her every quip seemed forced. The girls responded to her remarks with congeniality, but they railed against her as soon as her back was turned. They were aware of the reason for her outward liveliness; she needed them only to get over the hurt she felt on account of Saadat. However, since she was a favourite with all the teachers and always stood first in her class, no one had the courage to be rude to her.

Sensing this to be her opportunity, Shamman began devising ways of getting close to Najma. If nothing else was available, she would intercept her mail so she could hand-deliver it to her in her room. She also consulted her frequently on the meaning of a word or sought information about a useful book. Najma was always very polite. If, by chance, she found herself becoming too familiar with Shamman, she immediately drew back, bringing up some excuse for Shamman to leave the room, something which hurt Shamman deeply. Three days passed. A flurried exchange of notes continued between Najma and Saadat. But no one expected a reconciliation. During this time Najma came to Shamman's room often, cheerfully carrying on a conversation with her each time, but always she would become distant after a while and leave abruptly. On a few occasions the two of them met in the garden, but the silence that hung between them forced them to part hastily within minutes.

Final examinations approached. These examinations were like a grand festival. Many days in advance the girls begin offering each other salutations, flowers and fruit are exchanged, and many give and receive *dupattas*, saris and bangles. Actually there's more giving than receiving going on. In other words, the girls who have special favourites give generously, no matter how indigent they might be themselves; they might be barely subsisting on a scholarship and may be receiving books and money as hand-outs, but for the person they adore they will even steal, commit burglary or beg; for their darlings they will buy bangles for ten rupees, garlands, bracelets made from flowers, and bouquets for another five or six rupees.

The girls with the most devotees would receive the greatest number of gifts. In addition, on the day of the exam they would be draped with garlands and adorned with floral bracelets, and some of the cherished ones are so completely covered in flowers they remind one of a prominent leader in the midst of a cavalcade of admirers. Some devotees bedeck the cherished ones in gold lace and flowery adornments until they begin to resemble brides and who then enter the examination hall shyly, demurely.

The previous evening Shamman too had bought a heavy, one-and-a-half-rupee garland for Najma. She sprinkled it with water until she went to bed, and again and again she touched the fortunate petals which would embrace Najma tomorrow. If she could have her way she'd hide herself among these petals.

The next morning she was so nervous she missed breakfast. She kept shifting the garland from one hand to the other. How will she put the garland around Najma's neck? Surely even Sitaji didn't have as much trouble placing the garland around Ramchanderji's neck, but of course Sitaji didn't have these girls and eagle-eyed Matron to be afraid of. And these crude, unrefined girls tormented you endlessly. They stood around in the verandas, and because they had no favourites they took immense pleasure in making fun of the garlands and ridiculing the misgivings of the devotees, sometimes wounding the cherished ones and creating an unpleasant mood for everyone. The devotees got upset that these other girls regarded them as low as the singing girls of the bazaar, but these devotees are very strong-hearted. No insults, no reprimands can deter them from their path. They become unusually thick-skinned and shame-less and some of them were so persistent that even their families were fed up with their obsession. However, if these girls were threatened with the slightest bit of harshness they became hysterical. As a result everyone was compelled to be lenient with them.

When Najma appeared from her room draped in garlands, Shamman's steps faltered. With some difficulty she placed the garland around

Najma's neck and Najma rewarded her with a tiny smile. But instead of going to the examination hall she went to Saadat in the sick room. Surprised, Shamman followed her.

But she was forced to retreat in a hurry. Dragging her feet, her mind in a blur, she walked to the examination hall. What she had seen in the sick-room burdened her heart, making her feel as if someone had dumped tons of mud on it. Saadat was sitting on her bed completely healthy and happy, with the garland Shamman had offered Najma with such aspirations wrapped around her bun.

Saadat and Najma became friends again as if nothing had happened. Najma's exams were over and Saadat's commenced. Shamman had given Najma a one-and-a-half-rupee garland and Najma, in turn, had bought hundreds of garlands for Saadat, but she forgot to get something for Shamman. If Shamman had known she'd have bought one secretly for herself. Standing at the end of a line of girls loaded with garlands, she walked towards the examination hall with her head lowered.

'Shamman, you know I don't like garlands one bit. Here, I got these flowers from my garden, do you like them?' Bilquis turned and handed her a bunch of fresh flowers. Bilquis, a day scholar, was in class eight. Shamman felt as if someone had thrown a blanket over her naked body and presented her with more garlands than she could count.

Vacations began with the announcement of the examination results and the girls left for a two-month stay at home. The birds fluttered away to roost in their nests. A two-month-long roosting!

THE SECOND PHASE

16

Shamman returned to school to find everything changed. Bilquis's older sister, who had recently returned from England, was now the principal, and Bilquis and her younger sister were living in the principal's house in the school compound. Saadat had been told by the doctors to take a break from studies for a year because of failing health. Najma, having passed her exam, had transferred to another college in Lahore. To Shamman the world appeared bleak and desolate. Her heart burnt with loneliness, thoughts of Najma tormented her like an aching sore. How sad her life was. But there was some sweetness in it. Najma had once given her a photograph of herself which Shamman now found to be her best friend and companion. In retrospect she saw Saadat in a better light. Actually, if she didn't think of Najma, Saadat was really her best friend. If only she had never seen Najma and if she had, then? She couldn't think further than that, but she was sorry she had lost Saadat's friendship. Najma was like a flame with which one could warm one's hands for a moment, while Saadat was a cool stream, a friend with whom she associated compassionate behaviour and wonderfully lively times in class and outside. Saadat had a habit of laughing too much. She and Shamman often rolled on the grass in the garden, helpless with laughter at some trivial joke. Saadat was also very smart and helped her like a teacher and not only that, if she ever saw Shamman behaving in a disheartened or lazy manner, she scolded her severely. Shamman saw a glimpse of maternal affection and concern in her chiding, and times, just to annoy her, she'd say casually, 'So what, why don't you let me fail?'

'Stop, *ji*, don't talk nonsense, or else . . .' Saadat would say angrily.

'Or else, or else what?'

'Or else . . . uhh . . . nothing . . . come, my dearest sister, come.' And she'd put her arms around Shamman. But when Najma came into the picture everything was shattered and Shamman began praying for Saadat's death. Her ignoble emotions were transformed into satanic acts. God forgive her!

Shamman's friendship with Bilquis came about in a rather unusual way. One day they were both sitting on a bench resting after a vigorous game of tennis when suddenly Bilquis asked her:

'You were crazy about Najma, weren't you?'

'No, of course not, what a thing to say!' Shamman became flustered and started swearing her innocence.

'*Array*, you're lying to us, unh! As if we don't know, and you and Saadat had a disagreement.'

'No, not at all.'

'But what's the big deal? I too was crazy about Najma once, but Apa *bi* told me we should be crazy about boys not girls.'

'What? How awful!' Shamman jumped.

'Yes, because we can marry them and live with them for ever, isn't that right?'

'But . . . this is . . . Allah, don't talk such rubbish, Bilquis.'

'It's not rubbish. That's why I like *koriyale*, and I'm also older than you.' Picking up pebbles from the path, Bilquis started throwing them in the air.

'*Koriyale*?'

'Yes, *array*, *koriyale*, don't you know who they are? Come on, you're so stupid.' She guffawed and took a tumble on the grass. '*Array*, *koriyale*, you fool, black and white.' She rubbed her cheek on the cool grass and shivered. 'Poisonous . . .' The bell for prayers rang just then and they didn't finish their conversation.

Bilquis didn't come to the dormitory for the next four days so Shamman was unable to resolve her dilemma. Curiosity made her restless. Finally she couldn't stand it any longer so she consulted the dictionary. But there it said: '*Koriyale* . . . spotted, black and white snake, very poisonous, whose bite . . .' The rest didn't make sense to her. She couldn't understand why Bilquis liked *koriyale* snakes.

70

'Come now, tell me, who are *koriyale*?' she asked Bilquis the first chance she got.

'*Koriyale*? A piece of one's heart, life! Who else?'

'Unh. Tell me.'

Shamman kept pestering her for an explanation for days and Bilquis kept evading, until one day she showed Shamman a photograph. It was a handsome young man dressed in a black *sherwani* and white cotton pyjamas. All at once both girls broke into laughter. Oh, so this was *koriyale*! Black *sherwani* was the uniform at the university and the man in the picture was Rashid, Bilquis's brother.

Although Bilquis and her sister Jalees didn't live in the hostel, they sidestepped every rule and came to the hostel whenever it suited them; they were the principal's sisters, so who had the nerve to object? Because they enjoyed being with their friends they came often and soon Bilquis moved permanently into Shamman's room. But she often left without permission. Jalees, who was extremely ill-tempered, was Noori's classmate. They were in the same room, but they fought every day; Shamman and Bilquis would go to pacify them, help them reconcile, and soon the two of them, each wearing the other's *dupatta*, would be strolling together in the garden.

In the beginning Noori tried to become Bilquis's devotee and Jalees singled Shamman out for that purpose. But Bilquis humiliated them both with such ferocity that after some serious thought they turned their attention to a ninth class girl and became her devotees. But Bilquis continued to make life miserable for the two girls. Whenever she lost something she shouted at Jalees and Noori, accusing them of giving it to their darling. The truth of the matter was that once the poor girls stole two oranges from the fruit bowl in Bilquis and Shamman's room to present to their cherished one. Now, as a result of this, if Bilquis lost even her old, tattered sandal she would declare that Noori and Jalees had made an offering of it to their darling. This would make Noori and Jalees cry and they would beg, 'Please don't speak so loudly, she'll hear.' Shahjahan was double their size and when she heard Bilquis's name being mentioned she threw the girls out of her room. Both ran to their room in tears. In addition, Bilquis and Shamman started teasing them, making up taunting songs and humming the songs spiritedly in their presence. Noori and Jalees insisted, 'We swear Shahjahan Apa didn't throw us out, she said, "Please, kindly leave."' But Bilquis maintained that Shahjahan had pushed the two girls out of her room and also smacked them with her slipper. The poor girls, their hearts broken,

71

became Shahjahan's enemies from that day on. After this bitter experience they made no effort to be devotees again and spent most of their time playing pranks, plucking off unripe mangoes from trees, and harassing devotees.

Bilquis had five sisters, the oldest among them being the principal. She was beautiful, delicate and demure, and didn't look like a principal at all. All the girls adored her. Shamman herself might have adored her too, except that Bilquis had given her the facts about her sister. She was unsporting and got into a squabble when she lost a game of badminton, and she was in love with eleven men at the same time, of whom two were professors and the others 'koriyale'!

Because she was the principal's sister, Bilquis always got her way in the hostel. No one, except the girls who were sick, was allowed to bring food to her room; even if a glass was displaced all hell broke loose, but stacked everywhere in Bilquis's room were piles of small plates with leftovers spoiling in them. Matron saw all this and was forced to exercise restraint since the last matron had been fired simply because she constantly lodged complaints with the principal.

Every day Bilquis had new tales to tell about koriyale. She and Jalees had an ample store of koriyale; if you assembled all the lovers of the five sisters you would have a regular platoon. Gradually talk about the young admirers became routine around the hostel as well; using pranks and anecdotes as aids, brothers of some of the day scholars proceeded to enliven the half-dead life of the hostel. A little buying and selling, exchanging old books, getting some film developed, or carrying on a romance under the pretext of having prints made – this is how romance flourished.

And these men were extraordinary. If they're not doing anything else, they're sending Eid cards to the girls. The girls can barely make ends meet, they curse, but at the same time the cards are circulated all over the hostel, they're proudly and casually shown to everybody. 'Ohhh! Ooohh!' the girls are screaming. A man and a woman are kissing each other and there are curiously worded couplets penned underneath.

In time this malady spread further. Every girl had a story to tell about her romance with some male cousin. The list of Bilquis's lovers was endless. Each one of her brother's friends was a registered lover and whoever wished to start a romance only had to be friendly with Rashid Bhai and on this pretext arrived every day as an aspirant. All the liberal young men with revolutionary ideas in the university came to discuss social and political issues and to uncover ways of educating the younger generation in the practice of liberalism. Generally dressed in their night-suits, the broad-minded sisters socialised with these young men and played cards and *carom* with them. Songs were sung, heated discussions of a radical nature took place, and romance flourished, not in nooks and corners, but in full view of everyone. Principal Sahiba's house was incandescent with light and the five sisters sparkled in it like a cluster of stars.

Late into the night, Bilquis whispered stories of these visits to Shamman, continuing with her tales even after midnight. One or two lovers could be dealt with, but would you not tire of a whole army of lovers? Babar Mirza was Apa *bi*'s lover, but he also tickled Bilquis. Haider Mirza was nearly her father's age, but he was crazy about her; she had snatched three pens from him until now, one of which she had given to Shamman. She would have snatched his ring as well, except that he said he was getting a dainty little ring for her from Delhi.

'This ring will fit your waist,' he had said, holding her tightly between his knees, his hands forming a circle around her waist, tickling her.

All these stories exhausted Shamman.

'So are you in . . .'

'So will you marry him?'

'Look, who knows – let's see what happens.'

'But if you marry Haider Sahib, what will become of Abbas? Ansar will die, to be sure, and Ishrat? This midget Ishrat also loves you. What a shame. God forgive us!' Shamman felt sorry for all of them. 'Oh, the poor lovers! *Uff!* I'm tired.'

Most of these men with revolutionary ideas were poor, physically stunted, pock-marked and extremely dark; they wanted to luxuriate in the radiance of beauty in order to placate their souls, and, like moths, were in search of light. Jalees was the youngest of the sisters, but there was evidence that she would turn into the Nadir Shah of her time. The apprentices were already lining up. If only Bilquis would sift her lovers in a waste basket and give the discarded ones to the girls in the hostel who, unfortunate creatures, could only dream.

'Why don't you tell your story?' Bilquis would say.

'What? We have no story.'

'What a shame. No one loves you?'

Shamman's heart was filled with sadness and she blushed from a sense of inferiority. So, one day, after much thought, she named somebody, although she hated all her male cousins. And why not? Didn't they always torment her, and not one of them had ever acted in a way that the other girls prattled about so deliciously. Having no other recourse, she named Ishaq Bhai. But she knew that if he or his wife had the slightest inkling that she was making up tales about his love for her, all hell would break loose; Amma would beat her until she was senseless. Actually, with the exception of Ishaq Bhai, she despised everyone else. At one time she had also been friends with his older daughter.

'So he kissed you.'

In the first place Shamman hated the word kiss. In the second place, the very thought of Ishaq Bhai kissing her proved sickening. When he sucked in the milk froth left on his moustache, she felt nauseated.

'What? How can he love you if he doesn't kiss you?'

When Bilquis began to feel sorry for her, Shamman decided there wasn't any reason to feel sick if Ishaq Bhai kissed her from far away. Subsequently, she shyly admitted that yes indeed, he had kissed her. Later she recounted the incident of snatching Ishaq Bhai's pen, although she knew very well that he possessed only old worn-out nibs and scratched holders which not even an idiot would wish to snatch from him. But what did Bilquis know?

Shamman and Bilquis's friendship flourished to the point that they were in each other's company night and day and even studied together. Shamman liked Bilquis very much. Even more than Saadat. But she didn't know if less than Najma or more. Najma was something quite different. She was fiery wine and Bilquis was clear, sparkling, sweet water, although she was shameless and took off her clothes without any hesitation. Before going to the bathroom she removed her clothes and searched for insect bites on her body. Shamman felt very embarrassed when someone walked in and Bilquis was undressing, but Bilquis didn't seem to mind.

'Why, what's there to be shy of in front of girls?' she'd proclaim audaciously. Once when Matron reprimanded her, she said, 'Because you're built like a broken cart, you're jealous of the way I look.' Matron complained and wept bitterly, and Bilquis received a scolding as well, but she wasn't one to pay attention to anyone. Her body was indeed very lithe and beautiful and she often smiled to herself as she admired her reflection in the mirror. After a bath she never put on her clothes right away, wrapping herself in a quilt instead until she was feeling warm enough and all the hair on her body was glistening like golden filaments, and then she got out her clothes. But for hours she couldn't decide whether to don an off-white *dupatta* with the grey *shalwar*, or wear the purple one instead. She would consult Shamman. Her back to her, poor Shamman would offer her opinion. She was a little scared of Bilquis, because once or twice, while talking to her, she had felt the impulse to stroke her neck with her fingers, her soft, lissom neck which she kept cocked to one side coquettishly.

Rashid Bhai, whom Shamman had initially mistaken for Bilquis's lover, was endowed with the same family talent as the sisters. Wherever he went he left behind three or four wounded birds in his wake. Many of the college girls were crazy about him and several rich girls whom he tutored also adored him. He might not pass himself, but the girls who received two or three lessons from him were sure to pass.

'I swear by God, you'll fall in love with Rashid right away,' Bilquis often told Shamman. But Shamman wasn't allowed to step outside the hostel, so the question of falling in love did not arise.

But fate brought her together with Rashid Bhai in a most interesting way. On the occasion of the annual picnic, Principal Sahiba took along her brother and some other boys as well. They came in their own car and camped away from the girls behind some trees. Principal Sahiba had brought them along so that if one of the girls decided to drown they could help fish her out. Since they were all quite a distance away there was a sort of purdah between the two groups. But in their hearts the girls were thinking only of the boys. Again and again they wandered into the boys' area by mistake, laughing raucously and nudging and pushing each other.

'Shamman, do you want to meet Rashid?' Bilquis took her aside and asked. 'He's over there, behind that tree.'

'What? I'm in purdah.' Shamman became flustered.

'Uhho, come along now, I'll cover his eyes.'

After much difficulty it was decided that Bilquis would blindfold Rashid with her *dupatta*. But Shamman was still hesitant. Rashid was tall and lean, the *dupatta* covered his eyes and part of his nose, leaving in view only the lips which quivered delicately as he attempted to repress his smile. There was a jungle of thick hair on his head and locks of hair threatened to escape from under the *dupatta*. The top front button of his shirt was open, revealing his light brown neck and the veins that throbbed as he controlled his amusement.

'*Hee, hee, hee!*' He suddenly burst out laughing. Shamman and Bilquis started laughing too. He stretched out his hands towards them.

'*Array*, girl, where is your friend Shamsham? Tell her to shake hands with us at least.'

Bilquis pulled Shamman's hand, but Shamman refused to move.

'Look here, we'll take your hand by force, and no one should blame us if we do, all right? We're going to take off the blindfold now.'

Quickly Shamman placed her frightened hand in his and then tried to snatch it away and couldn't because Rashid was clasping it firmly.

'*Array*, is this your Shamsham's hand? No, no, this is the hand of a mouse.'

Shamman stuffed a corner of her *dupatta* in her mouth to muffle the sound of her giggling.

'So there's just one hand? And the rest of her? *Array*, Billee, does she have feet?'

'She does,' Bilquis said, holding her laugh in check.

'How many?'

'Two . . . ' More giggling.

'Really? And what about ears, Billee? She has ears?'

Bilquis cackled. 'Yes, yes.'

'And a nose?'

Shamman was doubled over with the effort of pulling her hand away from Rashid's clasp.

'Look, if you talk like this we'll not speak with you any more,' Bilquis finally complained.

'All right, let's skip that. Now, tell me, where's the nose?' Rashid started fumbling again. His fingers wandered probingly over Shamman's face as if he were blind. Eyebrows, eyelashes, nostrils, lips – where they paused momentarily – then down over the cheeks and to the hair.

'*Array*, Billee, she has no plait! What kind of a plait is this?' He began fingering her ear. Both girls were in stitches by now. Finally Shamman wrenched her hand from his and bolted.

'That's not fair, that's not fair! Run after her, Billee.' Rashid pulled off the *dupatta* from his eyes and tried to catch Shamman, but she made off.

But Shamman's reserve had worn off by now. A little later she and Bilquis made some excuse and accompanied Rashid to the fields to steal watermelons. There he pushed them knee-deep into mud. Later they went searching for damsons. With their *dupattas* spread out on the muddy ground, he broke off ripe and raw damsons for them. Rashid had devised good uses for girls' *dupattas*. He preferred to tie them on his head rather than see them on the girls' shoulders, and *dupattas* could be rolled so effectively into balls – how hard one could hit with them!

On her return from the picnic Shamman felt as if she had just come back from a journey through the clouds. Before going off to sleep that night she recounted every single moment of the picnic. Rashid's locks peeping from under Bilquis's *dupatta*, his restless lips, the throbbing veins in his neck, and soon she felt Rashid's hand crawling . . . on her forehead, her nostrils, stopping on her lips. She turned on her side abruptly and fell sleep.

The next morning Bilquis informed Shamman that Rashid had fallen madly in love with her.

'Don't be silly. How do you know?' Shamman's heart pounded violently.

'I can tell. Whenever I mention your name, he blushes, what else?'

Shamman herself blushed at the mention of Rashid's name. So the two of them talked openly and endlessly about Rashid. But Shamman could not meet Rashid, and as a matter of fact she was not eager to meet him either. This was only because she had already received a heavy dose that she hadn't been able to digest as yet; her waking and sleeping hours were filled with recollections of the happy events at the picnic.

But God blesses a lover of sweets with more sweets. Bilquis's birthday altered her world. Many of Bilquis's friends, including Shamman, were invited to the birthday party. Shamman didn't have a gift, so she wrapped a silk scarf she had and gave it to her quietly. But Bilquis brandished the scarf openly and later Shamman saw that while Bilquis was trying to put it on her head, Rashid snatched it from her and, wearing it like a *dupatta*, began teasing her.

'Ohh, Shamman, look, Rashid won't listen . . . please give us back our scarf.' But Rashid ran off with the scarf. 'Did you see, Shamman? Tell him to return our scarf, he snatched it from us,' Bilquis complained to Shamman who saw from the window that Rashid was playing hockey with the scarf tied around his neck.

In the evening all the other girls left, but Bilquis managed to coax Principal Sahiba into letting Shamman stay for the night. They were playing *carom* with Jalees when suddenly Rashid came storming into the room.

'Rashid, Rashid there's purdah here!' Bilquis and Jalees screamed and began covering up Shamman in *dupattas*.

'Who is in purdah? The girls have left.'

'No, no, Shamman is still here, Rashid. Apa *bi*, Rashid won't listen to us.'

'Now look here, if you complain to Apa *bi*, I'll, well . . .' Rashid threatened them. 'Purdah or no purdah, we'll play *carom* no matter what.' He pushed his way in.

After some deliberation it was agreed that Rashid would play with his face covered. Bilquis and Shamman were on one side, while Jalees teamed with Rashid.

'I say, let's bet some money.'

'One anna, one anna,' Jalees spoke up.

'No, no, Rashid will clean us out!' Bilquis screamed. 'Two paisas.'

'All right, if I lose I'll give you an anna and a tiny rap if you lose.'

'No! Not your rap,' Bilquis retorted fearfully. 'It's a wallop, I tell you.'

After great difficulty it was decided that if Rashid lost he'd pay the girls an anna and if they lost they'd let him slap them, but very gently. Because of purdah Rashid placed the silk scarf like a veil over his head and the game began in earnest.

Everyone was teasing Rashid by calling him a bride. The scarf was sheer and his shining eyes were clearly visible through it.

'Bilquis, he's watching everything,' Shamman complained in a whisper.

'Rashid, don't you dare!' Bilquis scolded him. 'I swear I'll kill you if you play any tricks.'

When the game was at its peak all purdah was forgotten. After he had won the game Rashid carefully readjusted his veil and rolled up his sleeves.

'Come on now, be ready for the rap.' He took Shamman's hand and, joining two fingers, got his weapon ready.

'Now look, not too hard, please.' Bilquis practically climbed over him.

'Well, isn't that something. You swallowed my anna, but now that it's my turn, you're protesting. I swear I'll break your bones today.' He braced his fingers again. As soon as he raised them, Shamman snatched her hand away with a moan.

'Did you see that? Your friend is so sly. She's moaning and I haven't even touched her as yet. Tell her to sit straight. It won't be my fault if my hand lands somewhere else.'

For what seemed like an eternity he kept scaring her off without really hitting her. It would have been better if he had hit her and had done with it. Just then Principal Sahiba's attendant appeared with orders that all the hostel girls should leave right away. Who was left there except Shamman?

'All right, so this rap is a debt.' Rashid let go of her hand.

'Rashid, dear Rashid, please escort us back to the hostel,' Bilquis begged.

A five-minute walk turned into a half-hour jaunt. For quite some time the three of them stood at the hostel gate, arguing. Rashid was insisting that Shamman say goodbye by shaking hands like civilised people, and Shamman, bashfully rooted to the ground, was scratching the varnish on the gate with her nails. Tired of the long argument, Bilquis finally pushed Shamman towards Rashid. Although Shamman tried to catch herself she still fell against Rashid's chest and tried to ward off the impact with her palms. With an exclamation of alarm Rashid stepped away and Shamman ran inside.

For a long time afterwards she pinched Bilquis and scolded her.

17

The exhibition had arrived, and Shamman was allowed to make several trips because of Bilquis. The exhibition is indeed a magnificent festival. Every year there's a tumultuous gathering. Corpses that have been asleep for a whole year are awakened by the trumpet of Israfil, and for fifteen days the world of desire is shot with the vigour of spring. Who has the money to shop and buy, and anyway, who is stupid enough to waste time buying and selling? A terrible commotion prevails. At every stall there's a crowd of black *sherwanis* and black *burkas*. The *sherwanis* don't have the nerve to stay away from the shadow of the *burkas*; if you're buying earrings, they're present, if you're sifting through bangles, they're pushing through with their hands, they're at the sariwallah's shop, heckling and hooting, they're crowding the entrance to the toy shop. In short, they're everywhere, hissing, the *koriyale*. As for the girls, they are bewildered and confused; if they complain they would be prohibited from coming, which means they're helpless. However, the world is hostile and desolate without the *koriyale*. What is left in the exhibition that is of any interest if you reproach them and send them away? These sparkling gems? These golden garments? No, not at all.

These riches belong to others. The impoverished student – he will discover a thousand exhibitions in his own liveliness.

Bilquis had been anxious for a long time to have her picture taken. Rashid had promised he would send the negative to his friend in England to have it enlarged. She and Shamman quietly slipped away when Matron wasn't looking and decided to go to the booth where you could get eight photographs for a rupee.

'Please take our picture quickly,' the girls told the photographer who was standing there. Like the university boys, he too was dressed in black and white.

'So you want a picture taken?' He smiled good-naturedly.

'Of course. Could you please hurry.'

'Yes, yes, certainly. Come and sit here on this stool.' He lit a cigarette.

Bilquis and Shamman decided they should put on some powder and lipstick; something, at least, to show up in the photograph.

'Do you have a mirror in the shop?' they asked diffidently.

'Mirror? Why not? Come with me.' He led them into a room in the back. They powdered their faces while he stood nearby, smiling.

'Why don't you put on some perfume too?' he said mischievously and began rummaging through his pockets.

'Perfume? Perfume?'

'Yes, perfume. You see, the picture will be perfumed. Look, I have some.' With that he rubbed some perfume on his fingers and dabbed it on their clothes.

'That's enough!' Shamman pushed his hand away roughly.

'All right, all right, come and sit on the stool now. Sit properly.'

They both began posing.

'Could you turn this way . . . yes, and watch the *dupatta* . . . actually I think you should take off the *dupatta* altogether.' He was paying more attention to their *dupattas* than to the camera.

'Allah, what a dreadful man,' Shamman whispered in Bilquis's ear.

'If you're going take a picture then go ahead, or else . . .' Bilquis mustered her strength and scolded him.

'But the powder on your cheek . . .' He smiled mischievously again, touched Bilquis's cheek softly, and blew smoke in their faces.

Both girls became so agitated that he probably took pity on them and moved back.

'All right now, ready.' Both of them were ready. After sticking his head inside the hood once or twice he finally said, 'Ohho, what did you do to your hair? Let me fix your hair first.'

'It's none of your business. Are you taking a picture or . . . Shamman, let's go.'

'Ohho, don't get angry now, please sit down, Shamman, oh, excuse me . . . I was only saying this for your own good, you know, because if your hair doesn't come out right in the photograph you'll blame the photographer, won't you?' He looked hurt. Finally both girls decided they'd let him fix their hairdos and, with his hand under their chins, he began arranging their hair. Bilquis pulled away her head which he had clasped tightly against his chest while he combed her hair. He laughed roguishly and turned towards Shamman, but suddenly they heard voices and soon three or four men came in. Shamman and Bilquis became apprehensive.

'We'll go now.'

'All right, goodbye.' Laughing, he turned to leave.

'Are you going?' one of the men who had just come in asked the girls.

'You, who are you?'

'I'm the photographer, *ji*, please be seated,' the newcomer said, glancing proudly at his black *sherwani*.

'So . . . who was . . . he?' Bilquis stuttered.

'Who? Oh, you mean Hameed. *Array*, he was here to pick up some prints. Come in, please, come in.' He tried to wave away their question.

'What?' The two girls looked at each other blankly.

'Come now . . . sit here.' The photographer started fiddling with his equipment.

'No, we'll come back tomorrow. It's late now.'

Both of them ran out of there in haste, their hearts beating uncontrollably. Matron had turned the exhibition grounds inside out looking for them. The moment she saw them she began scolding them angrily.

'*Array*, and we have been looking for you all this time,' both lied. Matron was familiar with these excuses, but because of Bilquis she didn't pursue the matter further. How many girls got lost in this fashion every day and then were found, and what fun it was to be deliberately lost. You don't want to be found and sometimes you wish you could be lost for ever in exhibitions and fairs and never be caught by matrons.

The next day they couldn't return to the photographer's shop, but that same *koriyala*, Hameed, followed them everywhere, sighing, singing verses. He would call his friends 'Shamman' and 'Bilquis' and the friends would respond with a bashful 'Yes, photographer sahib.'

'Come, dear Shamman, let's buy earrings,' one would say coyly to the other, imitating the girls.

'No, Bilquis, let's go and have pictures taken,' the other one would reply coquettishly.

Bilquis and Shamman were annoyed, but they were also amused and couldn't help giggling. As long as the young men followed them, they continued to exhibit outrage, but no sooner were they separated from them than their eyes eagerly sought them out, and soon thinly veiled remarks were being bandied about again.

At the gate that day a boy handed them a packet saying they had left it behind at one of the shops.

'It must be yours, Bilquis.'

'No, I didn't buy anything. Well, open it, let's see what's in it.'

When they opened the packet they found it was full of toffees and chocolates! And sweets! The girls screamed in joy and fell upon the contents of the packet. But suddenly they raised their eyes and glimpsed the *koriyala*. He tilted his head in salutation and they looked away angrily. 'Let's throw these away,' Bilquis suggested. But hunger pangs made them realise how foolish that would be. They walked off from there and after some initial hesitation both filled their pockets with the sweets.

Once the exhibition was over, Bilquis and Shamman began receiving love letters. Both girls would have been severely reprimanded if Bilquis hadn't told Principal Sahiba everything, although she did leave out the episode at the photographer's shop. The matter was covered up. Bilquis said that the *koriyala* had dispatched innumerable letters which Principal Sahiba had torn up and burnt. When the situation showed no signs of improving, Principal Sahiba collected all the letters and sent them to the principal at the university. The matter was finally laid to rest.

Rashid was brought in to take photographs of the annual play. The girls in the play didn't observe purdah in front of Rashid; if someone else had been asked to take photographs, there might have been repercussions, the unenlightened ones would have made a fuss.

Dressed as a young man, Shamman was beside herself with mortification because of the moustache she had to wear. Bilquis was her beloved, Rosalind.

'*Array*, Billee, who's this urchin?' Rashid asked in surprise, and Shamman threw down her sword and hid behind the bushes, absolutely refusing to be photographed. But pictures had to be taken and she had to kiss her beloved Rosalind's hand, and here she was, barely able to stand; her legs shook and her hands turned cold.

'*Array*, you urchin, don't stand so close to her,' Rashid said and Shamman began looking about her sheepishly.

Bilquis scolded him. 'What? Shamman is a duke's son, why are you calling her an urchin?'

'Oh, I see, so the duke's son had a tooth-powder moustache. Well done!'

'Liar, it's not tooth-powder, it's kohl,' Bilquis said, glancing lovingly at Shamman's moustache. 'My word, it looks real!'

If Principal Sahiba hadn't come and admonished everyone the joking and teasing would have never ceased and the pictures would never have been taken.

'Apa *bi*, in the next play I'd like to be a girl,' Rashid told his sister, Principal Sahiba. 'If girls can put on some black paint and become men, why can't I be a woman? That's not fair!'

When everyone was leaving, Rashid whispered in Shamman's ear: 'Now don't forget you owe us a rap.'

Exasperated and amused at the same time, she ran from there, laughing.

18

Rashid = Bilquis's brother

Shamman and Rashid's romance flourished. Every day Bilquis brought her a note from her brother. There would be nothing more in that note except the wistful old reference to the rap. Rashid addressed her as 'Shamsham', or 'urchin sahib'. Rashid invaded her thoughts completely. In the quarter-term examination she failed badly and cried with shame for hours. She was given a passing grade as a courtesy and Principal Sahiba set up a tuition for her in mathematics since that was her weakest subject. Rashid was appointed as her tutor. Where could you find a decent, upright man these days?

The relationship between a student and a teacher – what a romantic relationship that is. Romance bubbles at the slightest provocation; no one studies much. Rashid and Shamman talked for hours on end without any hesitation and then parted cheerfully with hopes of continuing their conversation the next day. Shamman had to go to Principal Sahiba's house for her daily lessons. As evening approached, the bungalow was transformed into a noisy assembly. Friends began congregating, an informal gathering formed in which life's issues were debated candidly and lectures were delivered on the subject of human rights; the moon, cut into five segments, was surrounded by stars, proper and refined romances thrived, and the bungalow resounded with laughter.

One day, while Shamman and Bilquis were sitting on the steps of the hostel discussing Rashid's newest pranks, the gate opened suddenly and some new students' luggage began arriving. It seemed there were several sisters who had arrived together, but no one accompanied the luggage.

The next day Principal Sahiba came in with two girls. The girls were not only beautiful, they also appeared to be very well-to-do. One was about seven, while the other perhaps fifteen or sixteen. Impressed by their fashionable, silken attire, the girls peeped from their classroom doors to catch a glimpse of them.

During lunchtime Principal Sahiba entrusted the two girls to Bilquis and Jalees. The four of them sat, very prim and proper, at the neatest end of the table and were served the food that had been brought over from the principal's house. The dining room was unusually clean today and the chipped enamel plates and the unpolished copper serving bowls were not present at this particular table. Instead, the table was set with new plates, the ones set aside for special functions. This afternoon the food also came in large quantities and because it was Friday, *kheer*, made from skimmed milk and not quite as sweet as it should be, was also served. Suddenly Principal Sahiba walked in, accompanied by a large, thick-set, beautiful begum dressed in shimmering clothes, and, going up to the new girls, the two women began chatting with them. The urgent whispering among the girls revealed the woman was the newcomers' mother.

The newcomers' mother also tasted the food and complimented the cooks.

'One doesn't get such delicious food even at home,' the mountain of fat, the nawab's daughter, said. 'So . . . nutritious!' How could she, the begum fatigued with obesity, tired of kababs and *parathas*, have any sensation left in her taste buds to judge the excellence of the *parathas*?

The girls got up to leave with the principal and their mother, and on their insistence Bilquis and Jalees also accompanied them.

In the evening Bilquis returned with the two girls, who were still wearing their brightly coloured clothes. Bilquis too had donned a beautiful *dupatta*. She stayed with the girls the entire time. There was quite a stir in the hostel and all the students abandoned their work to gawk at the new students. Their room was finally ready. Besides two very handsome beds and a dressing table, which was a novel object, there were tables, lamps, rugs, mats and silk curtains. In short, it seemed as if someone had set up in a forest an enormous bouquet bursting with colourful flowers and fresh green leaves.

Shamman had not walked past their room as yet. Since her friendship with Bilquis she had distanced herself from the rest of the students in the hostel. Because she was Principal Sahiba's favourite, she had fallen in the estimation of the other girls who thought she fawned over the principal, and was conceited and selfish. Today, while Bilquis was busy entertaining her new guests, poor Shamman sat alone and deserted like an owl in her room. During lunchtime Bilquis went to the bungalow with the new girls and, surrounded by mocking smiles and sneering glances, Shamman sat alone at her table, silently swallowing mouthfuls of smelly curry and dry rice.

When Bilquis came back to the room later to get some of her things Shamman tried to complain in a sullen voice, but Bilquis seemed to be in too much of a hurry to listen.

'Achi Nawab Sahib is here as well, he's wearing gorgeous clothes. Naseema forcibly gave me this *dupatta*, Apa *bi*'s orders are that the girls should not feel homesick, such a fuss, and she says we must all go to New Delhi the day after tomorrow to see off Nawab Sahib.' Bilquis was putting her things together in haste.

'And Cuckoo is just so cute, she's crazy about Rashid, she was straddled on his shoulders all day long.' She walked out with a sheepish expression.

School closed for three days and Bilquis and Jalees went away with the new girls to New Delhi to see off their parents. Shamman didn't get a chance to talk to Bilquis even after their return and Rashid was away at a match so she didn't go to the bungalow either. When she did go for her lesson she found the atmosphere greatly changed. Although she had persuaded Abba to pay Rashid thirty rupees, and that with a great deal of plotting and scheming, today she was being treated like an orphan receiving lessons as charity. Rashid wasn't present. Not much could be done when he came because he had to play *carom* with Naseema, and Cuckoo was constantly climbing over his shoulders. Except for Jalees and Bilquis, practically everyone was glued to the new girls like flies.

Naseema's dressing table was like a chemist's shop. Bilquis and Jalees constantly plastered their faces with this and that, and all day long the girls in the hostel gathered in their room, flattering them, fawning over them. In a short while Naseema had gained control of the entire camp. Nearly every girl was buried under the weight of powder, lipstick, old silk blouses, *dupattas*, or sandals. With Naseema and her sister was their nanny whom everyone called Baibay. The big, fat, strapping female was brusque with the fawning girls, but they were ready to kiss her feet.

The hostel rules didn't apply to Naseema and Cuckoo. Servants were not allowed in the hostel, but in their case Principal Sahiba had to give permission. In addition, they ate their meals in their rooms and used their own china. They had been given two rooms with attached bathrooms and storage areas. It was a standard house. No one was allowed to traverse their side of the veranda.

Very soon the make-up affliction spread. The poorer girls daubed their faces with red ink and the four-anna powder for pimples when they couldn't find anything else. Wherever you looked you could see red cheeks and artificially curled hair. If an electric roller was not available then heated steel rods were used to wind up hair. If real gold lace and spangles were not to be had, then pins and tiny golden leaves were stuck on *dupattas*. Because of the new girls, cloth merchants, bangle-sellers and fruitwallahs were now allowed to come into the hostel compound, and so what if there was a dearth of money? Loans were readily available. Who knows what treasure these girls had stumbled on, because after lending money to nearly everyone in the hostel, they still had enough left over to buy baskets of fruit and boxes of biscuits every day, and every day free goods were distributed, halvas were made, and parties were thrown. Today it's Cuckoo's birthday; the entire hostel has been invited to a celebration. Today Naseema is feeling down so she's making preparations for Bilquis's party, paying for everything, and to top it all Bilquis and Jalees are both getting new suits. Charity is providing succour to the devotees.

Shamman's maths was not as bad as Naseema's Urdu. Having spent her entire life in a convent, Naseema had now been sent to this Islamic school to improve her well-being. So, for seventy-five rupees Rashid began tutoring her in Urdu, geography and mathematics. Naseema was in ninth class. Although her English was better than that of many of her teachers, her skills in Urdu were at the level of class two. During the English period she came to Shamman's class. She gave correct answers even before the teacher had finished phrasing the question, which made her teachers beam from ear to ear. Naseema spoke constantly, and sometimes Bilquis too, and the teachers complimented them while the other girls, uneasy and mortified, could do nothing better than quietly submit to a shower of disapproval.

That was not all. Naseema proved to be better than everyone on the athletics field as well. Sometimes she cheated, but when questioned she would lapse into fluent English, thus intimidating the other girls, and meanwhile the teacher, who favoured English, forgave her every transgression with a sweet remark made in English. Shamman didn't know why, but from the very first moment she had placed Naseema in the role of an enemy. Whenever she and Naseema ran into each other, their eyes met brazenly and then both would look away. Rashid still had some amiable talk for her when they chanced to meet, but something had changed. It seemed as if he was slowly forgetting. Shamman was also no longer a favourite of Principal Sahiba, in the hostel she was like an outsider, and Noori, following Jalees's example, had become a permanent appendage to Cuckoo. So once again, Shamman was overcome by an indescribable feeling of loneliness, and so intense was this feeling that finally she rebelled.

First she attacked her books. Naseema was good at smooth-talking, but her general knowledge was near zero. In a few days Shamman was answering Naseema's rapid vocalisation in broken English sentences she had learned by rote. Having memorised complete pages, she overpowered Naseema. She stood her ground like a stubborn mule and responded in halting English to every smile and every snicker. She hated sports, but she practised in the blistering heat until, like a wounded lioness, she overcame all her opponents on the athletics field.

No doubt Naseema's favours were like a magic wand, but Shamman's stubbornness and her tenacity were not in vain either. Gradually all those girls who for one reason or another had fallen from Naseema's favour gathered under Shamman's banner. Naseema, dashing off to the bungalow to improve her Urdu as soon as classes were over, spent hardly any time in the hostel now. Cuckoo was also no longer the delicate little girl she used to be, while Baibay seemed to have very little control over her. After spending time in the company of rowdy, ill-mannered young girls, she would return covered in dust so that the Cuckoo whom students had once run from their classrooms to kiss and hug, now received slaps from her nanny before coming out of her room. And there was also a decrease in the amount of fruit at the hostel, one reason being that much of the fruit was now conveyed to the bungalow where Naseema and her sister took their meals most of the time.

Shamman was sitting quietly in her room. She now lived alone. After Bilquis left she didn't allow anyone else to share the room with her. She was busy memorising a speech for the next day when suddenly Bilquis walked in. She looked a little uncomfortable and contrite. Pretending to be searching for a book, she rummaged at the table for a long time. Finally, when Shamman didn't speak to her, she said:

'I've lost my poetry book. Could you lend me yours?'

Shamman silently placed the book before her on the table.

'Are you prepared for tomorrow?'

'Yes.'

'Here, do you want me to hear the speech?' Bilquis came and took the notebook from her. Shamman felt tears choking her throat. Words of reproach rose on her tongue, but Bilquis's downcast eyes silenced her.

'I tell you, by God, Naseema can't be a good speaker no matter what. Do you know, she doesn't even have the notes ready yet?'

'She can speak without any notes.'

'No, no she can't. Rashid has written such a wonderful speech for her, and she hasn't even looked at it.'

After a moment's pause Bilquis continued. 'Isaa and I have fought.'

'What? You're joking!'

'It's true.'

'But?'

'He's a cad. Do you know, this Sunday he . . .' She stopped in mid-sentence.

Shamman did not exhibit any curiosity.

'He said, "I have eight photographic plates and I'll take four pictures of Naseema and the rest of you." And it turned out there were only six and one he took of Jalees in shorts. Hunh! As if I can't live without the photographs.'

'There was only one left?'

'Yes, he said he'd have to get more from Delhi. And these girls can be so immodest . . . Rashid must have taken a hundred pictures, the poor fellow and now . . . Oh, how dreadful!' Bilquis became tearful. 'She doesn't study a word, and when Apa *bi* complained she immediately went and got her a cheque for two months' tuition. I don't know what's wrong with Apa *bi*, why is she so afraid of her?' Apa *bi*, the unfortunate woman, was the only breadwinner in a family of five sisters and one very spoiled brother.

'You were afraid of her too,' Shamman finally said.

'I say, my shoe's afraid of that witch! Hunh! She was the one who was always forcing me to do things. Do you know she's asked Isaa to come with her to their home in Musoorie.'

Bilquis left after pouring her heart out to Shamman. In the afternoon the sound of Matron and Naseema bickering with each other brought the girls out of their rooms. What had happened was that the cloth merchant had come and had been turned away on the orders of Principal Sahiba. When Naseema complained to Matron, she explained she had no choice but to say no, and this enraged Naseema. But in the end Naseema had to admit defeat and she left the hostel to buy what she wanted to. Matron couldn't say a word to stop her. However, in the evening a notice appeared on a wall across from the hall saying that no vendors were to be allowed in the hostel compound, and any shopping that had to be done would be undertaken only on Sundays and only in the room on the far side of the dormitories. All the girls read the notice and grumbled as if they had been planning extensive shopping sprees.

Three or four days later Shamman walked into her room to find Bilquis sitting quietly on her bed. For a few minutes Bilquis gazed at her silently then, turning, she threw her head down on the pillow and burst into sobs.

'My goodness, Billee, what's the matter?' Shamman used a loving tone with her after what was a very long time.

'Ohh, Shamman!' Bilquis put her arms around her and sobbed hysterically. Between sobs she recounted the story of Isaa and Naseema's romance. Isaa had already taken the ICS exam and with Naseema's father's recommendation he was sure to pass. And today, when Bilquis threw his album at him, he had the gall to be offended.

'You can have my album, Bilquis,' Naseema said in sugary tones. 'I'm getting a new one from Paris.'

'Hunh! As if Bilquis collects other people's discarded goods. And Isaa hasn't apologised either. Anyway, today I'm inviting Ansar and Abbas to tea and you have to come as well.'

A note from Principal Sahiba made it possible for Shamman to go. The gathering today was large.

Bilquis was all dressed up, but Naseema stubbornly refused to change her clothes.

'Billee, you should have taken the shirt that goes with this *dupatta* – I just can't stand printed georgette any more,' Naseema sneered, revealing the fact that Bilquis was wearing her clothes. Bilquis was forced to quell the anger that rose inside her like a storm.

Rashid didn't say much to Shamman, who had been trying unsuccessfully to get out a splinter that was lodged in his palm. During dinner Bilquis and Naseema had words for which Bilquis was reproached. Ansar went so far as to say that Bilquis was too fond of quarrelling. Bilquis left the table in a huff, leaving Naseema to snigger.

Before returning to the hostel Naseema had another row with Bilquis. Further complications were averted with great difficulty and once again everyone reproached Bilquis. Naseema had to return to the hostel alone because Bilquis didn't let Shamman go with her. Isaa, Abbas and Ansar insisted on accompanying Naseema, but Principal Sahiba told them it wasn't proper for the boys to be present in the vicinity of the hostel.

Tearful protestations helped Bilquis get permission for Shamman to stay the night with her at the bungalow, and her stories about Naseema continued late into the night. Some time before the girls turned in, Rashid came to their room on some pretext and the three chatted for a while.

'Please turn the light off when you go,' begged Bilquis, feeling lethargic.

He turned off the light and in the dark tried to grab Bilquis's nose, and then, letting go of her nose, he quickly pinched Shamman's finger before leaving the room in haste. Dazed, Shamman stayed awake a long time after that.

The next morning a notice appeared in front of the hall which said that anyone visiting the bungalow would first be required to obtain a permission slip from Principal Sahiba. Naseema received meaningful glances and, their heads together, the girls gossiped. That evening Bilquis's servant came to Naseema's room with a bundle containing all the things she had lent Bilquis. Naseema called the sweeperess and handed her the bundle without opening it first. Who knows how many shimmering *dupattas* it contained – shoes, albums, powder, lipsticks, earrings, rings, and pins – the girls gazed longingly while the sweeperess swept up everything.

Naseema and Cuckoo left for the hill station before the exams started and it soon became known they were not returning. Their furniture was left behind to be distributed among the less fortunate girls, but somehow that furniture found its way to the bungalow.

19

There's no recourse but to go home during the holidays. Shamman disliked being at home to begin with, but this time the holidays were a burden she couldn't endure. Noori went off to her paternal grandmother's house. Shamman felt very alone. Although she needed to improve her performance in several subjects, she could not bring herself even to glance at a book. The house was full and noisy, but Shamman had no friend here. One of her sisters-in-law had a baby and for a short while her loneliness was eased, but she still found everything to be wanting and clumsy. How methodical everything was at college. Not muddled and confusing like this.

A letter arrived from Bilquis and along with it a note from Rashid. Bare Bhaya opened the letter and read Rashid's note. A disturbance followed as a result. But Shamman was a clever one! She said that this was her friend's younger brother. And Rashid's words rang like a little boy's. He had asked for the old rap that she owed him, begging in his usual sad tone!

After some time Bilquis went to the hill station and the letters stopped. One of the letters informed her that Bilquis and Jalees were to continue their education in Nainital. When Shamman returned to college she discovered that Rashid had gone to England.

Shamman felt as if a film reel had suddenly snapped while running and the lights in the hall had come on with an abrupt flash, blinding her eyes with their brutal, piercing rays. Silent and fearful, she held her breath and cowered. When a child wounds a finger while she's being mischievous, she conceals the bloodied finger with her shirt and, cowering, hides in a corner. Frightened by sorrow and shame, Shamman's feelings also fell face down in some remote corner of her heart, perhaps to stay there for ever.

When Bilquis wrote again there was no mention of Rashid in her letter. Perhaps her eyes too were blinded like hers. Relentlessly pushing everything aside, Shamman forged ahead.

By now she had developed an interest in her family. She secretly learned to ride a bicycle and also improved relations with her brothers. Noori had been away at her grandmother's and returned from there quite hardened. She frequently got together with other girls in the neighbourhood and stitched odd-looking garments although she had no need for them. She would put them on by mysterious means, and when these garments became dirty they were washed and placed inside suitcases to dry. Having also learned about being in love from a distant cousin, she acted coyly at any mention of the first letter in his name. Shamman didn't tell her anything about Rashid, and what was left to tell, anyway? She deliberately referred to him as Rashid Bhai now, with special emphasis on 'bhai'.

In those days Ejaz, Shamman's *khala*'s son, came to live with them. Ejaz's father had died and his mother had remarried. His stepfather's behaviour towards him was worse than a stepmother's might have been; he treated Ejaz and Shamman's aunt very badly. That was why Ejaz had been sent here. Usually he sat silently in a corner, gaping wide-eyed like an owl at those who were talking. He didn't know how to be mischievous. People always pray for children who are not mischievous, but when they saw Ejaz they shuddered. Like a battered monkey he sat in one place, staring all around him with eyes that were at once hungry, ravenous and distrusting. He seemed to be pleading and begging even though he hadn't asked for anything. He was the first one to arrive at the dining table. While waiting for the others he would straighten the folds in the tablecloth and meticulously arrange the silverware, and when the meal started he'd sit patiently and eye the food fondly. He seemed to enjoy everything he ate; regardless of whether something was too salty, too sweet, or too sour, he devoured it with the same degree of relish. Usually he was the last one to finish and, taking the remaining piece of chappati, he would clean up the plate with it, roll it into a big morsel and stuff it in his mouth. This last morsel stayed in his mouth for some time and, although he washed his hands and mouth, he never gargled because he wanted to retain the taste of food in his mouth. Actually no one had to tell him to wash. Early in the morning he cleaned his face with water from the tap in the courtyard, wiping it neatly with his shirtfront. But he still appeared filthy, filthy with sickly-looking skin, matted hair and rumpled clothes.

His petname was Ajju. Who knows how the wretch had got that petname – who could have felt so loving towards him as to give him one? He was very obedient. Abba disliked the English cut of hair and the boys rebelled at having their heads shaved. But Ajju, on the other hand, came and promptly sat before the barber with his ungainly head and smiled away as the barber shaved off all his hair. Taking the two-paisa reward, he would knot it in his cummerbund. However, it didn't make Abba happy to give him the reward; he was adamant about his principle, but for some reason the sight of Ajju's shaven head irritated him. Everyone disliked his head, which, because he had slept on the same side from early childhood, was flattened like a softened melon. He laughed cheerfully when someone boxed his ears, which aroused a little pity, but the feeling was short-lived and within minutes the pity was transformed into annoyance.

Old and young, all laughed at him and made fun of him, the servants rebuked him, and his peers couldn't tolerate him, and to top it all, at Shamman's birth her aunt had put down a rupee in Ajju's name. Amma had remained silent because she didn't want to hurt her sister's feelings. The poor mother adored her son and whenever a festival came along she arrived with a new suit of clothes and sesame-seed *ladoos* for him. Like a dutiful son, Ajju presented the *ladoos* to everybody, but when everyone had declined them he had to eat the *ladoos* himself.

Besides being poor, Khala was also old-fashioned and coarse. For a hulking, full-grown boy like Ajju she'd bring a *kurta* with a floral print and a red twill scarf. Early in the morning mother and son would take baths with freezing water and, dressed in his stiff new clothes, Ajju went from bed to bed offering salaams. Smiling, holding her laughter in check, Khala would accompany him on his rounds. But everyone was disgruntled by this early morning disturbance and no one responded graciously to his salutations.

Whether it was pudding or cake, Ajju insisted on calling it *puteen*. It enraged Manjhle Bhaya when during a game of cards he said *hukam* and *eent* instead of hearts and diamonds. 'Ajju, you wretch, come on say salaam ... hold your nose ... here ... there ... and over there too.' Ajju would hold his nose and offer and bow in all directions. 'Now stand on one leg ... hurry, hurry.' Bhaya would rap his knees with his stick. 'No, Bhaya, don't, why do you hit him?' Khala would plead.

When Shamman set eyes on Ajju he appeared to her as a big, hefty curse. Her emotions ran amok and were driven to rebellion, she felt like digging her teeth into someone's flesh. And to make matters worse, the undiscerning aunt thought that if the childhood engagement were mentioned perhaps family members might be prone to treat Ajju less severely. So, she sat in the middle of the courtyard one day and began talking about her aspirations as Shamman's mother-in-law. Shamman was stunned into silence, but Khala's comments had a strange effect on Ajju. First, his eyes flew open and he gawked at everyone for a few minutes, then suddenly he blushed, and soon he bolted from there.

From that day on he behaved timidly and with extreme reticence in Shamman's presence. He was stupefied if she was around and if she happened to walk past him, he acted as if he were paralysed. This was the only sentiment, after his indestructible appetite, that had attacked Ajju with such force. The minute he stepped into the house he started behaving like a prospective son-in-law, and seeing him look so serious and reserved, as if indeed he were a hopeful bachelor, Shamman wanted to throw a shoe at his face and call him the worst names. There was another upheaval. The playful tomfoolery he always engaged in to amuse and please people ceased all of a sudden, and although he was bashful before Shamman, secretly he scrutinised every movement of hers.

At night the children's beds were placed side by side in the courtyard. Using some pretext or another, Ajju would slowly push his bed until it was close to Shamman's. No one thought he was doing this deliberately since everyone regarded him as an idiot. Only Shamman knew the truth. When everybody was asleep he stealthily stretched his foot and tried to pinch Shamman's toes with his. Shamman would get up and scold him, but he would feign sleep. All night Shamman felt as if there were mice hopping about on her bed, and she couldn't get any sleep because Ajju's hand was either on her ankle or her thigh.

'What is it, Ajju? I'll hit you,' Shamman would say, picking up her shoe threateningly. But she developed a fear of Ajju and began sleeping next to the old nanny in order to avoid him. On one side was a wall, on the other the nanny from whom she heard the same old rundown stories of kings and princesses which she knew by heart. Actually she didn't hear a word and just kept saying, 'Hmm, yes, hmm . . .' Her thoughts were elsewhere, in a faraway place, weaving the strands of a light-hearted, interesting story. She was the heroine of these stories and as for the hero, well, who could say no to her? She remembered a film she had seen not too long ago. *Heer Ranjha*. How artlessly Heer had seized Ranjha during a game of hide-and-seek! Her own ardent but innocent meeting with Rashid had been something like this . . . during the picnic . . . when she . . . She dozed off, the dreams lulled her to sleep, she felt she was in a swing going up, now down, and then she falls, the slippery ground tickles the soles of her feet and seems to run away from her . . . Bilquis's room and the *carom* board . . . Rashid sitting there with his head covered in Bilquis's scarf – she's in purdah from Rashid, isn't she . . . Rashid's roguish eyes peering at her through the gossamer curtain of the scarf . . . she loses . . . the winner, Rashid, holds her wrist and prepares to give her a rap with his fingers ... all at once she's swung around in an empty space, streaks of scalding hot water slither down her temples and her shoulders and she starts ... ohh! Ajju's hungry hands!

Waking up with a stifled scream, she noticed that Ajju was at the water containers, seemingly engrossed in drinking water. He gave no reply to her quavering condemnation and, finishing his drink, returned quietly to his bed. For hours afterwards Shamman trembled with fear, her blood pounding through her veins.

Her hatred for Ajju was now mixed with dread. All day long he looked utterly harmless and at night all she could see was a monster. His face had changed. He studied constantly, and strangely enough, his great hunger seemed to have disappeared altogether. He came to the table only after being sent for again and again, swallowed two or three morsels apathetically and left the table quickly. He had also begun to recognise the odour of soured milk, the stink of rotting melons, and the acrid taste of mangoes. Somehow, with the aid of memorisation, he did well in his exams and obtained a scholarship in matric. But not a day went by when Shamman didn't find him standing at the foot of her bed. He didn't touch her, however, he only paced restlessly, stooped, hesitated. One night he picked up Shamman's *dupatta* that was trailing on the floor, but then, alarmed, he dropped it on her and was immediately sorry afterwards; why did he relinquish the *dupatta* ... the attempt to retrieve the *dupatta* was thwarted by his trembling hands. Seeing Shamman toss and turn angrily he hastened to the water containers and quickly filled a glass with water.

She wished for his death. 'If only Ajju would die, if only he would die!' she muttered when she was half-asleep. He didn't understand what she was saying and bending over her he gazed at her moving lips. One night Shamman's patience finally ran out. She had gone to sleep with her hair still wet after a bath. Suddenly it seemed as if there was steam moving through her hair. She became frightened and, holding her head with both hands, started screaming. She felt stifled. Her mouth opened but no sound emerged. When she opened her eyes she saw that with his head cradled in her hair, Ajju was sobbing violently like a hungry dog. She hit Ajju with her shoe as he dashed from there.

The next morning she searched the whole house for her shoe, but there was no sign of it.

'I hit the dog last night with it – I don't know what happened to it.'

'What? The dog was tied up all night, where did the dog come from?' someone said.

'Maybe the drain was left open, it might have been a stray dog.'

'Yes, it was a stray dog, wild-looking.' Shamman decided to go along with the stray dog story.

'These wretched dogs sometimes carry people off, you know.'

'But what will a dog do with a slipper?'

'*Array*, they just make off with shoes for no reason. Kaleem Mian's bitch ran off with my new Delhi shoe. The wretched bitch ripped it up, it was in shreds when we found it.'

Conversation veered from one thing to another until it took off in a totally new direction, but Shamman's uneasiness was not dispelled. After all, she queried, where did the shoe go to? From that day Ajju's bed was transferred to the other side of the courtyard. Shamman heaved a sigh of relief. At last she was free of the wretch! After this she saw that Ajju became completely detached and was lost in his books; it seemed as if he had had his fill after being struck with the shoe.

Shamman's vacation was coming to a close. In another four days she was to return to school. One afternoon Ajju got heatstroke while walking home from school. No one found out at first, but when Abba reprimanded him in the evening for being lazy and instructed him to water the plants, he leapt to his feet. However, he hadn't gone a few steps when he tottered and fell. It was discovered he had a fever of a hundred and five.

Shamman felt as if God had answered her prayers and Ajju was about to depart. All night he was shaken by fever and delirium. Although Abba didn't keep track of what was going on in the house, he turned the house upside-down when someone took ill. There was a commotion even if the hen fractured its leg. Ajju's condition worsened; in his delirium he tried to bolt from the bed several times. Everybody in the house went to apply cold compresses on his forehead, but Shamman didn't even peek in his room. Finally her turn came and she was forced to go. She was determined, however, not to touch the wretch. But when she saw him lying unconscious she felt a tinge of pity and taking an ice cube she began rubbing it on his forehead. His forehead burned, his lips were chapped, and moisture seeped from the corners of his eyes. Ajju's condition was pitiful. Outside, the children were eating ice-cream, and although Shamman wasn't a greedy person, she was anxious to have her share. She tried to slip away quietly, but Ajju began chewing his lips from thirst and she applied the ice cube to his hot, burning lips. His lips touched her finger! She got to her feet with a start. Ajju opened his eyes and stared at her without blinking. A misshapen smile spread on his face. Shamman turned to leave. 'Shamman,' he tried to form the words hoarsely, but she was already outside eating ice-cream. Her hands trembled and her throat burned. The chilled ice particles scratched her throat. Putting down the cup of ice-cream, she blew on the tips of her fingers which felt numb, as if the blood in them had become petrified after coming into contact with a corpse.

She wet a rope cot and lay down on it to cool herself. It seemed as though there were heated rods running through her body. Her throat was dry and bland like a piece of paper, and Ajju's feverish voice kept writhing in her ears like the hissing of a snake. She could not understand why her emotions were in such turmoil.

The next morning when Ajju was moved so that his bedsheets could be changed, Shamman's lost shoe was found; Ajju was lying face down with the shoe clasped tightly between both hands. His temperature had dropped to below normal and his eyes were beginning to glaze over.

20

One morning Shamman woke up to find the house alive with a strange kind of hustle and bustle. Equipped with a long pole, the steward was attacking the cobwebs in all the rooms while the sweeperess was being scolded for not cleaning the gutter properly; Bari Apa, her mouth and nose covered with a cloth, was having the rubbish under the divans removed; china was being taken out of the cupboards.

Soon it became known that the uncle from Calcutta was arriving with his wife, his illustrious son Abbas, and his daughter Fehmida. Besides being the oldest son, Abbas had recently returned from England with a degree in engineering. This Chacha from Calcutta was a good-for-nothing, useless man. But no one knows how his son turned out to be a jewel; somehow he managed to receive a scholarship to study engineering, and poor Chacha's life finally turned around. Chacha, the unfortunate fellow, was treated by the family like a contagious disease. He had a habit of arriving at someone's house and remaining there until he was thrown out. Amma decided to observe purdah in his presence and the girls in the family appeared before him only to offer cursory salutations. For the most part he was left at the mercy of the servants who derided and ridiculed him. He stayed in one place as long as he could, then left in search of insults and rejection elsewhere. A school teacher took pity on Abbas and helped him, and today when Abbas returned furnished with the blinding glitter of a shining star, the whole family turned its gaze towards him. Manjhle Mamun and Chote Mamun arrived at the station with garlands, and as for Khala *bi*, she had made arrangements to have breakfast delivered to the travellers while they were still three stations away from their destination. At Shamman's house the good china was being brought out, as were floor coverings and carpets, and the room upstairs was being furnished.

Finally, after a long wait, Abbas Mian arrived in the company of his dastardly father, his incompetent mother, and his pimple-faced sister, Fehmida. Amma gave Abbas a tight hug and actually bestowed blessings on Chacha.

'*Array*, how Fehmida has grown,' Bari Apa said, embracing the young girl lovingly. 'You must sleep with Noori, all right?'

Khala *bi* turned to a cinder.

'I say, why should she give up the company of someone her own age to sleep with Noori? Daughter, go with your Sameena Apa, she'll help you wash. *Array*, don't stand there looking at our faces, Sameena, take your sister to the bathroom.'

Bari Apa was astounded. What has the world come to? Nobody cares about the plight of widows. People don't think twice about stepping on an orphan's rights just to clear the way for their own daughters. She was absolutely certain that Chacha would give the rightful candidate his consideration, but Sameena and Ahmedi duped everyone and absconded with Fehmida.

'*Ai*, Shamman, don't sit there like you're dead – send some hot water for Abbas's bath,' Amma said nervously; Bari was very hotheaded.

'*Ai*, Shamman doesn't have the brains to think . . .' Bari Apa interjected. 'Noori? Heat water on my electric heater and take it up to Abbas.'

But before Noori could heat the water Khala *bi* came down smugly, accompanied by Abbas who seemed to have washed already. Everyone stood there gawking in surprise. Smiling, she pulled a chair for him and opened her *paan-dan*.

Poor Chacha! He was flabbergasted and at first didn't understand why everyone was being so nice to him. He was very uncomfortable, the poor fellow, because it was he who was accustomed to flattering everyone. In the past when he stopped for a visit, his charpoy was set up in the area near the door and his meals were sent to him there on a tray. All this fawning by the entire family proved baffling beyond measure. However, soon he ascertained that the number of girls in the family exceeded that of the boys, who were also good-for-nothing for the most part. Flustered, he selected Sameena, and immediately thereafter began feeling sorry for Noori; Sameena was getting older, but Noori had the distinction of being an orphan; sometimes he leant towards Ahmedi, then showered Shamman with consideration. If he could manage it he would make them all his daughters-in-law.

His smallest request created a furore in the house. The mothers sent their daughters scrambling and were later embarrassed by their own impatience. A competition was in progress. In other words, let's see who overwhelms Chacha and Chachi with their pampering and wins the trophy – Abbas, that is. Bari Apa devised an entirely new technique; she instructed Noori to consult Abbas repeatedly on the meanings of English words. But Sameena was quite mature and it was on her that Abbas's attention was mostly directed. He regarded Noori as a child, Shamman as bad-tempered, and as for Ahmedi, poor girl, her face was blemished by pockmarks. Her fate was crystal clear.

Sameena responded coyly to Abbas's jokes. She had started knitting a sweater for him which Khala *bi* also helped her with. In the evening pachisi was played often and during the game Chacha delivered a chain of profanities as was his custom. Once, a long time ago, Amma had gone into purdah when he swore in this manner. Today all the genteel ladies of the house laughed clamorously, and Khala *bi* hid her face behind the fan and tittered. Chacha cheated at length, but was forgiven as if he were a naughty child. Chachi spat out streams of betel-juice on the spotless walls and waited for Amma to rise up in angry protest, but Amma remained calm and collected.

Although Abbas was most impressed with Sameena, the minute she dropped out of sight he immediately began his pursuit of Ahmedi and Shamman. He teased all the girls equally and it was his teasing that created a disturbance in the political circles; true, Sameena was the oldest and there was no room for argument here; Shamman's father had obliged Chacha with innumerable favours so there was no reason to object here; Noori was an orphan and in her case everyone was relying on Abbas's integrity and high principles. So, how will a decision be made? Everybody waited.

Actually Abbas was a very interesting man. As soon as he walked into the house the girls gathered around him on one pretext or another. And then either his button broke which Shamman or Ahmedi readily sewed back on, or Sameena discovered an invisible splinter in her finger which no one could remove and which hurt as if it were a spear. The remarks Abbas came up with while trying to remove the splinter made Sameena break out in a sweat.

'I say, there's only one cure for this naughty finger,' he would say with a laugh.

'Why don't you cure it then if you know what it is?' Sameena would look at him demurely.

'The cure is that a sparkling ring . . .'

'Don't.' Sameena would pull her hand away bashfully. Khala's face would light up.

'All right, come on, I won't say anything now.'

In addition to this, Noori's problems with English words multiplied, and Bari Apa was consumed with grief and misgiving. Chacha was exhausted from eating too much chicken and Chachi ingested so much carrot halva that her stomach rebelled. Sameena and Ahmedi's fingers and thumbs were sore from dyeing and crimping Fehmida's *dupattas*. Holding their breath, immersed in their duties, all of them waited patiently for the results. Let's see which side the camel sits on, whose fate stirs.

Shamman liked Abbas. Not because he had curly hair and hooded eyes, but because he made everyone laugh. Pinching your cheek without warning, suddenly resting his head in your lap on the pretext of a headache, asking to have the *paan* dropped into his mouth instead of in his hand and trying to squeeze your finger between his teeth while you were giving him the *paan* and inadvertently rubbing your knee or your thigh – he kept them laughing. In the evening they all sat covered in quilts because it was so cold and within the clouds of these quilts Abbas's hands bolted like lightning. The girls quivered with tiny tremors, they scattered, then gathered closer. The elders sat some distance from the playful antics of the children, submerged in their *paan* and betel-nut. But their ears were tuned to the children's voices.

At night all the girls whispered among themselves and the ember that Abbas had left was ignited. The girls, with the exception of Sameena, were frank with each other and there wasn't the slightest bit of envy in their hearts. Like *gopis* they danced together to the notes of Krishna's flute, and whenever Abbas was in the drawing room or the dining room, they forgot everything and flitted about him as if he were Krishna. As for Sameena, she was usually more occupied with taking care of Fehmida who called her 'Bhabi' when they were alone. But Sameena told her not to call her that in front of the others, and her shyness in Abbas's presence grew. All Khala *bi* could talk about day and night was gold lace and gold and silver tassels, and lately you could hear echoing in her storage room the sounds of Muradabadi and copper utensils.

Bari Apa was not negligent either. She immediately had her old bracelets sent away to the jeweller to be melted down and shaped into more fashionable anklets and she constantly talked about the special china dinnerware that she was going to get from Bombay or Calcutta. Why, if everything had to be done all at once, would she just not die from too much anxiety, the poor thing!

Shamman's mother didn't have the courage to open her mouth because within minutes Bari Apa would bring up the matter of her husband's untimely death and start wailing. As a grandmother, could she take away her granddaughter's match? Nevertheless, Apa continued to make cutting remarks.

'*Ai hai*, people don't refrain from sucking a widow's blood . . . *Array*, I say, there's no shortage for the others, but if an orphan gets lucky, why it's something. The Koran also says, first it's the right of the orphan and the widow . . . and then . . .' But Khala *bi* heard all this and pretended not to know what it meant. She was too busy preparing the dowry.

There was all kinds of speculation.

'No, my dear, you just wait and see, he's not going to marry Ahmedi, but as for our Noori . . .' Mumani tried to curry favour with Bari Apa.

'*Ai*, dear, see the oil and observe its flow,' Bari Apa said. 'Even if it's Shamman it would be something . . .'

'Well, let's see what happens . . . although your aunt is after him with a vengeance. *Array*, I say, yesterday she had a velvet quilt made – what a showy thing it is. I told her so right away.'

In short, it seemed as if the horses were on the racetrack; sometimes one was leading, sometimes the other. Or it was like an interview where all the candidates have done their best and now everyone is waiting impatiently for the outcome. Chacha and Chachi haven't proposed, haven't said a word. They eat and sleep and here everyone is on tenterhooks, unable to sleep or rest. It seems as if there's a wedding procession at everyone's door, but the bridegroom won't step over the threshold.

In the meantime Abbas had started playing hide-and-seek. When Ahmedi was cutting up betel-nut in the rear veranda, he suddenly appeared from somewhere and grabbed her; it was with great difficulty that she freed herself from his grasp and bolted from there. And then one day Shamman happened to walk into the drawing room and saw him with Sameena. Sameena ran away and when Shamman turned to leave, Abbas seized her hand.

'You won't say anything, will you Shamman?'

'Why not? You just wait,' Shamman said mischievously and laughed.

'No, no . . . look don't tell anyone . . . and listen . . .' He crept up close to her to whisper urgently in her ear.

'All right, I won't tell anyone, let me go now.' Shamman wanted to escape.

'Unhuh, you'll have to swear . . . swear by my head.' Abbas pulled her closer.

'All right . . . all right . . . I swear by your head. . . let me go now,' she floundered.

'But listen . . .' he tried to pull her in an embrace.

'Shamman!' He endeavoured to grasp a slippery fish and failed.

For a long time afterwards she trembled in exasperation. She didn't know why but being so close to Abbas had left her feeling sick. She could clown around with him, but from a distance. She found this intimate playfulness very distressing.

'Why?' she wondered. Abbas's hair was so much like Rashid's and his laughter was a little like his, but . . . so what was it that had turned her off? It's sickening to share a spoon with another person; spit from one mouth to the other mouth! *Uff!* And a few moments ago Sameena had run from his side . . . and . . .

Abbas's leave was coming to an end and the thought of leaving saddened him. The girls too became depressed, and all the elders were fearful, apprehensive. He was dodging; he was besieging the girls at night and during the day, and on the other side all the traps were open, grain was being scattered, nets were still being flung out, and the hunters, ready with bird-lime, were waiting hopefully.

Day and night there was talk of weddings, but Chacha and Chachi seemed to have lost their speech. Finally Khala *bi*'s patience brimmed over. Chacha's answer was like a hurricane that levels entire populations, leaving desolation in its wake. After the ICS exam the successful

102

candidates look so happy and content, and go about with smiles on their faces as they distribute sweets. And those unfortunate ones who have failed, they experience a sort of death. The massacre of a thousand aspirations, the slaying of a million ambitions. But if you discover that the government has, by illegal means, terminated the post of ICS altogether, then this would be referred to as a national and public death. And this is exactly what happened. Chachi gave everyone a verbal invitation to Abbas's wedding. The wedding that had been arranged with Master Sahib's daughter before Abbas left for England. Master Sahib was the one who had helped Abbas pay for his degree. The girl was dark-complexioned and poor as well, but she was clever and worldly wise.

Who knows how many dowries, bracelets and velvet quilts were demolished by this clever daughter-in-law. Suddenly Amma began to show affection for her chickens, carrot halva was not cooked again, the *dupatta* that went with the suit Khala *bi* had planned to give Fehmida got lost, and Ahmedi decided to keep the *kurta* and pyjamas for herself. The streaks of betel-juice on the walls cut into the heart like deep, elongated wounds. Chacha and Chachi departed suddenly in order to take care of important business, and Sameena's attacks began afresh. Noori's misfortune as an orphan re-emerged like a pus-laden sore and Mumani began referring to Ahmedi as the 'unfortunate one', as the 'ill-fated one'.

Chacha and Chachi left frightening, painful twinges in everyone's heart. Chachi packed two pillows in her luggage by mistake, and Fehmida forgot to return Sameena's silver earrings. Chacha soaked the cards with spittle, and, leaving behind longing and restlessness in a few simple hearts, Abbas went his way.

21

At the end of the summer holidays Shamman was admitted to a mission college. For the first time Shamman realised how big and expansive the world was. She felt that until now she had been crawling on the surface of an egg, slippery, colourless and without a base, but limited; no matter how much she walked she stayed where she was. As soon as she set foot in college it seemed to her that she was soaring in a train and when suddenly the train came to a junction she had to get off and submerge herself in the hustle and bustle she saw around her. Literary meetings, engrossing lectures, forceful speeches, eventful excursions, and tempestuous romances. The first informal chat between two girls was about admirers. Girls gauged each other's worth in this very manner. For example, the entire university was infatuated with Mary, the entire political science class adored Bina Rai, Sanskrit's Pandit *ji* had been in love with Kamla for three years now, Kishori was worshipped by the professor of Persian and, as for the other girls, the steward's *chacha*'s and *mamun*'s sons, and their neighbours were in love with them. At least that was their role in the college.

The rules were very strict; not even someone's real father was allowed to come in without a thorough check first. Despite these security measures the vast sea of romance surged and swelled and the matron with the coarse lips and chipped, yellow teeth had no control over these matters.

Matron, poor woman, was extremely unpopular. Her lover had been killed in the Great War, or he had abandoned her, but for some reason she was always trying to uncover any secrets the girls might have. As soon as it was ten, she immediately began her rounds to make sure the lights were turned off. Actually she herself commenced preparations for bedtime two hours in advance. First she bathed, then polished her face, curled the few hairs left on her head until they danced on her forehead like twisted wicks, donned a Japanese kimono with a swishing serpents print, and put on her flat-soled slippers. When she walked, her massive, aging body rippled and the serpents on her kimono seemed to be slowly coming to life.

Despite the fact that the girls loathed her, they were compelled nonetheless to curry favour with her every Sunday by saying nice things about her deceased lover whose photograph she kept in her room. The photograph was of a white soldier. The face extremely repulsive, at least a foot long and hard, the upper lip short and stretched, making him look as if he had clenched his teeth in anger, eyebrows missing, and a crewcut. The biology girls had a notion that a combination of Matron's seed and this white man's would have resulted in the birth of a bizarre mutation.

Matron could not imagine a girl without a lover, although she herself was like a nun. Once Prema's brother Narendar came to visit her and, since she was standing in the veranda when he arrived, she forgot to get permission first from Matron to see him and started talking to him. Shamman was with her that day.

The minute Matron discovered he was there she appeared on the scene huffing and puffing, all out of breath. Prema protested vehemently that this was her real brother, but, ignoring all her pleas, Matron reported her to the principal. Prema, however, was too clever for Matron. She obtained a few permission cards, addressed them to the principal with the message that Prema and Shamman could meet any family member and that Shamman could go and stay with Prema during the holidays, and then requested a BA girl to sign their parents' names on both cards. Afterwards these cards were secretly delivered to the principal's desk. When Prema was called in to the principal's office she mentioned the cards innocently. Poor Matron received a terse reprimand.

That Sunday Shamman went home with Prema. There were four or five other friends with Narendar and everyone got into one car. It was the middle of the afternoon, blistering sunshine, waves of scorching heat pressing down threateningly, but there were cool sparks coursing through Shamman's body. For the first time in her life she was in such close proximity to this many coarse-textured coats, over-sized shoes and hats that were totally unnecessary. Perhaps the boys were giving themselves airs just to impress the two girls. They were all extremely free with Prema, and one of them, whom everyone called 'Bittu', was dozing with his head on Prema's shoulder and at every bump his head fell forward on to Prema's chest. Grinding her teeth, Prema would clutch a handful of hair on his head and shake him. Finally the car drove into the compound and came to a stop in front of the veranda. Shamman's legs were stiff. With great difficulty everyone pulled their legs out and emerged from the car and, screaming and shouting, they all went in.

Shamman was the last one to enter the house. When she walked in she saw Prema embroiled in a wrestling match with somebody on the sofa. The boys stood around cheering vociferously. At last Prema fell from the sofa, defeated.

'Well done, Rai Sahib,' Narendar said, patting the opponent's back.

'*Array*, Shamman . . . Rai Sahib, this is Shamman.' Prema introduced her.

'Hunh.' He rolled his eyes behind his glasses. A long cigar dangled from his lips and, drawing in quick puffs from the corners of his mouth, he exhaled tiny strands of smoke. Strewn about on a table nearby were a palette and brushes and on an easel before him was the unfinished painting of a woman.

Shamman observed him while no one was looking. A muscular but slim build, tall, complexion the colour of molten gold, and a mass of hair brighter than silver. Faced with this strange appearance, Shamman was so flustered she forgot she was staring.

'*Ai*, what's this girl's name? She looks a bit wild.'

'Shamman,' a few voices screamed in unison.

'Chaman?'

'No, Shamman!'

'Come here, Chaman,' Rai Sahib said, blowing strands of smoke again. Shamman approached slowly. He got up and, coming close, began observing her as if she were some strange animal. A mischievous smile played on his face.

'Show me your tongue,' he said seriously and Shamman moved a few steps away from him.

'She looks hungry. *Array*, Prema, give this bird something to eat. What's your name . . . Chaman?'

'Shamman, Rai Sahib,' Prema yelled at the top of her voice.

'Shamman? What kind of a name is that? We'll call her Chaman. Give her some food. No, wait, why are you so pale? Don't you have any make-up?' Rai Sahib picked up a brush and put a smudge of red on her cheek.

Shamman rubbed her cheek shyly.

'You're so naughty, get away,' Prema complained and, elbowing him aside, took Shamman to the bathroom.

In the evening everyone went for a swim in the swimming pool. Shamman couldn't swim so she sat at the edge of the pool with her feet dangling in the water. Rai Sahib dived several times from the diving board and displayed feats that Shamman had never witnessed before.

'*Array*, who's this water crow?' he teased when he saw her with her feet in the water. 'Why don't you come in?' When Prema explained Shamman couldn't swim he whispered something in her ear and then dived into the water. Shamman waited for him to come up, staring at the water with her eyes wide open. Suddenly he screamed: 'Crocodile! Crocodile!' and Shamman was in the water with a splash. Rai Sahib fished her out. Bursts of laughter greeted her as she squirmed tearfully.

After an early dinner Rai Sahib, Prema, Shamman and the boys gathered in the drawing room. Everyone opted for dance performances. Prema displayed her newest lesson, and when she became fatigued a general cry of, 'Rai Sahib! Rai Sahib!' went up.

At first Rai Sahib remained silent. A few minutes later, setting down his cigar on the ashtray, he silently rose to his feet. The music continued to play and, standing still, he fixed his eyes on the wall before him. Then, slowly, he removed his shirt and threw it in the air and massaged his arm for a minute or two. And then . . . Shamman's jaw dropped in amazement. He spun around with an electrified swiftness and soon his rugged body was swaying to the beat of the music, just as if a marble statue had stretched and come to life. The body that only moments ago seemed a little aged was now springing like the strings of a sitar. The intricate movements of the supple joints, the solid arches of the calves, and the magnificence of the massive chest . . . it seemed as though the musical notes were being created by the supple motion of his limbs, the movements of the fingers, the stamping of the feet, and it was as if the rippling of his muscles had been transformed into a melody. The light from the lamp behind him brilliantly illuminated his wavy, silvery hair. All at once it seemed that the storm's pace had quickened, the instruments raced with heightened intensity, the god of wrath emerged from a mysterious sphere and thrashed with fury and rage, shaking the universe with a thunderclap. It seemed as if Rai Sahib was a towering mountain, his white dhoti swelled about his feet like foamy ocean waves, his silvery grey hair resembling the sun rising from behind a mountain.

The instruments fell silent. The dance had ended. But Shamman's mind was still in a whirl and when Rai Sahib shouted 'Hoo!' and clapped his hands in front of her face, she was suddenly lost for words, and if everyone hadn't started laughing she might have been reduced to complete stupefaction. Gradually a smile spread across her face.

'A scared mouse, that's what you are,' Rai Sahib said, holding her head between his hands. 'Now, would you like to learn to dance?'

Shamman revealed her teeth in a smile and nodded.

'Hunh! Did you hear that, Prema? This little girl says she wants to dance. *Array*, bring my kettle-drum, I'll teach her to dance.'

'What? I'm not a monkey.'

'Oh? Not a monkey? A bear then? All right, why don't you bring us some sweets and become our student.'

'First you teach me and then I'll bring the sweets.'

107

'What a fine thing to say. Why, first you pay the fees and then we'll teach you to dance. In two months you'll be dancing like a butterfly.'

'Shamman, Rai Sahib gobbled up all the sweets I brought him and didn't teach me a thing,' Prema said.

'Hmm, shush – now, what's your name, girl? Yes, Chaman, forget the sweets. All you have to do is to come here during the holidays and sew buttons on our shirts and we'll teach you to dance. Understand?'

'Buttons?'

'Yes, buttons. All the buttons on all my *kurtas* are missing. You know this Prema, she is useless, no good at all. All she can do is be naughty.' Prema smiled happily at this compliment and dropped herself in Rai Sahib's lap.

Shamman returned to the hostel with Prema after making a promise of sewing on buttons in exchange for dance-lessons. On the way back she talked constantly about Rai Sahib. When she fell on her bed that night she felt as though she had run for miles; entangled in the exuberance of the dance, her soul was still all wound up, still in a whirl. She didn't know why, but her heart longed to yield to some dynamic power, for the first time a tiny flower of devotion was blossoming in her heart.

'What is Rai Sahib's name?' she asked Prema in a tremulous voice.

'*Array*, silly, Rai Sahib is my father.' Prema was laughing.

'But . . . but Prema!' She sat up on her bed.

'What?' Prema turned on her side and asked.

'Nothing Prema.' Shamman became silent.

'We call him Rai Sahib, everyone calls him Rai Sahib. He's very nice, he loves me very much.'

Shamman experienced a twinge of annoyance. She felt like scolding Prema, felt like asking her why she let him love her so much, but she realised what foolishness that would be. She clutched her pillow to her breast and silently rocked back and forth, the creaking of her bed like a song which placated her thoughts.

22

Shamman had a Christian friend whose name was Alma. She was very outspoken and blunt. Her dark complexion was typically South Indian, her hair was as black as a bee, and she had big eyes which were shot with red like the eyes of sadhus; her lips were elongated and had a mauve tint reminiscent of the colour of unripened damsons, her face was always pulled down, she had high cheekbones, and the white of her teeth was tinged with a faint bluish pallor. When she laughed, her teeth, which were pointed and appeared like poisonous fangs, shone brilliantly.

The girls had strange stories to tell about Alma. Although she was a Christian, she didn't go to church regularly and if she did go it was only to sing in the choir with the boys. Her voice was very melodious and she also sang when she was bathing. In her room she had a picture of Krishna instead of Jesus, and before going to bed every night she knelt in front of it, made the sign of the cross, and then proceeded to read from the Bible. She said, 'I abhor white colouring and I feel sorry for the Christ on the crucifix, and feelings of pity incite feelings of rebellion in the heart instead of devotion, but when I see the happy, flute-playing Krishna Kanhaya, my heart dances.'

Then one day she threw out Krishna ji's picture and put up another picture. A monkey is perched in a tree, while another monkey underneath is prodding it in the back from below with a stick and smiling, it would seem, at a half-eaten banana that perhaps the other monkey had been eating and which is now in mid-air. When the girls asked her about this change she laughed in her usual fashion and babbled as was her custom. 'Krishna ji's flute was eaten away by termites – you see he was very fond of butter and a little butter remained stuck inside the flute and the termites got it.' And then she grimaced and continued, 'Well, he had nothing better to do than tease women. I hear he was very fond of married women.'

This angered the girls who attacked her and reported her to the principal. Not only that, she got into a tiff with Shamman as well.

'Why were all these prophets so devoted to women – as a matter of fact, Henry the Eighth was also a prophet . . .'

109

Shamman lost her temper, her eyes filling with tears in anger. Alma apologised quietly.

Three or four days later a change occurred in the picture of the monkeys. The monkey on the top branch became John Bull, the one below donned a dhoti, and the banana slipping from the hands of the monkey on top became the map of Hindustan. Alma's drawing skills were quite deficient, but she continued to make colourful alterations to that picture of hers, and, revealing her bluish-white teeth, she continued to howl with laughter.

Her tongue loosened to such a degree that she was again reported to the principal, with whom this time she had a long argument. Finally she emerged from the principal's office with a quiet and crestfallen expression on her face. Shamman didn't approve of Alma's opinions, but her look of dejection made her feel sad. Alma told her that the principal had warned that if she didn't mend her ways and didn't start attending church regularly, she'd be expelled from the hostel. Although Shamman was fearful of the way Alma talked, she tried to reason with her.

Alma left college and went to the university after the December break. She got a room in Kailash Hostel which had been specially established for girls, but she often came to visit Shamman. She gave Shamman some books on serious subjects which Shamman found extremely dull and uninteresting. Alma blossomed at the university and achieved academic success; not only that, she was also elected president of the union and began delivering impassioned speeches which endeared her to the boys and her professors.

23

What a difference there is between school and college. How far apart a Muslim school is from the American Missionary College. In one if a girl playfully donned a black *sherwani* and Turkish cap, the other girls would swoon, a commotion would ensue, fines would be levied; in the other the new girls were introduced in a very sophisticated manner to the university boys when the new term began. As a matter of fact, a special banquet was arranged for this purpose. The principal, the women teachers and the professors introduced students personally, stayed with them a short while and then left them to talk informally with each other. Preparations for this banquet began days in advance and, in addition to the refreshments, plans were made for a stage variety programme comprising plays, dance presentations and vocal performances. The girls worked feverishly on new clothes for this function.

The new girls were terrified at the idea of the banquet. It seemed as though some dreadfully indecent occurrence was anticipated, and many of the girls didn't inform their parents, thus committing the sin in secret. The older girls made fun of them.

'Shamman, listen, you'll have to kiss your partner,' Prema said impishly.

'*Hai!*' Shamman broke out in a sweat.

'Yes, you'll have to kiss him, and the next day you'll have to give the principal a list of all the boys you've kissed.' The other girls hastened with confirmation.

'That's right, and then the one whose list is longest gets a prize.'

'And . . . and if you don't?'

'Well, a fine for her who doesn't and in the annual report it's put down that the girl is mediocre, very bad.'

Shamman was so perturbed by all this her sleep abandoned her. What if Abba Mian received the annual report and he sees what's in it? She'll not see the light of day again. Her admission at this college had been achieved with great difficulty. For one thing, her father had suggested she continue at the school with special classes added on for her, and in the second place, ever since Muheet Bhaya had returned from England he had made a mission of opposing the idea of education for women. This was strange indeed because Hameed Bhaya forced even their grandmother to drop her purdah when he came back from England. Nani, the poor woman, tried to hide behind fans, but the water-carrier, the sweeper and the cook all came into the house. Young daughters-in-law calmly rested on charpoys nursing their babies, Khala *bi* continued to receive her massage without a care, and Begum Amma relaxed on her bed casually while the fourteen-year-old Meera kneaded her thighs. Poor Nani, on the other hand, trembled and quivered; in the beginning the water-carrier and the sweeper would cover their faces with their *lungis* when they came in, but now she, poor thing, veiled her face when a male outsider was in the house.

111

'Nani Amma, you're so old but you haven't given up being bashful in front of men,' Hameed Bhai would tease her, and poor Nani would turn and stare at him helplessly.

Who knows what those filthy, fetid gutters were where Muheet Bhaya had played his games and which had caused him to favour seclusion for women more than ever. He married the stupidest and the most unattractive girl in the family and launched a crusade against Shamman's education.

How long could Shamman escape the inevitable? The day of the banquet arrived. Shamman felt as if she had fever. All night she had been tormented by strange dreams. Sometimes she saw the university boys running after her, screaming and yelling. Sometimes she would see that she was slipping backwards on a shiny, glass-like mountain slope with her clothes all tattered and the palms of her hand badly grazed. And then she saw Matron walking in while she was taking a bath and, screaming, she tried to cover herself. When she recovered from the shock somewhat she opened her eyes to see Prema removing the blanket from her face.

'What happened? Did you have a bad dream?'

'Yes.' Still feeling apprehensive, she rubbed her eyes.

'You silly thing. You screamed so loudly you frightened me. Come on, get up now, the bell for breakfast just went off.'

That day she couldn't concentrate on anything. The other girls appeared not to have a care in the world. She peered at them closely looking for some signs of anxiety, but nothing was visible from their faces. Either they were very brave or, like her, they were pretending.

In the evening every room was topsy turvy with the bustle of girls getting ready. They were borrowing articles ranging from needle and thread to saris, blouses and earrings from each other. Shamman took out her cotton *shalwar* and her crimped *dupatta*. Today the *dupatta* seemed unsatisfactory. She was smoothing out the fine crimps which had caused boils on her fingers as she had painstakingly worked them in, when Prema walked in.

'*Array*, are you crazy, you'll wear a *shalwar* and *kameez*? The principal will be so angry you won't hear the end of it.'

'Why?'

'What do you mean why? Don't you know college girls should wear saris?'

'But the only sari I have is that one with the plaid design and I don't have a jumper to go with it.'

'You're out of your mind. Do you think a cotton sari will do for this banquet? I have a sari for you, come with me.' Taking Shamman by the hand, she dragged her off.

Shamman begged and protested, but Prema forced her to wear a purple sari with a heavily ornamented brocade border and a brocade pinafore with it. Shamman was only going to apply a little powder on her face, but Prema intervened again and put on lipstick and kohl as well. Then Shamman herself covered her wrists with bangles and slipped on earrings which were gold-plated, but looked real. Walking on high-heeled shoes made her feel as if she was tottering on the bridge of Sarat. The shoes were a little tight on the toes, but she decided to ignore the discomfort. Today, imitating Prema, she also put a *kumkum* dot on her forehead.

The hustle and bustle accompanying the banquet had begun. A look around revealed everyone dressed up stylishly. Their teacher, Miss Johnson, had also endowed her mannish-style dress with some feminine charm by wearing a small corsage; the little softness that was buried in her was showing through today. Matron too was wearing a tighter dress than usual, the different parts of her body bulging like rolled-up bedding secured with twine. Alma was also present. In her simple sari and her swept-up bun she looked like a *devdasi* from the Ellora paintings.

Shamman felt as if everyone was staring at her and was afraid that in a few minutes her heavy, *banarsi*-edged sari would become unravelled, leaving her exposed. Because she was not used to wearing a sari, every now and then she tugged at the end on her shoulder, kept fidgeting with the front pleats, and sometimes, fearing that the end on her shoulder had become too long, she furtively tucked in the excess material. Suddenly she felt as though the *kumkum* dot was digging into her forehead, pricking her, and in a few seconds it would explode like a pomegranate seed and drip down on to her face. The heavy, gold-plated earrings, meanwhile, pulled down her lobes.

The principal arrived and the introductions began. Quickly girls and boys were paired off so that in a very short time every girl was seen in the company of a young man. When Shamman recovered from staring speechlessly at these proceedings she noticed the nervous-looking young man at her side. She gave him a startled glance. The baffled expression on her face made him even more agitated and, stuttering, he began to adjust his tie. Like Shamman's first time with the sari, he too was probably wearing a suit for the first time.

When he recovered somewhat, he made a cup of tea for Shamman in imitation of the other boys, and offered her fruit. Shamman said 'Thank you,' in English and he responded with 'It's all right madam', although once in a while he made a slip and called her 'sir', at which, blushing with mortification, he would feel his throat getting dry. His nervousness amused Shamman and soon, using the memorised English phrases and sentences at her disposal, she was talking to him freely. Before long they were both conversing in English, embellishing the tiniest sentence with sophisticated and elaborate figures of speech. But in a few minutes their store of topics ran out and they were forced to turn their attention to eating, and the remainder of the time was spent in sipping tea since you did not have to talk while you were drinking tea. Between sips they gazed enviously at the boys and girls who were not eating at all and were constantly laughing. Suddenly Shamman felt as if someone had filled her throat with the filth of a putrid gutter and, in order to prevent herself from throwing up, she contracted her throat and hastily took a large gulp of scalding hot tea. It burned her throat and her stomach, and her eyes began to water. Her companion looked at her sympatheti- cally. He understood what the problem was. He too was not used to eating canned fish. You needed to train yourself to eat this particular fish and that training had to be undertaken in the bathroom and could be successfully completed only after having vomited several times. But for the moment two new birds were gazing longingly at the bars of their cage, their voices silenced.

Shamman saw that Alma was watching her closely and whispering meaningfully to the young man at her side. Soon she was tittering, her sharp, white teeth gleaming brilliantly. Embarrassed by that scene, Shamman and her companion looked away sheepishly.

Suddenly, taking aim, Alma threw a grape at Shamman. As if she was about to drown in the juice of that one grape, Shamman became agitated and frantically searched for her handkerchief. When she couldn't find it, her bewildered companion took out his handkerchief and quickly wiped her cheek with it. Shamman felt as if the *kumkum* dot had melted and spread all over her body, and the poor young man, after this one act of courage he was so disconcerted that Shamman couldn't help feeling sorry for him. Alma and her friend were doubled over with laughter. Then the two of them picked up their chairs and joined Shamman and her companion at their table.

'*Array*, mister, you're very forward ... I say!' Alma's companion slapped him on the back so hard that his spine rattled.

'Shamman, introduce us to your friend,' Alma said.

114

'This is . . . this is . . .' Shamman stammered.

'Well, you're so busy eating you didn't even ask his name?'

'No, no, that's not it,' he spoke up in Shamman's defence.

'*Array*, you've been eating for such a long time and . . .'

'No, no,' he stuttered, at which Alma and her friend again burst into boisterous laughter.

'And I say, you're a rogue, already . . .'

'The truth is, forgive me.' He turned towards Shamman. 'Actually I wiped your face because I thought you might get your handkerchief dirty.'

Thank God that with the arrival of Alma and her companion, Iftikhar, the stifling chain of silence was broken at last. In a short while Iftikhar's teasing helped break the ice completely, making Shamman and her companion feel less inhibited. Soon the programme commenced.

The next day Prema wanted to take Shamman home with her. When the two girls got ready and went to sign the register the matron informed them they needed to obtain permission from the principal; visiting a Hindu friend's home required more stringent permission.

They returned with long faces from the principal's office.

'What happened? Did you get permission?'

'No, we got a scolding and a fine.'

'Well, didn't I tell you, but you wouldn't listen,' Matron said happily.

'And Principal Sahiba said that since the fines were levied because of your efforts you should have this chocolate as a reward.' With that, Prema handed her the permission slip in which the principal had stated in polite terms that she should not be troubled with such trivial matters.

Don't ask what happened after this. Matron was so upset at this humiliation that she burst into tears and threatened to resign, which everyone knew she would never do. Shamman and Prema packed and squeezed in together in the front seat with Narendar. Just as the car was leaving the hostel compound, Shamman saw her companion from the night before; he was leaning against the wall as if he had deliberately stopped for something.

'Oh,' she said, when she recognised him.

'Who was that?' Prema asked.

'No one, it's, it's . . .'

'A boy? Hunh! I see.' Prema pinched her hard and Narendar gave her a sidelong look from the corner of his eye.

Moved by a feeling of sweet satisfaction, Shamman smiled to herself. When your dice hits its mark during a game of *carom* your heart sings.

In the same way something cool and mellow rushed through her mind. Prema dozed during the ride while Narendar, either consciously or accidentally, kept touching Shamman's thigh with his elbow. But she was somewhere else. She was far away, flying, flying ahead of the car.

24

The next day Shamman sat on a chair stitching Rai Sahib's buttons while he sat at her feet, telling stories and handing her one button at a time.

'Now don't sew it on with the wrong side up,' he said naively, turning the button over in his hands to look at it before giving it to her.

He was telling her stories about princesses, sorceresses and inn-keepers, stories she had heard a hundred times, but Rai Sahib added on little bits that he had made up himself. He kept bringing up the story of the innkeeper's wife who played *chausar* with every traveller, and who, when she was losing, made a sign to her cat who quickly extinguished the lamp.

'And she would change the pieces around in the dark, making the traveller lose the game,' Rai Sahib said animatedly.

'What? How can a cat extinguish a lamp?'

'Eh?' Rai Sahib started artlessly.

'Yes, how can a cat extinguish a lamp?'

'Like this . . . *Phooh!*' He imitated the cat. Shamman became helpless with laughter and he grinned like a child.

An expression of childlike simplicity blanketed his face when he was telling a story. The tiny creases on his face were transformed into faint smiles and the wrinkles of old age shifted from his eyes. How severe and sombre this same face was when he was reading the paper or working in his office.

In the evening Rai Sahib stretched out on a chair and called: 'Who's going to rub oil in my hair?'

Prema and Narendar started fighting. Prema contended that she spent most of her time in the hostel while Nari had Rai Sahib all to himself

116

constantly and still wasn't satisfied. Narendar said she had no idea how to rub oil in anyone's hair.

'Chaman will put oil in our hair, Narendar will massage our toes, and Prema will sit in our lap.' Rai Sahib made the decision for them. Prema got up smugly and immediately plonked herself into his lap.

Rai Sahib's hair was not completely white. It was tinged with a light greyness, like soft evening shadows on pure white mountain snow. The texture of his hair was such that a slight touch created static. How mysterious and mystical Rai Sahib looked with hair like this.

Shamman stroked his curls timidly. Prema was now lying on the grass, dozing. Narendar went off to see about the badminton courts, and Shamman kept plunging into the deep abyss of Rai Sahib's hair. His eyes were shut, but he wasn't asleep; his eyelashes quivered delicately. Watching the smile that played on his half-open lips, Shamman felt as if she were slowly sinking into soft, cool quicksand. The tiny throbbing veins at his temples pulsated as if harbouring another consciousness, a vein stretched across his forehead like a purple *qushka*, and the crow's feet at the corners of his eyes, the jaw so strong as if carved out of stone! A feeling of awe and unnamed fear overcame her and her icy and timorous fingers strayed to his neck without her volition.

'*Array*, what are you doing?'

The world rushed at her. Taken aback, Shamman nervously cracked her knuckles.

'You're tired, aren't you? Now go and wash your hands and then we'll have some *chat*.' Rai Sahib spoke lovingly.

He got to his feet and, bending over Prema, began tickling her ear with a blade of grass. Prema frisked like a little girl. Later they all had *chat* and coffee right there on the grass.

Forged permission slips continued to be used and Shamman's visits to Prema's house increased. Shamman got along very well with Rai Sahib. He was like a child when he played with them and openly cheated and often he and Prema ended up tussling with each other. Sometimes when he tickled Shamman along with Prema or pinched her cheek, she became very agitated and distanced herself from him for a while. But she experienced this strange desire to be a little child in his presence.

One day he squeezed her in jest and she started weeping. Rai Sahib was surprised and somewhat distressed by her reaction. He hadn't squeezed her that hard. When a smile appeared on Shamman's face he pretended to be offended with her.

During lunch he was talking to Narendar about matters related to the

117

estate and afterwards he shut himself up in his office. Shamman became tearful at his indifference; what if he was really angry with her? She suddenly wanted to flee to her hostel.

Lying in bed during bleak afternoons, she used to wonder why she was reduced to tears so quickly. Why did she feel tremulous in Rai Sahib's presence? Then she thought of Narendar. How quiet he was when the others were around, and how ill at ease he was when he was alone with her. She enjoyed his discomfort and became bold, and when he gazed at her with affection, she smiled at him condescendingly. She was not a child any more. She knew Narendar loved her. What is love? Narendar seemed like a fool to her; how clumsy, how inane his love was.

And Rai Sahib? He was like a god. She longed to lie prostrate at his hallowed feet until he slowly lifted her up and placed her reeling head on his chest, that broad chest from which emanated the spellbinding fragrance associated with sacred temples. She would flare her nostrils to inhale this fragrance, wishing for eternal sleep.

Prema had told her that after her mother died he didn't remarry and was everything to his children. Some people regarded him as a snob, others called him a mystic philosopher. Shamman saw him as the incarnation of a Hindu god. After having lived with Prema all this time she now found Hinduism to be a very exalted religion. Sometimes she secretly applied a *kumkum* dot on her forehead and examined her reflection in the mirror. Her own face appeared illusory to her. The tiny red dot seemed to engulf her face until it glowed, her eyes began to resemble Alma's languid, saintly eyes, and her hair seemed to twist like live serpents. She felt as if, enwrapped in icy cold flames, she was slowly smouldering ... at that time all she could remember was Rai Sahib's enchanting hair and his forehead which gleamed liked a bright morning light. She wandered in the depths of some strange darkness.

During dinner that day a discussion began about society and religion. Soon Prema was lecturing in a loud voice and Narendar too interrupted vociferously with his opinions. Suddenly Rai Sahib asked, '*Array*, Chaman, are you Hindu or Muslim?'

Everyone fell silent and looked at each other blankly.

'Why, if you're Muslim then our faith has been desecrated.'

'Rai Sahib, our faith isn't so weak that anyone can desecrate it just like that,' Prema said. 'There's no power in the world that can tarnish our faith.'

118

'Come come, that's all nonsense,' he dismissed Prema's vehemence. 'Chaman, tell us what you think.'

'Rai Sahib, look at me!' Narendar shrieked.

'No, no, my dear, if this girl is Muslim . . .'

'Rai Sahib, you . . .' Prema was speechless with rage. 'And what about all your Muslim friends?'

'As for our friends, it's another matter altogether, but this girl, why I had no idea, Ram, Ram.'

Prema and Narendar were both reduced to tears with embarrassment, and Shamman pulled away her hand fearfully from her plate. The severe expression on Rai Sahib's face remained unchanged.

'This is no joke. Now all of us will have to make amends, and we'll have to convert this girl to Hinduism. What do you say?' He lowered his head to look into Shamman's eyes.

'Well, here you are, I'll make you a Hindu.' Taking some water from his glass he sprinkled a few drops on Shamman's face and muttered something under his breath.

Suddenly Prema got to her feet, ran over to his side and, swinging in his arms, plunged her teeth into his shoulder.

'Oh, you wretch!' He rubbed his shoulder.

'Very well, you don't have to be converted. We just thought it would be nice, and we could have found a fat businessman for her and married her off, but . . .'

Shamman left the table and sat in the window, blinking her eyes as she tried to hold back tears.

'*Array, array, array*, our daughter is angry with us.' He came after her. For a long time he tried to pacify her, but she continued to sulk.

'Here I come, here I come.' He shut his eyes and extended his arms towards her. Shamman couldn't repress a laugh. Rai Sahib leapt forward, picked her up and put her down on a chair.

Shamman remembered a story. A man buried his friend and then realised he had left his *tasbih* in the grave. He thought he would go and retrieve it. He dug up the grave and saw that the corpse had disappeared. But then he noticed a window at the head of the grave. He went through the window and saw his friend sitting on a jewelled throne.

'I say, my friend, you're living in splendour,' he said.

'Yes, with your good wishes, I am fine, and here's your *tasbih*, you had left it behind.'

He said, 'Yes, I had come for the *tasbih* and now I've seen you as well. Well, *Assalaam alaikum*.'

'*Walekum assalaam.*'

When that man emerged from the grave he saw that the world had changed. His home, his wife and his children were all gone. A hundred-year-old man told him that yes, in the time of his great, great grandfather, there was mention of someone of this name.

So these are the wonders of the great Almighty. There the man just exchanged salutations, and here centuries had gone by. When Rai Sahib picked her up and put her in the chair, she felt as though she had swung through the starry skies and come to a sudden halt. Everything around her seemed to teeter and a sacred fragrance numbed her brain. She quickly rose to her feet and, lifting up a glass of chilled water with trembling hands, she carried it to her eternally parched lips.

25

This time no one came to take her home her during the December holidays. There were only a few girls left in the hostel and they were usually busy with something or the other. She and Prema stayed together all the time, but when Prema went home Shamman wandered about aimlessly all day long. Once in a while she sat on a dhurrie under a tree and read. In the evening the girls would go to see a film, leaving her to feel even more alone. Stretched out in an armchair, she would silently read from the *Ramayan*. She envied Sitaji's life in the forest. How lucky she was to be having a picnic with Ramchanderji and Lakshmanji, a picnic that lasted fourteen years! Alma used to say that it was just as well that Ramchanderji was banished to the forest, otherwise how would he have ever known about the sorrowful lives of poor people? How many people there are who are forced to live like animals, but who writes about them? If prominent personages tire of their opulent lifestyles and willingly renounce the world, they receive a lot of publicity, but no one takes any notice of the ones who are born ascetics into a squalid world.

In a short time she had read innumerable books of which *Jane Eyre* affected her the most. The last chapter where Jane returns to her blind

December break - stayed at school + read many books.

master appealed so much to Shamman she read it over and over again. And Tagore's stories, especially *Castaway*, made her weep. Hardy's famous novel, *Tess of the d'Urbervilles*, also touched her deeply. But the thing that shook her to the very depths of her soul was the poetry of Byron, Shelley and Keats.

When there were only five more days of vacation left Prema and Narendar came to get her. Shamman forgot that she was angry with Prema and sitting so close to Narendar didn't bother her either. When he crushed her foot as was his custom, she slapped his face while Prema, siding with her, also began pinching him. The car was flying, but flying faster than the car was Shamman. She felt she was already there in spirit ... Rai Sahib is scolding Prema and Narendar for not bringing her sooner, how anxiously he must be waiting for her, how his pearly teeth will shine in a smile when he sees her.

But neither did any pearly teeth shine on her arrival nor was anyone anxiously awaiting her. Rai Sahib was away on a hunting trip with some friends with no word as to when he would be back. The house looked bleak. Shamman was sorry she came. And to make matters worse, Narendar started behaving badly. In the afternoon, while Prema was taking a nap, he made a declaration of love to Shamman, and that too so crudely Shamman got really upset. But soon she was feeling a motherly affection for him. She smiled. Just as a mother lovingly refuses to give her child a fragile glass, so Shamman consoled Narendar, and when, despondent from a sense of defeat, he started sobbing, she wanted to hold the foolish boy's head against her breast and pat him to sleep. She suddenly saw herself as someone very wise and prudent and Narendar seemed to her a helpless orphan. The poor fellow, astonished by her patronising behaviour, was completely nonplussed. During teatime he appeared somewhat diffident and reserved.

Rai Sahib returned unexpectedly in the evening. Shamman felt as if her silent call had summoned him home. His khaki outfit was covered with dust and dirt, a fine layer of dust rested on his silvery hair like the shadow of clouds on the sun's surface, his complexion was more ruddy from having been in the sun, and when the string of stars gleamed between chapped lips, Shamman's heart beat with unusual force and she fastened her gaze on the heavy, muddy boots.

He downed a glass of chilled water as soon as he arrived and then, contrary to his usual practice, he sat down with his head between his hands. Prema and Narendar were very friendly with their father, but when he was like this they became tongue-tied; one reproachful glance from him and even a restless spirit like Prema cowered fearfully.

'What's the matter?' Surprised by the silence and the gloom, Shamman asked Prema in a whisper.

'He's probably tired, or maybe . . .' she stopped.

'What?'

Prema took Shamman aside to the far corner of the drawing room. 'Maybe he had a quarrel with Miss Philip. She had gone with him.'

'Who is this Miss Philip?'

'She's inspectoress of schools here and she was Rai Sahib's class-fellow. Actually they were engaged to be married, but Rai Sahib went to England and there he met Mummy and no one knows why, in two days they were married. *Array*, have you seen Mummy's new picture which Rai Sahib commissioned? Wait, I'll show it you. Anyway, she used to come and visit us when Mummy was still living. Mummy was Irish and she was such a simple person, Dadi used to make her do all the housework and she wore a dhoti too. This witch has been trying to trap him ever since. This Miss Philip, actually Rai Sahib likes her a lot, but he also teases her and then when she cries, he gets upset.'

'She's terrible,' Shamman said from her heart.

'Yes, but Rai Sahib never tries to make up.'

'Oh?'

'Yes, they meet somewhere at a party perhaps, and you know Rai Sahib, it's his habit to make you laugh and cry all at the same time. And so that day . . .'

'Prema,' Rai Sahib's ponderous voice resounded in the huge expanse of the hall.

'*Array*, my Chaman is here too. When did you come, my friend?' It seemed as if he had just noticed her. He smiled. 'Come on, help me out of this coat,' he said, trying to extricate himself from the heavy overcoat.

Shamman assisted him with the coat. His shirt was badly soaked in sweat and his skin was burning. That faint, mysteriously sacred fragrance jolted her, but she composed herself and sat down to untie his shoelaces. He quickly pulled away his feet and, bending, tapped her cheek gently with two fingers. Shamman got to her feet apprehensively and the valet began taking off Rai Sahib's shoes.

Shamman felt there were mice scurrying about in the dining room. She turned on the light and saw Narendar sitting glumly on a chair with his feet up. Shamman pulled up a chair close to him and pretended not to be aware of what was going on in his heart.

'It's so hot.'

Silence.

'It's a day for making ice-cream.'

Silence.

'Does Rai Sahib like *faluda*?' she asked casually.

Silence.

'Hunh! If only someone could open that window, and the fan isn't turned on either. It seems as though there's a fire somewhere nearby . . . could someone . . .'

Casting a scornful glance at her, Narendar got up and banged the window casements noisily.

'Nari, are you very angry?' she asked affectionately.

'No.'

'Really? Then why didn't you smile at the mention of ice-cream?'

Narendar could no longer hold back a smile.

'Ohho, so you were just play-acting? What a greedy one you are! Does anyone eat ice-cream in the winter?'

'You don't know that . . .'

'Hunh! As if you know a lot.'

'If you loved someone,' he began in English.

'Aha! Love. The boat of love . . . love . . . well, what next?'

'Ohh! I . . .' Narendar was exasperated.

'Look, Narendar, it won't do at all for you to scold me, yes, who do you think you are? And you call this love? It's nonsense. If you loved me would you hide your racket from me, or would you eat all the ripe loquats yourself?'

'Why all these lies? I broke off so many for you, but Prema snatched them away. Hunh!'

'All right, but what about the racket? As if I would have eaten your racket.'

Stamping his feet angrily, Narendar left the room. Smiling, Shamman sprawled on the chair.

'Here's the racket, and don't talk to me.' Suddenly Narendar appeared with the racket and threw it at her. Shamman looked at him for a few minutes and then broke into a laugh.

'Ohho Nari!'

'Don't speak to me, I've said that a hundred times, and if you do . . .'

Prompted by innocent feelings of motherly concern, Shamman continued to laugh.

'Oh Nari dear.' She placed a hand on his shoulder and gazed at him.

Suddenly Narendar pulled her close and clung to her like a bear. Scared, Shamman pushed him away, and scratched his face and pulled his hair. Like a beaten dog, the poor fellow cowered in a corner while Shamman, embarrassed and a little agitated, bolted out of there and ran right into Prema who was coming in.

'*Array*, what's the matter?'

'Umm. . . umm. . . it's nothing, Narendar here was hitting me.' She puffed her cheeks in mock anger.

'What, Nari, you wretch! Here's your racket and you were saying it was lost.'

'Yes, he's such a liar,' Shamman offered hastily in agreement.

'And why were you hitting poor Shamman? Hunh? Why?' Prema swatted Narendar's head with the netted part of the racket.

Swaddled in a blanket, Rai Sahib appeared suddenly and further trouble was averted.

Seeing Narendar, whose colour was rising from anger and mortification, he asked, 'What's the matter with Narendar today? Both of you must have badgered him. Isn't that right?'

'He's in love,' Shamman whispered, stifling a laugh.

'What?'

'He's in love, *love*, Rai Sahib,' Prema yelled.

'Who? Our Nari?' Rai Sahib looked worried.

'Yes, the poor fellow.'

'I'll kill you, do you hear?' Narendar roared.

'Oh my goodness! But who is he in love with?'

'There is someone,' Shamman said coyly.

'Liar! Hunh!' Embarrassment added fuel to Narendar's exasperation.

'Ahh! Poor fellow. Rai Sahib, our dear Nari is . . .'

'And Rai Sahib . . .' Before Prema could continue Narendar placed the handle of the knife on her finger.

At dinner the idea of Narendar being in love proved ticklish, especially for Shamman, who, finding this game extremely comical, laughed without restraint. Rai Sahib had also recovered some of his earlier joviality, and for a long time he remained at the table, quizzing them by making designs with forks and knives. But he only had some soup and retired early.

Shamman and Prema went to bed together. While Prema fell asleep, Shamman lay awake, thinking. She had developed a habit of staying awake and talking to herself. Every night, before sleep overtook her, she recounted all her feelings, emotions and experiences one at a time, reviewing and assessing each one until she finally dozed off. This bedtime activity was like a lullaby that helped her idle into sleep. The memory of Rai Sahib tapping her cheek with his fingers came to life all of a sudden and at the same time she started remembering things from her past that she had forgotten. Far away, ages ago Rashid had held her wrist in his hand so he could rap the back of her hand with two fingers . . . and then he let go of her hand. And that sad little rap was still throbbing in every fibre of her being. She placed her cheek on her wrist and the feeling of Rai Sahib's touch crawled into her wrist, as if infusing the half-dead wound with new life. She drifted into peaceful sleep.

The next morning she woke up late as usual and heard the sound of the college bell somewhere in the distance. When she was fully awake she realised that she was in Prema's bed, not in college, and this sound? Someone had dropped a copper plate. Her heart beat uncontrollably.

Rai Sahib was still a little dispirited and Shamman secretly cursed the Miss Philip who had distressed him so. However, his eyes lit up when he saw her and he teased her in his usual manner. Later he sat down at a game of cards with them and cheated as he always did. For some inexplicable reason Shamman was stricken with the longing to touch him; she sided with Prema when she got into an argument with him, and during the course of the argument he squeezed her finger in mock irritation. Immediately Shamman reacted as if she were a child. She wished his chest would open wide and she would disappear inside it with her head bowed, but she continued to sulk. Afterwards Prema went to give the washerman the laundry and Narendar, still upset and sullen, went to the veranda and pretended to be engrossed in a book. Just then Rai Sahib walked in and Shamman puffed her cheeks angrily. He puffed his cheeks in mock imitation and when Shamman laughed he sat down beside her. But Shamman was like someone who is obsessed. She got into a tiff with him over something trivial and when he heckled her, she broke down and started sobbing.

'Array, array, our Chaman.' Rai Sahib leaned over to pat her and she grew more agitated. Surprised, he examined her face closely and the serious expression on his face frightened her so much she suddenly clung to him, sobbing hysterically now.

Laughing, Rai Sahib patted her as if she were a child. With her head resting on his chest she breathed deeply until she was overcome by a feeling of drowsiness. Rai Sahib lowered his face to look at her and she pretended to be asleep. He continued to pat her for a while longer and then tried to move her slowly to the bed. All at once she clasped him with both hands; she was shaking.

'No, no, Rai Sahib,' she spoke in a stifled voice.

'What is it? Is there . . . *array* . . .' He was alarmed by the wildness of her gaze.

'I, I . . . No, Rai Sahib, don't let me go, Rai Sahib . . . Rai Sahib . . . Rai Sahib, I . . . I love you.' She finally said it in a dry, hoarse voice.

'What?' He looked at her with the eyes of a stranger.

'I love you . . . Rai Sahib, I . . .' Her voice choked from fear.

'Eh? All right, Chaman, go to sleep.' He tried to loosen her grasp on his arm.

'No, no, Rai Sahib, I'll die, please Rai Sahib, don't push me away, Rai Sahib, please . . .'

Rai Sahib recoiled as if he had been struck with a rock.

'Rai Sahib, I'll change my religion,' she groaned and Rai Sahib looked around him apprehensively.

'*Array*, Prema,' he called.

'Please don't call anyone, please, Rai Sahib, I love you.'

Standing aghast in the doorway was Narendar. When Shamman's words fell into his ears he turned red to the roots of his hair as if someone had cursed him heavily. Shamman's voice cracked. She fell face down on the bed.

Rai Sahib left without saying another word and Shamman wished she could descend into the earth along with the bed on which she lay, inside, deep inside the earth so she could hide in the earth's bowels. Sick with shame and fear, she remained in that position, her eyes shut, until evening approached. If only there was some way she could hide her face and flee from there. No one came to her room. But she knew that Prema and Narendar were whispering fearfully among themselves in the other room. What had she done? What will happen now?

Trembling, shivering, she finally came out of her room with her eyes lowered. On seeing her, Narendar immediately disappeared into his room; he too was afraid to confront her. Exhibiting womanly courage, Prema came forward gallantly. She was treating her as a complete stranger today. She spoke to her very politely and both of them went to the dining room and had tea in a very civilised fashion. Today there was no quarrelling over snacks, no snatching of biscuits. Shamman didn't have the courage to mention Rai Sahib's name. Prema handed her fruit courteously and Shamman too continued to eat quietly. But every once in a while she glanced at Prema out of the corner of her eye, and felt

126

be heard over the din. Not too far from her people are
[...]g over a game of pachisi and cards, and who's going to
[...]nts a drink of water? The servant is summoned and that
[...] that would awaken a corpse. And if she dozed off for a
[...]meone's yell of 'I got you!' would shake her into a rude
[...]

[...]t of her a huge tablecloth would be set out at mealtime
[...]te with undisguised relish. Shamman's soul hovered over
[...]rmoil, her eyes glassy when she viewed the dishes, her
[...] paralysed from the constant onslaught of food aromas.
[...]ributed her longing for food to avarice and a weakness of
[...]y were not distressed by her illness, but certainly everyone
[...]h it.

[...]ings went too far. Two elderly people sat down some
[...] her bed to discuss funeral prayers. They were facing her
[...]embroiled in their discussion she felt as though they were
[...]ay prayers at her funeral. One of the men was in the habit
[...]g ablutions round the clock, but the stench that emitted
[...]y was enough to drive you out of your mind. The other one
[...]eranged. Shamman was sure that anyone whose funeral
[...] offered by either of these two men would have a difficult
[...] into heaven. Then some other people joined in the discus-
[...]e topic under debate shifted to questions concerning the
[...]readth of the shroud. During this exchange a piece of paper
[...]illustrate shape and proportions. Feeling helpless, Shamman
[...]back to them and burst into tears and soon she was sobbing.
[...]men left she turned around and examined that paper model
[...]ud. How inadequate this garment was for an appearance
[...]Almighty. What difference would it make if a stitched suit of
[...]as used instead? She was more terrified of death now than
[...]er been before.

[...]h was not as horrifying as the anticipation of death. It seemed
[...]yone was waiting for her to die. She began to experience
[...]hatred. She hated everyone. Dead or alive, she had died for
[...] a long time ago. Or maybe she had never been born. Who
[...]? Who were all these people? True that she and her brothers
[...]s developed in the same mother's womb, but what difference
[...] make? A hundred tenants live in one building, they come and
[...] . . . on the roads are tongas, carts being dragged along, lorries
[...]bout – what are they to each other? No one, she told herself.

130

overcome with nervousness, as if she couldn't recognise her. Both girls
were extremely distressed. The two loving friends suddenly found
themselves in the parched landscape of alienation, distanced from each
other.

Their feelings had become scattered, as if a desert had suddenly
appeared between two friends and they couldn't even call out to each
other. After a long, heavy silence, Shamman finally and with great
difficulty, in a tremulous voice, requested permission to return to the
hostel. The swiftness with which permission was granted disheartened
her completely. And the driver, it seemed, had also been eagerly waiting
to take her back.

With heavy, tired steps, she walked into the empty hostel and into her
room where she fell on the bed and curled up without taking her shoes
off.

The next morning she was reluctant to face the other girls. No one
knew anything, but she felt there were long sentences written on her
face announcing her sin. She wanted to hide herself from questioning
eyes. So she was a slut, a promiscuous woman. She had tried to tarnish
the unblemished reputation of a saintly man, but God had saved him.
What had happened to her? How will these shattered fragments become
whole again? What will happen now?

The girls had started returning to college a few days before college
resumed. Prema will also come back. What will happen then? Will she
be able to see her face in the mirror? Her anguish grew.

The following morning she saw the girls with their heads together
over the newspaper in the library, glued to it like flies. Some were
reading out loud. Just as in the case of an accident the onlookers stand
around looking at the corpse, in the same way one group after another
was collecting around the paper. 'Ah, poor Prema . . . What a shame,'
she heard someone say and the books fell from Shamman's trembling
hands. Her eyes downcast, she waited silently like a criminal. But Prema
probably didn't see her. Her eyes strayed to the newspaper. The girls
had left. She advanced slowly and sat down in the chair. Rai Sahib had
died the night before from heart failure, the paper informed her. This
was an old ailment and he had suffered a sudden attack. She sat silently
with her elbows resting on the table. Then somebody shook her shoulder
and she got up and started walking.

'Where are you going?' a classmate asked when she walked right past
her classroom.

'What?' She started.

127

'You've passed your classroom. Where are you going?'

'Oh. I'm going to the sitting room, I left a map there yesterday.' She made something up and a good thing too, or else she would have been caught. The sitting room was on the other side of the veranda. She continued walking until she was sure no one was watching her, and then she turned around and walked to her classroom.

She didn't know what she studied that day, what she heard in class. She didn't cry, her tears had dried up when she cried incessantly night and day for her wayward Unna; to reveal her feelings was a sign of weakness. But every time her eyes fell on Prema's vacant chair she felt it was Prema who had died, not Rai Sahib.

Rai Sahib is dead! The very thought frightened her in a strange way. He had been cremated. How could this be? His hair, that crown brighter than the sun, could not be seared. That golden complexion and teeth which were like pearls – impossible, she decided.

Her nights terrified her; she could not get Rai Sahib out of her mind and finally she began to dread him, dread the Rai Sahib whose very presence had made her tremble with awe. One day she saw a sadhu's funeral procession. The sadhu's body had been propped up in a palanquin, his mouth was stretched over his teeth, and there was vermilion on his face along with smudges of turmeric and sandalwood paste. His skin was puckered and black like a rotting aubergine, and that faint redolence of decaying flesh! This spectacle deprived her of whatever courage she had left. Now she was afraid to be alone in her room at night. She felt that the sadhu was sitting at the head of her bed, and when she peeped out of one half-open eye and didn't see him she was sure he had hidden himself under her bed. Sometimes she felt as if, extending an arm from under the bed, he was stroking her throat, and there were moments when she felt his presence behind her as she made her way to her room or when she was alone in a dark place. One day she fell asleep while she was studying and she dreamt she was playing cards with Rai Sahib. Suddenly she saw that he got to his feet and started dancing. His muscles ballooned and vibrated, his tresses turned into serpents that rocked back and forth, his artificial teeth began to clatter to the beat of music, the cards lit up like lamps and slowly he advanced towards her. Shamman screamed, but he plunged fiery rods into her eyes. She continued screaming while she tried frantically to push away the flames from her eyes.

'Khun, khun,' he said and she broke into a run and she would have run all night if she hadn't hit her head against a door. She fell down.

When she awoke she saw Rai
that seemed to burn her head li
and tried to lift herself up, but
bore down upon her.

'Lie still!' It was the principal's

'The moment I turned the torch
like someone gone mad and then
herself had been frightened by her

So it was Matron whom she had
white hair, tied in paper rollers, sh
torchlight in her hand. Shamman wa

Later it became known that Ma
books even after the lights had been
the torchlight on her, she ran lik
Shamman had developed a high feve
condition she was sent home. For
pounded her body.

26

Her illness was protracted and uninteresti
long ago she read a book in which the h
beginning to the end and because of her illne
opportunities to be with her. He's helping h
drink her medicine, he's stroking her slen
delicate pulse, he's squeezing drops of gra
mouth. After reading this novel she was be
sick and the pleasing thoughts of those rom
pulse throb and her heart beat faster.

But when she did get sick, not only the helpe
as well shouted and shrieked in her presence.
were beaten while she watched helplessly, in
was winnowed noisily, turmeric and coriander
in the pestle and mortar, and on many occasions

After three months the fever was spent but it also wore her out completely. When she was finally able to walk from her bed to the chair on unsteady legs, she experienced not joy but a desire to weep. Her hair had fallen out, the skin on her hands and feet felt like dry burnt wood, and her face resembled the face of a corpse that had just jumped out of its shroud.

During that time Noori came and stayed for a month. She had been living with her father's family for over a year. Having tired of the fare at her parents' house, Bari Apa too had moved in with her in-laws and now taught at a local girls' school. Like a hissing, swaying snake, her youth scuttled away in the twinkling of an eye. Perhaps a blurred vestige remained. The old, shrewd mother-in-law mocked the youth that had fled; she was happy that her daughter-in-law was aging so rapidly and would soon be out of danger. That was why she had initially sent her to her parents' house; consideration of the family honour was bound to keep chains on the young widow's feet. Now the old crone regarded Bari Apa as a peer. By warning her of impending old age at every step as if it were the plague, she hoped to squeeze her of whatever life she had left in her. Like a living martyr, Bari Apa kept her head up and maintained silence.

She hated her mother-in-law. This was the witch who had made the three short years of her married life so unpleasant. Bari Apa didn't know that her married life was fated to be so short. She used to think that a day would soon come when she and her husband would be by themselves. If she had any idea that her husband was going to leave her, she would have covered the old woman's face with dust and made every effort to cling lovingly to those three years with her husband. The old crone was crazy about her son, but whenever he lavished any attention on his wife, she was burnt to a cinder.

'*Array*, I say, what is this constant fussing . . .' she'd screw up her nose and taunt and poor Bari Apa would break out in a sweat with shame. Hastily she would free herself from her husband's eager grasp and start sorting out spinach leaves. He'd sit at some distance, gazing at her longingly, making amorous signals, staring at her as if she were not his wife but a strange woman. But she didn't go to him.

As soon as he returned from college the old woman corralled him and opened up her bag of ailments before him. The moment he managed to get away from her, she immediately called the daughter-in-law to take care of some seemingly important chore. The daughter-in-law sat with a stone pressing down on her heart. Her hands would be occupied with

131

work, but her heart remained with the unfinished sentence her husband had whispered in her ear earlier.

'I say, *Dulhan*, you can go if you don't feel up to doing this, or else . . .' She chained her daughter-in-law's feet with more sarcasm. When she was absolutely certain that the daughter-in-law had given up all hope, her son's temper had risen to boiling point, and the danger of frolicsome pranks had been averted, then she let the daughter-in-law go.

Silently Bari Apa tolerated every injustice and comforted herself with the thought that one day soon these jibes and this taunting would be buried in a remote corner of the grave. That was why she also felt sorry for the old woman. She would see her laid out helplessly on the wooden washing slab in readiness for her last journey. Bari Apa had decided that she would observe the third day rituals following her mother-in-law's death with great pomp so that people would not complain that the old woman's provisions for the next world had turned to dust at the hands of an educated daughter-in-law. But she was sure that fortieth-day observances or third-day observances would not be adequate; without some kind of atonement the old woman could not save herself from punishment for her viciousness. Imagine getting by with just offerings and supplications.

But the old woman became a millstone round her neck, her nights became desolate and her days were filled with horrible thorns.

Since Noori was growing up the mother-in-law constantly admonished her daughter-in-law to watch her step, and mother-in-law and daughter-in-law became intent on finding a match for Noori. In addition to her many talents, Noori's certificate of orphanhood proved useful and soon an only son from a very rich family was coaxed into falling in love with Noori. His family resisted and made a fuss, but in the end they were powerless to prevent the match.

When Noori arrived she exhibited a very bashful and submissive exterior. Bari Apa embarked with great diligence on preparations for the dowry, daily expenses were slashed, and both mother and daughter began a life of frugality. Noori would wear old, shabby clothes with demure pride. Everything was being set aside for her dowry even though the boy was still studying for his matriculation and was to leave for England after his exams. Noori was to pass seven years of waiting in this fashion but, intoxicated with the ardour of dreams about the wonderful life to come, she ignored everything; she wore these tatters lovingly in anticipation of the wedding dress that she would don one day.

work, but her heart remained with the unfinished sentence her husband had whispered in her ear earlier.

'I say, *Dulhan*, you can go if you don't feel up to doing this, or else . . .' She chained her daughter-in-law's feet with more sarcasm. When she was absolutely certain that the daughter-in-law had given up all hope, her son's temper had risen to boiling point, and the danger of frolicsome pranks had been averted, then she let the daughter-in-law go.

Silently Bari Apa tolerated every injustice and comforted herself with the thought that one day soon these jibes and this taunting would be buried in a remote corner of the grave. That was why she also felt sorry for the old woman. She would see her laid out helplessly on the wooden washing slab in readiness for her last journey. Bari Apa had decided that she would observe the third day rituals following her mother-in-law's death with great pomp so that people would not complain that the old woman's provisions for the next world had turned to dust at the hands of an educated daughter-in-law. But she was sure that fortieth-day observances or third-day observances would not be adequate; without some kind of atonement the old woman could not save herself from punishment for her viciousness. Imagine getting by with just offerings and supplications.

But the old woman became a millstone round her neck, her nights became desolate and her days were filled with horrible thorns.

Since Noori was growing up the mother-in-law constantly admonished her daughter-in-law to watch her step, and mother-in-law and daughter-in-law became intent on finding a match for Noori. In addition to her many talents, Noori's certificate of orphanhood proved useful and soon an only son from a very rich family was coaxed into falling in love with Noori. His family resisted and made a fuss, but in the end they were powerless to prevent the match.

When Noori arrived she exhibited a very bashful and submissive exterior. Bari Apa embarked with great diligence on preparations for the dowry, daily expenses were slashed, and both mother and daughter began a life of frugality. Noori would wear old, shabby clothes with demure pride. Everything was being set aside for her dowry even though the boy was still studying for his matriculation and was to leave for England after his exams. Noori was to pass seven years of waiting in this fashion but, intoxicated with the ardour of dreams about the wonderful life to come, she ignored everything; she wore these tatters lovingly in anticipation of the wedding dress that she would don one day.

132

After three months the fever was spent but it also wore her out completely. When she was finally able to walk from her bed to the chair on unsteady legs, she experienced not joy but a desire to weep. Her hair had fallen out, the skin on her hands and feet felt like dry burnt wood, and her face resembled the face of a corpse that had just jumped out of its shroud.

During that time Noori came and stayed for a month. She had been living with her father's family for over a year. Having tired of the fare at her parents' house, Bari Apa too had moved in with her in-laws and now taught at a local girls' school. Like a hissing, swaying snake, her youth scuttled away in the twinkling of an eye. Perhaps a blurred vestige remained. The old, shrewd mother-in-law mocked the youth that had fled; she was happy that her daughter-in-law was aging so rapidly and would soon be out of danger. That was why she had initially sent her to her parents' house; consideration of the family honour was bound to keep chains on the young widow's feet. Now the old crone regarded Bari Apa as a peer. By warning her of impending old age at every step as if it were the plague, she hoped to squeeze her of whatever life she had left in her. Like a living martyr, Bari Apa kept her head up and maintained silence.

She hated her mother-in-law. This was the witch who had made the three short years of her married life so unpleasant. Bari Apa didn't know that her married life was fated to be so short. She used to think that a day would soon come when she and her husband would be by themselves. If she had any idea that her husband was going to leave her, she would have covered the old woman's face with dust and made every effort to cling lovingly to those three years with her husband. The old crone was crazy about her son, but whenever he lavished any attention on his wife, she was burnt to a cinder.

'*Array*, I say, what is this constant fussing . . .' she'd screw up her nose and taunt and poor Bari Apa would break out in a sweat with shame. Hastily she would free herself from her husband's eager grasp and start sorting out spinach leaves. He'd sit at some distance, gazing at her longingly, making amorous signals, staring at her as if she were not his wife but a strange woman. But she didn't go to him.

As soon as he returned from college the old woman corralled him and opened up her bag of ailments before him. The moment he managed to get away from her, she immediately called the daughter-in-law to take care of some seemingly important chore. The daughter-in-law sat with a stone pressing down on her heart. Her hands would be occupied with

131

overcome with nervousness, as if she couldn't recognise her. Both girls were extremely distressed. The two loving friends suddenly found themselves in the parched landscape of alienation, distanced from each other.

Their feelings had become scattered, as if a desert had suddenly appeared between two friends and they couldn't even call out to each other. After a long, heavy silence, Shamman finally and with great difficulty, in a tremulous voice, requested permission to return to the hostel. The swiftness with which permission was granted disheartened her completely. And the driver, it seemed, had also been eagerly waiting to take her back.

With heavy, tired steps, she walked into the empty hostel and into her room where she fell on the bed and curled up without taking her shoes off.

The next morning she was reluctant to face the other girls. No one knew anything, but she felt there were long sentences written on her face announcing her sin. She wanted to hide herself from questioning eyes. So she was a slut, a promiscuous woman. She had tried to tarnish the unblemished reputation of a saintly man, but God had saved him. What had happened to her? How will these shattered fragments become whole again? What will happen now?

The girls had started returning to college a few days before college resumed. Prema will also come back. What will happen then? Will she be able to see her face in the mirror? Her anguish grew.

The following morning she saw the girls with their heads together over the newspaper in the library, glued to it like flies. Some were reading out loud. Just as in the case of an accident the onlookers stand around looking at the corpse, in the same way one group after another was collecting around the paper. 'Ah, poor Prema . . . What a shame,' she heard someone say and the books fell from Shamman's trembling hands. Her eyes downcast, she waited silently like a criminal. But Prema probably didn't see her. Her eyes strayed to the newspaper. The girls had left. She advanced slowly and sat down in the chair. Rai Sahib had died the night before from heart failure, the paper informed her. This was an old ailment and he had suffered a sudden attack. She sat silently with her elbows resting on the table. Then somebody shook her shoulder and she got up and started walking.

'Where are you going?' a classmate asked when she walked right past her classroom.

'What?' She started.

127

'You've passed your classroom. Where are you going?'

'Oh. I'm going to the sitting room, I left a map there yesterday.' She made something up and a good thing too, or else she would have been caught. The sitting room was on the other side of the veranda. She continued walking until she was sure no one was watching her, and then she turned around and walked to her classroom.

She didn't know what she studied that day, what she heard in class. She didn't cry, her tears had dried up when she cried incessantly night and day for her wayward Unna; to reveal her feelings was a sign of weakness. But every time her eyes fell on Prema's vacant chair she felt it was Prema who had died, not Rai Sahib.

Rai Sahib is dead! The very thought frightened her in a strange way. He had been cremated. How could this be? His hair, that crown brighter than the sun, could not be seared. That golden complexion and teeth which were like pearls – impossible, she decided.

Her nights terrified her; she could not get Rai Sahib out of her mind and finally she began to dread him, dread the Rai Sahib whose very presence had made her tremble with awe. One day she saw a sadhu's funeral procession. The sadhu's body had been propped up in a palanquin, his mouth was stretched over his teeth, and there was vermilion on his face along with smudges of turmeric and sandalwood paste. His skin was puckered and black like a rotting aubergine, and that faint redolence of decaying flesh! This spectacle deprived her of whatever courage she had left. Now she was afraid to be alone in her room at night. She felt that the sadhu was sitting at the head of her bed, and when she peeped out of one half-open eye and didn't see him she was sure he had hidden himself under her bed. Sometimes she felt as if, extending an arm from under the bed, he was stroking her throat, and there were moments when she felt his presence behind her as she made her way to her room or when she was alone in a dark place. One day she fell asleep while she was studying and she dreamt she was playing cards with Rai Sahib. Suddenly she saw that he got to his feet and started dancing. His muscles ballooned and vibrated, his tresses turned into serpents that rocked back and forth, his artificial teeth began to clatter to the beat of music, the cards lit up like lamps and slowly he advanced towards her. Shamman screamed, but he plunged fiery rods into her eyes. She continued screaming while she tried frantically to push away the flames from her eyes.

'*Khun, khun*,' he said and she broke into a run and she would have run all night if she hadn't hit her head against a door. She fell down.

When she awoke she saw Rai Sahib stuffing her nose with something that seemed to burn her head like the fire of hell. She screamed again and tried to lift herself up, but several elongated pigeon-shaped faces bore down upon her.

'Lie still!' It was the principal's voice.

'The moment I turned the torchlight on her she began scratching me like someone gone mad and then she dashed away from me.' Matron herself had been frightened by her behaviour.

So it was Matron whom she had mistaken for Rai Sahib's ghost. Her white hair, tied in paper rollers, shone like a silver crown. She had a torchlight in her hand. Shamman was lying on a bed in the infirmary.

Later it became known that Matron discovered her asleep on her books even after the lights had been turned off, and when she turned the torchlight on her, she ran like someone crazed. By morning Shamman had developed a high fever and while she was still in that condition she was sent home. For three months typhoid brutally pounded her body.

26

Her illness was protracted and uninteresting at the same time. Not too long ago she read a book in which the heroine remains ill from the beginning to the end and because of her illness her lover has innumerable opportunities to be with her. He's helping her up in his arms so she can drink her medicine, he's stroking her slender wrists looking for her delicate pulse, he's squeezing drops of grape juice into her parched mouth. After reading this novel she was beset with the longing to be sick and the pleasing thoughts of those romantic moments made her pulse throb and her heart beat faster.

But when she did get sick, not only the helpers but all the other people as well shouted and shrieked in her presence. Children squabbled and were beaten while she watched helplessly, in the front veranda grain was winnowed noisily, turmeric and coriander continued to be ground in the pestle and mortar, and on many occasions it so happened that her voice could not be heard over the din. Not too far from her people are raucously fighting over a game of pachisi and cards, and who's going to get up if she wants a drink of water? The servant is summoned and that too with a roar that would awaken a corpse. And if she dozed off for a few minutes someone's yell of 'I got you!' would shake her into a rude awakening.

Right in front of her a huge tablecloth would be set out at mealtime and everyone ate with undisguised relish. Shamman's soul hovered over the food in turmoil, her eyes glassy when she viewed the dishes, her sense of smell paralysed from the constant onslaught of food aromas. Her family attributed her longing for food to avarice and a weakness of character. They were not distressed by her illness, but certainly everyone was fed up with it.

One day things went too far. Two elderly people sat down some distance from her bed to discuss funeral prayers. They were facing her and were so embroiled in their discussion she felt as though they were preparing to say prayers at her funeral. One of the men was in the habit of performing ablutions round the clock, but the stench that emitted from his body was enough to drive you out of your mind. The other one was quite deranged. Shamman was sure that anyone whose funeral prayers were offered by either of these two men would have a difficult time getting into heaven. Then some other people joined in the discussion and the topic under debate shifted to questions concerning the length and breadth of the shroud. During this exchange a piece of paper was used to illustrate shape and proportions. Feeling helpless, Shamman turned her back to them and burst into tears and soon she was sobbing. When the men left she turned around and examined that paper model of the shroud. How inadequate this garment was for an appearance before the Almighty. What difference would it make if a stitched suit of clothing was used instead? She was more terrified of death now than she had ever been before.

But death was not as horrifying as the anticipation of death. It seemed as if everyone was waiting for her to die. She began to experience feelings of hatred. She hated everyone. Dead or alive, she had died for her family a long time ago. Or maybe she had never been born. Who were they? Who were all these people? True that she and her brothers and sisters developed in the same mother's womb, but what difference does that make? A hundred tenants live in one building, they come and they leave . . . on the roads are tongas, carts being dragged along, lorries running about – what are they to each other? No one, she told herself.

130

ached from the pressure of her forceful embrace. Within minutes the two of them were deep in conversation. Bilquis was at her aunt's to conduct a lively romance. Her aunt's house was a regular recruiting office where nearly all the eligible bachelors in town made an appearance. Not only was the aunt adept at providing opportunities for her own daughters, but she also opened the doors for daughters of relatives and friends. She was such an expert now that she matched a girl with any boy of her choice. Her opponents endeavoured to thwart her, but were helpless in the face of her strategy. All the unwanted boys were hurled out of the garden like poisonous weeds, their visits suddenly deemed extremely undesirable.

Bilquis qualified in every way for her aunt's services. In order to achieve refinement and a true fashion sense she had enrolled in an English-medium school for a while and came out of there perfectly honed. The strange thing about this girl was that she talked proudly and openly about every womanly wile used for trapping men, owning up to artifice, selfishness and deception with total candour.

'I don't like Issa at all, but when he heard me play the sitar he lost control. Jalees played the violin, but she was too bashful.'

'Munawar is such an idiot. You know he looked all over for a book by Bernard Shaw for me? He is a real bookworm, says he's going to be a professor. Now tell me, Shamman, how many years is that, at least four, right? Who's going to let me wait that long? Akhtar is a superintendent of police, he's been badgering me, but I haven't given either of them an answer as yet. I swear if Akhtar doesn't get me a ring like Padma's I'll die before I agree to an engagement.'

'And Khalabi says Akhtar is all right, but I say Musa has a lot of property. Do you know he has three cars and . . .'

From the club she took Shamman to her aunt's and the next day both sisters arrived unannounced at Shamman's house. Shamman's house was not such a bad place but, because of indifference and a lack of good taste, only a few damaged chairs, one or two divans draped with soiled dhurries, and a few rope cots without sheets on them constituted the total seating that was available.

Embarrassed and humiliated, Shamman brought them to her room. Actually it would be wrong to call it her room. There were a few suitcases piled against a wall, standing before another wall was a china cabinet, dangling from the ceiling on the other side were winter supplies, and in another corner stood the long pole used for clearing cobwebs which had obviously never been moved; spiders and lizards ruled the terrain unchecked.

'Let's go to your room,' Bilquis whispered and Shamman, filled with shame, just wanted to die. There had never been a shortage of money and now the pension was sufficient to run the household smoothly. But it wasn't as if the living was grand before the pension, although there were at least fifteen servants who remained idle for the most part, and crowding the outer courtyard were four or five cows, horses, dogs and hens. A few stools could be found in the outer courtyard, but inside the house even when important ladies came for a visit, charpoys and cots were hurriedly dragged out and covered with sheets to provide seating. Shamman had never told anyone about the way her house looked. As a matter of fact once or twice she had even made something up to tell Bilquis and Jalees. She regretted having been born in this house. She wished she had been born somewhere else, she often wished she was the only cherished daughter with just one very well-educated, brilliant brother. How she longed for a bungalow, sofas and horse carriages, for loving uncles and doting aunts . . . if only that bungalow had a lawn with orange and loquat trees from which she would break off fragrant flowers with her delicate fingers, but . . . all this was not available to her even in a dream. All her dreams had always been horrible and frightening, inhabited by witches and ghouls.

Taking Bilquis and Jalees with her, she retreated to a quiet corner of the courtyard. This corner was also filled with garbage, broken bricks, and old and battered furniture. But without standing on ceremony, Bilquis calmly spread a piece of newspaper on the step and made herself comfortable. Jalees went off with Noori to listen to stories of her romances and pick tamarinds.

For hours, their heads together, Shamman and Bilquis talked of this and that. Bilquis told her that she was vigorously involved in preparations for marriage, which consisted of choosing a mate from among many candidates. Selecting one out of all these boys, and discarding the others like peanut shells, was just so hard for an emotional girl like Bilquis.

'But whom do you really love?'

'Well, as far as love goes, I really love Abbas. We've known each other since childhood and we share ideas and interests.'

'What? Liar! First you said you were madly in love with Ansar, you said he's patriotic and this and that,' Shamman retorted irately.

'He's very patriotic, but tell me, my dear, how will he support me? You know, I must admit I like a social life.'

'Bilquis, you're too crafty. One doesn't think of things like this when one's in love.'

'But actually I'm really in love with Akhtar.'

'Hunh! Akhtar or his new car?'

'Oh, you're so silly. I don't like his car at all. I swear if you see Musa's car you'll just die.'

'But what about love?'

'Well, one falls in love with someone poor, but . . .'

'But?'

'But one has to marry someone rich. Isn't that right?'

'Why? You're talking just like a prostitute.'

'Hush! Why? And so what if it is like being a prostitute? It's the same thing.'

'What?'

'I mean, look, it's the same as . . . Oh, I don't know, you're always arguing. My goodness, what are we saying . . . Shamman, do you know, I said my prayers yesterday.'

'Oh?'

'Yes. Akhtar said . . .' She hesitated.

'What did he say?'

'He saw me with my head covered and said, "Come, I'll take your picture and send it to *The Weekly*." I suggested it would be better if I were standing on the prayer rug. But you know, Shamman, I looked really awful standing, so I sat down and held out my hands like I was praying . . . and after taking a picture . . .' She broke out laughing.

'What? What?'

'That same terrible thing, he kissed me, the wretch!' Bilquis spoke demurely.

They were both laughing when Ejaz came out of the veranda looking very suave as he casually swung his racket in the air.

'Oh, I'm sorry.' He feigned surprise and turned to leave.

'Who was that? My goodness, he looked just like Fredric March.' Bilquis squeezed Shamman's arm.

'He's a cousin, a distant cousin.'

'Really? What a sly one you are.'

'Why?' Shamman smiled.

'He's such a dear, I swear. I bet you are crazy about him.'

'Hunh! Never.'

'Oh dear, what bad taste. I swear he's ... look, he's looking in our direction. He must be staring at you.' Bilquis spoke coyly.

'Be quiet, you fool!' Shamman pinched her. An unrecognisable emotion stirred in her heart, but she kept thrusting it away angrily.

When Bilquis and Jalees were about to leave, Ejaz appeared again and started talking to one of the servants. As soon as Bilquis's car had left he turned towards Shamman, but she quickly went in.

During dinner Ejaz deliberately squeezed himself in the seat next to Shamman. He didn't hear what Bilquis was saying, the wretch! He tried to engage in sweet talk with her, but Shamman got up on some pretext and changed her seat. Later he came and sat alongside her while she was preparing *paan*.

'Will you give us one too, but don't make it too strong,' he said brazenly. As Shamman handed him some, he tried to grab her finger. Angry, Shamman let go of the *paan*. She had no taste for this outmoded practice; she despised those mute lovers whose souls speak, but who never open their mouths to utter a word.

'Let me help you,' he said when he saw her with a book.

'I'm done,' she said, shutting the book mischievously and, slipping her feet into her shoes, she made off from there. She knew what he was up to. Today he seemed like the old Ajju to her, fluttering around her like a buzzard does around meat. Shamman was deliberately repulsing him; seeing Ejaz huff and puff longingly filled her with an immense satisfaction.

For two days he hungered, but Shamman did not give him a chance to speak. Then one night he came out on some pretext and first, as was his custom, he pretended to be looking for something, after which he got a drink of water. With some effort he downed a whole glassful. Holding her amusement in check, Shamman lay still. He turned, but Shamman saw out of the corner of her eye that he was coming back.

'Shamman,' he whispered.

'What is it?'

'Can I sit here?' But before she could formulate a reply he was sitting on a corner of her bed.

'Shamman, can I say something? I've been trying to, for many days . . .' His voice got stuck in his throat.

Shamman's hands and feet became numb, all her senses converged on one spot and became constricted, she held her breath.

'You know I have two more years of training and then I'll get a good

138

posting somewhere, and the inheritance from Chacha Mian is also quite substantial. I think I'll buy a bungalow in Simla as well.'

A bungalow and garden . . . orange blossoms . . . Shamman's fingers began to twitch.

'I think a person of my status should have an educated wife. Isn't that right?'

'Ejaz.' Shamman tried to stifle her breath.

'Yes, Shamman, these people are all backward, they don't understand anything, everything is in your hands now . . .'

'In my . . . hands?' Shamman clenched her fists tightly so that this mysterious treasure would not slip from her hands.

'You know that friend of yours . . .'

'What?' Shamman stopped breathing.

'Yes, Bilquis is an old friend of yours, isn't she? If you want you can help me get married.'

'But . . .'

'Now look here, don't make excuses, my dear. Anything you want, anything at all. You like that leather-bound Hardy collection, don't you?'

'But,' she interrupted him, 'Bilquis has very high standards, and I'm very sorry, Ajju,' she continued stubbornly, 'she's a different sort of girl.'

'But Shamman, I'm very broad-minded.'

'What I mean is girls these days want culture more than they want broad-mindedness.'

'So . . .'

'And they also demand a good family, society. Bilquis's admirers are mostly from nawab families, and anyway, you think your inheritance is some vast estate that . . .'

'No, I didn't say it was.' Hunger and defeat floated in Ejaz's eyes.

'This is all nonsense.'

His head lowered, Ejaz left. She lay still, silent. She didn't think. All she sensed was that she had thrust her hand into an orange bush and had been stung by a poisonous viper. Surging and sizzling, something resembling poison darted towards her head; she didn't try to ward it off.

Was she about to fall in love with Ajju? God forbid! The very idea made her laugh. So what was it? She didn't think it was necessary to provide an answer to this question.

Before Ejaz left, the question of his marriage came up. He was somewhat depressed. Because Shamman's father had done so much for him, he had the right to be considered first. But before anything could be said to Ejaz, Shamman told Noori that she was willing to marry any animal except Ejaz. A commotion ensued as a result, there were shows of pitiful lamentation, but once she was back in college she flatly refused to have anything to do with Ejaz, and so brazenly that the whole incident assumed historical significance in the history of the family. Ejaz was bewildered and embarrassed. He made no mention of Bilquis. And Shamman? Using tremendous force, she began slipping from every hold. Rebellion! Every vein in her body vibrated with disdain. She was amazed at her own strength. She had slapped everyone in the face, she broke hearts, ground hopes into the dust. Ah, how cruel she was!

27

On seeing Alma, she ran to embrace her. She could pass through the fires of hell with a smile if she had her hand on Alma's shoulder. She had brought her a present this time, hadn't she? For Alma. She was going to place a new rebel into an old rebel's lap. Alma plunged her bewitching stare into Shamman's fearless eyes and smiled.

'Why?' she asked briefly.

'Because my heart says so!' Instead of providing detailed accounts the new rebel dug her feet firmly into the ground.

'Good!' Alma said, joyfully. 'You're right. No one should have the courage to say "Why?" to us. Come on, let's go.' The guru clasped the pupil's arm.

That same day Alma introduced her to the union president and secretary. With great speed Shamman observed that facet of life in which you emerge out of your shell and see something other than yourself.

When she went to Alma's room she was somewhat taken aback. Lying on Alma's bed, reading a newspaper, was Iftikhar, the union president. Feeling uncomfortable, she was about to retrace her steps when suddenly Alma appeared from the bathroom with a towel wrapped around her head like a turban. She introduced Shamman, who had not spoken to Iftikhar since their brief meeting at the banquet. Telling Shamman to make tea, Alma started drying her hair.

'No milk, and one teaspoon of sugar,' Iftikhar swung his head around and ordered.

'He doesn't take any milk in his tea, he squeezes a lemon in it instead, the fool,' Alma provided clarification.

'Lemon?'

'Yes. Have you ever had Russian tea?' Iftikhar asked.

'Russian tea?'

'Yes, you use lemon with Russian tea. You should also try it, it's very tasty.'

Shamman picked up a lemon quarter and squeezed it in her cup.

'No one else is here as yet, and Satil is going there directly.' A meeting of the liberal and progressive members of the union was to be held as a picnic in an open field.

'Will Miss Boga be there too?'

'Of course. She will be there whether anyone else is or not. Why do you ask?'

'No special reason. Actually I dislike the wretch. Is she a woman or . . .' he stopped in mid-sentence, then continued hurriedly. 'How nice it would have been if we could forget to take her.'

'*Array*, she'll come flying on her motorcycle. Have you seen her new motorcycle?'

Shamman had been stirring her tea intently. Iftikhar looked at her closely.

'Now the cup is getting a scrubbing,' he said, raising an eyebrow. 'How long will you stir it? You'll make a hole in the base of the cup.' Alma revealed her shiny teeth in her characteristic smile and, suddenly flustered, Shamman hurriedly swallowed some tea. Sick to her stomach, she covered her mouth with her handkerchief and retched.

'This . . . this is Russian tea?' The milk had curdled from the lemon juice and brownish-looking shreds now swam on the surface of Shamman's tea.

'This is great! Listen, if you use milk then you don't squeeze in lemon.' Iftikhar made a fresh cup of tea for her. 'Not everyone can appreciate Russian tea.'

After tea they left for the appointed place outside town where they were having the meeting. Some of the students were on tongas, some rode cycles with girls on the back. Miss Boga, with the well-known college athlete Satil Singh seated behind her, hurled mud in everyone's eyes as she zoomed past them on her new motorcycle.

The sky was a clear red; it seemed as though it had been painted over thickly. The dry air dragged autumn's half-dead leaves all over the place. Although the breeze, having lost its edge, was gentle, yet its every blow made one tingle with liveliness. Small groups of young men and women were scattered casually under bare trees. The unusual and pleasant meeting between two opposing camps had created a spring-like atmosphere. Male voices became heavier and female laughter grew more melodic.

The number of girls was naturally limited, so each group had been assigned one girl as a special gift. This was how Shamman got separated from Alma and ended up in a completely dull and uninteresting group. A literary discussion commenced in the most cautious and prudent manner, but in a short while everyone's ability was spent and Shamman began to feel stifled. In Alma's group the select pearls of the university glimmered, their radiance blinding. In another part of the field, Miss Boga, surrounded by a few reckless boys, was trying to sing humorous songs in English. The flesh on her arms rippled as she clapped wildly. Iftikhar was under a bush observing a line of ants with intense concentration, as if that was what he had specifically come here for. Shamman's companions, who for the most part were Alma's admirers, were seeking excuses to approach Alma somehow, but they were forced to stay with Shamman; their hearts were actually dancing to the beat of Alma and Miss Boga's laughter.

This stifling silence unnerved Shamman. If she could help it she herself would run off to be with Alma, or at least find out what problems Iftikhar was trying to solve tangled in the bushes like that. The witless silence of her companions was making her seethe inwardly. Who knows how much longer the atmosphere may have remained congealed if Satil and Alma hadn't started arguing hotly. Satil was Alma's equal in every way, and although she always left him behind in every competition, when she looked back she would see him winning. An enviable feeling of rancour existed between them. If one was night, the other was day, Satil was as dull as a flat plain while Alma was full of surprises, Alma was extremely sharp and bitter, Satil extraordinarily carefree and amusing. Along with cricket he dabbled in English poetry as well and that is how their conflict began. Alma maintained that Satil's shoulders were like a gorilla's and his chest like that of a bull, but he was as far away from poetry as Tagore was from a game of bat and ball. This particular topic never failed to generate serious discussions whenever they were together. They were both quick-witted, so people waited eagerly to hear their opposing points of view.

Today Alma was proclaiming that the only cure for Hindustan's eternal enslavement and instability was absolute destruction. She said that this dying nation didn't need the elixir of life, it needed a poisonous gas so that it could be completely annihilated. Plague cannot be cured with calcium shots, it has to be treated by branding with hot steel; this centuries-old poison will be squeezed out not with balms but with more poison.

Using calculated, cultured language Satil was suggesting that her half-baked theories were ridiculously ineffective. She wasn't a doctor that she should be familiar with the cure.

'He who doesn't amputate a decomposing limb and tries to massage it with soothing oils is not a doctor, he's an ass. It's useless to try and revive these worms that have been putrefied for centuries. All that's needed is a little petrol.'

'Yes, but they're weak, they're not dead.'

'So they should all be made to play cricket.' Boisterous laughter echoed in support of Alma's response.

'Yes, and given a small dose of poetry as well.' No one except Miss Boga applauded. Her laughter was so uproarious it drowned out every other noise. Alma called her the heavenly mother. Miss Boga wanted to view life as an air-filled balloon floating about lightly. Now working on her third master's degree, she appeared to crave a master's in every subject under the sun, but Alma was of the opinion that it wasn't learning she was after; she had got used to life in the university and her life was reduced to nought outside the university walls. She didn't know how to communicate with anyone except college students. Actually she had made several attempts to put down roots for a new life, get a job somewhere, but nothing worked. A horse used to being hitched to a carriage is hesitant to prance about in an open field. She took charge of every newcomer, gave him a tour of the university, showed him where everything was, listed all the guidelines and, like a loving mother, she protected them from minor disasters and the pranks of the degenerate older students. But every new victim eventually became the hunter, got tired of her sheltering, and ultimately made her the object of his tyranny.

Alma told Shamman that at one time Iftikhar too was her favourite, but he began hating her from the day she exhibited her love and devotion for him in a very crude manner. He was nonplussed. Before that came about, this very Iftikhar used to lie on her bed for hours. She would knit while he read with his head on her knees.

These days she was showering all her attention on Satil. She had already knitted him two sweaters, and drove him everywhere on her motorcycle. To every word that came out of his mouth she responded with 'Wonderful!' and 'Marvellous!' Although she had a stable relationship with Alma, she felt it was her duty occasionally to give Satil a pat on the back. When Satil ridiculed Alma's revolutionary ideas, she screamed. And when Alma said something biting, she coddled Satil as if he were a child who had been beaten, which made colour rush to his face. The boys had spread a rumour that she was about to adopt him. and the textile mills in Gujrat that belonged to her father would be his one day.

Like a losing wrestler, Satil went for the throat:

'What does a woman have to do with politics . . . there's only one purpose in her life, and that is . . .'

Alma's eyes flashed with hate. She usually felt helpless in the wake of this line of attack by Satil. But before Satil could expound further on a woman's only function, Iftikhar arrived on the scene and disrupted the showdown. With Iftikhar's ascendance, Satil's presence, like the moon, lost its lustre. He never tussled with Iftikhar. As a matter of fact, he proudly admitted defeat.

With great alacrity Iftikhar immediately organised a game of hide-and-seek. One of the young men was blindfolded and all the others stood around him in a circle. In a short while the inexperienced boy became a practice shield; for hours he circled around and couldn't catch anyone. By this time Miss Boga had exhausted herself from constant shrieking and laughing. Her face, drenched in perspiration, was ruddy like a freshly baked cake, her limp, bare arms, on which freckles sat like a block print, flailed the air frantically, her bra straps had slipped off her shoulders, and the hem of the sari had become shorter. When no one paid any attention to her suggestion that one of the boys should come forward and get caught, she abandoned all the rules of the game and embraced the blindfolded young man herself. He immediately recognised her, but the poor fellow was embarrassed no end later when his friends guffawed meaningfully at what had happened.

Detached from the game, Shamman was lost in a world of her own. Not too far from her was Alma, staring spitefully at Iftikhar's well-built body while he stretched out on a bed of dry leaves. Satil said something and Alma's poisonous teeth shone like a wolf's fangs. Satil responded with a sarcastic smile and dropped his heavy body like a rolling pin on the leaves. Like small flames the tiny, crisp leaves crackled briefly and were silent again. Scornfully picking up a lump of earth, Alma hurled it at a tree trunk in front of her. Satil broke into laughter, which, it seemed, had been concealed in that lump of earth and was scattered on impact into tiny particles.

Shamman tried to force her arm free. Iftikhar had caught hold of her arm while she was lost in thought. She was startled as though a real thief had grabbed her. Like the tight grip of a rope, Iftikhar's fingers grew more powerful; he wasn't one to let go. He yelled, protesting she was unfair and was cheating. At the same time Miss Boga was overcome by a fit comprising clapping and shrieks. Shamman had no choice but quietly to submit to having herself identified, even though Iftikhar had already recognised her. But pretending otherwise, he groped her nose, hands and feet and made everyone laugh hilariously, especially Miss Boga who was completely out of control.

'Come on, tell us, is it someone from our group?'

Miss Boga continued to skip on both feet.

'A moustache? No, no moustache. Who can it be? Satil? Abbas? Qadri? Dutt?' He continued play-acting until Shamman became tearful.

'Oh it's you, I'm sorry.' He executed a comically exaggerated bow and Miss Boga shrieked with laughter again.

Iftikhar teased her so much that Shamman felt she had been taken out of a bundle of rags and placed on a high pedestal. The president of the union was no ordinary person; if he showed an interest in someone then there was a special reason for it. On their return she was offered rides on ten or so cycles and Miss Boga invited her to sit with Satil.

'Yes, you can sit in his lap,' she suggested naively.

Satil hitched up his shoulders invitingly and Shamman felt like slapping Miss Boga just as she used to slap the houseboy when he brought her water in a dirty glass.

That night Shamman stayed in Alma's room. Their conversation centred on different topics, but every now and then Satil's name came up, making Alma grind her teeth in anger.

'But do you know something?' she said, raising herself on her elbows.

'What?'

'Why . . . why I hate Satil?'

'I don't know.'

'Opposites always attract. Fire blazes with greater intensity in the

145

presence of water, the proximity of darkness makes whiteness shine even more brightly.'

'Hmm,' Shamman pondered.

'Is it possible I'm in love with Satil? I'm just wondering.'

'Who knows, perhaps you might fall in love with him.'

'Well, maybe. But do you know . . . what kind of love that will be?'

'No, I don't.'

'When I see him I'm tormented by shocking emotions and I feel as if I am a lump of flesh, as if . . .'

'What?'

'Never mind, you won't understand.' Her eyes shut, Alma got lost in her own thoughts for a few minutes.

'Shamman . . .' she whispered, 'when you see Satil, you feel you want to do something forbidden, isn't that right?'

'Don't, God forbid! I hate him.'

'Yes, yes, the hatred is there . . . Oh, you can't understand.' Alma became sad. 'Look, this happens, there are certain kinds of people in the world who arouse your maternal instincts and others with whom a few minutes of conversation is enough.' She tried to explain.

'But there are some men with whom you want to have a lengthy agreement and with whom you want to share a long journey.'

'What journey?'

'The journey of life.'

'But Satil?'

'Yes, wait. And then there are a few with whom you want to, just once, for the sake of experience . . .'

'My goodness, Alma!'

'And then later they make you recoil, the very thought of them makes you sick, you feel like picking them up and throwing them somewhere far away and forgetting about them.'

In the dim light of the room Alma's honey-coloured complexion appeared lifeless like moss on the walls of dark caves and the expression in her eyes grew desolate and strange.

'What a strange girl you are,' Shamman spoke, as if to herself.

'A strange girl? Maybe I am a strange girl . . . maybe.' She didn't continue.

After a moment's silence she said, 'Shamman, when I rummage through my heart I find savage thoughts hidden there which I hastily cover up again. I'm afraid that one day they will jump out and seize me . . . Shamshad, if I let these ghouls out . . .'

146

'What ghouls?'

'These . . . these who dance about haphazardly in my heart, but it's awful, it's terrible.'

'You're just superstitious, Alma. Is this something to worry about? That scoundrel Satil!'

'No, no, don't be afraid. I don't do what I say. You know, when I've thought something through . . . anyway, go to sleep now, you're tired.'

'No, I'm not sleepy, go ahead. Look Alma, don't have anything to do with this wretched Satil . . . I don't know why he scares me.'

'Scares you?' Alma leaned towards her. 'Are you afraid of him too?'

'What else? Such terrifying eyes.'

'*Array*, you fool, this fear . . . this fear – now how can I tell you, oh, why don't you understand?' Alma was piqued by Shamman's inability to grasp her meaning.

'And what was he saying – woman has only one function – what is that?'

'Oh that? Well, the same function you'll never comprehend. He's always saying that woman has been created for man's pleasure.'

'*Uff*, how terrible! What a scoundrel! So you lost your temper?'

'No, this is not what made me angry, it was something else . . . did you see him when he was lying on the grass?'

'What do you mean?'

'Unh! How can I tell you? You'll start saying, *uff*, God forbid and what not. For example, if I tell you that there's a special kind of man who . . . who . . .'

'What?' Shamman asked fearfully.

'Who causes a strange kind of yearning in your heart. Now take Iftikhar, for instance. I don't love him, and he's really strange, but I want my first child to be fathered by him.'

'Alma!' Shamman felt as if all the air had suddenly left her lungs.

'Yes, you silly thing, and how I long for him to . . . to . . .'

'May you die!' Shamman was visibly upset.

'But I can't tolerate Iftikhar on a long journey.' Alma yawned and slipped into the covers. 'I'd get tired, I'd get tired of him in two days,' she said sleepily between yawns.

good passage

Once she became Alma's pupil she had to move to Kailash Hostel. The principal reprimanded her for her association with Alma, but was eventually forced to throw her out to teach her a lesson. Before Shamman came here she had made such plans, hoping that she would have an exciting time after she had gained her freedom. But when a bird's feathers have been clipped once, it remains imprisoned even when it's free, and the clipped feathers don't grow back in this life and even if they do they reappear all out of shape and crooked. In addition, when you are burdened with your own protection you become short-sighted; where's the pleasure in telling silly lies and making excuses to yourself? Saying you're going to the lecture and heading off to the cinema instead – there was no need for this any more. Soon she had had her fill of freedom. She felt as if no one cared about her actions any more; she could be doing anything and no one was bothered. It was as though people were slowly shifting the burden of their shoulders to hers, liberated from someone else's prison, she was now becoming tangled in the chains of her own responsibilities. Her being was divided into two parts, one in the role of the protector, the other the protected.

She bumped into Satil on her way to the library.

'I'm not so insubstantial that I can't be seen,' he said in mock annoyance.

Shamman had started using glasses recently. She took them off sheepishly and began wiping them with her handkerchief.

'Yes, yes, clean them properly and then look at me. A six-foot object isn't so slight that you need a microscope to see it.'

Shamman couldn't help laughing. Satil broke into a laugh as well. He was going out for a pencil, but now he could use Shamman's pen. Alma was right. One felt like a lump of flesh in Satil's presence. He casually pulled off the pen from her shirt neck and before she could protest he dashed off to take down some notes. Crestfallen, Shamman sat at a table in the far corner of the room.

falling in love w/ Satil

Despite all her efforts she couldn't ignore Satil. Again and again her gaze travelled to the corner where he sat turning pages, poring over books. His elbows resting on the table, he was flipping through a massive dictionary and muttering something to himself at the same time.

Every once in a while he rested the tip of the pen against his lips and bent over the book intently. His tight sports shirt was sculpted to his shoulders and chest and his strong neck, because of vigorous exercise, gave the impression it was moulded in steel. He shifted repeatedly in his seat. His muscular body was slender and taut like the statue of Adonis. Under thick eyebrows his conical eyes were dark and alert. When he pursed his lips in the middle of a thought he looked just like a child pouting stubbornly. *she did not want to have these feelings*

Shamman snapped her book shut irately and ground her teeth for some reason she could not understand. Why was she angry with Satil? With a pounding heart she remembered Alma's words. Her imagination transported her to strange and faraway places, revealed scenes to her she knew nothing of . . . dark corners, desolate caves, and dense clumps of trees barely visible . . . the crackling noise of dry autumn leaves . . . but wait, this was the sound of Satil changing his position on the chair. Satil! Satil! Satil! Why? Why was he overpowering her thoughts? She slipped out of the library without waiting for her pen and went to lie down in the common room.

She could not help laughing to herself. This was not her weakness, it was Satil's strength that was wearying her. The same strength that decent men find in a harlot selling her beauty and which forces them to worship her. Shamman did not know that just as indecent women stick out their chests and, swaying their hips and radiating promises of delight and pleasure, they crush men's hearts, in the same way some men also exhibit their bodies in a cheap and tawdry manner. Every movement made by Satil seemed to cry out: 'Look at my powerful laughter, these thighs, this broad chest, take in your fill!' Rubbing the pen on his lips was such a crude way of sending a message. Shamman felt nauseated.

There were heavy curtains in the room and a strange, mysteriously soft darkness prevailed. Occasionally a curtain fluttered in the wind, a tiny beam of light sobbed and was soon dissolved into this pleasing darkness. The veins in Shamman's head felt like dry, cracked leaves; she was afraid that if her attention wandered even the slightest bit they would snap and shatter.

'*Array*, what are you doing here?' It was Satil who, wearing rubber-soled shoes and treading softly, came in so quietly she didn't know how long he had been standing behind her chair. Shamman jumped. She felt as if she had been taking a bath and suddenly someone had opened wide the doors of her bathroom. She quickly collected herself and sat up.

'Here's your pen.' He rubbed his cheek with it. His eyes betrayed why

149

the pressure on Shamman's finger was prolonged when he handed her the pen. Startled, Shamman let go of the pen.

'*Array*, did you burn your hand?' He blinked his eyes rakishly.

Without waiting for her answer he proceeded casually to examine the paintings on the wall. When he finished and Shamman thought he was leaving, he leaned against a stool, stretched a few times and then turned to face her.

There were servants walking about outside in the veranda and the library wasn't that far, but Shamman's heart beat uncontrollably, as if she were running from an unknown fear in some barren, lonely place where all the escape routes are blocked, and enormous reptiles, their mouths wide open, are leaping towards her from all sides. Even if Satil had taken a large knife and chopped her up into mincemeat, she would not have had the strength to move a finger. But Satil was no fool. He hated raw fruit. He would sit patiently under a tree, licking his lips, waiting for the fruit to ripen and become juicy. And finally the fruit would fall into his lap.

Satil left, but for a long time afterwards she kept remembering the Mullah *ji* she and Noori used to spy on when they were children. She made a quick escape from the common room.

There were two groups in the university. One that was a favourite of the professors, the other a favourite with everyone and watched closely not only by the university administrators, but also by the government. Alma and Iftikhar were the leaders of this group. Some people were of the opinion that Iftikhar was merely a crafty brawler; his tongue was so sharp that within minutes he roused the entire university, but the moment a new thought came up in his head, he put an end to the most riotous altercation. For that reason the administration was always calling on him to help out, no matter how small the task. As a matter of fact, guests and chairmen for special occasions were selected on his recommendation. The university could find no excuse to expel him, and if they had he would have been seen harnessed in a clerk's yoke a long time ago.

He was an ordinary-looking man. Most of the time he wore a witless, moronic expression on his face. People said this was not his real face. Only the principal had seen his real face and that too in the privacy of his office and for a brief period of time. Or, sometimes, he forgot himself and the onlookers caught a glimpse of the real him. Like a wolf he stretched his lips back to reveal his teeth, and silent rebellion against

leaders of rebel group w/in college

centuries of enslavement smouldered in his eyes. His health was never good; he was constantly coughing and sneezing.

Naturally Shamman's eyes sought out Iftikhar again and again. Although he hardly talked to her, when they met it seemed as if they had known each other for years, and she deemed it her duty to close her eyes and obey his every command. Shamman was slowly shifting from the group of admirers to the group of those who were admired, and in the new union elections she won a place as a member. Her self-confidence grew gradually until finally it was bordering on egotism. Now she saw Alma as someone like herself, only more intelligent and bright. She was no longer overpowered by Alma's enchanted eyes and her poisonous teeth, and began to hear echoes of an unfamiliar tinkling in her own laughter. However, Iftikhar and his ambiguous behaviour continued to bewilder her.

In those days the meeting of the All India Students' Association was held in Allahabad and, no one knows why, other, more deserving candidates were pushed aside and Shamman was elected to the group of representatives.

Shamman gaining self-identity + confidence, knowledge of herself as a strong person

29

A letter from home informed her that Noori was getting married. She arrived to find Noori in her room, cloistered before the wedding, according to custom. Noori got up and ran to Shamman to embrace her. They were not in the habit of showing affection for each other, but for some reason both suddenly felt overwhelmed with emotion. At night they slipped affectionately into the same quilt and talked late into the night, their conversation centring on subjects any girl might share with a childhood friend on the eve of her marriage. Stories, old and new, about her husband-to-be, tales of a mother-in-law's loving quarrels with her daughter-in-law, references to glittering ornaments and anklets. With the help of her grandmother and other relatives, Noori had conducted a romance from a distance. Her dowry was like an ethereal quilt with thoughts of her husband woven into every stitch. The romantic treatment at the hands of her mother-in-law and her sisters-in-law along with the clothes and other gifts from her husband-to-be's side had enabled her to get acquainted with her husband-to-be. She had become familiar with every characteristic and every single quirk of his.

'He hates henna, he can't stand dark colours, and he agreed to wear a *sehra* after a lot of fuss.' The same old tawdry ruses typical of every bridegroom, but Noori mentioned them as if they were something extremely unusual and wonderfully strange.

'Says he won't let me wear a long veil. Now how will I go before Bhai Mian? I'll just die.' She had familiarised herself with her husband-to-be's relatives after her engagement and called each one by name, just as he did.

'He shaves every morning, otherwise his cheeks become so rough, it is just unbelievable.' She said this as if she had been stroking his cheeks for years. What a strangely wonderful thing the imagination is. Where no one can go, not even a bird, there you can easily travel in your thoughts. Noori was secluded from him before the engagement and now he was returning from England after a stay of three years. Shamman felt like asking, '*Array*, girl, who told you all this, that his stubble is rough, his moustache tickles, and his palms are smooth?'

Shamman didn't ask for any details, but she was sure if she had Noori would have given her particulars about her peaceful wedded life to come, her children's petnames, description of household accounts, everything. Who knows how long she had been busy with life's addition and subtraction. People thought Noori was too immature, she wouldn't be able to carry the burden of a married life. These naive mothers! No one knew that she had been a seasoned grandmother from the time she was a young troublemaker.

Putting Noori aside, Shamman began pondering over life's many tangles. The female is a puzzle. At the age of four or five she's like a canny grandmother, making people touch their ears and wonder that if she's such a terror now what will she be like when she's older. As soon as seven or eight years pass, there's a dramatic change; the adult language and mature behaviour disappear, their place taken by a strange disorderliness – clothing is in disarray, everyday speech is marked by uncontrollable stuttering, and colour rushes to the face a thousand times. Turbulent new changes and fresh predicaments make such an assault as to cause total bewilderment, and like the plague an awareness of her pubescence paralyses all thought and action.

Noori was fast asleep, but Shamman did not shift her head from her shoulder. She looked closely at her soft, warm body, her face rosy with dreams, her dirty clothes fragrant with *ubtan*. Woman! Was it a woman, who was going to be adorned like a delectable slice of halva and presented to a new guest? She would be bathed and doused with fragrance so that if there was any odour at all it would not be detected; the bride would be smeared with sugary syrup and placed in the bridegroom's mouth and, once the morsel was swallowed, the lion is ours. This temporary gloss will wash off in a few days and the bride will simply be a wife. The word 'wife' made Shamman shudder. It seemed to her that there were dozens of babies and thousands of worries sucking on Noori's young body like leeches.

'A woman has only one function . . .' She remembered Satil's words.

Suddenly she recollected the Allahabad meeting, especially the last gathering which took place under the open sky, around a bonfire. People were sitting in clusters, discussing important world issues. The intermittently deep and low voices of the boys were interspersed with the sounds of the girls' voices which echoed like the tinkling of silvery anklets, while the 'crunch, crunch' of peanut shells fell in between, creating a special music. The fire was slowly going out, but sometimes a group threw peanut shells into the fire, causing a flame to leap up for a moment.

That day she felt so many glances piercing her body, and instead of thrusting them away she held them against her breast and caressed them. How many coats and mufflers were showered on her when she felt chilly; everyone seemed anxious to suffer at the cost of providing her comfort. What strange pleasure there was in this tribute, of seeing every forehead lowered. She didn't know whether it was coincidence or something else, but she found herself with Iftikhar's coat. She felt stifled suddenly; along with the smell of cigarettes there were other troubling fragrances as well that overpowered her senses. It wasn't as if she had worn a hundred coats before this and could recognise these fragrances.

She secretly rummaged through the pockets. How careless Iftikhar was. There was all kinds of rubbish in his pockets; broken matches, a few pencil shavings, one or two programmes all frayed and worn, in the other pocket peanut shells and a letter which she couldn't read because there wasn't enough light and which, for some reason she couldn't understand, she quickly hid in her *koti*. When the meeting broke up she began looking for Iftikhar.

'What is this? I gave you the coat just because everyone else was throwing coats at you, and you made off with it. Why, I'm freezing – either you cover me with it or else . . .'

Hearing Iftikhar talk like this made Shamman fearful.

'Take your coat,' she said, mustering her strength.

'What? And you? Do you want to die?'

'What I'm wearing is quite warm.'

'Oh, let me see – I've burnt my hand!' he said in mock alarm, touching her *koti*. 'All right, now don't pretend to be so brave, go to your tent and slip under the covers.'

'But I'm not sleepy. I'll get my own coat. Please take it.'

Both walked together to her tent and, instead of taking back the coat, Iftikhar picked up her quilt and wrapped himself in it. They came out again.

'What is this fragrance?' Iftikhar asked, rubbing the brocade of the quilt against his nose. Shamman didn't remember what she said. An awkward silence hung between them; they felt uncomfortable in each other's presence. Iftikhar lit a cigarette, then threw it down and crushed it with his shoe.

'Hunh!' he roared sarcastically.

'What is it?'

'You want me to go away. Here, take your quilt.'

'What?'

'I know it doesn't mean that you hate me . . . I . . . I mean – well, never mind.' Spreading his hands, he shrugged. 'I know that you like me.'

'I, what . . .' Shamman stuttered irately.

'Yes, and there's no need to lie. That is why I want to talk openly with you today.' He placed a restraining hand on her arm. 'I'm much older than you, I've been kicked around quite a bit by life, I understand a great deal. I like you, and . . . what was I saying?' He was suddenly lost.

'Yes,' he continued after a pause. 'For this reason I want to say something very important to you.'

'Yes.'

'You're very naive, and this is not something to be proud of.' He immediately clarified his point. 'Naivety is not such a treasure that anyone should be proud of it. So, in my opinion . . .'

Another pause. 'You've never loved anyone.'

Shamman remained silent. For some reason she felt diminished in confirming what he had said.

154

'And I have spent all my life travelling in that desert. I've loved so many times I've lost count now. A mother's love to the love of prostitutes, beggar women and women who are even more debased than that – I've had everyone's love. But the love I have for you . . . What is this!' He sounded annoyed. 'Now don't think that I've never loved anyone more than I love you, no, it's not that – it's just that when I see you my heart is assailed by strange emotions.'

He continued. 'You won't understand. Seeing my feelings for you grow I have felt as if . . . as if, well, it's as if I give you my coat and I know it will be safe with you.'

Shamman was afraid that he might have seen her taking the letter from his pocket.

'You won't be able to steal anything from it. Even if I entrust my love along with all its beauty to you for years, you won't cheat me, and I can't tell you how important this feeling is for a man. I mean for me.'

He paused. 'But why?'

'Only you can say.'

'Me? I can't tell you why, because I don't understand it myself. What can a simple, naive girl like you give me that I couldn't find in my countless wanderings? I can travel a great distance with you without tiring.'

Shamman was reminded of Alma's long journey.

'But our paths are separate.'

'Why?' Shamman struggled with the words as if some unknown power had wrapped its hands around her neck.

'Because . . . because you're square and I have become round from being pushed about mercilessly by life.'

'But buffing makes a diamond more valuable.' Shamman was embarrassed at her own boldness.

'What? But I'm just a stone. You think I'm pretending?' He was annoyed.

'No, no I don't.'

'Hunh! Do you know why I wrapped myself in your quilt?'

'No.'

'I was reminded of my past when I saw it. You don't know this, but I had a sister. We were very good friends. I still remember we used to get into a quilt just like this one and play trains. Today when I saw this quilt – don't laugh, why do you laugh? As soon as I set eyes on the quilt I was seized with a desire to play trains again. When I run into you I always want to tease you, but I stop myself because I'm afraid you

155

might misinterpret my intentions. You know, Shamshad, I have pinched the women I have loved, but the memory of the way my sister tweaked me under that quilt never leaves me, it's part of my very being. My sister died, and I never had the good fortune to have a love like hers again.'

For a few minutes he scratched with his nails the gold stars on the edge of the quilt. Then, as if he had remembered something, he said, 'We used to eat *urad khichri* for breakfast. My sister was small and slight in build. I used to jump on the bed, making her roll over me. She wasn't allowed to eat butter because of her cough, but she would insist on having some, so our mother would roll up a tiny ball of cotton on the *khichri* in her plate. Not knowing the difference she'd eat the *khichri* happily. One day I told her, "Sajjo, this isn't butter, this is cotton." "Cotton?" she said in amazement. And when she discovered Amma's trick, she broke into tears and sobbed. I felt very bad. Have you ever eaten *urad khichri*?'

'Yes.' Shamman felt tears choking her.

'And . . . *array*, what kind of nonsense am I talking about?' he said sheepishly. 'Oh my God, you must think I'm such a fool.'

'No, not at all, I . . .'

'Liar. You are telling yourself, he's an idiot. Of course, I like you and instead of taking you in my arms I'm talking about *urad khichri*.'

'So what? You like me as your sister.'

'What? No, not at all. I consider those men absolute hypocrites who cast women who can be their lovers as sisters. But perhaps you're right. I'm tired of falling in love with women, that's why I can't stand the word "wife". But still, I don't want you to be my sister, God forbid!'

'Why?'

'Because that can't be. I can't lie. I have often experienced feelings for you that are not the kind of feelings I would have for my sister. You won't understand just yet. A day will come when you will understand the meaning of these words without any effort. Is it possible that you regard me not as your brother but as your friend? A friend with whom you can be completely open?'

'Why not?'

'If my sister had lived, she would never be just a sister. Even if she were married she'd be my best friend.'

'Won't you get married?'

'What do you mean by marriage? If wearing a *sehra* and getting on a horse and receiving a girl after a stamped agreement is marriage, then I'm better off remaining a bachelor. Actually . . .'

156

Shamman blushed.

'You're against marriage, I mean against *nikah*?'

'Absolutely. *Nikah* is just a promise which is sealed and stamped so that the parties don't go back on their word. Just think for a minute, how can such an important undertaking be strengthened by signatures on paper? Marriage is an act, it's not an oath.'

Shamman understood nothing.

'But why do people have *nikah* then?'

'They are idiots, that's all.'

'What?' Unable to argue further, Shamman laughed helplessly.

Noori turned on her side and her head rolled over from Shamman's shoulder to the pillow. Shamman bent down to look at her. Perhaps she was dreaming of the most colourful moments that awaited her. Her lips were moving slowly and her eyes were half-open. In the silence of the night Shamman was seized with a longing to look into her eyes and catch a glimpse of her shimmering world. But Iftikhar's words echoed again in her ears and dragged her back into her world.

'Of course it's stupidity. What if a woman tells me she doesn't trust me and wants me to say in front of four witnesses that I will . . .' Noting Shamman's discomfort, he stopped. Then he continued quickly. 'So I'll say, "Begum, be on your way. If we can get something without having four men as witnesses, then . . ." '

'But this is unfair,' Shamman said hastily.

'Why?'

'Because what will those women do whose lives are ruined in this fashion?'

'Why do you say that? Aren't men's lives ruined too?'

'But people make life unbearable for women.'

'And they don't do that with men?'

'But men don't care.'

'So, who told women to care? Come on, say "society".'

'Of course.'

'And who created society? Did it hatch itself out of an egg?'

'No, of course not.'

'If we have created society, we can destroy it too.'

'But there are other predicaments too that only women have to suffer,' Shamman offered apprehensively.

'You mean children?'

'Yes.'

'My, what kind of a woman are you that you consider your greatest

157

duty to be a predicament? That's why they say women should not receive too much education.'

'*Array!*' Shamman was speechless. He laughed at her helplessness.

'But the children that will be born . . .'

'They will be bastards?'

'Yes.'

'Oh, this is too much. Your ideas and mine are worlds apart. I consider that which is prohibited and that which is permitted to be all the same. Only the person who follows the rules of nature has the right to be a human being.'

'But I mean, what about social problems?'

'So why don't you say you don't need a husband, you need a bank book.'

'Well, that's one way of looking at it.'

Seeing Iftikhar a little lost for words saddened Shamman.

'You're right,' he finally said. 'For years I have searched for an answer to this question. I haven't found it yet. Perhaps we'll get the answer in our lifetime.'

It was late and they began walking back to their tents.

'Yes, and there's one other thing I wanted to tell you and I forgot.' He extended the quilt towards her, then stopped midway and asked, 'Can you give me this quilt?'

'The quilt?'

'Yes, not in exchange for the coat, but free.'

'Please take it.' She is the one who should feel gratitude, she thought, not him.

'Salaam.' He touched his hands to his forehead in a comical gesture. 'Oh yes, another thing. I'm going to leave for the sanatorium soon. The doctors have told me I have TB. *Array*,' he smiled at Shamman's reaction. 'This isn't something new. It's an old ailment. Twice I've spent time in Bhawali. But this time I may have to stay longer.'

'But you don't look so ill.'

'No I don't look ill, but people are afraid I might pass on the disease to others. It's contagious, you know.' He laughed meaningfully. 'Our generous government has assigned me a bed in "B" class and the entire cost is the responsibility of the university and the government.' He continued laughing.

'When a gutter in the middle of a thoroughfare is filled with garbage and filth which begins to fly in all directions, smearing the faces of the passers-by, then it is the government's duty to clean it for the sake of the public good. Thank God I was spared the Poona Jail, or else . . . oh, what foolishness all this is.'

Before he left he said, 'Yes, promise me one thing. I've taken this quilt from you, but I also want a promise.'

'Yes, what is it?' She was getting impatient.

'Whenever I give you advice you must promise to take it, I mean any advice which will keep you away from trouble.'

'I'm not afraid of trouble.'

'I know, but I don't want to drag you into my furnace. I don't want a positive promise – you can think about it, if you think . . .'

'You've misinterpreted my silence.'

'So . . .'

'I promise.'

'Come with me then.'

He took a pen and paper and, holding her hand, made her sit next to him. The entire camp was plunged in the slumber of oblivion. Two crazy people put their heads together and wrote a few lines.

'Now close your eyes.' Iftikhar placed his hand under her chin and turned her face the other way.

'Oh!' Perhaps the nib of the pen pierced the tip of her finger too sharply.

'Write.'

'Shamshad.' Shamman signed her name with trembling fingers.

'*Khuda Hafiz.*' Covering his face with the quilt, he disappeared into the darkness.

Shamman woke up. She recounted the dream in detail. Composing her flustered senses, she grasped the chain again. Her eyes wide open, she seemed to be watching the moving flap of her tent still. Today, today someone had shaken and stirred her and placed her at a new crossroads in life. For a long time her senses tried to snap off the ropes, but far away in the distance she saw a long road emerging. Today, as a symbol of her adoration, she had drawn a sign with her own blood on the forehead of her god. She hadn't known her blood was so red, and this name, 'Shamshad', stretched like a red flag until it seemed to cover the horizon.

She glanced at the unwed bride. Tomorrow she too will bow before her god. Noori will diminish and exist only as a man's woman. Rocked by feelings of pride and satisfaction, Shamman idled into sleep.

30

During the wedding Shamman discovered that in a way she was now older than many of her elders. She teased those old crones until they were squirming helplessly. Taking the very same objections once directed at her, she bent and twisted them a little and hurled those objections at the older women this time, and in such a comical manner that these one-time objectors became sheepish while the onlookers were driven to laughter. Shamman succeeded in reducing to tears the old ladies who had censured with such remarks as 'My word, can you imagine? In our day young girls were not so shameless!' 'God forbid! Look at the neckline, you can see everything!' and 'What is this ceaseless cackling, this unending commotion, are these girls or horses?'

She derived great pleasure in teasing these women. With unabashed impertinence she interrupted everything they said, as if she was determined to avenge the years and years of rebuke and censure at their hands. But she realised she should feel sorry for these old women. Can youth be suppressed with criticism and rebuke? It's always old age which suffers defeat. When a person is faced with autumn's crushing touch he spitefully takes out his frustration on youth. Mirthful laughter is just '*Hee, hee*', romance is seen as lasciviousness, and youth becomes synonymous with shamelessness. When old women see the slender, soft arms and well-rounded bodies of young girls, they feel anger at the sight of their own skinny, half-dead bodies, they feel knives raking over their hearts. They pray for youth to be shrouded in autumn's blanket so it can be buried with them, so it can become as lifeless and pallid as they are.

All the girls at the wedding were younger than Shamman and also quite unsophisticated. Although the two or three boys she saw were timid and dull, she quickly mingled with them so that they too could see how an educated girl behaves. There were a few other educated girls there as well, but unlike Shamman they had not had the opportunity to associate with boys. For them boys were still romantic, heartless rogues whose voices had the power to make them neigh like mares tied up in a stable. Although they were cursing the boys openly, the girls deliberately traversed the areas where they were sure to run into them. And once they had bumped into the boys they bolted away so shy and bashful that one would think something had been actually snatched from them. Later, for hours, drenched in perspiration, they'd let their hearts beat uncontrollably.

And the boys too contributed amply to the excitement of this game of hide-and-seek.

'The wretch! My heart's still pounding, I'm still shaking.' Remembering the delicious collision, the girls would whisper excitedly to each other and shake while waiting for the next collision. In addition to these girls there were others who had latched on romantic associations to their sisters-in-law or mothers-in-law-to-be, and were as coy in front of them as a new bride is in her husband's presence. Now who can stop them from this romantic indulgence?

On the one hand there's this colourful atmosphere, on the other, there's everyone standing around in an open field under a professor's watchful eye and asking, with a forced smile, 'How are you?' As if a boy and a girl are truly concerned about how the other is doing.

Shamman felt that this freedom was in reality a confinement. People are right. Women should remain in purdah. It's true, how much more fun there is in playing hide-and-seek when you are behind a veil; you could hide from whom you want and show yourself to whom you wish. Those who are homely must find seclusion particularly useful. A tiny glimpse ensures the onlooker's interest; it's not as if you're standing in open view of the other person with every fault glaringly evident.

That is why if you look through the literature of the old days you'll notice that all women are exquisitely beautiful. A woman was either a beauty or a youthful maiden, and now she is referred to as doctor, nurse, sweeperess, or just woman. Why did she turn from a beauty to just woman once she emerged from the veil? What happened to all her ploys which she employed to break hearts and wreak havoc? Why did the arrows from her glance become blunt and why did the blades of her eyebrows lose their sharpness? Well, the thing is, once she emerged from the veil the secret of powder, kohl and *missi* was exposed. Everyone came to know that the eyebrows have been plucked into the shape of a bow, the eyes have been blackened to resemble nights shot with lightning, the lips are red like the petals of a flower thanks to lipstick, and the cheeks are aglow with rouge. There is as much dearth of beauty in Hindustan now as there was before, but the removal of the veil from faces has also lifted the veil from the eyes. Women have been cheated.

When the bridegroom arrived in the evening the women joined ranks like hungry flies. Those who were in seclusion were momentarily flustered, but soon they too got into the spirit that prevailed. A man, even if he's a bridegroom, has so much allure that even the most sensible of women lose their composure in his presence. And to make matters worse, there were two or three *shehbalas* who had tagged along with the groom. At first a few old crones blared away, but it was the younger crowd that eventually took over. It was decided that the *shehbalas* could stay as long as they made firm promises to hide their faces in *dupattas* borrowed from their relatives. Watching the mischievous eyes of the young men twinkling through the *dupattas*, Shamman was suddenly reminded of the day of Bilquis's birthday when Rashid was given permission to play *carom* with the girls if he covered his face with a scarf.

'My word, where did these appendages of the bridegroom come from?' Shamman asked in mocked anger. One of the boys with sharp eyes like that of a pigeon-fancier mumbled something under his breath, at which his companion nudged him with his elbow.

'He's mad,' one of them offered in defence of his friend.

'Don't call him mad, he's demented.' He rolled his pigeon-fancier eyes again and muttered once more, at which his companion instructed him to keep his mouth shut.

As long as the groom was wrestling during the *arsi-mus'haf* to catch a glimpse of the bride, the boys were on the lookout to pinch the girls. It seemed as if there wasn't just one but six or seven *arsi-mus'hafs* in progress. The girls were shouting in exasperation, but made no attempt to budge; they were fighting back with determination.

Noori burst into hacking sobs when the time came for her to leave. Shamman chafed.

'Now come on, don't pretend. You were dying to get married, weren't you?'

'Oh . . .' Noori sheepishly fiddled with her nose-ring.

'Or are you crying with joy because you had to go through all this trouble to get married?'

Noori was silenced. For some reason her tears also disappeared.

'No one is forcing you to get married. Why did you agree to the wedding? Get a divorce then.' Noori's silence compelled Shamman to continue showering her with harsh and uncharitable words.

She felt Noori was like a cow. Having made a deal for her youth for a *mehr* of ninety-one thousand rupees, she was now leaving with a man. Not like some fool, but all properly with signatures on paper so that if she writhes painfully later the noose round her neck can be tightened.

And that idiot too was making his purchase to the accompaniment of drums and trumpets. What was the difference between this transaction and the hundred others that take place every day in the market? Those are small-scale businesses, like the ones involving different kinds of hot, spicy snacks, and this is an extended contract lasting as long one of the parties doesn't defraud the other, and if that happens the transaction blows up. *what Shamman wished would happen*

But when the bridegroom began walking away with Noori, Shamman had this feeling in some corner of her heart that Noori hadn't been sold, but that instead this man who had clasped her to his breast was about to place chains on his existence. This very Noori, this young, inexperienced girl, will dig her claws into his being in such a way that he will abandon the rest of the world and, handing her the reins, walk on the path she chooses for him. How unfortunate that men think of women as a man's shoe, a creature with a weak intellect, and God knows what else. But when this very shoe strikes them on the head their ego is shattered. Suddenly she saw all men as victims, and all women laden with gold and rupees as tyrants who controlled men's incomes just as blood-sucking industrialists controlled the blood and sweat of poor workers. They demanded payment for their bodies – instead of getting payment from hundreds, they got it from only one man.

Then why do men regard women as weak? Perhaps because in this way they can disguise their own weakness. A tyrant never announces his tyranny, it's only the cowardly who give vent to their feelings by roaring like a lion. But a woman? A woman is like the ruler who fools his subjects by pretending to be their servant. Her ploys are so clever and dangerous; instead of being ashamed of her femininity she sees in it something sublime.

The women were singing. Their voices were tremulous:

> We, father, are the cows tethered to your peg,
> Where you'll lead us, we will go.

'How admirable is their meekness – as if they're dumber than cows and oxen,' Shamman said to a girl sitting next to her.

'Of course, sister. They're so innocent.'

But doesn't a cow attack with her horns? The ox is actually always duped. How can an ox working the water-wheel go after anyone with his horns, when does the poor thing get time to harass people? But the cow, on the other hand, why, what more does she do besides chew cud

163

and give milk? What does the cow care if the calf didn't get milk and someone made *kheer* with it instead? Cows don't have to move their hands or their feet, and still people worship the cow, and no one takes any notice of the ox.

She felt worse now. The singers were making fun of the bridegroom. She wanted to go up to them and scratch their faces. Wretches! The oxen too have life in them.

THE THIRD PHASE

31

When she returned from the wedding she felt she had buried two relatives, Noori and Iftikhar. Noori of course had no interest in anything except the recounting of her groom's mischievous behaviour. All day long she would sit among friends, excitedly whispering anecdotes in their ears. God knows what these friends were looking for even after they knew all there was to know. Perhaps they were motivated by that same fervour which makes people derive vicarious pleasure from reading smutty stories and tales.

And Iftikhar? From Allahabad he went straight to Bhawali. The professor who was in charge mentioned casually that he was sorry Iftikhar wasn't there, adding that he had gone to the sanatorium to get treatment for his old ailment. Afterwards he said a few words of prayer which seemed quite forced. Shamman knew very well that no matter how much God liked Iftikhar, if the world didn't want it, Iftikhar could never leave Bhawali completely cured, although people would hasten to rest the entire blame for his death on the angels of death and fate.

In Iftikhar's absence Satil automatically took over the leadership of the affairs at the university. He was also backed by the affection of the principal and the professors. Who knows what ploys were used to elect him to the position of union president. Alma was somewhat upset; she neither opposed nor supported Satil, nor did she take part in any matter relating to the union. She seemed frightened. When her experienced eyes became clouded with fear, her face began to resemble the face of a child, her laugh was self-conscious, and her teeth resembled blunt fragments of china.

Instead of being impressed with Satil's rise to power, she seemed to be apprehensive of it. But the union suddenly came to life. The number of progressive members increased rapidly, meetings were organised feverishly, new rules and regulations were set in place, new divisions were developed, drama and art sections were formed, schemes for rural uplift were laid out, and demonstrations began.

For a few days Shamman felt ill at ease. She couldn't get used to the idea of seeing Satil in Iftikhar's place. Life in college and the university is like a bubble. As long as it's afloat it reflects the myriad colours of the rainbow, but the minute it bursts everything disappears. The same Iftikhar whose presence was like the guiding star in the university had today fallen into the darkness of anonymity. The walls did not feel his absence. It was as if he was a tiny particle of sand and no one knew when he was blown away by a gale. For three or four days people did call Satil 'Iftikhar' by mistake, but in no time they got used to the new order, and soon Satil's eloquence and his handsome build erased Iftikhar's memory from people's hearts. Alma continued as secretary, but Shamman had to take on the position of treasurer. Overwhelmed by the weight of the new position, Shamman found herself propelled into association with the progressive group.

As long as a diamond remains in the darkness of the mine it's a useless stone. Unless musk is rubbed, it is no more than a tiny ball of noxious matter. No one besides Satil had probed enough to know that behind Shamman's anxious and fearful exterior there existed the hidden embers of rebellion and self-reliance, that enclosed in this flat, silent, stony breast was a smouldering fire just waiting to be awakened, and that once aroused all the slumbering powers were going to bubble furiously. Even Shamman had not been aware of this aspect of her personality. At first she considered the thought of this new Shamshad to be a figment of her imagination, but then she too saw a glimpse of it. She felt blinded by its radiance. Far, far away she saw this new thing elevated to a high place. Fighting the forces of opposition, where had this sacred strength been all this time? How insignificant and dull the old Shamman looked in comparison to it.

'There is something that only she has been blessed with!' And very soon she found within herself a mysterious appeal, a silent strength and a hidden elegance. With Satil's help she tried to identify and understand this new personality that had caught her unawares. She embarked on a study of literature and philosophy, developed an interest in poetry, and soon the old cracked shell broke, and from it emerged a solid kernel. She crushed the brittle shell and threw it away. She made an attempt to understand the core that had been exposed, but the more she comprehended the enigma, the more complex and convoluted it became. It seemed as if there was a new Shamman playing hide-and-seek with her. The minute she was close to touching her she dissolved and floated away from her. There were times when she felt she had caught her but, before she could examine the features properly, she slipped from her, making Shamman run after her with renewed vigour. Sometimes, during her pursuit, she ended up in a desolate, frightening corner where she found herself alone, the illusory Shamman having dissipated once again. Overcome with fear in this barren and unfamiliar place, she became fearful and fled from there, baffled and confused like someone who is lost. — understanding Sahil + loving him

How different Satil was from what Shamman had imagined him to be. Buried in the magnificent structure of flesh and blood was a philosopher poet whose heart brimmed with compassion and love, whose inner life yearned to sacrifice everything for his land, his nation. On the surface he appeared as someone who was worldly and fond only of sports and amusement. But no one knew how many tears were embedded in his smiles, the moans tangled in his laughter could only be heard by those who were perceptive. The fear that Shamman always felt in his presence was altogether unfounded, she discovered; he just looked like a scoundrel. How many kinds of snakes are there which look poisonous but are as harmless as mice in reality? He also had a sharp sense of humour and often his jokes left people in stitches. Because he was president he was obliged to keep everyone happy, which he did successfully.

Satil

The progressive party rapidly became more cohesive and the membership continued to increase. All at once Miss Boga gave up her Gujarati brocade and started wearing homespun cotton. Shashi, a new girl, was another person who used only indigenous products; her dishes were of Gwalior china and all the furniture in her room consisted of the best examples of craftsmanship from Kashmir and Mysore. She wore clothes made of silk from Murshidabad and georgette from Mysore, and her saris were from Madura. Her entire family was known as a family of leaders. Her father was a staunch nationalist and took her along with him to every political meeting where she would sing 'Band-e matram' into the microphone. She was married and her husband was in England.

In spite of their nationalist leanings, there was quite a bit of fashion governing their lives. They spoke English at home, terms like 'Mummy', 'Papa', and 'Auntie' were in common use, the young girls all wore frocks and had short hair. Although their souls had become European, their skins were still native.

Nobody in Shashi's family was employed by the government. Her eldest uncle had gone so far as to relinquish his title, and had been to jail several times. Cotton trading was the family business in which everyone from the family was readily absorbed. Who then would want to have a job which resulted in bondage to the government? Secondly, their business also helped the country's economy, although some people thought that Lalaji was more concerned about his profits than about the profits of the country. True, the homespun vogue helped the nationalist business prosper, but the workers remained as hungry and deprived as before. They wore coarse material before this and now too received the same. However, cheaper products imported from Japan did give some of them the chance to wear silk; the poor also became familiar with the feel of brocade; the sweepers and low caste workers also got to play with Japanese toys, while the daughters of orderlies were fortunate enough to receive crockery and glass tumblers in their dowries. But how long were these Japanese goods to last?

The meetings of the progressive party became increasingly more interesting as time passed. Every member was ready to lay his life on the line. Most of these people were men who had suffered at the hands of ill fortune and were despondent. Ahmed was in love with a Christian girl who had spurned him cruelly and lavished her attentions on a professor instead.

Rahman was in love with his uncle's daughter whose greedy father had turned Rahman away because he was unable to secure a government job and had vowed to serve his country; for three years he sat for various civil service examinations, but only at the insistence of his family. Having devoted all his time to serving his country, he didn't wish to get involved in any trivial business now.

Anwar was in love with a girl who attended the Women's College and whose wavy tresses and slender waist had turned him into a poet. It was hoped that very soon he would become the most progressive poet of his time. Moving away from the traditional path, seeking new directions, his poetry was unique. His romantic heroine, entirely different from the antiquated heroines of *Zehr-e Ishq* and *Gul Bakaoli*, was a broad-minded college beauty, who, instead of being hardhearted and unfeeling, was madly in love with him. However, helpless in the face of ruthless society, she had been forced into marriage with an ICS officer. But Anwar's poetry predicted that a revolution will take place and all these restrictions will be broken, society will be annihilated, the skies will rain blood, and both the earth and the sky will become red and red storms will sweep across the entire world, and engulfed by these red flames all evils will be obliterated – the red flag of freedom will fly high, the worker will rule, and at that time Anwar will love his heroine without any constraints, and he will unravel her raven locks, imbuing the atmosphere with their musky fragrance. And what will happen next? No one knows what will happen next.

And then there was Anand with whom the town's entire population of prostitutes had fallen in love. He went to them without paying anything and they also gave him free liquor; liquor is necessary for every artist, and he was a true artist. He had made a deep study of Russian literature, and after translating for some years he started writing his own fiction and there was evidence that very soon he would have a place among the front-row writers.

Barkat was a strange, obsessive character. He was doing his master's in history, but the better part of his time was spent in furnishing information on sexual subjects. James Joyce and D. H. Lawrence were his spiritual mentors whom he referred to at every step, and he had begun to regard sexual liberation as more important than union with Brahma. He spoke very fluently and people were often convinced by what he said. Shamman didn't have any reason to dislike him and didn't oppose his views with any degree of severity, but still, when he was alone with her and embarked on psychological analyses, she broke out in a sweat.

'Man is worse than an animal. Until he is given a religious, social and legal certificate, he should not love.' He emphasised the word 'love', using it in a meaningful way. He didn't believe in the kind of ineffectual love which involved sighs and sleepless nights. It was only passionate love that he was interested in. Prostitutes aroused his sympathy greatly. He had such hair-raising tales to tell of their lifestyles, their financial difficulties, their living conditions, and the diseases they were stricken with that Shamman would begin to feel sick. God knows what filth he plunged into every day. Shamman was angry at the prostitutes; why were the wretches so filthy? Why didn't they do honest work, *array*, why didn't they work a millstone, stitch clothes, and lead respectable lives? But she knew these prostitutes weren't fools. If working a millstone and sitting at a stove were easy they'd already be doing it.

'But what's the cure for this?' she'd ask Barkat sometimes.

'The death of capitalism.'

'How?'

'The way it happened in Russia.' And for hours the two of them would study the features of Russia's revolution.

In short, everyone in the progressive party was special in one way or another. Love and romance, betrayal and cruelty, poverty and unemployment, all this had made them eccentric.

One day Shamman returned from college to find Alma sitting on her bed in her room.

'*Array*, have you been sitting here long?' Shamman asked a little sheepishly. Her conscience berated her. What promises they had made to each other after Iftikhar's departure, but with the new elections a distance had developed between them and now things were so bad that Shamman was on this side of the road and Alma on the other and if by chance their eyes met, both of them immediately looked away; it was as if they hadn't even seen each other, as if the other's presence was an illusion. But today Shamman put her arms around her and, holding her tight, gazed at her face for a long time.

What had happened to Alma? This was not the same Alma. Her eyes, aged even more, looked like they were enveloped in celluloid. Her cheekbones were more prominent and her hair seemed thicker than before. Instead of bursting out with tinkling laughter, she was smiling bitterly, the smile on her face not a true reflection of her true feelings, but more like a mask. There was no hostility in this smile, no sweetness and no hidden sarcasm.

Then they started talking. They chatted for a long time, about Iftikhar, about this and about that.

'Sometimes our every move is foiled,' Alma said suddenly.

'What did you say?' Shamman lowered her head.

'I said, we think of one thing and do another.'

'What do you mean?'

'Shamman.'

'Hmm.'

'Have I changed?'

'No, of course not.' Shamman glanced up and down at Alma. She thought she saw something, but she shrugged the thought away.

'But the doctors think I won't be able to sit for the exams. If the news spreads . . .'

'You . . . you . . .' Shamman stuttered.

'Don't be scared. My illness isn't contagious, you won't catch it.' Alma laughed derisively. Her laugh reverberated like a clatter in Shamman's ears as if someone was rattling a steel box filled with rocks. Alma's teeth shone like poisoned nails and her eyes became clouded. Now Shamman understood why her cheekbones were more prominent and why her hair appeared thicker than before.

'Won't you tell me anything?' Shamman asked, even though she had surmised quite a bit already.

'What's there to tell? I have a child in my belly.' *Alma pregnant*

Shamman jumped as if the roof had fallen over her head, but then, embarrassed, she quickly composed herself. Why is it that nature's laws appear weak and worthless when compared to social mores? If one thinks carefully it becomes clear that nature has no restrictions on a woman who wishes to be a mother, but society demands a tax. Shamman was proud of her open-mindedness, but before we become open-minded we have to change our habits. Shamman pulled herself together. Her thoughts leapt like wild does. At the time the two friends had returned from that picnic and talked, Shamman was still very naive. But not any more; now she understood the meaning of Alma's words. She remembered the night when she turned towards a new juncture. Recalling the fragrance of Iftikhar's coat brought back the memory of that night in its entirety. And then she thought of her quilt which Iftikhar had wanted to take with him.

'I know what you're thinking,' Alma said slowly.

'Me?'

'Yes, you're telling yourself that I'm very unfortunate, I have committed a sin. That's not true. I don't consider this a sin, but . . .' That bland smile returned to her face. 'You won't understand. Actually I have committed a sin.'

'Alma!'

'I have committed a grievous sin. I deceived my soul and satisfied my body.'

'What nonsense is this, Alma? What do you mean?'

'Hunh? No, I didn't know what I was saying.' She was silent for a few minutes. Then she began again. 'You've forgotten, remember I told you that . . .'

'Yes, that you wanted Iftikhar's . . .'

'Yes, yes. That's what I mean, if only that were so.' She was plunged in thought. 'If that were the case I would keep his gift close to my heart for ever.' She sat up hastily and began blubbering. 'The devil that is growing in my body is Satil's gift, and, and . . . I gratified the need of my body, but my soul is still hungering. I'm going to Bangalore this week, I'll have the operation there.'

Holding her breath, her eyes flying open, Shamman tried to make sense of what Alma was saying. 'Why?'

'You probably think all this is very strange, but because I hate Satil and he hates me, we can't come to an agreement. Just think, how can I tolerate this sin of his? The operation will be a testimony of my intense hatred, I can reject his precious gift.'

'But he won't feel remorse or sadness.'

'Oh, but that's what you don't know. Imagine for a moment that you throw a party for me, place a delectable morsel in my mouth – now how will you feel if I spit out that morsel at you?'

'Oh Alma!'

Alma burst into bland, raucous laughter again.

'But . . . you have a share in all this too.'

'Yes, yes, but if something falls on the ground and is covered in mud, there's no need to clean it and eat it. Instead, one should accept one's loss and throw it away.'

'Does Satil know?' Shamman asked after a moment's silence.

'Yes. When I told him he puffed up his broad chest like a film hero and asked me to marry him.'

'What did you say?'

'I said, "I'm not ready to make a four-paisa deal with you, how can I make a commitment for the rest of my life?" and when he started making other promises I said, "I'm going to Bangalore for the operation." The poor fellow's face fell.' She let out a full-throated laugh.

Alma left. Shamman sat thinking for a long time. Satil had been in a bad mood for days. Suddenly she wanted to go to Satil and ask him to open his heart to her. A careless, cruel man like Satil – was he really feeling insulted on account of Alma's behaviour? Leaving aside marriage, creation is man's first duty. God hasn't made man so he can spend his entire life just attending universities and toiling in offices. Creation, no matter what form it takes, is man's most important reward, and perhaps, seeing his reward being wasted, Satil is remorseful. Perhaps if Alma had wept and become hysterical like ordinary women, his feelings might have been different. But now he was irked by her disdainful

172

rejection. He may not be experiencing any regret at losing a part of himself, wondering instead what right that eccentric girl had to degrade him.

A few days later Alma left for South India. Shamman felt deeply saddened by her departure. Alma muttered something vague about the question of her return, neither yes or no. Her answer was strangely philosophical. At the station she embraced Shamman closely and kissed her.

'I won't be seeing Iftikhar again. If you happen to see him give him this kiss for me. I don't know why, but I have this feeling that I'm not going to live long.'

'Don't talk rubbish!'

'You silly thing. I don't mean physically. No, physically I'll live a long time. But my soul is dying.'

'How dark your thoughts are!'

'I know you'll regard this as absolute nonsense. But when we Hindustanis go beyond the allotted limit, we receive a jolt and are forced to turn back. This darkness exists in our blood. As far as our imagination is concerned, no one can compete with us in that sphere. In our dreams we can even conquer the seven regions of the underworld, but when it comes to action, we are left behind. Take Iftikhar for example. He's so intense, so sincere, but only in theory. If even one-third of him were to materialise into action he would become a great and genuine leader of Hindustan. But if he knew that I . . .'

'Iftikhar is broad-minded,' Shamman said, remembering her last conversation with him.

'No matter how broad-minded he is, this blot will darken him too momentarily. What is left in my life anyway? Just constant reproach from my conscience.'

'But what about serving your country, something you have already taken on?'

'That undertaking has also proven tragic. There's nothing left, everything is vile in this world. We start something with such excitement, but soon selfishness, separatism and avarice come in the way and erase everything. We don't really know how to do anything except engage in hollow talk and applaud noisily.'

'But surely there's a reason for this.'

'Reason? Our innate nature. We may go anywhere, achieve great learning, but we can't remove this element from our blood which has been the cause of our destruction over the centuries. We are born to be enslaved and to worship others. Gandhi *ji* tried to free us from bondage and what did we do? We turned him into a Mahatama and started worshipping him. That intense national fervour was focused on the meaningless adoration of a god.' Alma had been transformed into a philosopher while strolling on the railway platform.

'When we are tired of worshipping one god, we create another god. We don't care that it's black or white. If someone asked us to live in this world without a god, we'd never agree. I've read about your religion. But western and eastern religions are different, as different as domestic liquor is from French wine; one is the intoxication of a sophisticated philosopher, the other the wild exhilaration of home-made liquor. Religion suffers a strange fate here in Hindustan. Right away Bhawani Mayya and demons take over.'

'But you . . . you're a Christian?'

'All this me and you business is utter nonsense. We're all rocking in the same boat. We take off our dirty garment and eagerly put on new raiments, but in a short while we're rolling in the dirt again. We run after everything new, not to use it to create some newness within ourselves, but only to make *it* shabby. We're like the spider that entangles the prettiest moth in its web and mangles it until it's unrecognisable. Whatever you throw into a salt mine will turn into salt.'

'So in your opinion Hindustan's ailment is incurable?'

'No ailment is incurable,' she said after a thoughtful pause. 'But our doctors are still standing by the patient's bed trying to come up with a diagnosis. One says it's arthritis, another proclaims that it's all in the blood. And yes, that's true. This blood, this Hindustani blood, has turned black.' She stared into the distance pensively.

Although Alma's health had deteriorated, her body had the bloom of a flowering fruit tree. Shamman began observing her closely. Suddenly her throat constricted with emotion. If a tree begins to fight with nature, how long before it falls down? What if a mango tree refuses to allow the fruit to grow after the appearance of the flowers? But that can't happen. Only humans have the right to rebel; if they are not ready to fulfil nature's demands, they can't be coerced. But she couldn't understand where Alma had learned this lesson of defiance.

Alma's train departed and, like parts of a puzzle, a thousand questions became tangled and untangled in her head. Her heart was heavy, and the wistful kiss that Alma had left on her lips for Iftikhar smouldered like a live ember. Will her keepsake remain safe with her? If only people were not such cowards.

174

On her return she found Satil sitting on a bench on the lawn. He was observing the path of a worm that had crossed between the spaces in the grass.

'These worms eat away the roots of the grass too,' he said, pointing to a long, chain-like creature.

'Have you started studying botany?' Shamman said, a sarcastic note creeping into her voice.

'No, no. A few minutes ago I was asking the gardener why the tennis court is slowly becoming spotty and . . .' Seeing the tremulous smile on Shamman's face, he stopped. 'You've just seen her off,' he ventured self-consciously a moment later.

Shamman couldn't help breaking into a laugh. How naive men are. They always try to cover up the fire in ashes. Sitting here feeling sorry for himself as if he'd just broken a glass. Shamman sat down beside him.

The difference between the oppressor and the oppressed is almost illusory. If Alma had dealt the appropriate punishment Satil would not be tormented by his conscience. Her indifference had added to the feelings of quiet suffocation. How much better if a slap is administered right away so that your emotions can be saved from stumbling and foundering.

'I told her I don't care about my father's threats, my mother has quite a lot of property,' he said in a protesting tone and Shamman felt sorry for him. Even now people attach so much importance to property and the threats of parents, as if money can be the price for conscience. But why was Satil presenting this defence in Shamman's presence? Perhaps his ego wanted to pick up its shattered pieces by using a sense of persecution as a cover.

'Won't you play tennis?' He stopped her when she got to her feet, as though he was afraid to be left alone.

'My racket is upstairs in my room.' Although she was determined to overwhelm Satil with condemnation and rebuke, suddenly, and she didn't know why, a feeling of maternal affection arose from somewhere; why torment someone who is already in tears?

When she returned to her room after playing three sets of tennis, her conscience showered her with reproach. How shameful that she was comforting her dearest friend's enemy. She drooped with dejection, feeling as if she had just returned from dancing at Alma's cremation. Frightened, she quickly splashed some cold water on her face and promised herself she would not talk to Satil again.

But she was helpless. An important member of the union now, she could not keep away from Satil. Whenever he wanted to he arrived at her door for consultation on some important matter. In the classroom, outside class, in the library, on the tennis lawn, at the dining table – in every corner of the university Satil began descending upon her like a persistent cloud. She felt as if she were being pulled into a tiny dot. Why was this loop stifling her? Why was her power of resistance becoming so weak and sluggish? For three hours Satil read worthless poetry to her in the library and she listened.

Sitting on an armchair, her feet curled under her, she was watching the encroaching darkness crawl up slowly. The last rays of the setting sun had imbued the room with an enchanting colour. All at once a whiff of lavender startled her. Extricating her mind from the magic of this aroma, she turned quickly to find Satil standing behind her chair. Drenched in perspiration after a game, he was asking her a question. His long, hairy arms were bare and his calves shone with sweat. She didn't know what happened, but suddenly she couldn't breathe, she felt as if someone had buried her in a pile of flesh and swung her around. With faltering breath she got up and ran from there.

She hurriedly gulped down water from the bathroom tap and then, leaning against a wall, she tried to collect the scattered particles. Later, feeling sick, she fell on her bed in a stupor.

At the dining table, despite his insistence, she couldn't give Satil an appropriate reason for having bolted the way she did. And she didn't really know the reason either. And yet she had wanted to run and she ran without a word. It is said that many animals run about frantically seeking refuge before the onset of a storm.

And Iftikhar? The very thought of Iftikhar made her feel exalted. What did Iftikhar have that made him so attractive? As far as looks went, he didn't stand up to Satil. It wouldn't surprise her to discover that Alma too had been seeking Iftikhar in Satil's body and, disappointed, she had turned away. Examinations approached and, forgetting all the hatred and appeal and fear associated with Satil, she drowned herself in her books.

32

Shamman found it extremely tedious to spend her time chatting aimlessly all day long while waiting for the results of her exams. Because she had been living in the hostel the house seemed like an inn to her now. For the first time after her BA she had the opportunity to examine the world around her with leisure. The number of children in her family had increased four-fold. Her brothers were busy working while her sisters-in-law were engaged in adding to the progeny. It seemed as if everyone was busy dragging life along as if it were a rickety cart. No one wanted to stop for repairs. The joints were loose, the slats were ready to slip, the roof had disappeared, and the base was full of holes like a sieve, but the yoke on the oxen's neck was strong and the prodding with the stick continued. If you wanted to stop someone and ask, 'Listen, where are you headed?', the answer, offered in bewilderment, would be, 'Nowhere'. Once you come into this world, where can you go except towards the grave? Stumbling, foundering, everyone is headed in that direction in the hope that's where heaven will be, that once they've arrived there they won't have to worry about the office, they'll get female attendants and palaces studded with jewels. Amass whatever you can with both hands for that life. Once you get there stuffed with all that's needed, all will be well. So what if the world becomes hell in preparation for heaven?

During the holidays she received letters from Anwar, Barkat, Abbas and Satil. Alma and Iftikhar maintained silence. Shashi's husband returned from England quite the westernised businessman. Miss Boga undertook research in philosophy. And Shamman? After getting her results she didn't know what to do with this new Shamman. There were several fashionable slats available to help pull the carriage of life but some had a weak axle, others a loose rudder. Jobs in the civil service were limited, in the police fixed, and the forestry department was saturated. Observing the turbulent times, Miss Shamshad accepted a job as headmistress of a national school.

The school's building was an abandoned bungalow built some years ago by a man of wealth for his favourite courtesan, the construction situated on the outskirts of the town so that people would not harass him. Unable to cope with lizards and mosquitoes, no tenant stayed here

177

for long. The furniture in the school, comprising benches and a few tables, was a donation from another wealthy man, while yet another rich and important personage, whose ancestors had an interest in literature, insisted on providing a library. Because the municipality wasn't forthcoming with a pit for disposing of rubbish, all the worthless and trashy books imaginable, which in addition to their authors only the publishers must have read, arrived in a state of horrifying decrepitude.

As for the students, the number of girls registered on paper was more than the total number of girls ever born. There were four teachers who received a salary of twenty rupees per month and were given a receipt for thirty rupees. The unfortunate creatures were helpless at the hands of widowhood or poverty and had no affinity whatsoever with the idea of education. The two female custodians present were a legacy from the days when the courtesan had been around; both had served her well. A steward carried on the functions of Manager Sahib's cook, valet and chauffeur, and also maintained the role of his children's 'governess'; during the inspectoress's visit, dressed in a brown coat and white belt, he also served to present salutations respectfully. All the school's usable tables and chairs were transported to Manager Sahib's drawing room when school was not in session. The four teachers usually spent most of their time stitching fine coverlets and muslin *kurtas* for Manager Sahib's children. In addition to this, they were very fond of embroidery and multi-coloured thread and, neatly and diligently, they embroidered 'Sweet Dreams' and 'Forget Me Not' on his pillowcases.

One of the teachers, Razia Begum, received a receipt for thirty-five rupees for a salary of thirty rupees a month. Every month Manager Sahib offered to pay the extra five rupees from his own pocket, but never came around actually to doing it. When Razia Begum first arrived, Mrs Manager threatened to ingest Phenyl and tincture of iodine. Razia Begum was an elderly widow with a stocky build. Besides the Koran Sharif, she had some knowledge of Urdu and basic Persian. She must have been pretty once, but white spots on her face made her look quite unattractive. People maintained that the spots were old, but Mrs Manager was of the opinion that these spots had appeared on Razia Begum's face as a result of her prayers, that they were a curse.

Except for the shrewd female custodians, everyone was quite impressed with Razia Begum. The custodians had been her confidantes at one time and were on friendly terms with her, especially the older crone, who called her Rajjo *bi*. Most of Rajjo *bi*'s time was spent in shelling peanuts and knitting sweaters for Manager Sahib. The patterns she created were so intricate they made your head spin. She was no teacher. Her girls either spent their time unravelling yarn for her or pressing her head, while the custodians sat around recounting stories of the courtships going on in the neighbourhood, or discussed the blunders made by the senior teacher – Shamman, that is.

There had been two other headmistresses before Shamman, but each made off after three months. For some reason, the attention of the Muslim families was suddenly directed towards education after Shamman arrived on the scene. In no time two Christian teachers were hired, and admissions rapidly increased. Using a graduate headmistress as bait, Manager Sahib brought in some girls from upper-class families as well. But these upper-class girls came surrounded by crafty nannies and ayahs, gave themselves airs as if they were made of glass, and then their cars and carriages came to pick them up and off they went.

Shamman's arrival was followed by a total upheaval. With her leading, Manager Sahib strutted about as if she were a wondrous new marvel.

'I say, does one find educated girls among Muslim families?' And it was true people stared at her as if there was a snout hanging from her face. Fortunately the inspectoress turned out to be a college friend of Shamman's and because of this old association the school received a government grant; instead of sitting out in the veranda, Manager Sahib could now sit in the drawing room, although he was always feeling ill-at-ease while he sat there, especially when the inspectoress suddenly came for a visit. And Shamman also became quite well known for her patriotism.

All at once the world changed. New furniture, maps and pictures appeared. The girls, who were used to sitting on the floor, now found themselves sitting on benches, and Shamman vigorously undertook repairs of the building; a fight was launched against lizards, Miss Thomas and Miss Alexander actually started making timetables using blue and red ink, the tattered library books with brittle pages were carefully and diligently restored. For a few days even the female custodians sat perched on benches like aging parrots, Razia Begum hid her store of peanuts, and suddenly the steward struck the gong suspended in the middle of the doorway, his ears turning red from the effort, while the workers in the dilapidated garage interrupted their chit chat and their smoking to look at him and smile.

But after only a few days the enchantment of these restrictions was dissipated. Her legs crossed on the chair, Razia Begum started knitting Manager Sahib's sweaters again, the custodians resumed their usual floor positions in the doorway, their baskets open before them, while the mallet used for striking the gong was taken to drive a nail in a wall and was eventually tracked down to the Islamiyat teacher's room where it had been secured for cracking betel-nuts. Operating with a western-style patience and seriousness, Shamman tried to pick up the rapidly dispersing pieces, but it seemed as if some unknown force was at work. The minute her back was turned one thing or another slipped and within minutes got out of control. Tables, chairs and flower pots went to Manager Sahib's house on loan for a party and were never returned. The steward returned to his old job, and the two Christian teachers became more and more intimate with the masters of the neighbouring national school. The only functional books in the library were taken away by Mrs Manager and her friends and when they were finally returned to the library they were in tatters, the pages heavily soiled with turmeric and oil stains.

Razia Begum actually initiated a permanent siege in which the two female custodians took active part. All day long the girls wrestled under the mango and the berry trees, while Shamman continued to be tormented by the feeling that some unknown power was bent on destroying the structure she was working so hard to erect. The more strict she was the more rebellious her staff became.

Razia Begum and her compatriots were cause enough for consternation, but one day Mrs Manager arrived unannounced with her brood of spoilt, filthy children, intent on inspecting the school. Nobody knows why and how this job had been assigned to her. Actually the real reason for her visit was something else. She had discovered through a very reliable source that the girls were picking mangoes from the trees and consuming them indiscriminately. These precious mangoes, small, tart and raw, were not only used to make pickles and chutneys, they were also used to provide Mrs Manager with a year's supply of tangy chips for use in food, and Manager Sahib himself was extremely paranoid about protecting them.

'Well, I'm not going stand watch over them,' Shamman said brusquely after listening to her tirade. 'I've warned the girls, but what can I say to the teachers who break them off to dry them into tangy chips?'

'Yes, sister, this is the trouble. I've told these wretches so many times, but no one listens. And this Razia Begum, she's the leader. Now tell me, sister, is this the age for chewing on raw mangoes? The old mare!'

'When I told her not to pick the raw mangoes, she said she was making pickles for you.'

'Such rubbish! For me indeed! If she could help it she'd pickle me as well. You don't know . . .' She moved closer conspiratorially.

'What can I tell you, sister,' she began mournfully. 'This school is just a front. A father of six children, and just look at his behaviour. God help us! All sorts of miscreants were after this Razia at one time and this man has entrusted the care of respectable girls to her. I said once, "She's not going to teach them to read or write, but yes, she'll give them some lessons in how to be coquettes."'

Holding her laughter in check, Shamman patiently listened to her story. She left after exacting a promise from Shamman that she would keep a strict eye on the mangoes. For a long time afterwards Shamman kept thinking about Razia Begum, whose youth had faded, but who still seemed to have something dangerous that was making Mrs Manager so nervous. If it had been someone younger there might be cause for concern, but why did Mrs Manager see a threat in the person of a relatively unattractive woman her own age?

'I make pickles too, but he prefers the one that wretch makes. He'll give anything for her chutney. I tell you, one day she'll make chutney out of him.' She had spoken with such confidence.

So was Manager Sahib really in love with Razia Begum? Shamman chuckled to herself. The romance was definitely unusual, and spicy as well. In other words, one could also entrap lovers with the aid of pickles and chutneys. She had never imagined while she ate chutney that it could serve such a romantic function.

Shamman's room was in a more lively area of the school compound. She had cultivated a small garden in the front where she sat in an armchair in the evenings to watch the children playing in the field across from the school. Round the corner from her room, separated by an adjacent veranda, was Razia Begum's room which she shared with one of the female custodians. After school she placed a small rope cot outside and settled down to embroider Manager Sahib's pillowcases. Why did Manager Sahib need so many pillowcases? His wife probably did away with them. The 'Sweet Dreams' embroidered by Razia Begum stole her sleep no doubt. Now that the mango season had started, she was often seen peeling mangoes to make chutney. Shamman forgot her books and newspapers and tried to study her instead. Razia Begum seemed to be a very clever and experienced person; she could not have led a very simple life. If only someone could turn back a few pages of her life's book. She called Manager Sahib 'Bhai Jan', but in such a way that the word *jan* drove Mrs Manager to distraction. It is said that one woman understands another woman, but still, what was this thing that frightened her so?

To help out with organising registers for admissions and everyday attendance, Manager Sahib dispatched two masters to the school who came every day in the evening and would assist the two Christian teachers practising subtraction and addition starting from the basics. Putting down more than the actual number of dots, adding the month's attendance and subtracting it from a year's attendance, and then mixing this and that – all this was done along with how many girls take drawing, how many take Persian, and so on.

Sometimes Habib and Akram came together and sometimes Habib came alone. And when the matter of the registers was resolved, these visits did not end. Now they made trips on the pretext of borrowing books, the books they needed apparently available in no other library in town except in Shamman's library. Finally Habib's attentions became unbearable so Shamman started loosening his claws so he wouldn't feel he was being kicked out, but the more you pulled him out the more firmly he became entrenched. He would come and sit in Shamman's presence stammering and flustered; Shamman was forced to smile at his pitiful nervousness. Soon he began arriving dressed up in clothes more expensive than he could afford and, when rejected by Shamman, became an even more ardent devotee, but silent and meek, as if he were a question himself. But his tongue had been silenced. Altogether, his behaviour was quite ludicrous.

This was not his fault. For the first time an educated boy from an illiterate family finds himself talking to an educated, respectable woman. He had seen a lot of girls no doubt, but only in hide-and-seek games, and now when he sees a walking, talking real woman, he has no recourse but to become an admirer and fall in love. It's not surprising to see an ordinary person walking about, but when you see a juggler tumbling from the tip of a bamboo pole you're wonderstruck. In the same way, like a magician Shamman had bewildered him into shocked silence. He was interpreting these confusing feelings as love. Shamman was irked by his attentions. The fact that you're of the opposite sex can't compel you to respond to love, nor does every man have the right to fall in love with every woman.

Shamman felt sorry for him and was also annoyed by his behaviour. She could see what his future life was going to be: a small house, an ordinary wife, and several children growing up in poverty. These people forsake their station just once to fall in love, even if it's one-sided, but failure is inevitable. But perhaps they consider it their good fortune to love and be rejected. This boy of limited means, from a middle-class family, goes out of his way to find the daughter of a well-to-do professor or the only daughter of his boss in whose office he works as a clerk for forty rupees, and proceeds to fall in love. If by some fluke he succeeds in getting his way he is dumbstruck. Running away with her shatters his dream, he's thirsty even when he's drowning in water; he's in love just so he can have that on his record, so he can sigh and tell stories of this romance to his bride. He feels belittled in having a prostitute as his wife's rival, he's never in love with his wife, but he spends his entire life slaving for the little brats she produces, becoming a machine in the process. When she's sick he allows himself to be flustered, and if she is angry with him, he pleads and begs forgiveness. He places his beloved on a pedestal, but he regards her as less innocent and chaste than his wife.

Feeling the need for some fresh air, Shamman strolled in the direction of the mango trees. There she saw Razia Begum standing on a rope cot under a mango tree, smacking mangoes with a stick to make them fall. She didn't know why, but the sight of this elderly woman, stretched like the sphinx and attacking raw mangoes, annoyed her. Mrs Manager was right. There's a time to be doing this sort of thing and truly, it is not at all proper for aging mares to pounce greedily on raw mangoes.

Seeing Shamman approach, Razia Begum quickly jumped off the cot and, smiling bashfully like a young girl, started adjusting her *dupatta* over her head. Shamman couldn't understand what made her behave in this coy fashion. She was middle-aged but, acting young and timid, she said, 'Oh, oh,' looked sheepishly about her, smiled with her eyes lowered, and kept fussing with her *dupatta*. This kind of behaviour riled some people, but it was perhaps this very demeanour that overwhelmed Manager Sahib.

She lovingly gathered all the mangoes and walked off towards her room. Razia Begum was a very fastidious person. Her small room was an example of her orderly nature and good taste. Draped over her doorway was a vine of pink flowers, and in the vegetable patch grew spinach plants and mint. There were also some flowerpots. In the evening she sprinkled some water on the bricks in front of her room, donned nice clean clothes, and sat like a begum on her small chairbed while the female custodian gave her the neighbourhood news. Although she wasn't very fashionable, she tried to wear as well as she could what was in vogue. Her pyjama was always a little short, but she put on a jumper or a *kameez* instead of a *kurta* and because she was in good health whatever she wore looked good on her. Usually she was drenched in pleasant-smelling attar. Mrs Manager, on the other hand, was inept and always dressed badly. There was always a child with her, nagging for her attention. She neither had the time to put jumpers before *kurtas*, nor did she have any talent for making chutneys and pickles. After her wedding she had become a permanent pickle herself. The house was like a bundle of rags and, although Manager Sahib was a completely uncultured man, he too was sometimes so exasperated by the disorderliness in the house that he made some excuse to leave and came and sat on Razia Begum's nice clean chairbed, looking as if he was enjoying an evening at a club. Razia Begum didn't observe purdah in his presence, but she had an odd habit of standing coyly behind something and talking, so that only part of her was visible and close enough so that some of the fragrance from her clothes could reach him. Manager Sahib was a serious-minded man and quite unpopular due to his frankness, but as soon as he saw Miss Razia he would begin teasing her.

'So how is your bad temper today?' This was how he greeted her every time.

'Did you have a another quarrel with the sweeperess?'

'Why should I quarrel with her? You've spoilt her, she doesn't listen to me any more.'

'Your *kurtas* are ready, should I give them to the steward or will you take them?' she'd ask without looking at him.

'No, no, I'll take them,' he'd say, flustered all of a sudden.

'That jar of pickles I sent to your house and was broken. Now if you want more pickle please send a container.'

'Yes, the kids broke the jar. I'll send another one.'

'Send me your old sweater, I'll unravel it and knit another one with a new pattern.'

'What? You'll unravel a sweater?' He would smile in amazement.

'So what? What else do I have to do?' she would say, breathing a deep sigh. Only a few days back Shamman had asked her to number the books in the library and she had started complaining that she had too much work. And now here she was, ready to unravel a whole sweater and knit it over again.

On the other front, Habib's behaviour had become quite unbearable. Now when Shamman sent a message saying she was busy, he would leave a note for her. Gradually this note with a few lines scribbled on it took on the form of a regular letter consisting of several pages, and in addition to being hand-delivered, his letters also began arriving by mail. If, by accident perhaps, Shamman did see him, he would sit before her looking very nervous and uneasy. His conduct irritated her. She didn't know why she hung on to him. There was no reason to suppose she would ever have any kind of a relationship with him, but she had to admit she found his attentions oddly comforting. He didn't make her heart beat uncontrollably, nor did she break out in a cold sweat when she saw him. Still, there were times when she waited for him just so she could have the satisfaction of depriving him of her company.

'Tell him I'm resting,' she'd say, and it maddened her when he sent back the message that he would wait. She hated men who, like a rubber ball, kept bouncing back even after they had been hurt. He should lower his head obediently. Well, she punished him for his foolishness by going out the back door to see a film or do some shopping. On her return the first thing she wanted to know was how long Habib had waited, and if she discovered that he had become numb with waiting she smiled in satisfaction, reprimanded herself sweetly, or ignored the matter altogether.

One day the steward came and told her there was a man to see her. She was about to say 'I can't see him,' as was her custom, when the bamboo screen was lifted and she saw Iftikhar standing in the doorway with one hand on the screen, the other grasping a corner of the woollen shawl over his shoulders. She didn't show any alarm, nor did she allow a storm of intense shock to surface by gesture or a change in facial expression. She suffered the reverberation of this massive turbulence with a simple 'Oh.'

Iftikhar had become thinner and more unsightly than before. His hair was dry and awry, he wore a shabby, worn-out shirt and a cotton *koti*, and around his neck was a frayed, dirty muffler. He had changed a lot, but for those who knew him, it was now easier to recognise him. He had removed the mask from his face which he wore constantly while he was at the university; his features were a true reflection of his inner feelings, his mutinous eyes now openly reflected antagonism while a permanent sneer played on his lips. His health seemed to have deterio- rated and he was in an irritable mood. His laughter was tinged with a certain hysterical pitch which he made no attempt to disguise.

'Are you still as simple and cowardly as ever?' he asked in a

185

patronising tone.'My clothes smell and I probably have fleas. Do you mind if I sit on your bed?' He sat down without waiting for her answer.

'When did you return from the hill station?'

'Eh? Hill station? Oh . . . yes, I was in Bhawali for my health, wasn't I?' He broke into a laugh. 'You don't know anything?'

'No, I don't.'

'But I have been in touch with all the news about you,' he said, somewhat agitated. 'I read about your job here in the newspaper and I thought I should go and see you. You don't know that our hill station has now been established in Poona where we work the millstone for six hours and . . .'

'What? You were in jail?'

'Where else? Do you think they would reward me with a title?'

'And what about the others?'

'The entire group was arrested.'

Shamman stared at him dumbfounded. What group? Why was the group arrested? She didn't know all the details, but she didn't want to embarrass herself by asking. All she knew was that Iftikhar was a dissident and always a suspect, but today she discovered that he had also become a militant. For a moment her timid nature was alarmed by the idea that he was a militant. Then her fleeting strength returned. Iftikhar was wrecking himself for his country and his nation. Sacrificing his youth and his life, he had vowed to seize freedom with both hands. Those who thought like him were increasing in numbers with each passing day, this small group slowly spreading in readiness to encompass all of Hindustan. An awakening had begun. The old relationship between the farmer and the landowner was changing its garb and all of Iftikhar's dreams were being transformed into action, but how slowly this was happening, at a snail's pace. Why is everything in Hindustan prone to crawling? You need centuries to turn your head from one side to the other!

At mealtime Iftikhar swiftly touched and smelled everything, trying to recognise what had been laid before him, but his appetite was dead.

'What is this?'

'It's turnips and meat.'

'Turnips? I remember this was once my favourite dish. My mother used to serve it with a thick buttery chappati in a copper plate. We used to sit next to the stove and eat and when the butter started congealing we'd take out a live ember from the stove and place it on the plate. My

186

sister loved lemons.' He was trying to shake up the roots of forgotten memories.

'Shall I send for lemons?'

'No, no, it wasn't me who liked lemons, it was my sister.' Then he silently broke off large pieces of bread to put in his mouth as if telling her that lemons were not going to bring back the past. Lemons have embraced the mud in the grave. What can lemons and turnips do now?

'Did you hear from Alma?'

'No, I didn't.'

'She's a schoolteacher now, teaching God knows what. She was thrown out from the first school where she took up teaching because it was said she was misleading the girls.' He smiled. 'The stomach's demands tighten the brain as well as the hand. As long as you're in college you're having fun either at the expense of your parents or aided by scholarships, and afterwards you can either be a clerk or starve. All your high-mindedness is finished. Do you know what happened to Dalip? He was arrested and now he's a chauffeur for the same viceroy whose car he had tried to blow up. When the viceroy's car drives off, he's there saluting the clouds of dust and the tyre marks that are left behind. But don't think that his defiance will be buried in this dust. No, this sentiment will continue to fester within him and when he dies this unrealised aspiration will be transferred to his children as a permanent characteristic. Mehboob's father managed to save him somehow, got him a government scholarship and sent him abroad. He has returned as a professor from there and is now teaching at some college.'

'What about Miss Boga?'

'Oh yes, I forgot. She's doing a course in nursing at the King George Hospital. As a result of a beautiful gift I received in jail I had to spend two weeks in the hospital. She hasn't changed at all. She is working diligently to finish her course.'

'I heard she was getting married.'

'What? Married? No, she won't get married until . . .'

'What?'

'Well, until someone takes pity on her and first takes away her virginity.'

'Oh God!' Shamman blushed.

'Yes, yes, you don't understand. She . . . she's a very strange creature. She's the type of woman who becomes a mother the moment she's born but who is terrified of marriage.'

'What do you mean? How?' Shamman didn't know what he meant.

'When I say she becomes a mother I mean she is imbued with maternal feelings, but regards marriage as a repulsive act until . . .'

'Look, let's drop this subject. I don't know what you're talking about. Tell me, what are your plans now?'

'I have to leave by the evening train. Why don't you make some plans for both of us?'

'Would you like to see a film?'

'Anything you say is fine, but I'm not that interested in films. They have no other purpose except inflaming emotions and I'm already feeling quite emotional.'

'Oh my, what kind of a mood are you in today!'

'I'm right, you know. Just think, what pleasure can I derive from watching someone fall in love? Actually comedy makes me furious. There's that good-for-nothing idiot, not doing a day's work and having a good time, and here we are . . .'

'All right, let's see a tragedy. How about *Devdas*?'

'Nonsense! Tragedy makes me even more uncomfortable and as for Devdas, I want to spit on him.'

'Oh God, why?'

'The damn fool! Should have run off with the girl.'

'That's it, we're not going. Why don't you say you don't want to see a film?'

'There's a park nearby, isn't there?'

'Yes.'

'If you won't be expelled from your job for being seen with me, let's go there and enjoy the fresh air for a while. I have been living in tombs for too long. Actually,' he added, 'there's one good thing about films.'

'Thank God you found something good.'

'There's a lot of advertisement for our hidden diseases. Have you noticed that there's a drug advertised with every ad for a film? You don't understand?' He looked at the annoyed expression on Shamman's face and laughed. 'Do you girls pretend or are you really naive?'

'You can think what you want.'

'*Array*, my dear, what do you see in the gutters after the cheap liquor following the late show? The scenes from the film are enacted lying down in the gutter.'

Shamman remained silent.

'Some of the more fortunate ones discover their Sulochanas and Madhavis in the red-light district, and others . . .'

'What?'

'Nothing. You'll be repelled. Let's forget it. These topics are either too sacred or too obscene. I don't understand why we become so incensed when our faults are mentioned. Well, let's drop it . . . Tell me about your school. Do you throw your weight around with the teachers?'

'No of course not. I'm not in the habit of giving myself airs.'

The shadowy light of the moon was making the silence even more mysterious. There were signs of life in the park everywhere around them, but accompanied by a stillness, a quiet whispering. Moonlight and silence had mingled to make the sounds of voices rise and fall at the same time.

'Will you be surprised?' Iftikhar said, intoxicated by the atmosphere that prevailed.

'At what?'

'If I say that I am very fond of you.'

'No.' Shamman clutched her unsteady heart.

'And is it necessary that I tell you that you're the first girl who has affected me to this extent?'

'But why?'

'I don't know.' He sounded surprised at himself. 'I don't know why I'm saying all this. Do you know I've been in love not once but a hundred times, at least I've thought so and I've tried to convince myself too, but no . . . I don't want to convince you.'

'Nor do I have the right to believe anything,' he said in response to Shamman's silence.

'Maybe.'

'And this could also be an illusion.'

'Perhaps.'

'Then why did I come to you the moment I was released from jail, as if you have the balm for my old, putrefied wounds and the moment I see you I'll be cured immediately?'

'Perhaps this too is an illusion.'

'Oh, don't torment me. Shamman, for God's sake try to understand me and if you understand something, please explain to me as well. Why do I exist? What am I?' Like an innocent child he stared at her pleadingly.

Shamman's eyes filled. What could she give him? She doesn't have the cure for Iftikhar's ills. He wasn't even asking for anything. Ahh, he was like an orphan child who has wandered far away from his home and does not remember his parents' names. Who can guide people who are lost like this?

'Shamman, I long to love someone, I long to love someone with all my heart. I no longer have faith in anything, I don't trust anyone, I even feel like laughing at God's existence. I'm repelled by love and angry with God because He exists. Who needs Him? I agree He created this universe. So is that supposed to be a favour to us? Why is He so fond of being worshipped? And if you don't worship Him, He threatens you with hell. Tell me truthfully, do you like this cross-eyed, crippled world? On this side there's too much elevation, and on that side it's too flat. In some places there's so much water and then there's barren land stretching endlessly. I feel like taking this world in both hands, kneading it and then reshaping it into something beautiful and refined that would make everyone happy.'

Shamman couldn't help laughing at his childishness.

'But you said that every ailment can be cured. You're a dissident and you're losing hope?'

'I'm a dissident, but my soul is accustomed to fascism. Dissension is as far from us as the sky from this earth.'

'Will this distance never be lessened?'

'Perhaps it will some day, but will I still be alive?'

'*Array*, what about your scheme then?'

'A few bombs went off, three or four trains collided, the viceroy's car had a narrow escape from a tyre blow-out.' He laughed loudly. 'More than half the workers are in jails working the millstones and no one even knows the difference. Look at these callouses.' He spread out his hands.

'Oh my God! Why do people go to jail?'

'Well, they say no one is convinced of your nationalist spirit unless you've been to jail, just as you can't get a government job unless you have a stamped university degree. Unless you have a certificate from jail, you can't dance on the political stage. For this reason sometimes you have to make a special effort to go to jail.'

'What nonsense.'

'Yes, just a hoax. Actually the truth of the matter is that our leaders have no other proof of their nationalist fervour except their eagerness to go to jail. If these millionaires don't spend a few months in jail, how will they fool the public, how will they be deluged by flowers?'

'But everybody is not a millionaire.'

'Yes, and those others have no other device they can use except protesting on the streets, and immediately '*Amma jan*' shuts them up in a dark cell. *Array*, these are matters you can't understand like this. If you really want to understand, come out in the open, and you'll have to wear coarse linen, not this fine muslin.' He shook a corner of her sari with his hand. 'You'll get boils on the soles of your feet.'

For some reason Shamman thought of Miss Boga again.

'Why is Miss Boga training to be a nurse?'

'To vent her feelings. She can't have a husband and children, but at least she'll have patients.'

'Come on, she was always an advocate of pure love.'

'What do you mean by pure love? The love between mother and son?' Iftikhar seemed bent on lecturing her today.

'No, I mean friendship, compassion for each other.'

'There's no such thing. Friendship between a man and woman develops for one purpose only and that is . . .'

'Oh, please don't! You can't make every woman your wife.'

'You're right. Not every woman can be a wife, but . . .' He ran his fingers through his hair while looking for the right words to continue. 'But Miss Boga's feelings are not love. They have neither the warmth of a mother's unselfish love nor the passion of a beloved's ardour. She's like a dying ember, no, actually she's cold like ice and lifeless like mud, a sort of shabby, worn-down intensity.' He fell silent.

A few minutes later he spoke in a whisper. 'And my love? What is my love like? How do I love? How enchanting this darkness is that surrounds us, you're here, and with you my yearning, unsatisfied soul, but not for a moment would I think of dragging you down to this level where my imagination has placed you. Am I so honourable? Hunh!' He almost spat out the word 'honourable'.

'You think you're being very honest by branding all your virtues as weaknesses and all your strengths as faults?'

'God forbid! But I don't consider honour to be my domain. Do you think I want you to certify my decency?' He seemed irked. 'If I wanted to, I could, right here in this isolated place . . .'

'You can't do anything.'

'Why?' Iftikhar's face fell.

'Because you're not as bad as you have imagined yourself to be.'

'Why?'

'For your peace of mind. You're one of those people who derive immense satisfaction from belittling themselves, perhaps because they think by doing that they've washed away their sins.'

191

'Sins? But which idiot believes in sin and redemption?'

'Your conscience.'

'No, not at all. Conscience is just an illusion, nothing else. Whatever I do . . .'

'You do because you think it's bad and the result turns out to be good.'

'What?'

'You may agree or not, but I know you're good at heart.'

'You're forcing me to be good?'

'Yes. If I didn't believe that, I wouldn't be sitting here alone with you.'

'You're very narrow-minded.'

'You can think what you like. Come, let's go now, it's getting chilly and you might get sick.'

'So, what do you care?'

'I care. Your life isn't as insignificant in my eyes as you've made it out to be for yourself. You still have to do a lot in this world and I must keep you alive for the world.'

'Oh, just for the world, not for anyone else?' He looked downcast. 'I'm tired of living for the world. You want to keep me alive so I can continue suffering?'

'I'm the world too.' Shamman was amazed at her boldness.

'Oh.' His head lowered, Iftikhar remained lost in thought for a long time afterwards.

After Iftikhar had gone, Shamman's thoughts wandered. She placed Iftikhar and Satil on two scales. The very thought of one was like a backward thrust, while the other, surrounding her like an intoxicating vapour from all sides, overpowered her senses. She had sat with Iftikhar for so long, but not once did she experience the savage emotions that overwhelmed her the last time she was in Satil's company. What was this that had caused such a silent stir in her life, this unknown, restless stab which was at once sweet and bitter? She was driven by a desire to give everything up for him, she felt a hunger in her crying out like a beggar's call. What was all this? Why? She could not find an answer.

33

Shamman was reduced to distraction while attempting to reassemble the school's broken pieces. The female custodians snitched portions of potatoes and meat from the lunches that arrived for the students in the afternoon, and the teachers misappropriated the rest. As a result, the girls remained hungry. At first the custodians ignored the warnings and then, when some severity was exercised, they devised another move. They threatened the girls, 'Don't you dare finish all the food. Leave enough for us!' This ploy could not be kept under cover for long and one day someone complained about the tyranny of the custodians. On being questioned, the custodians began sobbing violently.

'What can we do, Miss Sahib? Three children, one crippled mother and one good-for-nothing brother – how can we all manage with just six rupees? This wretched stomach, we can't destroy it either.'

'We're spending so much on the education of our girls and barely have enough for ourselves – how can we provide for these custodians as well?' the parents protested noisily on the other hand.

'Rent along with feeding and clothing four other people besides ourselves – how can we make do with twenty rupees?' the teachers screamed.

Shamman felt as if she were in a charitable establishment, not a school. This wasn't a place of learning, this was a permanent orphanage for the destitute and the impoverished where everyone from the top of the ladder to the lowest rung was enervated. She started giving the female custodians two rupees each from her own purse. Whenever it was possible she invited the teachers to dinner, and every month she paid the fees for two or three indigent girls. But she discovered very quickly that the more she tried to satisfy hunger, the more that hunger increased. If you give a paisa to a beggar soon you'll have ten more to deal with, and if you refuse to help there are some spirited ones who will not hesitate to call you names. In other words, you get hit with reproof for your generosity instead of being rewarded for it. Every Thursday the custodians went out begging in the neighbourhood. Teachers, unfortunate creatures, didn't have the nerve to beg nor were they young enough for streetwalking. Bereft of home or family, what other source of income can they have besides the charity of the schools? They trembled constantly as if they were cows about to be slaughtered.

But Razia Begum strictly observed a policy of defiance. She did not teach the girls anything. All day long she embroidered intricate patterns for Manager Sahib. Shamman complained about her in her report, but Manager Sahib intercepted the report for perusal before it could be sent to the inspectoress of schools and the complaints were quietly done away with. Razia Begum's influence grew at an alarming rate. Payoffs to ensure promotion came into effect. Along with mango chutney she started turning the school into chutney. With Manager Sahib on her side, she began conspiring behind Shamman's back. News about Shamman's visitors travelled to Manager Sahib and he suddenly seemed intent on exhibiting moral fervour. He hinted that Shamman's mode of dress and her lifestyle might be a factor in keeping away girls belonging to respectable families. He knew everything about her. When she woke up, when she went to bed, what she ate and why.

'But who told you?' she would ask in amazement.

'I have to keep tabs on everything, you know,' he would say, wearing a mysterious smile on his face, as if a manager had to perform the function of a CID officer as well. 'I have to boost patriotic zeal in order to obtain contributions, and so the character of the teachers . . .'

Shamman was burned by the word 'character'. What do people think character is? Is it a shrine at which they must lower their heads in the hope of redemption? If a teacher is the worst slattern, but she does her work well, she's a thousand times better than an instructor crafted from sacred clay who is good by necessity but who is engaged in destroying her students' present and future.

'I say, the girls receive notes.'

'What kind of notes?' Shamman controlled herself.

'You know, obscene notes, sent by degenerates. Why don't you do this: gather all the girls who receive these notes and give them a thorough scolding.'

'But how do we find out who gets these notes? First we'll have to catch them.'

'So catch them, I say.' As if notes were pigeons that could be surprised and caught. Anyway, this kind of bird-catching required special experience. These letters didn't arrive by mail. It's the girls who help each other; helping with this exchange of notes is routine. What else can the teachers earning twenty rupees per month and the custodians who are forced to subsist on six rupees a month do except earn a few extra rupees by helping with this exchange? If you reproach the girls the parents hasten to attack you. What do their innocent daughters know of such ploys? And it isn't easy to catch these innocent daughters; they are extremely clever. A thousand tricks are employed to enable the passage of letters from one place to another, and most of the time the letters are from girls to girls. You have to be a seer, too, in order to trail such correspondence.

Along with all this came the examinations. Arrange the benches so the girls can't cheat, have the copies ready, and then spend the whole day supervising. The time for inspection also drew near. Now check the registers to see if all the useless information is filled in or not. What techniques were to be used to cover up the amount that Manager Sahib had misappropriated from the funds allocated for needlework and library books to pay his mother-in-law's debts? Manager Sahib was quite nervous about this matter.

'Well, I say, why don't you put down in the register that the money was spent on flowerpots and seeds and that's that,' he suggested.

'But where are the pots and the seeds? What if the inspectoress wants to check?'

'Just say the girls broke them by accident. I'll have the Chungi officer deliver some old, cracked pots. There are innumerable pots like that lying around in the public gardens. Some I'll send down from my house, and you have flowerpots too, don't you?'

'I distributed mine before the holidays. Who was going to water them?'

'Oh what a shame! Anyway, that's all right.'

'And seeds?'

'Well, just put down that they didn't grow, they were defective. What do you say I get you some from the grocer's shop?'

'But that doesn't account for all the money.'

'Some items related to needlework I'll send from my house.'

'All right.'

'And I'll get some books from the bookseller. Now be careful they don't get damaged because they have to be returned. What about refreshments?'

'That we'll take care of, but what about the hostel? We receive separate funds for it.'

'Don't you worry. Actually I've already made arrangements. Those rooms in the east wing, I'll have fifteen or twenty cots placed there, and my wife will provide the sheets. If you have any extra sheets and pillows you can bring those as well.'

'But this is full-scale deception. What respect can we have in the eyes of the inspectoress after this deceit? What if she finds out?'

'Now there's no way she can find out anything unless . . . anyway, you're the head of this school and I'm sure the school's welfare is foremost in your mind. Do we have a choice? You see, if we want a government grant we have to do everything. Don't worry, I'll take care of everything. All you must do is when she comes . . . oh, I forgot, the poem.'

'Poem?'

'Yes, the poem. Have you prepared it?'

'Prepared the poem? Why?'

'I say, in honour of the inspectoress. My goodness, I nearly forgot. You see, when she comes and sits down, have a pretty little girl place a garland round her neck. She should be wearing nice clean clothes. I think Superintendent Sahib's granddaughter will do just fine.'

'But she's not in our school.'

'I say, everything goes. No one is going to check the registers to see whose name is down. I think you should send for her in the morning, right?'

'As you wish.'

'Oh yes, and after the garlands, have the girls sing the poem . . . oh, you don't have the poem ready, do you?'

'I've already said I don't know how to write poetry.'

'Ohho, what's so difficult? Last time Razia Begum wrote the poem. If you find it somewhere we can use it again. We'll just change around a few words here and there. Or else, let me see, maybe I can come up with something myself.' He strained to cast himself in a poetic mode. 'Hmm . . . hunh?' Suddenly he got it. 'Look here, you know the national high school? They've had several functions and they must have at least a hundred poems lying around. I'll send for them right away. Oh Nanhe, you wretch – oh, excuse me – look here, boy, run over quickly to Masud Sahib and tell him Manager Sahib says salaam and wants the poems.'

'Poems?' the boy mispronounced the word uncertainly.

'*Array*, yes, you donkey, just say, *uff*, you're an idiot – oh, excuse me. Anyway, I'll get them myself. You'll receive them by tomorrow and you can make the appropriate changes. I'll have the school decorated one day in advance and make sure you start the exams from Monday. Plan the Urdu exam for that day.' The inspectoress didn't know any Urdu. This was the only way to avoid an academic inspection.

All the pots available in the vicinity arrived. Some of them had mint plants growing in them, others green chillies, but at least the veranda became abundantly green. The bookseller charged ten rupees for a loan of five hundred books. Who had the time or the inclination to see that most of the books were not only unfit for the girls, they were not fit to be read by anyone? The majority were cheap, smutty novels like *Husband and Wife*, *The Nights of Bliss*, and standard copies of the *Kok Sastra*. All these books were bedecked on the shelves along with other rubbish from here and there. Old magazines, telephone directories and outdated registers were covered very neatly and shelved in such a way that an onlooker would be instantly overwhelmed by their size and, in addition, perceive the trick with the covers as a reflection of organisational skills. The badly scratched benches were polished with oil and water. Calendars and pictures were glued to the walls to conceal their state of disrepair. The girls had been asked to come dressed in neat and clean clothes and they came wearing garments fit for their wedding day; the school turned into Raja Inder's court with much noisy tinkling and jangling of bangles and anklets.

Another clever ploy was used as well. Teachers completed the first half of the paper on the board for the girls to copy so that if the inspectoress was bent on examining their answer sheets and had brought along an expert with her, she would find college level questions solved on those answer sheets. School authorities have to be aware of any tricks the inspectoress may come equipped with.

In addition to this, on tables and in cupboards were examples of the needlework done by the 'girls'. Many of these things had been bought from the bazaar. Some items, like tablecloths, *paan-dan* covers and a model of the Taj Mahal in gold thread, had been borrowed from various households and these, along with Razia Begum's 'Goodnight' and 'Sweet Dreams', were elaborately displayed. Quite a few of these things were imported while others had machine-embroidered patterns on them, but the display was arranged in such a clever way that these items were not within easy reach of anyone who wanted to pick them up and examine them. That was not all. There were other articles, still incomplete, that were on loan from the neighbouring school.

The hostel had been furnished as well. On the cots were pillowcases stuffed with whatever could be found and thrown over them were sheets and bedcovers. On two or three tables nearby some books had been

197

arranged. There, the rooms are furnished. As for the girls, several were selected from different classes with instructions that they should immediately come and offer salutations when they were sent for.

Finally, the inspectoress arrived with the pomp that accompanies a wedding party. To receive her at the gate, which had been decorated with a large welcoming banner and streamers, was Manager Sahib, along with the steward and the school's two Christian teachers. The inspectoress holds a godly position in the world of education. She has the same distinction as Lat Sahib, the governor. And all she generally did was make a tumultuous appearance, scold and reprimand, and then leave.

'Why this cobweb? What's this brick? Whose doll is this?'

Someone should ask her why it was so terrible that if on the two occasions she visited in a year she had to suffer cobwebs and pot-holes. Come decorously, wear garlands, listen to poems presented in your honour, partake of the fresh fruit and delectable sweets procured especially for you, some of which we'll quietly pack up for you to take home so you can taste them at leisure. That's it. Don't interfere any more than this and don't make lists. Why bother with a full report when the chief inspectoress never comes and if she does it's only for a very short time? A cursory report of a cursory inspection, otherwise your own department will get a bad name. In the first place we're Hindustani. Deceit, mismanagement, fraud, these are our birthright. In the second place we are one of the underdeveloped nations. You're wasting your time. What do you care if the receipts carry forged signatures, which, using his left hand, Manager Sahib executed himself, why bother about the thumbprints that students and custodians have stamped on false reports in the register? Why do you embroil yourself in this mess?

And if you still persist, your character, your secret relationships, and details of your trips will be unravelled by means of the local newspaper. In addition, you will be branded as a racist. It's not much of an expense, just four or five rupees. The smooth-talking editor will slash and scatter six generations of your forebears into bits. Whatever deception we have prepared for you, take it all as it is and present it to your superiors. Share with them if you like the silver box and the sweets we're offering in gratitude for this inspection.

After receiving a garland from the superintendent's granddaughter, the inspectoress chose a rather crooked path.

'What's your name?' she asked sweetly.

'Unhunh, no,' the spoilt granddaughter replied, and Manager Sahib felt his life ebbing.

'Oh, she's so shy. Come on, daughter, speak up, tell your name.' He hastened with assistance. Actually he had forgotten the girl's name.

'Waheeda,' someone prompted.

'What class are you in, Waheeda?'

'Speak, child, speak, Waheeda, come on, don't be scared. Why are you scared?' The girl wasn't scared at all; she was glaring sullenly at the inspectoress and Manager Sahib, meanwhile, grew pale with fear. The girl did not budge.

'She just visits every now and then, you know, she's not in any of the classes – she's from a rich family and when she comes here the public is encouraged.' Manager Sahib remembered all the tricks.

What? The inspectoress refused to have tea or breakfast. Someone must have tattled. The inspectoress who came last year – how nice she was! She sat serenely, listening to the poem and constantly nibbling on food at the same time like a cow. This one was too much.

'These are Chungi's pots.' She immediately recognised the pots.

'What? Chungi's? My goodness!' Manager Sahib had become paler and weaker from a combination of forced amazement and fear and, in a desperate attempt to disguise his bewilderment, he bent down and closely examined the numbers on the pots. The stupid steward had forgotten to erase the numbers!

'Oh, that's right, they are from the Chungi,' he said with a sigh of relief. 'The public parks officer donated them to the school.' There, another contribution cut down.

'There are too many pots, no more are needed. The funds will be withdrawn.' She brushed the row of pots with her stick.

What happens is that if you baffle the inspectoress in the first round, then she timidly complies with everything, but if you don't make the right move then you've lost her; bellowing and roaring like a mad elephant, she will trample everything in her path. Like a wild mare this new inspectoress was kicking in every direction. But Manager Sahib had dealt with the worst of them. Who knows how he did it, but he made most of the books disappear so that she couldn't figure out the cost by examining the ones that remained. But, despite persistent requests, she didn't see the needlework. The exam ploy also backfired. At first she looked at a few answer sheets, then spoke to the secretary in whispers and finally announced that because there was an exam in progress the academic inspection would take place another time. When? She couldn't say. The visit would surprise them like an unannounced bomb.

Later she adopted a masterful strategy. She decided that for the time being she would test the teachers instead of the girls. The ground shifted from under Manager Sahib's feet. Completely flustered, he started running around like a scared camel. In all this commotion the pots that had been placed in precarious positions toppled and fell, and the 'Welcome' sign along with the poles and the wooden racks came down over him. Suddenly exhausted and complaining of the recurrence of an old stomach ailment, Razia Begum retired wearily to her room. The other teachers felt they had been widowed. Only the Christian teachers were trapped, but that was just as well.

During this time Manager Sahib corralled the girls to come and sing in the hope that music might alleviate the gravity of the situation. It is said there is great power and magic in music, candles that have been extinguished come to life again, crazed elephants bow down their foreheads. But what a catastrophe! The poem had been given to the girls without any alterations. Hearing a poem read in honour of the district commissioner, the inspectoress burst out laughing. Manager Sahib, who all this time had prevented his legs from collapsing simply by using the strength of his imagination, began shaking violently and, feeling completely baffled, also broke into laughter.

'Sing something else,' came the order in a sweet voice.

'Yes, yes, sing something else. Sing "My desire is on my lips like a prayer" . . . come on, wretches, don't look at my face, start.' Darting frantically from one end of the row of girls to the other, Manager Sahib instructed, 'Sing . . . yes, "My desire".' But the girls, dazed and shy, kept bending and stooping to hide behind each other.

'You see, Miss Sahib? I'm tired of them. You don't know how low our nation has sunk. These are all girls from poor, lower-class families where no one can even read. I'm tired, tired of telling them, teaching them . . . for God's sake, girls . . .' Fearful of his whimpering tone, the girls started 'My desire is on my lips', but despite all their efforts they couldn't bring anything to their lips.

'All right, sing that one, "Better than all the world" . . . come on, start now.'

With great difficulty a girl dragged a fifth note and dropped it at 'all'. The note was very high and it seemed as if an eagle had dropped an egg, flown away and then, turning, had fallen after it. Finally, after much wheedling, nudging of elbows, hiding of noses behind *dupattas*, another girl picked up and stretched the note again and using low-pitched notes began giving proof of Hindustan being better than all the world. It was dreadful.

'That's enough.' The inspectoress rose to her feet. The girls, hurt and embarrassed, stumbling and foundering, ran off like wounded does.

'We know what your school is and why it was established. But we are forced to be lenient with an underdeveloped nation. This is the government's policy. In reality this school does not have the right to remain open for even two days.' She spoke disdainfully as she wrote 'Satisfactory' on her report.

Manager Sahib heaved a sigh of relief. The crisis was averted and it hadn't been all bad. Quickly he grabbed the box of *gulab jamuns* which the inspectoress hadn't touched.

'Ah, what do these brutes know about the taste of these morsels?' he said, looking at the sweets lovingly, and walked off.

All day long Shamman felt dejected. Leniency? But why? Everyone regards those who are inferior with pity. They're weak, they're illiterate, they're useless, and therefore deserving of charity. If this is so then the underdeveloped nations have the right to continue scattering blackness and stagnation over the rest of the world. Why doesn't someone pour petrol over these people and burn them as if they were worms gnawing at the roots of the nation's tree? Keeping them down and continuing to push them into an abyss is inhuman. It is said that violent storms and hurricanes destroy even the waste and debris that is in their path. Oh God, when will that storm rise here which will dissolve all the baseness like an impermanent dye, and wash it away with the sludge? At least then people will stop pushing baseness towards even greater baseness.

34

The inspectoress presented a report that seemed straightforward, but some verbal exchange resulted in delaying the grant for months. The school was threatened with further inspections. Manager Sahib was drained from running around. This year he had trouble getting his

201

children everything they wanted. His wife begged him to abandon his public service and go back to his law practice; they would make do with whatever he earned, but at least he wouldn't be hounded by people from all sides. He owed the teachers four months of salaries. The steward revolted suddenly, handed in his resignation and, changing his profession altogether, got employment as a bricklayer. The gatekeeper and sweepers ran off, and the houseboy disappeared with some items of furniture, leaving a commotion in his wake. Flabbergasted, Manager Sahib, the poor man, darted about in all directions, his jaw hanging in bewilderment. When the door on a cage with wild birds falls open without warning and all the birds flutter and escape, the birdman lunges this way and that after his birds and when he can't grab even one, he sits back on his haunches wearily and calmly watches the flight of the birds. 'Fly away, what do I care . . . fly off to wherever you want to go and take me with you.' Manager Sahib was also exhausted now and, sprawled on Razia Begum's chairbed, he calmly surveyed the destruction of the school.

For some time Shamman was nonplussed, unable to think or act clearly as she tried to find her way in this baffling storm. Although there were better schools than this for her to observe and study, she thought it was cowardly to abandon a place where one had made a break in one's journey only because it was on fire. She had no idea what she should do or how. Without giving it further thought, she left for the Department of Education in Allahabad.

The grand building which housed the Department of Education did not in any way appear to have any connection with education. It looked more like a place of business. One area reminded her of a hospital. In the corridor she saw a row of women who looked anxious and fearful and were there no doubt in anticipation of a job opportunity or a scholarship. All of them looked feeble, sick, distressed and needy. It seems as if after being turned away from every other department, the last place where you can find a promise of sustenance is the department of education. Either they weren't able to get a husband because they were poor or homely, or they were widowed and the relatives on whom they had become dependent had thrown them out. They're here because of the children. They're not interested at all in education, their brain is a dishrag, not only can they not teach, they don't even have the energy to read, but they're here. Of course the education department is also obligated to advance the cause of women's education; why not let this human debris and dirt go in as part of the first load and eventually better material will follow suit.

One of them was nursing her baby and at the same time complaining about her in-laws in a loud voice, recounting their tyranny which had forced her to come here. Another was scolding her child and pouring lamentations about society's shortcomings into the ear of a third woman who was sitting next to her. In other words, here was a picture of what was to come. No matter what happens, what schooling or training is provided, these minute defects are in the genes, they will persist generation after generation. Shamman felt she should go back instead of trying to make an attempt to preserve such a system of education. She should go home, get married and increase the number of impoverished and beleaguered human beings; this is her national legacy. What is to be gained from this mental torture? If the seed is defective, why wait for the plant to mature and bear fruit . . . but . . .

She had gone only so far when the orderly told her to go in. After hours of exhausting debate it was decided that the department would take the school under its wing. The headmistress would remain at her post, but the rest of the staff would be replaced. The question was, what about Manager Sahib who had invested all his money in the advancement of the national school? The receipts showed a substantial investment. Well, that question was shelved for the moment. The national stamp was removed from the school's dossier and it became a government school.

When the school bounced back dressed in a new garment it drew attention to itself in no time. Admissions increased. Manager Sahib made frenzied efforts to get his money back and found himself in a state of extreme distress; it seemed as if he couldn't do any work. His wife was making his life more and more unbearable. Bewildered by all these ups and downs, he married Razia Begum and established two fronts instead of one and had to deal belligerently with a life more spicy and pungent than mango chutney. Then came the news that he was suffering from attacks of depression.

The number of Christian and Hindu girls was on the rise, but the attendance of Muslim girls diminished. The new group of teachers arrived with such confidence that it was difficult to ascertain at first whether they were vigilant or just lazy and whether they taught well or not because most of these teachers, having spent twenty years each in one department, were quite resourceful. A perusal of one twenty-year record revealed the teacher had not stayed for long in any one school.

That was typical of government jobs; if you're tired of one place, on to the next with a transfer. Whenever a teacher had trouble with the headmistress and everyone else down to the female custodian, and her creditors starting beating her door down, she would go whining and snivelling to the inspectoress and have herself transferred. Now how could someone like that be intimidated by Shamman?

However, despite all this the machinery of the school continued to perform smoothly, its wheels whirring like the flow of a pleasing song. The admissions were satisfactory, the results were satisfactory, the instruction was satisfactory. This atmosphere infused with satisfaction on all fronts had created an unsatisfactory weariness, an indolence and lethargy. It was as if a thundering, swirling stream had suddenly begun crawling on flat, level land. In this sluggish life everybody is treading silently along the path of life with their eyes shut. If there is a collision, you sidestep and continue ambling. Life moves slowly. The same sleepy 'tun, tun'. The hour wakes up at the prescribed time, stretches, and then dozes off again, its every movement either taking you forward two steps or pulling you back two spaces. On the languid furniture sit drowsy teachers who long to shake up the hour to make it move faster and faster. Why is the minute hand so ponderous? Does it have to take provisions for the after-life with it? And if the second hand accelerates its swing just a little perhaps its motion will wake up the world. If time didn't move so sluggishly, so surreptitiously, man would not have been so lethargic. 'Tick! Tick!' He too would move swiftly like the parts of a machine.

And the atmosphere too is ponderous, as if there's some immense storm brewing. One push and the dams will open, and then no one knows whether there will be a shower of ambrosia or of flames, but an involuntary expectation weighs heavily upon everyone. An unknown load seems to sit massively upon the shoulders. What will happen? When? And why will it happen? No one knows! But it will happen, something will happen. Inexpensive cloth, grain costing only cowries, but cowries are not available even in exchange for blood. Why is there so little money manufactured? The copper pots and pans in the house – they can be melted down to make cowries.

The stifling atmosphere became heavier. People inhaled the air and shook their heads meaningfully. Like worms and reptiles that dart off to their sanctuaries when a storm is approaching, there was a flurry among the businessmen in the bazaars. They started amassing gold and silver and began hiding it in the bosom of mother earth; the blast of the storm will not be so powerful as to make mother earth spit out her trust. Suddenly the red star in the sky burst open like a wound and people saw blood dripping from it. An invisible miasma arose from all sides and a silent thunder shook hearts and minds.

The war broke out

The ripened sore erupted and a torrent of pus gushed forth. We have to see whom it drags along in its current and who is saved. Germany attacked Poland. Why did Germany suddenly feel this itch? England and France, compatriots of the oppressed, ran forward with banners of freedom.

'We are no longer your friend,' they told Germany. But like a stubborn child, it continued to expand. At this end, Russia too felt some tingling and joined the ranks of martyrs. In the flash of an eye two greedy children cut up Poland in half as if it were a sweet biscuit, and devoured it. There, that's the end of that.

And what will happen next? Poland too will become a slave. Well, Hindustanis have been in bondage for centuries. Hunger sharpens the appetite and the elements strengthen the body. Flesh is just a useless excuse, the real thing is the skeletal frame, and to keep it together, the cover of skin. These human skeletons, black and crooked like aubergines, covered with sores and bruises, whom nature has crafted with its own special hands and then, incinerating them in the scorching sun and waves of torrid air, it swaddles them in dust and dirt, hardening them like a pumice stone, these cannot be affected by bondage. But how will the delicate creatures of the north, which shrivel at the slightest touch of even a sharp glance, endure this type of tyranny?

While working on worthless matters in her office, Shamman's thoughts often wandered far away. The blue curtain hanging in the window protected her from the curious eyes of the people on the street, but where the curtain ended she could see the legs of those who walked by and sometimes she sat for hours observing the pace of these legs. Going past her window would be dark, crooked and withered legs, skinny legs wrapped in torn and dirty dhotis, infirm legs splattered with mud and dirt, and sometimes disfigured legs cringing from the weight of a heavy paunch. Once in a while she would also see a pair of legs encased in satiny trousers and sparkling-clean socks. She was tired of sitting there. The whole world seemed to turn into legs and stride past her office window. She felt sorry for them. Don't they get exhausted? How long have they been walking and how long will they walk? No one protects them from the cold and frost, from the heat of the sun.

Every day a new storm of legs sped past her window. This storm arose from the nearby mill and travelled towards the city. Immersed in fetid syrup and rotting molasses, the weary current flowed this way every day. Some time before the mill closed for the day, a lonely leg accompanied by a wooden stick slowly and painstakingly lumbered by her office. It was Shamman's custom to throw down a paisa when she heard the 'thak, thak' of the wooden stick and then wait as a dark, skinny, shrivelled hand reached into the filth of the gutter and cleverly drew the paisa out. Then, saddened and listless, she watched the leg disappear. Why? Why do these legs, these blackened skeletons, come into the world? This led to the thought that if these skeletons were not so scrawny, how would the Taj Mahal be seen as the world's eighth wonder? If so many beggars and flies didn't buzz around on the main steps of the Jamia Masjid, what proof would there be of the splendour of the Mughal era?

If, God forbid, the Germans go crazy and develop designs on Hindustan as well, what will happen to these ageless mausoleums, this sacred earth that we adorn with lush green fields just to satisfy our yearning to till the land, these long roadways that we tar with our blood and sweat so they can swallow dust from automobiles? When we come out of the factories, will the steps of the Jamia Masjid still be there with the vendors from whom we buy hot, tasty kebabs? When dark, dense clouds roll in and the rain pours in misty rhythms, the nightingales will sing, cuckoos will heave sighs of longing, and lovers will dash to these very mausoleums to quench their thirst for love. But these fascists will annihilate our places of celebration, they will pilfer the bones of our ancestors, the bones for which we have shed rivers of blood through the centuries, which are more precious than pearls and diamonds, and which are Hindustan's pride. It is the duty of every Hindustani to give up his life to protect them. *Culture will not change + modernize because all it cares about is protecting the family, the community*

The morsel served by Poland proved unsatisfactory and the beautiful lady of France was swept away next. These animals are not ashamed of raising their hands to a woman? The Rani of Jhansi was also a woman. How feminine she was. See the last embers of the slowly dying funeral pyre in this spirited beauty . . . but the shower of benevolence cooled it in one downpour. What good are these embers in this land of bones?

The clouds did pour and poured without restraint. Dams broke and torrents gushed forth. But why is Hindustan still arid? Has the viper not inhaled the odour of Hindustani blood as yet? This dark blood is very fetid no doubt, although a mixture of some white particles has created a muted brown appeal in it. But it still requires many more transfusions.

206

Why is the 'Better than all the world' Hindustan still sheltered from the tangles of the swastika? Every nation in the world has looked at Hindustan lovingly, everyone was inspired by a concern for improving and developing it. The Aryans arrived to teach the black-skinned Dravidians. Even Alexander was tempted. Iran and Afghanistan felt waves of affection, the Tartars ground their teeth and kissed it, the Mughals swept across it with their love and warmth, and then the scales of European businessmen began to rock. Hindustan's hospitality spread out a tablecloth before them all, waiting on them with folded hands. 'Here's everything, eat your fill, and take what you can back with you. We'll sleep on empty stomachs so that your granaries can be full. All we ask is that you allow us to be your orderlies and your ayahs, so that we can bow our black foreheads before your whiteness.'

The weather changed. Shamman became restless. This stifling atmosphere was becoming even more putrid. She was very uncomfortable and felt anger. At whom? She didn't know. The teachers' lethargy had been transformed into anxiety. Who knows what wind will arise from where, blowing away who knows whom? A nervous scuttling had begun. The war was thousands of miles away, but there was a secret dread buried in every heart.

Driven by anxiety, she took fifteen days off from work and decided to go somewhere far away. She didn't know where she was going even when she had arrived at the railway station. The first train was heading for Madras. She boarded it. Where is she going, to whom? She didn't feel the need to figure out all that. Why did she need a destination? If she had to travel, why be bothered with a set plan? She had a third class ticket and, from a Hindustani's viewpoint, she had the necessary paraphernalia for completing a journey. In a short while the commotion typical of rail travel provided a taste of life's last journey. Sick, broken, ungainly human beings, dressed in dirty, foul-smelling, shabby rags were heading for God knows where. Perhaps they too didn't know what their destination was. She felt anger as well as amusement. What foolishness to travel and that too in a third class compartment. There were times she wanted to get off at a station and go back, or else lie down on the tracks so that this tiring journey could end once and for all. But then she wondered about that. Transmigration is an uncertain phenomenon, and it's so confusing. You don't come into this world again and again to get a taste of these jolts in the train, these crowds, this rotting food, these smells. Whatever it is, grab it with both hands in this life.

In changing trains one encountered the pleasure of going from one world to the next because for third class passengers it is difficult to obtain even a place worse than an animal shed. She had to spend four long, dragging hours resting against her holdall at the platform. The second class waiting room was locked and there was an Englishman resting in the first class waiting room. With the exception of this white man, all other people, black and yellow, were piled on top of one another everywhere on the platform.

Every vendor seemed intent on selling his wares to her. She was tired of saying no to them. In addition to the beggars, she was attacked by orphanage workers, people toiling for shelters for widows, and those engaged in the sacred work of caring for the cow. She was extremely irritated by what she saw. If you go to an orphanage you are hard pressed to find a single orphan there, and a shelter for widows has no reason to exist when there are so many men around. And why do you need these shelters when there are streets available for orphans and for the women there are the *kothas*? Anyway, these are matters that are best left alone.

Again and again her gaze travelled from a small boy who had been staring closely at the bananas that peeped from her basket like alluring courtesans, to the dogs that ran around in all directions as if busy with some important task. The boy was extremely animated. His elderly ayah had to wrestle with him to keep him under control and repeatedly threatened him with references to his mother who was off somewhere. But the child had an uncanny ability to spin. He would jump up and execute a somersault without warning and overturn everything in his path.

'That's not nice, baba,' the ayah would say and for a while he would stop. But soon his body would be attacked anew by waves of motion. First he kicked the canvas holdall, then he started pulling at his shoelaces, his head rolled like a movable toy to his left, right, front and back, and within minutes he had turned into a tiny, dynamic earthquake.

He gazed longingly at the bananas. The stamp of 'that's not nice' had made them even more attractive and desirable. He couldn't understand how the innocent desire for such sweet and delicious bananas could be tinged with the bitterness of 'that's not nice'. He knew that the ayah was a liar and often used similarly unpleasant ploys with him. He ran towards the engine several times; does this massive whistling giant pull all these carriages? He was also fascinated by the newly wed couple. The bridegroom in the front and behind him, her *dupatta* tied to him, the bride. If Ayah would let him, he'd swing a few times by that *dupatta*. Ayah didn't let him jump on the weighing machine either and forbade him from marching on the row of suitcases as well. Finally, feeling helpless, he would stand still, watching passers-by, his face involuntarily mimicking the expressions on their faces.

'Would you like a banana?' Shamman asked the boy, tired of being alone.

'No,' he said quietly, looking at the ayah from the corner of his eye. 'Taking someone else's thing is bad, isn't it?' He spoke excitedly and turning his attention from the bananas he proceeded to scatter the luggage nearby.

For some time a group of sickly looking young men had been loitering around her, humming, making suggestive gestures. A reflection of their suppressed and stifled desires danced nakedly on their faces. To vent their feelings they swore, using epithets that would be impossible to translate into action. Standing on the platform were many *burka*-clad figures playing football with the crippled intellects of these men. Close by was a bride, who, her veil lowered, was engaged in bombarding them. A nice-looking boy sat holding a sex manual in English, his posture enabling Shamman's glance to fall on its illustrated subject matter each time she looked in his direction. For nearly an hour he had been trying to memorise the one picture. He was aware that the women sitting nearby could see the picture and when he happened to catch their eye, a lewd smile spread on his face, making him breathless. Using this strange and silent form of exchange, he was communicating secretly with the women in *burkas*. He was also receiving responses, some nervous, some filled with loathing, some extremely curious. The coquettish bride's face was concealed, but, overcome with exhaustion, she stretched coyly. The child's innocent eyes, which were engaged in conducting a love affair with the bananas, were slowly becoming lewd and brazen like the young man's. He was stamping his feet in exasperation, and spitting. A few times he spat on the ayah as well and then, just to provoke her, he shoved his finger into his nose, sucked on the buttons of his shirt, and undid his shoelaces.

A brawl ensued among the amorous young men for some reason. The epithets became increasingly more original. The basket with the bananas and the water pitchers came under attack while bewildered legs slipped, assuming different positions. At first the boy was nonplussed by this commotion. Then his eyes brightened, his cheeks turned red, and he started laughing loudly, screaming at the same time.

'Bananas! Bananas! Ahha, bananas!' The sight of the trampled bananas was driving him to ecstasy. He ran towards the fray to take part in it, but the ayah pulled him back and plonked him on the holdall.

When things quietened down somewhat and the boy stretched out face down on the holdall, Shamman opened a box and took out some chocolates and biscuits.

'It's not nice,' the boy shouted without moving.

'Ayah, bring the child to me,' Shamman ordered the ayah.

'Memsahib, he's very naughty. His mother is shopping, she said she'd be back by two, but who knows when she'll be back.' Finally the ayah was forced to let the child go to Shamman.

'What's your name?' Shamman filled both his hands with chocolates.

'Memsahib, he misbehaves all day long, doesn't study, he's very naughty.'

The boy didn't eat the chocolates. Instead, he lined them up on the suitcases and started clapping. The ayah continued to lament his bad behaviour. Shamman observed the child closely. He would build a tower with the chocolates and then hit it hard, making the chocolates scatter, after which he laughed triumphantly at the destruction he had wrought.

'What will you be when you grow up?' Shamman asked him the question that teachers are most fond of asking.

'I'll ... I'll be a soldier.' He looked at the constable, who, after dispersing one brawl, was now leaning against a pole waiting for the next breakout. How dull would this world be if these riots didn't take place. Then constables would have nothing to do except lean against poles, dozing. If the boy didn't make small towers and strike them down, what else would he do except break up luggage and spit on his ayah? If only these constables and these children had something else to do as well.

'Does Mummy hit you?' Suddenly Shamman felt that the boy probably asked for a lot of beating. A few times she too wanted to squeeze his beautiful, red cheeks and hug him hard. The child wrinkled his brow at the mention of his mother.

'She's very naughty, Mummy!' the boy said irately and Shamman had the feeling that she had known the boy for a long time. She's seen him before somewhere. How fresh his lips were. Some people resemble fruit and sweets; no sooner do you see them than your nose is filled with the aroma of popping corn. There are others who smell like fresh grapes and slices of pineapple. He was like a section of an orange that she wanted to taste.

'I have a gun. It's in the bedding. Do you want to see it?' The boy attacked the bedding roll diligently.

'No, no, baba, you can't open the holdall,' the ayah with the English deportment rebelled.

'I'll tear it.' The boy glared at her.

'How can you tear it? Mummy will beat you so much.'

'I'll shoot Mummy with my gun . . . *thain!*' the defeated soldier said, puffing his red cheeks.

'No, no, that's not nice,' Shamman said patronisingly and he cast a distrustful glance at her too.

'You're also naughty. Mummy, Ayah, everyone is naughty, I'll shoot everyone . . . *thain!*'

The boy's anger aroused Shamman's affection. Such a small child and so many enemies. Oh, the poor little boy.

'I'm sorry.' The boy's voice was strangled in his throat as he spoke angrily to the woman who had just made an appearance. The little giant of anger and revolt positioned himself upright on the holdall.

'What? You!'

In the midst of a crowded platform two bewildered friends fell into each other's arms like shunted rail carriages coming together.

'Alma, you?'

'Where are you going?' they both said at the same time.

'I'm on holiday. And you?'

'I'm going home. You must come with me.'

'Why didn't you answer my letters . . .' Just then the train pulled into the station and they had to run. Alma talked to one of the railway guards and got permission to have Shamman with her in second class.

Like little girls the long-lost friends spent a great deal of time asking each other questions. Who had the time to listen to answers? Alma was on her way to Bankipur. Shamman decided to spend her holidays there. There wasn't enough time to listen to all the stories in the train, and the stories weren't that brief that they could be told effectively in one sitting.

Alma gave the child a resounding slap. He was twisting his foot around while changing his clothes. He screamed once very loudly and was silent after that. Not a tear fell. He said something with his blazing red, insolent eyes, his nostrils flared from the force of emotion, but the milk dropped to a simmer just as it was about to come to the boil. He quietly submitted to having his clothes taken off, but the expression on his face gave the impression he was being skinned.

'I'm hungry,' the boy said indignantly.

'Ayah, give him a biscuit.'

'I'll throw away the biscuit. I want rice.'

Alma ground her teeth and raised her hand again, but Shamman caught it in mid-air.

'Why do you hit him?'

'You, you don't know . . . he, he . . .' Alma's throat was constricted and she grimaced like a child who had been beaten. Shamman didn't say anything. Her head turned, she became lost in thought and the train raced on.

35

'You want to know why I hit him?' Before turning in, Alma started pacing up and down in her small room. The boy slept with the ayah. The house was tidy and clean, but for some reason a stifling atmosphere prevailed. Some of the rooms were in a state of disrepair and had been closed up for years.

'I want to kill him. Do you know I tried to destroy him, I placed my own life in jeopardy to get rid of him, but each time my good health came in the way. I tolerated him in my womb as if he were a loathsome disease. I cursed his existence at every step, and finally gave birth as if he were something I had to vomit out.' She spoke animatedly. Her eyes were still sizzling and dark, but a fine curtain of weariness clouded her gaze which one glimpsed only now and then. She had put on some weight and the waist that once stretched like a tiger's torso had thickened. The delicate flower-laden bough was now an empty branch. But her mind was virgin still and wished to remain virgin, even though her body had become a mother.

'I refused to nurture this cactus, but there was too much milk and I was forced . . . oh!' She cringed and sat down close to Shamman as if she wanted to take refuge in her lap. 'Believe me, Shamman, I clasped this viper to my breast. It is said that when an infant's chaste lips touch a mother's body the nymphs in heaven burn with envy because they can never be mothers. But, Shamman, people lie. Only I know how my soul spat at me all the time this viper's offspring sucked on my blood.'

'Don't be so upset.' Shamman lovingly pulled her closer.

'You don't know . . . oh, you don't know.'

'Alma, you're so upset – is this all because he's illegitimate?'

'Shush, you silly girl! If Satil's child was more sacred than the flame of the gods, even then he would torment me, crucify me. No magic, no benediction can purify him. When my conscience collided with the body of an animal . . .'

'But how is it that innocent child's fault?'

'Fault? Hunh! You didn't look closely. He is the same.' She became fearful. 'The same, the very same viper!'

And suddenly Shamman remembered the feeling she had had on first seeing the boy, that she knew him from before; it wasn't just her imagination. The boy was a miniature version of Satil. The same robust build and buoyant gait, the same passionate spirit. So Alma was justified. Nature was mocking her. If the child had resembled Alma, her self-love might have taken over. But the man who was always the recipient of her hatred overwhelmed her in such a way that he merged himself in with her blood. Love and hate. At the apex both assume a form that makes it difficult to distinguish between them. The deity and Satan – their worship converges at a point and comes to a standstill. How fine this point is so that even the eye of the mind can't discern it.

'But Alma, you're very broad-minded and if society treated a child like this you'd call it cruel.'

'Society disapproves of such a child because he comes into the world without first being showered with society's incantations, and I . . .'

'No. He enters the world without society's permission. You hate Rolly because he came into the world without a command from you. In the same way society . . .'

'But why? What does society have to do with this?'

'So that the number of helpless beings does not increase. You know that the responsibility of something like this falls on the woman, the man doesn't bear the brunt at all. Now just think: if the stamp of marriage isn't there, what will a woman, whose economic status is near zero, do?'

'I see. In your opinion illegitimate children are a burden simply due to economic reasons?'

'Of course. Think. Why shouldn't a mother love a child according to nature's rules? Isn't the child a part of her body? The giver offered a benefaction and the receiver took it. Why then should the father be afraid, why should the mother quake?'

'Because raising this child is a burden.'

'And after marriage?'

'All men suffer that because they deem it their duty to do so.'

'A duty imposed by society?'

'Yes. But by now man is so used to bearing this burden that he considers the child "his". The word "his" is enough to satisfy his feelings of egotism.'

'And he doesn't consider that which is illegitimate to be his?'

'He's forced not to, and legally the child isn't his either. Without a legal contract the child's mother is also a stranger to him.'

'But the mother? Why should the mother hate this child?'

'Why?'

'Because the child didn't bring a wage earner with him. The onus of his upbringing becomes a chain around her feet and tangles her up.'

'Shush, all this is nonsense! Mothers want to destroy such children for one reason alone, and that is that they hate the man who fathered the child. They avenge this hatred by twisting the child's neck.'

'God forbid! God forbid! I consider such a woman to be an animal.'

'You're silly. Animals are not so heartless, nor are they so stupid. They don't set dates and have weddings . . . have you ever heard of a donkey wearing a *sehra*?'

Both broke into spontaneous laughter. The dark clouds scattered.

'Alma, you're crazy. No matter whose child he is, he's so lovable.'

'Rubbish! He has no brains, he's just like a lump of flesh. I don't pay any attention to his schooling. I have no idea what he's learning in school.'

'What are your plans for his future?'

'My plans . . .' Her eyes blazed again.

A fierce scream arose from the boy's room followed by more screams which rang through the whole house. Both of them leapt up, Alma in the front, Shamman running behind her.

'No, no . . .' The boy was face down on his bed. Alma picked him up and for a moment Shamman thought she saw a gleam of soft light in her eyes. But suddenly the boy slipped from her arms with a violent shriek.

'I'm sorry . . . sorry . . .' he howled in dread. A shadowy expression of concern flitted over Alma's face and was gone.

'Silent! Be quiet!' She began showering him with blows and she might

214

have strangled him if Shamman and the ayah hadn't dragged her out of the room. For a long time afterwards she trembled from the impact of her emotion. It seemed as if it was a giant she had just wrestled with, not a child.

'I'll finish him one day ... I'm not afraid of dying, but this life sentence ... my life ...' Like an angered lioness she paced furiously in the small room. Tormented, she clasped the fingers of one hand with the other, then pulled them apart forcefully. It seemed as if someone had woven a web around her mind so that the more she pulled at it, the tighter it got.

'But it's not the child's ...'

'He's not a child,' she said in a loud voice. 'This is *he* himself, he has taken this form to torment me, to destroy me. He didn't think the shame was enough and now to trample me under foot ...'

'Are you mad? You're the boy's mother.'

'No, no, I'm not his mother. If you can become a mother simply by giving birth, then ... then ... no, if a cactus winds itself around a cambeli vine, would you start calling the vine a cactus? If a snake finds its way into this vase, will the vase turn into a snake hole?' She squeezed the vase on the mantelpiece with both hands. 'You can't understand my pain.' She turned abruptly and the vase hit the floor with a melancholy thud. Alma gazed apprehensively at the worms that came out of the vase and scurried to take refuge in different parts of the room.

'No, no, this can't be, this can't be ... this can never be.' She acted as if she had lost her mind. Shuddering, she bent down and attempted to put the broken pieces together with trembling hands. Shamman was afraid for her. She tried to drag her away and seat her on the bed, but Alma's rage took over.

'Before I'm in pieces like this I will toss him in the dirt and throw him away.' She ground her teeth as she spoke. Her face resembled that of a monster. Shamman was repelled.

'You're pretending, Alma,' Shamman said scornfully.

'What?'

'Yes, you're enjoying putting on this act, you're lying.'

'Shamman.'

'All right now, don't give yourself airs. I didn't expect you to talk like this in my presence. You love your child and you're trying to fool me.'

'What? Love?' Alma seemed ready to flare up again.

'Don't lie to me, I know what is going on. You love Rolf very much, but you want to display that love by blanketing it in false hatred.'

215

'You . . .'

'Be quiet! I didn't think you were so mean-spirited. Alas, you have shattered all my pleasant dreams like the vase. You're a coward and a deceiver. How liberal you are, indeed. Call illegitimate offspring legitimate, but start taking refuge under cover of illusory ploys. Don't keep lying in my presence, don't make me lose all respect for you. Tell me truthfully – didn't you turn your motherhood into an ogre? What ideals you bragged about once, but your conscience is taking a beating from your intelligence, your maternal instinct. It is not true that you never loved Satil.'

'Shamshad . . .'

'Don't talk any more nonsense. You adored him, but your vanity didn't allow you to admit that. This philosophy of yours that the soul and the body are two separate entities is absolute rubbish. How can it be that your body loved Satil, but your soul hated him? You crazy woman, the heart and the soul can be deceived, but the body can never be duped. When the time comes it tells the truth. But you don't want to admit that you loved Satil and your soul is punishing you for desiring him, and because you couldn't have him, you're punishing the child for this burning loss, forgetting that he is also your child. Just think for a minute, you silly girl, think of the myriad weaknesses that are concealed in this strength you think you're displaying.'

'Why would I be afraid to hide my love?' A note of helplessness crept into Alma's voice and it cracked. *Shamsaan speaking to Alma*

'You're afraid of yourself. Alma, there's no one you're more afraid of than yourself, you don't have the courage to speak the truth to yourself. And you have another terrible weakness, which you'll never admit. You profess to be very strong, but actually, you're afraid of society.'

'Hunh! You think you can say all this and the whole world will believe you.'

'You've started lying a lot, you've turned life into magical incantations. Tell me truthfully, what name did you give the school for the boy?'

'Rolf. Why do you ask?'

'No, give me the full name.'

'Why?' Colour rushed to her face.

'You see how embarrassed you are at the mention of the father's name?'

'What do you mean? These are personal matters.'

'Absolutely, and I have no right to interfere. Forgive me, I won't say anything else.'

'His father was not good enough . . . and in the second place . . .'

'And in the second place you didn't have a certificate with his name.'

'Yes.' Alma looked apprehensive.

'And that's all you're angry about. So here's the truth then, isn't it? Do you see the fate of your ideals?'

For a short while an awkward silence hung between them. Restless, the two friends breathed wearily. It seemed as if both of them were tired. Outside, the moon was struggling to emerge from under a cloud and the breeze rippled through the leaves. It was late. Far away in the distance wild jackals cackled sleepily.

'You were always a coward, that's why you always attacked everyone so viciously. And these feelings you have about the child, these are nothing but an expression of the revenge being exacted by your numbed maternal instincts. Don't fight the mother in you, you'll suffer terrible defeat.'

Seated on the bed, Alma twisted and wrung her hands. Pain and helplessness surfaced on her fatigued face. Wrinkling up her discerning eyes, she burst into tears like a child. Silent tears travelled down her black, sickly cheeks like glimmering streams. Driven by facial tension, her upper lip moved back to reveal her teeth, which were still pointed, but didn't look poisonous any more.

'Get rid of this delusion,' Shamman said, helping her place her head on the pillow. 'What's there to be ashamed of? Rolf is such a beautiful child. I never think that Satil has a part in his creation. He just seems like my dear Alma's pretty little toy. Listen, Alma . . .'

But Alma had dozed off into deep sleep. Shamman's lullaby had summoned the slumber that had been evading her for years and, like an innocent baby, she became oblivious in the twinkling of an eye. Shamman, however, could not sleep. She slowly straightened Alma's legs and went to stretch out on the divan. Her thoughts sped from her like horses without reins.

Alma had aged after only one child. Nurturing only one plant had drained her completely. The delicate waist, the firm body, they were gone. Shamman glanced at her own body and the aroma of ripened grapes filled her nostrils. She remembered the grape Alma had thrown at her a long time ago. And Alma? Like a pit that's been sucked dry. What had she done to herself?

She thought of Satil, the afternoon when he had been rolling on dry

217

leaves, and then she gazed at Alma's withered cheeks. Her heart ached. She wanted to get up quietly and kiss those wet, melancholy cheeks. The slumbering Alma, on whom the waking Alma rode with a sword like a sorceress, looked so innocent. The disdainful arches of the eyebrows had slackened and, instead of resembling a *devdasi* of Ellora, she looked just like an ordinary woman. Her breast moved in the rhythms of motherhood. Perhaps in a dream she was kissing the boy whom in her waking hours she had given the role of her delusion's gatekeeper.

The next morning Shamman tried to make friends with Rolf. The child was extremely intelligent and perhaps just to annoy Alma he had sneaked Satil's intelligence. Like him he raised his eyebrows and glared darkly as he talked. Rejected by his mother, the boy latched on to Shamman with a passion. And he was stubborn like Alma; if there was something he wanted there was no way anyone could dissuade him from obtaining it. Alma looked at him with quiet eyes, but was embarrassed to express any affection, behaving as if she had taken off all her clothes in public. The seedling, buried for four years, had become sickly and lifeless.

Gradually her reserve crumbled. At first the child reacted with distrust, exhibiting anger. Then, astounded, he became friendly. The river's dam was broken. It seemed the gushing current had become more forceful because it had been held in check all this time; it was no longer easy to stop its flow. All day long Alma's eyes followed Rolf and, when he was out of sight, her gaze wandered restlessly in search of him.

When Shamman was leaving after having stayed longer than her intended two-day holiday, Alma clung to her and wept. She had softened. When the torrent of a stream falls upon the earth it creates gashes in the earth. The current of love fell upon Alma's starving motherhood with such force that it became a well. Mother and son came to see Shamman off at the station. When the train moved, Shamman heaved a sigh of relief. She was happy that she had brought together two children who had been angry with each other.

Shamman helped Alma soften + reconnected Alma + her son Rolf.

218

36

The heat was at its maximum. It seemed as if the sun had lost its way and was slowly coming closer. The world is in a whirl. Germany has incinerated France. Spreading its wings wide, the Nazi eagle has swooped over the lovely lady who carried the banner of freedom for centuries, the goddess of art and literature. Free France left the enslaved France sobbing in the Nazi jungle and took refuge in England. The liberated fantasies of all the nations which were buried under Nazi pressure came together in England. How nice it would be if this beloved son, this treasure of England, this Hindustan, could also be free from its mother's lap and breathe the air of freedom; thus a liberated Hindustan would be born in one of its corners.

Tired of the drudgery at school, Shamman started going to the club. But she didn't feel any better. She didn't know where her peace of mind had taken off to. Her life was dragging itself forward sluggishly. That was when she met Mansur. He was from a very wealthy family, but his heart was filled with love for the country. He wore coarse cotton and owned many fabric shops where *khadar* was sold.

She had the chance to travel to the village with him on a trip which was undertaken for the purpose of rural reform. The delightful picnic proved extremely gratifying. Zamindar Sahib was also a progressive, although he had a passion for hunting, and was a very good friend of Mansur's as well. The villagers arrived wide-eyed in droves to see the people who provided them with their cakes of grain and flour. They were overwhelmed with reverence, bewildered, as if they could not believe that there was such a thing as rural uplift. They had never felt a need for it. They had become so accustomed to bowing their foreheads that their very feelings had become numb. The plough and the oxen are the riches with which these farmers have cleft the earth's bosom, extracted grain from it, not for themselves, but for throwing into pits. These farmers embrace only the *havan*, they believe they will have eternal redemption if they keep the gods happy.

But these simple illiterates have another characteristic. They tire quickly of one master and, when their noses are thinned on one side from rubbing as they worship, they turn towards another god in order to breathe. That is why their noses are so sharp. They haven't the slightest idea what will happen if the German wheel turns. Unending oppression has made them completely fearless. They don't know that Germany is bombing Britain. So used to peace, how will they endure this conflagration? What will happen to them when they discover that the world is not just comfortable rooms, it is also the sun's blaze, the chill of ice, and gusts of wind?

But these starving, naked beggars don't belong to anyone. Hindustan's riches and its wealthy inhabitants can be conquered, but its straining, struggling paupers and their silently mutinous hearts cannot be won over.

In the evening the entire village received orders from the rulers to offer prayers for the victory of the rulers. The temple bells clanged vociferously and calls to prayer echoed from the mosques, but the hearts of these dejected farmers remained mute. What curses can they have for any enemy when for centuries they have been praying for the longevity of their own enemies?

The evening meal was delightful. Zamindar Sahib had arranged for the game to be roasted along with which came buttery chappatis. The gramophone played late into the night and the next morning everyone returned to the city. The first instalment of national reform wasn't so bad after all.

Isolation forced her to turn to the newspaper as her friend. Actually, the news was very interesting now. The most scant information about any new battle in Europe created a commotion. Country after country was slipping into Germany's massive jaw. Dark clouds were hovering over the *sarkar*'s golden ornamentation. Hitler's rapacity was on the increase. The *sarkar* was nervous; what had taken years to accomplish was now threatened with destruction. No one could be trusted. That same Germany which had been forced to grind its nose into the dirt by the standard-bearers of fairness, now seemed intent on stampeding like a mad elephant.

Third term examinations came along. Who started this system of examinations? What are they but a way of tormenting both the examinees and the examiners? Study for fifteen days and then a pile of meaningless papers. Something, no matter how nonsensical, has to be written down and then to give marks for it becomes the job of the examiner. Who knows what the real purpose of these marks is.

Pacing up and down in the examination hall made her feet swell. Give this one a drink of water, bring that one ink; one forgot to bring her pen, another one had an accident with her nib. Run with blotting paper, ruler and knife. This habit of borrowing and lending is a mystery; why don't people also borrow noses, ears and eyes along with inkwells, paper and pencils?

Shamman decided to go home for the December holidays. In the evening she packed all her luggage and sat down comfortably in an armchair to rest and pass some time dozing before leaving for the station. This time she was quite homesick. A whole year had gone by since her last visit. Who knows what shape the family will be in? She wondered how many teeth Amma had lost; it might be just as well if she's lost them all so she could be fitted with dentures and suffer no more discomfort. How many more children does Manjhu have? The sixth was a boy, or was it a girl? It has been four years – who can remember? And who knows what the total is now; after all, Manjhu was very fertile. Poor Sanjhli tried everything and couldn't produce even a baby mouse, and now her husband is reduced to a skeleton. The sisters-in-law are probably the same; they don't get along with anyone, not even their husbands, the babies don't stop coming. Well there's a need for children. It's wartime. The boys will become soldiers and return as the wounded, while the girls will bandage and nurse these wounded. What pleasure does man get from all this breaking up and repair?

The orderly brought in a <u>telegram</u> and Shamman's thoughts were scattered.

Come to me.
Iftikhar

Her heart knocked against her ribs. The four words were transformed into an enormous stack comprising countless words. She read the telegram over and over just to make sure she hadn't missed anything. Her heart burned. A splash of water on the face of someone dying from thirst and that too so scant that the thirst only flares up further. That night she left for Bhawali.

Where is she going? Very soon she forgot that she was being pulled along by the cord of a kite and, tossing about on destiny's hands, she was getting closer to the wheel. Hidden desires and fettered dreams broke free of their ropes and sprinted away from her. These last few years her dull life had blanketed her emotions with a cemented layer of constraint. Her dress had been reduced to a simple, rather homely-looking sari and an unattractive blouse; in order to encourage moral

she become simple

221

decency among the girls she abstained from wearing fashionable clothes.
Her life had sunk into permanent sadness and monotony. But today she
felt as if, bursting through the cemented layer, a small seedling was
raising its head, a withered yellow shoot was finding itself flustered by
the awareness of a new warmth.

Last month she had sent Iftikhar a little money and some warm
clothes. A few vitamins he had mentioned in passing in his letter, and a
sweater she had knitted with her own hands, she had mailed only
recently. She remembered how the blasts of Iftikhar's coughing fit
reverberated in her head during their last meeting. If it were possible she
would take off her skin to provide warmth to his shrunken body. It is
no longer difficult to donate blood to another person. She decided this
time she would make every effort to transfer a little of her blood to his
body. Her eyes shut, she transformed herself into blood and raced
through Iftikhar's body. A shy bride in red! How effortlessly she could
be one with him there. Wearing this blood-red dress, the bride crawls
quietly into his heart, slips into his lungs, kisses his cheeks and dances
on his lips! Iftikhar was so gracious; he had never even touched her
hand. True, he drew her towards him with a magnetic charm, but only
so close that she felt the faint enchanting glow without being singed by
it. And then he slackened his grip so that she fell back in surprise. If he
too were audacious, and like Satil his body had the power to consume
like the plague, she would never look at him again. Would she
experience this same feeling of intoxicating exhilaration if a bucketful
of honeyed nectar was overturned on her?

How sacred their relationship was. That day when she entrusted her
quilt to Iftikhar she had also wrapped her dreams in it. When, during
the interminably silent nights of isolation, she heard frightening voices
laughing all around her, screeching, 'Alone! Alone!' she quietly sneaked
her lone shivering soul into this quilt.

She had an old photograph of Iftikhar in which he was staring at
some faraway point in the distance. The lower half of the picture was in
light while the left side was engulfed in darkness. The spirit of resolution
danced on his lips and it seemed as if the force of darkness pressed upon
his face, but he was struggling resolutely with the current. This picture
always remained close by her.

Recently Iftikhar had sent her some poems. These were burning,
revolutionary poems but his heart also sang the sweet songs of love. In
these vibrant verses he had seen Shamman's fluttering yellow sari which
had captivated his heart and his mind like a kaleidoscopic dream. And

222

he talked to his melancholy heart in the loneliness of the night. Shamman had hummed these verses so often they were now etched on her heart like dark, shadowy lines. The papers were fragile from the moistness of her tremulous breast. In the dry and craggy atmosphere of the school these few sprinkles kept fresh the flow which had almost shrivelled from a lack of appreciation. Iftikhar's letters kept her femininity alive, otherwise she would have long become a successful teacher who inspires dread in her students and fear in her colleagues. The successful teacher is she who forgets questions relating to masculine and feminine genders and becomes a ruler for drawing lines. In the face of this unpoetic embodiment of erudition, laughter should be stalled, faces should assume expressions of seriousness and respect, shoulders should not droop, pens should start racing and notebooks be straightened, a military order should prevail, and rules should become monarchs. But the delicate mist of these verses saved the plant from withering away.

The train was overcrowded due to some festival. There was a terrible rush in the third class compartment; people were clustered together like beehives. Arriving an hour and a half late, the train maintained its routinely casual speed once it was on its way again.

Iftikhar sat in the sunlit veranda of the sanatorium with Shamman's quilt thrown over his feet, and he was wearing the sweater she had knitted for him. Spread out before him was a heap of papers. He shook hands with Shamman. This was the first time he had been so forward, and Shamman didn't know why. Freeing her hand quickly from his, she sat down on a chair nearby and began looking at the papers. They were mostly hospital bills and prescriptions.

'They're no good to you.'

'Why?'

'They say women are afraid even of mice.'

'I'm not one of those women.'

'But these don't have mice in them, they have vipers,' Iftikhar said, but Shamman didn't hear him.

'Oh yes, I don't know when that new pullover will arrive, but I'm clasping my old friend to my breast.' He stroked the pullover lovingly. This was the same sweater into which Shamman had knitted her dreams. How grandly it was attached to his chest, that same shrunken, weakened chest, the overflowing reserve of love and mellow emotions; how the very thought of proximity with that chest made her tremble.

'I ran short of yarn. I'll parcel it as soon as I get back.'

'One shouldn't eat anything touched by a TB patient, but this fruit over here is fresh. Help yourself and cut some for me as well. The knife should be in the drawer.'

'I'm not so superstitious. Don't bother if you don't know how to entertain your guests.'

'Oh, so you're a guest.'

'Yes.'

'Hunh!' He got up to get the knife from the drawer and said in a whisper, 'They who rule my thoughts, who pursue me in my dreams, who steal my slumber, how easily they become guests . . . I hate such guests!' He spoke in mock anger and Shamman's heart lurched.

'I read in a story somewhere that the most enjoyable way to eat fresh fruit is to dig into it with your teeth, and it's even better if there are four lips instead of two sucking the juice.' Iftikhar was bent on being poetic today.

'Did you hear something?' he said.

'What?'

'Hitler has vanquished so many countries. It's our turn now.'

'How terrible. Man is chewing on man's bones.'

'That's what will happen. If a lion remains hungry it will attack its master first. These Nazi lions were just waiting for the whip to be slackened. And now they have the opportunity.'

'Poor Poland.'

'Well, the worms will be ground in with wheat. But their time has come. You'll see how their world will be turned into dust. They've crushed innocent people for too long, now it's their turn to be in the grindstone. The hot ashes they have showered on others for years will be converted into a flaming ball by fate and returned to them – see how the cowards are sneaking into their holes like worms. And they want us to feel sorry for them, they want us to sympathise with their cause, curse their enemies. *Array*, we who have been praying for the welfare of our enemies, what can we say to your enemies? But no one knows us. We tire of a master very quickly. And now history is issuing new orders, new portions will be handed out, what has been sown will be reaped. Those who have played games with the blood of others will have a chance to behold the redness of their own blood. This arrogance will also have to suffer at least a nosebleed.'

'But these wretches are very powerful.'

'That's not true. They just like to brag, their heads are bare, that's why they've spread out their hands before Uncle Sam. You'll see, they'll rub their noses for every dollar. And Uncle isn't that naive. Uncle and nephew are running this Raj together and as long as they live the wealthy and the starving will continue to exist side by side.'

'But they won't help this time.'

'*Array*, why won't they help? They're traders after all. So what if it's a trade of corpses instead of cotton? Secondly, they're terrified of the flat noses.'

'Come now, what's so special about Japan? There isn't a thing they make that's done right.'

'*Array*, Shamman, you're gauging Japanese power by the quality of their goods? You silly girl, these are for the Hindustanis and for them it's a great deal. You don't know how bad things are . . .' He began making mincemeat of the apple peels.

He continued. 'And you'll see, in the end the worker's spade will win. And this spade will shatter the false order to bits. The blood of innocent people has not been shed in vain. Chewing on the bread growing from this blood, the red nation will emerge. Peace will be smashed, a storm will arise, the bosom of the world will be rent. And what will happen next? I don't have the answer to that question. Perhaps one day I will.' Iftikhar's pale face was flushed from the intensity of his emotion.

'The defenders of oppression have started out to protect culture and justice. This same sentiment was asleep in some siren's lap in 1857. Iron is slashed only by iron. And Hitler is steel!'

'But how can their strength . . .'

'Just the ploys of a wolf who finds himself threatened by a lion. They will be wiped from the face of this earth. You'll see.'

'But what does Hindustan have to with this? The Europeans have always been at each other's throats. What difference does it make to us? We're slaves still and will be always.'

'You're right, Shamman, why should we burn our fingers in another's quarrel? But you're forgetting, we're slaves and along with our master, actually before the master does so, we have to sacrifice our blood. But that day isn't too far in the distance when you won't find the word "bondage" even in the dictionary. Do you know why I called you? Do you remember our pact at the camp or have you forgotten?'

'I'm not so stupid.'

'Do you know that even then you were the one I selected first. You don't know how much the country needs your sacrifice. And you have the courage and the intelligence. You're strong-hearted and bold. Now tell me, what can you give?'

'What do I have?'

'Whatever you have, a paisa, a blind cowrie, anything. The party badly needs funds, it's surrounded from all sides, the work that had been done so swiftly has slowed down, but we're afraid it might stop altogether. The Kanpur sector is in a great deal of trouble. All the papers have been impounded, many of our workers are rotting in jails, but the ones who are free are hiding like bats in old ruins, in nooks and crannies. Do you know where the best sanctuaries exist?'

'No.'

'In the *kothas* of the singing girls. You're surprised. A respectable woman does not have the courage or the wits to hide such lawbreakers. Who can recognise a man at a courtesan's *kotha* when he is drunk? People think he's a degenerate of the worst kind, that's all.'

'But what does your assignment look like?'

'This is a secret. Why do you think I'm sitting here quietly? No one bothers with me here and my companions can visit me very easily under the guise of relatives. I hope you'll forgive me, but I've listed you as a relative as well. I haven't been presumptuous, have I?'

'Come now, don't pretend.'

'Thanks. And because of lack of funds, these bills . . .' Suddenly silent, he tried to conceal the papers.

'You're insulting me.'

'Who, me?'

'Yes.'

'God forbid! *Array*, you can skin me alive but don't give me these looks.'

Shamman burst out laughing.

'Then give me those papers.'

'Don't bother with them.' Iftikhar tried to dodge, but Shamman snatched them from him. If two hundred and seventy-five rupees were not paid right away a twenty-four-hour notice would follow.

'Now I know what kind of a relative you regard me as.'

'But you see . . .'

'Just be quiet. I don't trust you any more.'

'Is this your final decision?'

'Yes,' Shamman said reluctantly, softened by the warmth of his subdued voice.

'Won't you accept a fine? Like holding your ears and doing sit-ups?'

'No.'

'Well, in that case I've also decided. Ask me what it is.'

'I won't ask.'

226

'Ah, I feel like swallowing some poison so I can end this squabble once and for all.'

'My, how nice you look when you act like a child.'

'You think I'm joking? The world has turned against me and now you . . . I can't tolerate this other world's anger.'

'Then tell me, why did you hide this from me?'

'I'm sorry . . . come now,' he said twisting his earlobes. 'Forgive me.'

'On one condition.'

'Ohho, is there any condition left which I have the right to agree or disagree with?'

'Yes, otherwise you would not have hidden these bills from me. If you had regarded me as your own you would have handed me these bills and ordered me to pay them.'

'Oh!' Iftikhar said in a stifled voice. His head was lowered and, despite all his efforts, tears gathered in his eyes. 'But . . .'

'You'll have to atone.'

'Listen.'

'No, goodbye.' She turned to leave.

'Sit.' He caught hold of her arm. 'You know, your sweet anger may make me audacious.' He looked at her warmly. 'Why are you so fond of playing with fire? I hope you don't get burned one day.' He let go of her arm hastily.

Shamman fell into the chair helplessly. An awkward silence grew between them, broken only by the beating of two hearts.

Taking out a few hundred rupee notes, Shamman slipped them into an envelope and slid them across the table.

'This is a loan. Return it with interest.'

'Oh, so this is how it works.'

'Why not? Why should you be let off the hook?'

'And if I can't pay it back?'

'Then I'll get it from you on judgement day, with an interest of seventy to a rupee.'

'Don't joke. You know my disease and then the work I do.'

'Allah! Leave this wretched disease alone.'

'I want to leave it, but it won't leave me. What prettier reward can I receive for eating in hotels and sleeping on footpaths?' His lifeless eyes glimmered with the old, smouldering defiance. 'Revenge! Revenge!' screamed the sharp creases on his face. Collecting himself, he swallowed his medicine and grasped his head between his hands.

'These wretched germs, these chains at every step,' he said, staring

227

wistfully at Shamman's face. 'When will you come again? Actually, now I don't need you, I don't need your solicitude.' Shamman's face fell. 'Because whenever I wish I drag you here with the force of my imagination and at that time you're not bashful with me and I have no fear of germs.'

She left in haste.

37

On her return she found a telegram waiting for her. 'Come immediately,' Alma had written. Because she hadn't given instructions about her mail, Shamman received the telegram several days late. Nevertheless she left immediately. She took along a toy gun, a box of coloured bullets and some chocolates for Rolf.

She was in the veranda when the old ayah grabbed her by the shoulders and stopped her.

'Don't go in. Just fall asleep.'

'That's all right, I won't wake him up. Where's Memsahib?'

'She sleeps. The whole day she does like this.' Ayah became the picture of grief. Surely the old woman had lost her mind. She should tell Alma to find someone else. She advanced.

'Didn't I say, you can't go in.'

'Why?'

'Why? Ohh, why?' A deadened voice drowned in pain emerged from the room. 'Why? Why?' The curtain was lifted and Alma came out. She looked like a savage, her eyes bulging, her hair awry, a sight worse than a corpse. She was burning with fever.

'Alma, what's the matter?'

She stared wide-eyed at Shamman. Perhaps a small part of her brain was still working.

'You, you've come. Did you bring him? I've boiled milk for him and . . .'

'What is it, Alma?'

'Ohho, I told you, what kind of friend are you . . . the doctor will be

228

angry,' the ayah started scolding Shamman again. 'Bai has had terrible shock,' she whispered in Shamman's ear.

'Why did you take my Rolly? Bring him here . . . you're very naughty.' Alma smiled bashfully.

'What?' Shamman was nonplussed.

'Ohho, you got a gun for him . . . that's good, he was crying for it . . .'

'The baby died . . .' the ayah said in a tearful voice.

'What? Rolf is . . .'

'Lies! All lies. . . they're all liars . . . they're deceiving me . . . I'll sue everyone . . . *thain! thain!* . . . There, I got them!' Aiming an imaginary gun, Alma cackled gleefully.

'He had pneumonia . . . three days and he was gone.' The old woman with the wrinkled eyes curled up her shrivelled nose and whimpered. 'Memsahib was out of her mind right away. I said, you can't do anything, he's Christ's lamb, he called him. But she kicked me, she says go away, I don't want you. Where can I go, I say. But she doesn't listen. Where can I go? There is no one . . . no one, even my husband is dead.' She sniffled. 'That neighbour, he says Mrs Paul is unlucky, very unlucky.'

'Hunh. Get someone to bring in my luggage, Ayah.' Shamman was bewildered by the ayah's garbled speech. She dragged Alma back to her room.

'Come on . . . where are you hiding him?' Alma asked her mischievously.

'Alma . . .' Shamman wanted to clasp Alma to her breast and sob unreservedly.

'Why don't you speak . . . now look, don't play any games with me . . . otherwise, remember I have a lawyer and I'll sue everyone . . . oh . . .' Alma paused as if in the middle of a thought and cupping her hand to her mouth she called, 'Ay . . . ah . . . Ay . . . ah.'

'Coming, Memsahib.'

'Ayah, baby needs hot water for his bath . . . make sure it's just right.'

'What does Memsahib say? Baby took his last bath. Now . . .' Ayah heaved a long sigh. 'The angels give him a bath with holy water, Christ . . .'

'Get out of here! Go away.' Shamman scolded her and tried to push her out, but the ayah stood her ground stubbornly.

'Why scream at me like this, Memsahib, I'll tell the doctor.'

229

'Just shut up, Ayah! Alma, take heart, what have you done to yourself?' Shamman began untangling Alma's hair lovingly.

'Then bring him,' Alma pleaded in that same desperate tone.

Ayah muttered, 'Nobody listens . . . I say baby is dead . . . all day she does this.'

'Lies, all lies.'

'You say lies for Christ . . . you can't do that.'

'Ayah . . .' Shamman glared at her.

'Christ's anger . . .'

'Leave the room, go.' Shamman pushed her out roughly.

'I go, I go, but you call me for this? Memsahib doesn't eat anything . . . The heavenly father will be angry.'

Shamman locked the door.

'She's only making you more agitated. What have you done to yourself?'

'Everyone says he's gone . . . did you take him?'

'No.'

'Swear.' Alma shuddered fearfully.

For eight days Alma was suspended in a struggle between life and death. On the ninth day her fever subsided although she remained weak for a long time afterwards. Both of them avoided talking about what had happened, even though they were aware that they were both always thinking of the same thing. Alma had given him birth and had raised him, but Shamman had loved him no less. During the Dashera holidays last year they had excitedly shopped for educational toys for him.

'Come on, say "Auntie".'

'No . . . Chaman.' His eyes gleamed in mischief and he ran away from her. Hearing him say 'Chaman' reminded her of Rai Sahib. He too was handsome like him, and so playful. What does God have against spirited human beings?

Alma had started worshipping him from the day mother and son came together. Forgetting the filthy nature of the seed, she was busy tending the plant. She had hundreds of pictures of him, many that she taken herself, and of these Shamman too received copies. Shamman was taking part in his upbringing from a distance. The moment she saw a useful book or toy, she immediately bought it for him and parcelled it to him. She read books on child psychology just for him. For hours she and Alma sat with their heads together trying to figure him out as if he were an intriguing riddle.

And as long as Alma tried to destroy him he remained unharmed, but the minute she began loving him, he left her, leaving her motherhood gasping for life. After the fever broke Alma's state of mind improved somewhat. She told Shamman that when she had lost hope she had sent for her. She thought that because Shamman had brought them together, she could also snatch him from death's clutches. They say illegitimate children are very rugged. Why then did Rolf appear like a puff of air and was lost? If it were another mother, she could be comforted with words like, 'Have a little forbearance, God will give you another.' But for the mother of an illegitimate child this remark is an insult.

'Alma, get married.' Shamman tried to reason with her.

'Hunh! To give birth to new Rolfs? You don't know ... it's not a joke to cut off a piece of flesh from your body and throw it away like this. Oh Shamman, the anguish that I suffered when I gave birth to him has become tenfold with his death. Oh, the anguish that's more stifling than death ...'

'You probably feel this way because your position is different from other mothers. If a child has been raised in a loving atmosphere then maybe it wouldn't be so hard ...'

'Perhaps. Maybe a time will come when I'm not so afraid. There's a professor here who has been after me for a long time. He knows about Rolf, the poor man was very attached to him and he's very open-minded, although I'm not such a coward that I can't tolerate derision nor was I ashamed of being Rolf's mother.' She was silent again.

'Why didn't you get married?'

'Because I was afraid that I might be unfair to Rolf again. I was a mother and I acted like a witch, but as you said, it was an unwitting mistake. But I didn't want to make that same mistake again. I never gave him all of what was rightfully his.'

Shamman left Alma and came home to her family. Because she had been away for such a long time she felt like a stranger in her own home. Occasionally she was indulged like a guest, but she had no fixed place in the house. Most of her time was spent in the drawing room during the two months of holidays; she didn't have the comforts of home people generally enjoy. As far as the family was concerned, she might as well have been married.

The room was like a waiting room. Her things were viewed as novelties and she had the feeling she was on the main road somewhere. No matter how hard she tried she couldn't have the seclusion to which she had become accustomed. Family members regarded her as a temporary annoyance and forced themselves to keep a control on their everyday idiosyncrasies. Even if they disapproved of her presence they tolerated her as they would a guest. Her room was the most well-ordered so the children's interest was always directed there. Guests too were brought here to be entertained, and her writing pads, envelopes and pens were generously utilised by everyone. The world had advanced so much but the chaos in her house hadn't undergone any change. To make matters worse, the sisters-in-law had come from families where children's nappies were habitually set out to dry on the dining table, meals were taken sitting on the floor in the kitchen, grain was stored in the bathrooms, and baths were taken in enclosures secluded by hanging a curtain on a line. In her absence the drawing room was used to store broken rope cots, chairs with no seats, old, ripped *moorahs* and teetering stools. The china and all the floor coverings were also kept in this room in cupboards. Whenever she came she dusted and cleaned a few chairs and divans so that they became fit for use.

Since her father's retirement everything in the house was kept only as long as it worked. If something was damaged or broken, no one bothered to have it repaired and, like an orphan, it was shunted into the pile of rubbish. The house was full of items that were on pension. It was the community dump. This unspeakable condition reminded her of Hindustan's general malaise. Don't government officers stretch out on charpoys and chatter, while on the desks the same old spicy, oily snacks and tea are served? On the desks lie mismanaged registers smudged with turmeric and ghee stains, dried-out inkwells, crooked nibs, and cracked holders which are used more often for inserting drawstrings through pyjama waistbands than writing.

Meanwhile Germany decided to bathe the world in blood in order to purify it. Poland was divided, and as for the rest of the world, how many more days will it remain whole? This triangle too can be transformed into a swastika with one swirl of the compass. Important personages will conduct conferences. Who really cares if Hindustan remains whole or breaks? Isn't there enough breakage in the world? There are times when one feels like taking a mortar and hitting this triangle so hard that it shatters into pieces, like Britain and Japan.

Her own family also needed a jolt. This was an ordinary family where the number of dependants kept increasing while the wage-earners continued to age rapidly from exhaustion. The stairs were in a danger-ous state of disrepair and everywhere the cement was eroding. If only some terrible disaster would hurl the slothful inhabitants of these ruins into a desert, where, free of the dark seclusion of this house, they would be forced to build new havens for themselves.

Germany began showering fire over London. A wave of blazing joy raced through the trampled hearts of the hungry and the starving, those whose blood had been drained to adorn this grand city. Ahha! What fun it will be! These buildings, tall as mountains and endowed with the beauty of paradise, will scatter like bundles of chaff. The dainty British women, and the men, as flimsy as blossoms, will turn into the kind of rubbish that is thrown out of a butcher's shop to be mauled by dogs and clawed by vultures. God's wrath will pour from the skies, the earth will spew lava; giant roadways will turn into deserts and hotels will become ruins. The blood of 1857 will spill over, this dark blood spreading everywhere like darkness.

Hitler is also an Aryan. The same Aryans who invaded Hindustan. Now these Aryans will come here, like Hanuman *ji* who went to destroy Lanka with his tail on fire. In the same way there will be a shower of flames which will consume all the demons and, like burnished golden idols, the gods will emerge again. Then Hindus and Muslims will place garlands around each other's necks, the Hindus will worship the mosques, and the Muslims will bow their foreheads before the temples. Two brothers will embrace and give vent to long-suppressed emotions.

Why be scared of this bombardment? What is the value of these firecrackers for the worms who have suffered famine and disease along with poverty and helplessness? Every now and then enough of them are trampled under cars to become dust. But this dust is not lifeless; it will burst into flames, and, like a restless soul, it will dance for years, rankling in the eyes of the world. So many times the Hindustani triangle was conquered, but its aching, impoverished hearts could not be overcome. These hearts don't belong to the toadies who sit in the courts of the rulers like some grotesque creatures, wearing their cast-offs. No, these hearts exist in those rotting, shabby cottages which leaked during the reign of the Aryans, continued to weep in the time of the Mughals, and to this day have a hundred holes which no one has been able to repair. How can these hearts be affected by another's pain when a centuries' long oppression has numbed their spirits, turning them into unfeeling stone? Now they don't even care if it's the *salim shahi* slipper that kicks them harder or the foreigner's boot. Pain no longer has any effect on them.

Political predicaments engulfed life like a silent war, but not with a vigour that would awaken the populace from a centuries' old lethargy.

When the west reverberated with the clanging of tanks and the thunder of guns, Hindustan presented the drama of *ahimsa*. What could be better than this? Someone is trying to wake you up with loud screams and you swallow a ball of opium and turn on your side!

The school also became an arena for political discourse. Discussions took place, were followed by condemnations, and then tears were shed. The Hindu girls were all for *ahimsa*. The Christians were extremely nervous, as if with Islam and Hinduism their crucifix is also in danger. What will happen if they don't take sides with the *sarkar* and the white Raj vanishes? It's only a difference of colour; these brown and yellow creatures are also Christ's lambs and, in addition, along with similarities in dress and comportment, children say 'Mama, Papa, Auntie and sister' so sweetly. And who knows Hindustani anyway? What they wear may look like sacks, but they are frocks, the dark, goat-like feet are encased in shoes which may be second-hand, but are high-heeled at least, while the side-parting and the curls are every inch western! What's the difference? If the sahibs are forced to leave Hindustan, what will these ayahs and bearers do? The brown man can't give them such a high salary, especially when he himself is used to sitting crosslegged in the kitchen for lunch and dinner, and when his own children are raised by maternal and paternal grandmothers. Sure, there are a few wealthy people around, but they too aren't very generous. Secondly, when the sahibs leave, who knows who will come next, or if ayahs and bearers will remain in fashion? The matter of the spinning wheel is another enigma. It is said Gandhi *ji* will give everyone a spinning wheel and a goat and say, 'Go and spin yarn and drink goat's milk.' No tea, or chocolate or biscuits!

The Muslim girls neither cared for the goats nor were they interested too much in spinning. They were to have Pakistan. Along with the Taj Mahal, Moti Masjid and Laal Qila, the entire hallowed world, under the silvery moon's shadow, happily engulfed in fasting and prayer, would slowly slide towards paradise. Their allotted portion was about to be handed to them. A copper 'P' was already selling at every *paan* shop. Now all they had to do was wait silently.

But Congress was reluctant to give them the portion. If, in an effort to vie with the creation of Pakistan, Sikhistan and Maha Sabhastan also came into existence, Bharat will shatter with a loud bang and the *jhumar* adorning the Himalayas' forehead will scatter. And what if, giving in to the invitation of the Khan brothers on that side, Pakistan decides to make advances like Mehmud Ghaznavi?

Holding aloft the banner of progress, time marched on very rapidly. Assemblies and gatherings were characterised by a new fervour. Programmes were developed, impassioned poems were recited, food and alcohol were freely consumed, progressive papers, progressive organisations, progressive journalists and progressive poets were born, and revolution went into effect full force. The privileges of free life and love, free birth and free death were extolled. Existing limitations were broken to construct new angles. Every man whose hair was awry, whose eyes flashed, whose clothes were a trifle unusual and somewhat shabby, who sported a briefcase containing some passionate verses and burning stories, spirited articles and fine photographs, a few simple memories and charming letters, was a progressive. He became thoughtful suddenly in the course of a conversation, he talked to women very freely and somewhat carelessly and roughly, mentioned love the first chance he had, allowed his hands to wander over female clothing without knowing what he was doing, looked at these garments as if seeing them for the first time, then smiled meaningfully and, blushing, proceeded to discuss their style and importance. In addition, he stressed the physical allure and bodily attributes of every notable girl he talked about, he already had a passion for her, he knew about her old and new lovers, her sound and unsound children. Along with all this, he was well-versed with the names of all American, Russian and French revolutionary writers and their works. Having translated their works, he had served the world of letters, and of course he was a writer himself, a poet, or a journalist that is, and signed his name with an unusual flourish. He suffered from an inferiority complex, the sort which had helped give rise to such great thinkers as Hitler and Napoleon, and in addition was anguished, starving and sensitive. He used his friends to keep himself supplied with fine clothing and his fill of alcohol. He forced people to put him up, and was only a dissenter along the lines of the principle, 'What's yours is mine and what's mine is *not* yours.' Not only that, he had also experienced the naivety of village girls and the artifice of girls who were educated. He supported every kind of woman – daughter, wife, prostitute; although he spat at rich girls, his love for them had turned him into an ascetic. Weary of life's harshness, he had now become accustomed to getting free alcohol and frequently falling into the gutter.

There can be another branch of progressives as well. Those unfortunate ones who have been forced to inherit substantial estates, who have failed in all elections and selections despite reliable endorsement, who don't know what to do, how to pass their time. They are obliged to live in their ancestral palaces, use high-quality furniture, attend important official and non-official meetings for which they have to forgo their national dress and don suits stitched by western tailors, they are forced to sit in grand drawing rooms, drink tea in teacups imported from Italy, and discuss revolutionary ideas with poets and writers, seek out beautiful girls in *mushairas* and literary meetings, and sit with their hands folded, waiting for the revolution to come about.

Like life's other carriages, revolution's cart cannot be pulled along by a single ox. The presence of females was essential, especially those who were independent in their thought and didn't care what the world was saying. Shamman was attacked on all sides by progressives; for some reason she was quite well known for her nationalist fervour, even though she hadn't performed any notable feat as yet. Like sweetness to which the ants are drawn guided by its aroma, nationalist fervour too cannot be hidden and people manage to seek it out.

The first day Nawabzada Samad arrived in the company of some zealous workers. For a long time heated discussions continued over informal cups of tea. He left after extracting a promise from Shamman that she would attend a forthcoming meeting. Nawabzada Samad was a spirited, handsome young man and was forced to use the non-revolutionary prefix to his name. As a matter of fact, his friends called him just Comrade Samad. The other man was a revolutionary poet who, having abandoned the beaten path of romantic poetry centring around such legendary lovers as Laila and Majnu, had taken on the task of attributing tragic romance to such figures as doctors, nurses and schoolteachers, and instead of horses and rapiers, he had written in praise of trains and automobiles.

The third person was a professor whose work had been judged decadent by the government. With great pride he proclaimed that people trembled when they read his articles. The prurience found in his work was renowned. He asserted that the moment he set eyes on a woman, the power of his imagination made her clothes disappear in a cloud of smoke, that his gaze could penetrate seven barriers and travel to the other side. Shamman heard this and quaked. She wished her clothes were made of a thicker, more durable yarn.

One was an engineer. Because he was a government official he had to bring about revolution surreptitiously. He was very unhappy with the income from his ancestral lands. As long as he stayed in England he constantly marched in all demonstrations, dressed in *khadar*, waving a flag. He had specially taken a *khadar sherwani* and tight-legged pyjamas with him from Hindustan which looked particularly good on him. Although the processions were long and he froze to death, yet for that day he avoided wearing an overcoat. On his return his landlady presented him with hot water bottles and tea. She had a great deal of sympathy for these brown boys who had made it possible for three of her daughters to be saved from working as maids and live instead like queens in Hindustan. She longed to go to her brown son-in-laws' brown country and, sitting atop an elephant, hunt cobras and lions, eat *pulao* and kebabs in gold and silver plates, and feel with her own hands the jewels piled in small antechambers.

On the day of the meeting Comrade Samad came in his car along with some of his cronies to pick her up. There was an immense crowd and the programme was quite interesting. Poems on revolutionary love were recited; the progressive, revolutionary poet, overcome with inebriation, radiating like the image of talent and artistry, intoned merrily. Every verse of his poem leapt like a flame. This was followed by powerful articles which proved that present-day obscenity is worthless as compared to the obscenity in the works of older writers. When the forefathers were so bold, why is it that their offspring remain so far behind? To ignore this literary legacy would be extremely inappropriate. Even if you inherit leprosy from your forefathers, you should clasp it safely to your breast.

There were several women present, but one in particular possessed a special place in the area of patriotism. Several butchers were ready to cut off her nose, which didn't scare her one bit, and she was, as a matter of fact, proud of it. She was a special flame from Nawabzada's candle. No one could make out what she said because the hall echoed with whispers during her speech. People were busy discussing and assessing the rumours rampant about her. Another woman came next, but she was rather dull. The poor woman looked like an oil lamp compared to this flame. Her hair was out of place, she looked flustered, and wore an extremely downtrodden and defeated look. She was known for her eccentricity and confused state of mind.

The meeting was exhausting. When she got home Shamman quickly fell asleep. Around one o'clock she was suddenly awakened by a sound. She wasn't afraid of burglars, but at this time of night the appearance of an honest person would also make one fearful. Bracing herself, she asked, 'Who is it?' There was no reply. She leaned back on her pillow and strained her ears. Her body became taut from the pressure of concentrating with such intensity. She heard a light knock, as if a wandering soul were rapping against the window.

'Shamman.' The wind whispered against her ear, as if a familiar voice was calling out to her. But this voice had deceived her often.

'Shamman.' This time her doubts were dispelled. There was somebody outside the window calling her name.

'Who is it?'

'It's me . . . don't be afraid, it's me, Iftikhar. Open the window.'

'Eh?' Shamman opened the window apprehensively. Her illusion was there before her in its earthly garb.

'You?'

'Can I come in?'

'Yes,' she said, moving away from the window.

'But think, there's danger behind me.'

'Danger?'

'Tell me quickly, so that I may try elsewhere . . .'

'Come inside,' she said in exasperation and opened the window wide.

'Don't regret this later.' He paused for a moment on the windowsill, then jumped in.

'What's the matter?' Shamman asked, shutting the window tightly.

'Let me catch my breath.' Breathing heavily, he collapsed on the couch and was silent. Shamman put her shawl over her shoulders and sat down on a chair nearby.

'These wretched lungs!' He pressed his hand against his chest. 'They won't let me take even two steps. That was a narrow escape.'

'What happened?'

'The same, the same . . . who else is fond of making me run like this? Life has become a continuous run.'

'Police?'

'Eh?' he started, but was soon lost in thought.

'I've never told you this,' he began again weakly, 'and what's the use, you're headmistress of a girls' school, you . . .'

'I'm not afraid of anyone. I'm an employee, not a slave.'

'But . . .'

'Leave it be – tell me, are you hungry?'

Iftikhar glanced at her silently in answer to her query, then began looking through his pockets for something. Shamman walked off to the kitchen.

'Do you know what's happening?' he asked when she placed food before him. Chewing the morsels of food hastily, he added, 'There are plans afoot to crush Russia. Why did Hess jump in? Russia is running scared of Finland . . . these wretched teeth will have to go, they're no good . . . these imperialists want to get together and devour Russia . . . and if they succeed by any chance . . .' He grimaced at what he saw in his mind's eye. 'But Germany . . . Germany is no fool, it won't be duped by them.' He appeared to be consoling himself.

'But Hess, what about Hess?' Shamman blushed at the stupidity of her own question. 'Politics is such a strange game. One minute all these important goings-on and the next children's pranks.'

'I'm going Shamman, try and remember me, and if you forget me, don't ever tell me, I won't be able to endure it. I don't know why I have this feeling that I'm alive only because of you. In my most despondent moments it's your thought that sustains me, and now it seems as though I first started looking at the world through your eyes . . . oh, what am I saying?' He fixed his stare on the floor.

'But for what crime?'

'You'll read about it in the paper. It's the old case, the one following the strike in Kanpur. Let's not talk about that . . . I didn't come here to burden you with all this nonsense, I came to . . .' He fell silent.

'Before I went away,' he continued, 'I wanted to come and ask for strength and courage . . . Pray that I don't lose faith along the way.'

Shamman's throat was constricted.

'Give me a little betel-nut.'

She said nothing.

'So, shall I go now?' He stood in front of her, rubbing his hands together anxiously.

'*Khuda hafiz.*'

He stood uncertainly without moving for a few seconds. He looked perturbed. Shamman's heart was pounding.

'All right. *Khuda hafiz* then.' He turned slowly towards the window and opened it with shaking hands.

'I'm leaving, and I wanted to say that . . . that doctors have told me my disease is no longer dangerous . . . now the germs . . .' He stumbled, then jumped suddenly from the window and disappeared in the darkness. Shamman saw just a glimpse of his flushed face. Biting his lips, he was trying to hold back tears; his nostrils were flared and the veins in his neck stood out from the pressure of restraint.

Her face covered with both hands, Shamman stood before the window a long time. Then she fell on the bed and burst into sobs.

38

Shamman soon wearied of the non-revolutionary antics of the revolutionary organisations. She presided over one or two meetings and also shared the work enthusiastically, although a close scrutiny would reveal that her work was in name only. It was customary for the organisers to write the speeches, provide resolutions and prepare the paperwork for the female speakers. All the women had to do was to tread on the path designated for them, and that too consisted of arriving on the stage in such a state of nervousness that the helpers had to come up at the last minute with the paper they were to read from. What an unreliable individual a woman is. She promises to deliver a lecture and forgets all about it, people come to get her at the last minute and she suddenly remembers that the speech she had been assigned has not even been looked at as yet.

'Oh dear, I completely forgot,' she says smilingly after making the biggest mistake imaginable. This was her right as a woman and not to use that right would be absolute foolishness. No matter how important the problem at hand, women's attitudes will not change; they'll just sit there calmly as if they're in their father's house.

If the meal is delayed and the quality of the food is unsatisfactory, it's the cook's fault; if the house is a mess, it's the servant's fault; if the laundry is dirty, it's the washerman's fault. Nothing is ever their fault. If they become prostitutes, it's society's fault; if they're duped, the blame is placed on their femininity and naivety; if they're robbed, if they elope, if they're sold into prostitution, it's the tyrants who receive blame.

There was no school that day and Shamman had no work. Actually the headmistress has no need to work. She must have the qualities of a police inspector. If she can somehow manage to make four teachers do the work of eight she is truly helping the department of education. The orderly came in and told her a woman wanted to see her. She wasn't available, Shamman told him. A woman's appearance may mean many different kinds of problems. She may be a spy sent by the enemy to gossip, she may be the mother or sister of a student intent on having the tuition fees waived, or she may be asking for a double promotion, as if grades were the rungs of a ladder that a headmistress can help the students climb.

The orderly returned saying that the woman's behaviour was odd and she wouldn't listen to him. He hadn't quite finished talking when she walked in. Taking off her *burka*, she immediately sat down.

'Are you Miss Gupta?' she asked Shamman without wasting a second.

'No.'

'Kamini Devi?'

'You're mistaken, I'm . . .'

'Then you must be Zehra. Isn't that right?'

'No. What do you mean?' Shamman spoke irately.

'Oh God, then who are you?'

'It's none of your business. If there's something you need to speak about . . .'

'I say, sister, I have a lot to speak about, but only after I know which one you are . . . errr . . . what was that name . . . yes, Tasneem. A curse on my memory.'

'No, I said you're mistaken.'

'No, my dear, I can't be mistaken. For this sector these are the only names. All right, never mind. Tell me, no one is listening to our conversation?'

'No. Please say what you have to and leave.'

'Yes, yes of course, don't get upset, I'll leave, but . . . whatever your name might be, dust on the name . . . you know him, Iftikhar Ahmed?'

'What?' Shamman was sure she was dealing with the CID, but she wasn't a fool.

'Don't deny it, I beg you, for God's sake, for the sake of *panjtan pak* . . . look, sister, you have to show your face to God . . . for the sake of your loved ones.'

'What do you mean? Leave at once or else . . .'

'My dear girl, I'm not scared by these empty threats. I've seen more of the world than you, I've suffered an ill-fate. What's the use? Tell me, did he proclaim you to be his mother, sister, or beloved?'

'I think you're mad. Will you leave or . . .'

'My conjecture tells me that . . . sister – although you're not very beautiful, but you are reasonably attractive.'

'You won't leave?'

'I'll leave, but not before I've said my say and heard your side of the story. I think you were the beloved . . . your demeanour betrays you. May God preserve you, so shy you are.'

'What do you have to do with all this?'

241

'Nothing, what can I, miserable, ruined creature that I am, have to do with all this . . . only that I'm that wretch's wife.'

'You! You . . .'

'Yes, you can see the certificate if you don't believe me. Here, I knew you would think I'm lying. Look, "Husain Bibi, wife of Iftikahr Ahmed, sect Sayyed".'

'What do you want?' Shamman's gaze was lowered.

'That's more like it. Are you married or single, by God's grace?'

'You tell me what it is you want to say.'

'So, by God's grace, you're unmarried. At least your face seems to show it. But only God knows what's hidden from us. These days there's hardly any difference between married and unmarried women.'

'Stop your nonsense and say what you came here to say.'

'So, sister, here's what I wanted to convey. What did you find in that worm-eaten kebab? Don't take offence if something slips out of my mouth. I've been in despair because of him since I was fourteen, if I've had one moment of peace you may devise what punishment you want. I never see him. There are three children. I've stayed with relatives, suffered at the hands of nephews and sisters-in-law – whatever Allah sent my way I suffered. But now sister . . .'

Shamman felt herself growing numb. The woman's sobs took away whatever strength she had left.

'I lost, but you, all educated flies by God's grace, you still tolerate him. It's not your fault, that's how he is, may God curse him! He's not good looking, but for some reason women are crazy about him, and not only the young ones, it's the old hags as well. I hear one of them wanted him to be her son. I've heard he was going to marry one of them.'

'Which Iftikhar are you talking about?'

'I'm not mad, you know, the Iftikhar who was in college with you, Shamshad – yes! That's your name, now I remember. He has your photograph, don't think I'm lying, I can give you proof. But first you must listen. You know this nawab, his sister has adopted him as her brother. Now I'm not so stupid that I don't know what this brother and sister business means, these wretches blush at this brother and mother relationship. *Array*, I say, if you want to do something like this, go ahead and do it openly.'

'Well, what do you want?'

'Tell me this, did you give him money?'

'No.'

'Don't lie. I have your letters in which there are references to the money you gave him. That's not all, sister, excuse me, but you also knitted him sweaters, you burnt your hands making halva for him . . .'

'Can you show me my letters?'

'I don't recognise your writing, but the postmark with the name of your town will tell . . .' Like a magician she started rummaging through her satchel. She extracted a bundle of letters and placed it in her lap.

'I . . . don't try and snatch them from me,' she said suspiciously, turning to one side.

Shamman felt weak with embarrassment because for one moment she had been tempted to snatch the symbols of her imprudence from this tyrant's hands and . . .

'These . . . these blue envelopes . . . why don't you check them.' Shamman took a blue envelope from her with trembling hands. There was no need to open the envelope and check. The truth had bared itself and was dancing naked before her.

'Don't worry, I haven't read any of these. I don't have the energy to read this rake's love letters. And, my dear girl, in the beginning I stole them, I read them, I burnt them, but now I disregard everything. The ones who write to him haven't given up, but I'm exhausted.'

'What do you want?' Shamman asked in a deadened, meek tone.

'*Array*, sister, what can I want . . . you know what I want.' She settled on the bed and crossed her legs under her. 'You see, this good-for-nothing fellow became everyone's favourite, but me, no one wants me in their house. "Come on, get out, do some work, you're strong as an ox," they'd say. As if I'm just fond of wandering from place to place and begging for help. At one time I was no less than anyone. An expensive house went to ruin. My father-in-law lost his eyesight and every penny was spent, and as for his penniless son, he dumped me at my parents' house and left, although he would be back to give me children every year. Only last month he came to visit you. I caught him at the station late at night and then he gave me the slip when he went to the waiting room. But I wasn't about to let him go. I hid near the railway gate and as soon as he appeared I followed close behind. I was there when he jumped out of your window. I would have come to you right then, but what good would it have been, and I've also heard that when women are with their lovers they don't hesitate to kill. He wouldn't come to my rescue, he'd strangle me if he could help it. But sister, I hadn't seen you until then. I can see you're from a good family, there's a look of reticence in your eyes.'

Shamman wished she were blind and deaf.

Husain Bibi continued. 'You don't know how many liaisons he's had, how many women are praying for him, and he's also making the government dance. This trip to Bhawali, this was also a trick. I was happy that at least now he's dying and I'll be a widow and be entitled to receive charity and have something with which to raise my children.'

'Why don't you tell me . . .' Shamman floundered in a stifled voice.

'And all this that I've been telling you, that's not enough? By God's grace you helped the father for so long, now maybe you can do something for the children. You have the right to say no. I'm just happy I met you, happy to find out that you're respectable and you won't abandon your honour. Ahh, could you get me some water, a curse on it, my throat is so dry.'

Shamman poured water from a jug, put some ice in it and presented it to her.

'May you live long, sister, you'll be rewarded for helping someone in pain.'

'Here's my bank book, here's a pair of earrings and these bangles . . . in addition to this, if there's anything else you see here that you want, please take it.'

For a long time Husain Bibi riffled through Shamman's bank book.

'You haven't saved anything.'

'Whatever there is, is right here.'

'Hmm,' she said thoughtfully, 'I'm leaving tomorrow.'

'Today the post office is closed because it's a holiday,' Shamman said numbly.

'These earrings are nice, why don't you wear them, your ears look so bare. The bangles were made in Delhi, right?'

'Yes,' Shamman forced herself to say.

'They're nice. I'll have something like this made for Qudsia. Even that scoundrel loves her. Last year he left two hundred rupees for her; actually I wrested them out of him – I made every minute so miserable for him he had to cough up the sum eventually. He also gave me two sweaters, he said unravel them and knit sweaters for the children so I knitted one for Aslam and one for the baby. A little bit of yarn was left over. God's curse on these women! How generously they knit for him. And wool is so expensive.'

Shamman listened quietly to everything.

'All right, sister, I will be leaving now . . . here are your letters, take good care of them.'

'And the money?'

'Now let that be, sister. I too have an unmarried daughter, growing fast like a berry tree. My dear girl, you haven't seen the world as yet. If you really want to, give me whatever you may have lying around.'

Shamman turned her bag inside out and counted one hundred and forty rupees for her.

'May God bless you. You should get married, my dear. What's the use of bringing dishonour to your parents' name? These pimples on your face, grind some mustard in with milk and rub that on your face, and by God's grace, you'll have new, whiter skin in no time . . . Well, I'm going now.'

She opened the door and walked out noisily. Like a lifeless mound of earth, Shamman sat still, watching the bundle of orphaned letters before her. So this was the harvest from her garden of love.

The orderly came in to tell her that the car was waiting to take her to the meeting. She had to deliver an important lecture today.

'Say I'm not here.'

And in truth, she felt she was even less than 'not' at this moment.

39

With a feeling of astonishment she saw that the shadowy darkness of evening was making the room look smaller. Frightened, she shrank and retreated. Where had she been all this time? When Husain Bibi left it was still day. So in what region did her spirit spend these four or five hours? Her brain had become numb along with her feelings. She didn't move, but her heart continued to beat, the lungs exhaled and inhaled, the blood proceeded to course through her veins, but where was she? She wasn't asleep, nor was she awake, she didn't hear anything and she didn't see a dream – so, what was she doing?

The force of restraint had paralysed her feelings, causing them to fall into some deep abyss, out of which they were now slowly emerging. Suddenly they raced, as if pulled up by a special force. Lanterns came to life on the streets, the tongas sprinted one behind the other, in the distance a train whistle tooted, a massive steam-roller, after a long day of hard work, was lumbering back to its depot, lorries jammed with people swayed like elephants as they made their way to nearby towns. New tunes and new songs raced into her ears. She felt as if she were hearing the breathing of the earth for the first time. Having remained dead for so long, her eardrums had become unaccustomed to these sounds, wincing with every new voice as if it were completely unfamiliar, strange.

So the world was still here! Just as alive and well as before. Only she had disappeared. She was disappointed that her absence had not made the slightest difference to the order of things; the journey didn't come to a halt if one tiny part among a thousand others in the machine loosened and fell off. Nothing happened. In the presence of all the elements, why should the caravan of life have stopped simply because she wasn't there? The engine of daily life thundered on, changing tracks, whistling.

She immediately got to her feet and took a few steps to test herself. She shook her hands and moved her feet. Every piece was working, the parts were functioning, the nuts and bolts were in place. She hadn't noticed anything while she was losing them. The light must have gone off in the twinkling of an eye. But while she was getting back what had been lost she was aware of everything. No one had turned the light on in her room. No one could come into her room because of respect for her position. And what if she were totally lost? These respectful servants would not have come looking for her and even if they had, it would be too late to regain anything. She would have been lost on this bed. The worms would have come looking for their share.

She began trembling with fear. She suddenly longed to run out of this small room and jump into the arms of a massive crowd, embrace it with both hands and say, 'Please let me drown in your midst ... hide me, surround this frightening loneliness from all sides and make it disperse ... and don't let me get lost again.' And then perhaps, that touch of life will make this despondency that had accumulated on her like years and years of dust, disappear.

Why did her room smell musty and frigid like a graveyard, as if it had been closed up for years? The orderly hadn't kindled frankincense as yet. But all at once the smell of frankincense terrified her; that deathly aroma will surely turn this room into an old grave. What should she do? What should she do? Where should she go? To whom? For a long time she wondered what to do with her shattered being, how to gather all the scattered fragments and put them all together again.

'Mother! Mother!' she called in silence. She wanted to scream for her mother, not the mother who was in her father's house, who used to satisfy her needs, who gave life to her and then forgot all about her. No, she wanted the mother in whose warm, loving lap she could curl up like a tiny bundle and forget this chill in her soul, whose soft, delicate hands would rub her tired back and, pressing her eyelids, squeeze out the tears that were trapped inside her temples.

'Wait, wait, wait a while longer,' she told herself softly. 'Wait just a moment longer and everything will pass, this dust-ridden wind will subside, this storm will abate . . . drink a glass of water . . . cool, cool, water.'

Like an obedient child she removed the cover of the thermos. Cubes of ice bobbed in the water like diamonds. The light from the window fell on them, making them shine lustrously. Her own breath struck the empty insides of the thermos, kissed the diamonds and returned to embrace her face. The contours of her face relaxed into a smile. She placed her mouth close to the thermos and breathed heavily a few times. Sheets of cool air slipped into her throat. She touched one ice cube hesitatingly. *Array!* A chilly kiss spread into her body like a scorpion's poison. She felt emboldened. Lowering a finger tentatively, she clasped an ice cube; a tickling sensation travelled from the tip of her finger to her elbow. The translucent cube floated in tears. Restless from the contact with the heat in the palm, it tossed about this way and that. Without knowing why, she placed her thirsting lips on the cube. Her mouth was filled with the taste of blood. Hurriedly she took out more cubes and, filling her mouth with them, she began chewing until the chill spread to her tongue and down her throat. But she continued to munch on icy peas. After she had finished the cubes, she poured the murky water into a glass. Like a greedy drunk she wanted to squeeze out the last drop. Putting the thermos aside, she turned to the glass, but the sudden movement of her arm caused the glass to spill over and then jump to the floor with a melodious clangour. The fragments fluttered like live birds.

She pouted like a small child who drops a glass of milk. Suddenly her feelings became tangled up, her maternal instincts commingled with the child in her. The intensity of her anger and heartache subsided like froth on soda. For one brief moment she wanted to pick up the crystalline pieces of the broken glass and chew them like the icy peas. But 'That's not nice,' a voice in her head reproached, and she lost her temper like a spoilt child. Grinding her teeth, she kicked the fragments forcefully with her foot and scattered them all over the room. Glimmering particles burst and flew about like half-dead sparks. She enjoyed that. It made her feel as if the clouds tangled in her temples had suddenly loosened and trickled down. She picked up another glass from the table. First she raised it against the light; a rainbow of colours darting back and forth along the rim ... the table away from her, how small it looked, the bed and the chair as well ... *array*, and she too was so diminutive ... the books as big as a watermelon seed, the stool and the clothes pegs as big as buttons. If only she too were a tiny doll, seated on a chair. Why was this delicate world beyond her reach? Which door should she enter from? Annoyed, she put the glass back and, turning to the cupboard, took out a new set of glasses. Soon each glass was drowned in the tinkle of her silvery laughter.

So what? She'll get a new set. Blue, yellow, pink, one of each colour, and then she will laugh along with the fragments. Someone knocked. Fearful, she started concealing the fragments.

'Sitar master is here,' the orderly said.

'Tell the wretch to go,' she wanted to say, but she changed her mind.

'I'm coming,' she said, trying to restore the tone of authority to her voice.

Swiftly she adjusted the folds of her sari and straightened out the wrinkles. Slipping her feet into slippers, she went to the mirror, daubed some powder on her face, wiped off the excess with a towel, fluffed her hair with a comb and, removing a smudge of powder from under her left eye, she burst out laughing.

When she was playing the raga *jayjayvanti* on the sitar, her eyes fell on her toe which was bleeding. But she didn't stop playing.

'One should be wearing a strong shoe when one is kicking.' She rubbed her toe against the carpet.

Before going to bed she shut both doors carefully and latched them, and also pulled the curtain at the window. When she had satisfied herself, she walked tiptoe to the bed. Slowly she pulled the mattress to the floor. Turning the fan on to full, she lay down straight on her back. The spine, accustomed to bending along special curves, had to keep itself straight.

'No ... every curve will be erased, this crookedness will have to be straightened,' she ordered and slipped into a deep sleep that had evaded her for years.

40

On waking up she realised that the day had advanced and she had missed the news. Someone was singing the opening of a lively raga in mellow tones. She finished tea in a leisurely manner and picked up the paper.

'Germany attacks Russia.'

She sat up quickly and read the bold headline again which was to be etched in blood on history's forehead. She wasn't as surprised by Husain Bibi's visit as she was by this news. But, for some reason, she smiled. One had to smile when the news appeared in a new guise each time. Until yesterday Russia and Germany were in an embrace, cuddling each other, and today this battering had started. There had been some speculation, but no one thought it would happen so soon. June 22 will live in history as a memorable date.

Array, she must get up. The shops will be open. This new development will definitely affect prices. It wouldn't be such a bad idea to buy winter supplies as well. She took the school van on the pretext of running an important errand and went shopping.

Today she was drawn to all the bright colours. *Banarsi* edging will become more expensive in a few days, and the price of satin has already gone up. She needed a coat as well. She should buy two of everything. More than half of her money was spent on clothes. With the remainder she bought dinnerware, cutlery and other miscellaneous household items. She had once seen a woman wearing gold nail polish; her dark brown hands were sinister-looking. Anyway Shamman did like three or four shades and, after some debate over different brands of cosmetics, she decided to opt for a whole set of Max Factor. For the first time in her life she wasted an entire month's income on such items. As far as cosmetics go, both imported and exported merchandise will do, and who really cares about clothes? If anyone asks she could say she had bought the fabric before the clamour for *khadar* started, before she became a progressive. It's foolishness to burn it, therefore one is forced to wear it.

How many different advantages a sleeveless blouse has. Less fabric, cooler, and more comfortable. And if you wear it in winter under your coat the shoulders of the coat won't puff out. True, a sleeveless blouse takes getting used to, and you have two-toned skin, dark from the wrist to the elbow and light in the area that was covered by the sleeves. So what if people think you've just started wearing it – what can they do?

That same five-seater belonging to Comrade Samad which always felt constricting, seemed roomier than ever today. On one side sat Comrade, on the other the poet of revolution and still there was enough space, and she didn't mind at all when they repeatedly lit cigarettes or used some other excuse to squeeze her from both sides. She wasn't upset when their hot breath warmed her arms and her neck, or their restless calves collided with her sari. Pretending not to notice, she looked away casually, providing them as she did so with a view of the most attractive angles of her face.

The problem with a sari is that the portion on the shoulder keeps slipping, causing the revolutionary poet's eyes to rotate like a top. And what's that crawling on Samad's neck, making him lift his elbow again and again, nudging Shamman's side each time? She leaned forward and asked Professor Rehman the time, although both Samad and the poet were wearing watches; she was more interested in Rehman at this moment.

The debate at the meeting was riotous. But everyone was somewhat flustered. No one knew which viewpoint to endorse and which to oppose; there were as many opinions as there were voices.

'Russia is stupid. They should have joined forces with Germany and annihilated imperialism.'

'This is just pretence, there's no real conflict.'

'No, the news is true. All night the British were dancing with joy. The monster that threatened them is now pursuing their enemy, their oldest enemy. Now they'll get together with Germany and give it a real beating.'

'*Array*, today these traders of peace will present a two-anna offering – years of wishing and praying have borne fruit.'

'No, they will side with Russia, perhaps not actively, but at least verbally, and then they'll stand to one side like a bat and wait for the winning party to emerge.'

'In the end they will divide and devour both the defeated Russia and the vanquished Germany.'

'For the moment they will support Russia, and they should too. Russia's death is the death of humanity, and it seems that humanity is aging rapidly.'

'It will probably take no more than two months to pound Russia.'

The swastika twirled like a top and enlarged its sphere, and Shamman, meanwhile, embarked on romantic relationships. Today she was with Comrade Samad in his car, tomorrow with Engineer Sahib, one day with the poet, immersed in his verses in some shabby restaurant, the next with Professor Rehman in a badly lit library. One week with the superintendent in his tent hunting quail, the following week on the banks of a river in a small tent, laughing boisterously between sips of coffee. Shamman had become very bold. Because she was eating less her body was leaner, her fingers longer and more supple. But the joints in her ankles had become very delicate so that even a short walk made them ache, and if she rubbed them she felt so ticklish that she scratched her skin roughly with her polished nails. Comrade Samad kissed the marks on her ankles when he was alone with her. The revolutionary poet had compared them to wells in which his heart bobbed on lonely nights. Engineer Sahib thought that when he had been separated from her a long time, these marks would be like scattered skeletons in the desert, reminiscent of some grand caravan. Professor was a writer and every sentence he uttered reflected his literary bent of mind. Shamman was frank and open with all of these men. They walked unannounced into her room, then exhibited sheepishness at her flustered behaviour, and like baby goats romped on her bed, put on her saris as part of mock dress-ups, and gambled, wagering her bangles. Each bangle, valued at ten rupees, travelled from one pocket to another. They pressed her clothes to their noses to preserve her scent in their minds so that when they were separated from her they could recall the scent and experience the turmoil connected with the remembrance of past times.

She had cut curls so often from her thick, wavy tresses for them to place in lockets that she was afraid she might not have any hair left. The poet rubbed the hair on his lips when he was lost for inspiration. Flowers from her bun, her old, smelly handkerchiefs and other such unromantic things were pressed between the pages of books as keep-sakes. She didn't know how many flowers, yellow, white and red, she had presented as virginal gifts to people, how many apples and glasses of juice had been sucked on by four lips . . . but she was still thirsty.

Iftikhar had taught her a wonderful lesson. If you want to train a lion, keep him hungry, if you want to rule a people, keep them hungry. These few whites who are ruling over millions of blacks are doing so in accordance with the policy of hunger. The smell of food should enter the nostrils, mouths should water, the tongue should hang out, but don't give them food. No one remembers the taste of food when the stomach is full. Let it travel down the throat and it's gone. Just keep it limited to the lips, away from the throat!

She did not hesitate to give the men all kinds of tasks. Suddenly late at night she would have a yearning for coconut oil, either because the present oil had developed an odour or because she just didn't like it any more, and she'd make them run in the car despite the fact that petrol was so scarce these days. They got special rations of petrol from the government for important 'work', or else they obtained it from the black market which was thriving as usual. She made them travel to Delhi or Calcutta on a search for the newest colours in georgette. In addition to all this, she made them change her pillow slips, wring out her cushions, and put a drawstring through a waistband with a tiny hairpin.

She gave each the impression that she socialised with the others just as a formality, and it was he who had broken her heart. When she was too intimate with one, she wanted the others to see her. If there's food cooking on one stove, the embers on the other should not go to waste; something or other should be cooking there as well. This was a very useful ploy and the greatest secret of her victory.

She never went anywhere alone now. Without her 'sanctuaries' she felt apprehensive and fearful. If she went shopping she took them along with her. They followed her proudly with packages, shoeboxes, boxes of biscuits and bundles of fresh vegetables; they transported an entire month's provisions to the car for her and if, on returning home, she discovered that the coriander looked wilted, they gladly went back and exchanged it. This was not all. They happily ran a hundred other errands for her which, if their wives mentioned them, would cause them enough embarrassment to want to drown.

She usually found herself entangled with the Professor, arguing, quarrelling. He was candid and outspoken to the extent of being cruel. Sometimes Shamman wasn't sure if he was the hunted or the hunter in disguise. She didn't know why, but whenever she found him staring at her she longed to cover herself with a steel blanket. Quite a few times she flung arrows at him, but it seemed as if the arrows hit a stony crag and returned. And to crown it all were his eagle eyes and his mocking smile. Angered, Shamman came back each time determined to exercise greater caution. But she didn't admit defeat and continued searching for the enemy's weak spot. Once she decided to stake everything on a single strategy. Her heart was pounding. What if he kicked the dish she was offering? She tried to probe him by using a few cleverly devised questions.

'To whom will you dedicate your new book?'

Professor looked at her sceptically. 'Whoever passes the test.'

'What's the admission fee?'

'Nothing, and a lot.'

'Oh, who can win with you? Now how can we idiots understand such a deep, mystical answer like that?'

'So you're teasing again?'

'Oh, you're so cynical.'

Professor threw a dark glance at her and she quickly snuggled closer to the poet. No indeed, this is not a snake you can play with. A short while later Professor came and stood next to her.

'Are you angry with me?' he asked, pushing down on her toe with his shoe.

'Of course not.'

'Then what was the meaning of that statement? The book is being published and will be dedicated . . .'

'To whom will it be dedicated then, your dead mother?' Shamman asked irately.

'My mother is alive.' Professor took offence.

'Oh, I'm sorry. The father's name then?'

'He's deceased.'

'Ohho, what nonsense! The one you think is alive is dead, and the one you think is dead is alive. Then to your wife?'

'I don't have a wife.'

'And if you did have a wife you would have committed the folly of dedicating it to her.'

'What's the use of speaking without first listening? I say that a wife is absolute foolishness and if you do have a wife, then not only do you dedicate your book to her, but also your intelligence and common sense.'

'Unh! Go ahead then, go one step further, dedicate the book to your mother-in-law.'

'Why are you getting upset? How about if I dedicate it to my beloved?'

'Come on.' She couldn't believe her ears.

'But I don't like the poet's words at all.' He was referring to the revolutionary poet's dedication.

'You're a fool.'

'Maybe I am, but there is no sitar in my dry and lonely life so no one is plucking the strings with a pick. I'm sorry, I hope you don't mind.' He smiled cunningly.

'Why should I mind?' But she did mind and she wanted to scratch his face. 'Well, how about the other collection, *Leaps*, you like its dedication, don't you?'

'Oh my God! "The glow of the sun" – archaic, and "whipping glances" – sadism?'

'I'm not talking to you, go away. What has the poor fellow ever done to you? Why are you always making fun of him? True, he's not as crafty as you are.'

'I'm crafty?' Professor asked brightly.

'Of course. And he's so simple.'

'You don't know what a clever man he is. He's a favourite with the nawab's wife. Do you know he's getting a stipend from four different places?'

With a jolt a few moments from her past forced their way forward, but Shamman pushed them back with both hands. She thanked God she had never felt sorry for the poet.

'Do you remember the day when you broke all my bangles?' She changed the subject swiftly.

'Yes, I remember.' Professor seemed piqued, as if it was a crime to forget such an important incident.

'Were you sorry?'

'I shed tears when I saw you cry. All those pearls are gathered in my handkerchief.'

'It must have been washed by now.'

'No, but anyway, water doesn't have the power to wash away such pearls.'

'Anyway, now listen, what if you phrase your dedication like this: "To those broken bangles . . ." no, just "To the broken bangles".' She had decided that if Professor disagreed with her statement, she'd turn the whole thing into a joke, but he was in a strange mood today.

'You're very clever.'

'And on the cover a picture of broken bangles. What do you say?'

'Why not?'

Seeing that she had him where she wanted him, she advanced quickly. 'Come, I'll draw your picture.' She clasped his wrist and dug her nails into his flesh. Before his afflicted hand could seize her she darted out of there to the garden, where, in the presence of everyone else, he had to

254

talk loudly about the weather and politics in a very cultured tone. For a while he panted like a thirsty ox, then left.

To the Broken Bangles was published and appeared in bookstores. But events took an unusual turn. The poet guessed something was afoot. Recently Professor had been making his appearance at the oddest of times in order to discuss important matters. One day the poet arrived and proceeded to sulk. Shamman exhibited patience for a little while, but then she lost her patience.

'But how does any of this affect you?'

'It's not affecting me, but you shouldn't encourage everyone like this, as if, as if . . .'

'As if, as if nothing! You're just jealous he's gone ahead of you.'

' "To the broken bangles": what a stupid and meaningless line.'

'I say you're stupid and meaningless yourself, yes!'

'What a compliment. Do you know that my name appears on the list of poets who are considered the best?'

'Hunh! All the best poets are fools!'

'Miss Shamshad! You have no right to insult me.'

'And you have no right to eat my brains. My mind is benumbed from having to listen to all your silly poems.'

'I . . . I . . . you . . .'

'What's this "me" and "you"? Some romance this is – no matter what's going on, one has to listen to these mile-long poems. I'll say goodbye to such love, I'm better off being alone.'

'I thought you were a champion of literature and . . .'

'Excuse me, I'm not a champion of literature at all. I listened to your poems just to humour you. Please leave and stay away from the confines of the girls' school. There are daughters of respectable people here, this is not a brothel.'

'And until now . . .'

'Until now it was as I wished.'

'I . . . I've strangled myself . . .'

'Good, now go and bury yourself . . . go.'

'I'm leaving, but I never thought you would be so sadistic . . . but . . .'

'Please leave now and you have my permission to get rid of these ifs and buts, go and tell the rest of the world that I'm base and immoral, tell them I was your mistress, go.'

After the poet left Shamman was racked by a fit of laughter. She was grateful no one else came to see her that day, because she was like a sword out of its sheath. Anyway, everyone was busy. Military conscription had begun in Comrade Samad's estate and he had to relinquish his role as comrade and, donning his mantle of landowner, had to revert to nurturing the role of squire. Literary and progressive meetings also lost their edge and were about to fall apart. Two or three people went to jail and the policies underwent change. Most of the members now shifted their attention to 'work' related to the national war. The battle for Russia was transformed into the world's battle, and for this reason was now mankind's battle. Engineer Sahib left for Beirut on an assignment which paid him four times more than anything he had earned before. The world became a dull place. Hitler sprinted all over the place. Japan too was beginning to sneeze; the chill was increasing in the eastern isles and there was a need for a bonfire.

Shamman was in a very bad mood for no special reason when Professor arrived. His boldness was increasing; he was the only one remaining now, like a lone branch on a tree. He was here for the sixth time asking for a lock of her hair or something else as a keepsake. Actually he had worn out all the components of clandestine dealings. The romance, after having been repeated the same way ten times, had putrefied, all the words and expressions had become commonplace. Political passion had also subsided.

The question of hunger was being raised again. Military conscription seemed to be swallowing up the blind, crippled, everyone; those who until yesterday did not have even a penny, were now dressed in military uniform and strutted about, giving themselves airs. Swaggering and cocky, everyone is a lieutenant. Tension decreased with the lessening of hunger. All this agitation takes place in order to fill the stomach's reservoir; fill the stomachs as much as possible, and then place these stomachs in front of guns and you won't even hear a squeak out of anyone. Despite all this a certain kind of selfishness and carelessness prevailed, as if this wasn't a war, it was a traders' exchange. Grab as much money as possible, now is the opportunity; people have needs and they also have money to buy goods, fill their pockets with rubbish. A war fund had been established and money was being raised by arranging entertainment shows – everything is there, except the heart. Why should the heart be in it? For whom?

Professor had gone too far with his attentions. Shamman was tired of everything and everyone. All the others had gone, but for some reason he persisted stubbornly.

'Suggest a name for my new book,' he said ebulliently.

256

'Name? Why do you need a name? Can't a book be published if it doesn't have a name?' She was chafing already.

'By name I mean title.'

'Yes, I know enough Urdu to know that. Any title will do, it's all the same.'

'You mean, not give it any title?'

'Sure, what's wrong with that? It's appropriate for a book that's unknown to have no title.'

'What do you mean?'

'I mean if you attempt to plagiarise other people's ideas and try to become an author . . .'

'Who are you talking about? My ideas are based on research.'

'No doubt. Tell me, how many times have you gone to a village and had yoghurt drinks there and eaten cooked mustard leaves and smelled the aroma of the mustard stalks? How many innocent village girls have you raped and how many bastard children have you fathered? Such nonsense! You just sit here and prattle. And you think you've set out to reform society? Hunh!'

'I don't believe in social reform at all, I'm not a leader.'

'Well, what's the use of blackening paper then? Except for supporting prostitutes, there's nothing else you want to do. Tell me, why are you so much in favour of prostitutes?'

'I . . .'

'You go to them and you feel depressed and you want the government to forget about the war and concentrate on decorating the homes of prostitutes, replace their flickering lanterns with electric lights?'

'And why not?'

'But why have you forgotten your own home in your eagerness to improve the prostitute's lot? There are others who are also starving, why do you feel pity only for these unfortunate wretches?'

'You can say what you want, but they're a part of society and my sensitive nature won't allow me to see any part of society rotting away.'

'Oh, these poor things. There are hundreds of other women rotting in their homes.'

'Well, how can I write about them? How do I know how many brothels exist behind curtained doors and what's going on there? Anyway, I'm not interested in the plight of the housewife . . .'

'Why should you be? Your entire interest is riveted on the prostitute.'

'Of course. She is helpful to me, she's mine, and this woman behind

257

the curtain whom we refer to mistakenly as an educated woman, what do I get from her?'

'All right, let's concede your point. But you profess to be a realist.'

'So? Do you have any objection to that?'

'No, I don't have the right to object, but this is what I ask: you know the prostitute very well, but what about men who suffer? Have you sought them out? Or are you always going to portray men as tyrants, heartless brutes, deceivers, capable only of fathering bastard children? You claim to be very liberal, but you too think that honour and chastity are attributes of women only, that men are free of all this folly.'

'What?'

'Yes. And you think you're defending women, in other words you keep telling women that everything that's right and proper for men is a sin for them. This is your justice and your open-mindedness?'

'You turn everything upside-down and you don't listen.'

'How can I listen? What's there to listen to? All this is only for vicarious pleasure. Tell me, why do your accounts of nudity stop at a woman's breasts?'

'Eh?' Professor burst out laughing.

'Well, take a look at your own nakedness . . . a rapacious assault and that's all.'

'You're very upset today. Drink some cold water to cool your anger.'

'Should I tell you why this obscenity is written?'

'You won't stop at my insistence . . . go ahead, tell me.'

'The breast is the centre of beauty, and it's enough to find satisfaction by playing with it.'

'All right, I give in. What did we start out with and where are we now? It seems as if . . .'

'What?'

'You've received a fresh bruise.'

'Bruise? Hunh! How did you know?'

'By your sheepish expression and your tearful discourse. Why are you blaming me for your wounds? Are you going to hold me responsible for the crimes of all men? You've spoken at length, but do you have the courage to listen to me now or will you ward me off with the shield of femininity?'

'I'm not a coward.'

'Well, listen then. I feel sorry for you.'

'Thanks. But what's the reason for this generosity?'

'Sometimes I feel pity for no reason at all.'

'In that case I have doubts about your intelligence.'

'Yes, perhaps we are both to be pitied. You got lost in an attempt to find yourself and I've lost precious time in my struggle to understand you. For once I turned away from women of the streets to study, to use your words, a respectable woman, and at every step I was blinded by dust thrown in my eyes. And after all this time I discovered that no matter who a woman is or where she is, it is foolish to try and understand her. She's not there to be analysed, she's there to be used. Yes, there's one other thing. I did surmise that you're not an ordinary woman, but you're suffering from some very colourful misconceptions. You think you're extremely intelligent, although that's not the case at all. You are extraordinarily outspoken and smooth-talking, you have a special talent for bandying words.'

'Hunh! And what else?'

'And don't try to be overly sensitive. I think that it's admirable you can suffer and then laugh obstinately, but that doesn't mean you're brave and strong. You're a coward, you turn a wound inflicted by a needle into a shield. You think that the way you treated all of us was a sign of strength? No, not at all. This fear, this desire to protect your femininity, these are all signs of your cowardice.'

'You're recounting your follies as my weaknesses.'

'Follies? You call it a folly? To come out unscathed like an ice cube after exposure to your smouldering heat was not cowardice or stupidity. It is the height of courage. And when we appreciated your delicate glass by curbing our desires, you thought you were making fools of us? We were having fun at your expense. Whatever we wanted from you we got. By God, not once did I experience the desire to step any further, and why should I have? What invaluable thing could you give us that we couldn't get elsewhere for less? And anyway, you know that your allure isn't so great; for example, did you think Samad Sahib would choose you over his title? Engineer Sahib left you and went to Beirut. Do you think you could have stopped him? Who knows how many women like you he leaves behind at every station? You can't achieve the status that his stupid, illiterate wife has. You're a flame, but you don't have the warmth of a mother's breast. You can burn but you don't know how to apply a soothing balm, you can break, but you can't put together.' He chuckled. 'Tell me, does anyone really care for you?'

'You kick in the shin and the eye is punctured . . .'

'I'm sure no one does,' Professor interrupted her roughly. 'There's danger everywhere in the country, people are trying to protect their

259

loved ones, but no one knows that you are alive, that you also need protection.'

'I can protect myself.'

'Yes, I know that you are so clever you'll save five or six others with you. You're quite used to indifference and lack of consideration from other people. The world has inflicted so much pain on you, you've become insensitive, and that's why your attack is so dangerous. By treating the poet in this way, you've avenged an old lover who probably abandoned you and left you sobbing.'

'You're very clever.' Shamman spoke as if her tongue had dried up.

'Forget my cleverness. And I pity your loneliness. You're like the street on which people walk all day and night and still it remains alone, silent and lifeless. Please forgive me, but often I've seen the pain of loneliness floating on your face when you're in a crowd. When you're hurting, you laugh and when you're happy there are tears in your eyes. Everything about you is a deception. Well, it's one thing to deceive the world, but I think it's stupid to try and deceive yourself.'

'Are you making up the plot for your new novel by any chance?'

'In my stories you'll find people, not corpses, people who are alive or who have died a natural death. Of course I must admit I haven't seen too many corpses like you that laugh and breathe. Please don't take offence, whatever I have said has come from a sense of compassion. Tomorrow I'm leaving. There's an offer from the BBC. I wish I had spoken the truth to you earlier.'

'So you do agree that you are a liar.'

'Of course. Truth is always eclipsed in the presence of a liar. That's why I always lied, but today when you began telling the truth, I lost my reserve as well. I'm glad it turned out this way, and the truth is . . .'

'Come on, say it, don't hesitate to speak. Your lies and the falsehoods uttered by the others have wearied me. I want to hear the truth from someone, so please say what you were saying, even if you think it will be like a shoe on my face.'

'Then listen. Actually – and please forgive me if you feel slighted – I have never asked you to marry me. No one can make a long-term contract with such an unprincipled, rude person. Unless I were out of my mind, I would not attempt to have any other relationship except a temporary one with an impetuous and capricious woman like you. Marriage is one thing, I wouldn't even want to be your neighbour. Do you see how we can't get along for even a minute. We know each other too well!'

260

'Oh, so this was the truthful admission that was supposed to hurt me?'

'Yes, but you're neither hurt nor have you suffered any damage. I know you're beyond any real feeling. Your ego has been kicked so many times it's transformed into a shameless lump of clay. Because so much has been snatched from you, you now pick up everything and throw it away yourself.'

'What's the use of collecting rubbish?'

'Your eyes now see diamonds as stones.'

'And one of those sparkling diamonds is you perhaps . . .' Shamman burst into derisive laughter.

'Let's forget me. You and I are of no importance to each other. But you spurned the poet, that was not nice. Do you know he's been hired to work for the war propaganda with a salary of six hundred rupees a month?' Professor smiled roguishly.

'In your opinion his faults have been washed away by the six hundred rupees?'

'Weaknesses are a result of poverty. You don't know what terrible filth hides in these breasts soaked in lavender. What I want to say is that war is knocking at our door, everything is becoming expensive and scarce and it might be a good idea to snare a worker who will come to your assistance when you're in trouble. I'm a useless person, and anyway, I'm too involved with prostitutes. By the way, can I ask you something?'

'Yes, ask quickly and . . .'

'Have you ever been kissed by a man? Oh, don't bother to answer, your saintly lips are a testimony to your chastity. I wonder . . . what will it be like to conduct an experiment . . .' Professor threw down his cigarette and stared at Shamman with a strange expression on his face. Before she knew what was happening, he bent down, held her head between his hands, and softly kissed her defiant lips.

'Get away . . . you scoundrel . . . you savage.' But who was it that she was pushing away? Taking long strides, he left the room, got on his bicycle and soon he had disappeared around the bend in the road. 'Wait, wait,' she said as she felt a mutinous horse stamping in some remote part of her brain, 'everything will be all right.'

'But what will happen now, what will happen?' the angry rider asked, tugging at the reins.

'Nothing, nothing, let it go this time . . . there's no time to think, the veins are taut, the slightest pressure will break them . . . come, lie down quietly on the bed ... slumber stands nearby ... you won't have to wait too long.'

Like a dutiful daughter she walked to her bed, lowered her head on the pillow, stretched out slowly, and shut her eyes.

'Today it acquiesced,' she thought once before falling asleep. 'What if it doesn't the next time? It would be difficult to appease this raging brain.'

Her body drifted into repose, but her mind continued to sob apprehensively. She looked behind her and saw in the distance a road that wound about like an undulating cobra pursuing her. She wanted to return, to wipe out this frightful mark and in its place draw a new line, a neat and clean line. But these curves had become too firm, like a steel wire. Her eyes closed, she began running on these crooked lines.

41

'This is the wrong side, this is the right side.' During a needlework class she spread out the cloth on the floor and examined it closely. But she couldn't be sure. If only there was some power that never lies, never deceives, that would come and whisper in her ear that this side of the fabric is the right side. What will happen if the girls do the embroidery on the wrong side? The items to be sold at the fair organised in aid of the war effort would go to waste.

Already, she had slowed down. It seemed as if gradually the machine was rusting, nuts and bolts had disappeared, and the handle failed to rotate. The new library books hadn't been numbered as yet, the registers were incomplete because the attendances had to be added and averaged, the prospect of all this addition and subtraction was stifling her, the receipts were also piling up without signatures, and the final inventory for the furniture had been delayed. What will happen? How will this machine be dragged along? And to make matters worse, this fabric! Several times since this morning she had paused during work to think. The teachers were also divided in their view of the fabric. But she had no faith in public opinion. The masses know nothing; they shut their eyes and agree to everything.

In the end she tried to reassure herself by drawing lots in secret. Placing two small chits in a box, she shook them up and picked out one, but ohhh! she wasn't satisfied. After being deceived so often she no longer trusted anyone or anything. What if the ballot was also lying? Playing a trick to entrap her? And if such delicate workmanship is completed on the wrong side, how will it be unravelled? The entire material will be riddled with holes, becoming mincemeat, and then how will these holes be darned? These minuscule bumps will rankle in the eyes, will make for sleeplessness.

Why is this intricate, ornate kind of needlework so popular in Hindustan? Europeans embroider such nice, large flowers, attractive as well as easy and simple. But here things are so cramped, so stiflingly close together that one has difficulty breathing; everything is tangled up! The creation of a muddled brain is sure to be knotted and snarled. Who can unravel it?

As the time of the fair approached she became more and more anxious. The fair and the war fund be damned! What will the money be used for? For dressing and healing wounds. On the one hand more and more effective ways of wounding are being invented, on the other, nurses are being rushed to counteract them. This beautiful needlework will take the form of thousands of tanks and bombs to be used by man on man. Bodies will be crushed, rivers of blood will flow, the oppressor and the oppressed will be bound together with the same rope.

And these innocent soldiers? No sooner did the war start than their value increased. Now everything is theirs – the country, the magnificent buildings. As long as there was peace no one bothered to look at them, but today when the god of war has opened his mouth wide, keep dumping in as much as you can as if it were a mill. And afterwards? When the game is over, everything ends. The tanks will be melted down to produce railway tracks, the guns will become fast-moving automobiles, some of the metal will fall also into the soldiers' laps in the shape of medals which will eventually become rattles for children. When the maimed, dying men are exhausted and spent there will be a reconciliation and the soldiers will come home with their amputated legs and arms. And until the imprudent ones start fighting again, they will rust away like weapons in permanent disuse.

When the war ends schools will close, dinner parties will be held, and the soldier? What will become of the soldier? He'll be melted down to give shape to thieves, criminals, and starving, naked beggars.

Someone should ask, 'You wretches, why do you fight?' Agreed that the population has increased tremendously and you can't come up with a solution. But just think for a moment: how do those mothers feel who have given birth? Fortunate are the women who remain infertile; if they had to give birth to these soldiers they would understand what torture it is to lose sons.

Shamman's head was in a whirl even before the time came to be lauded for the fair's success. Her power of restraint weakened and her sanity floundered, so she took leave of absence and went home. You want to be with your family during the war, you long to be immersed in another's being. Anyway, once in a while you should attempt to rediscover what it feels to be loved by family members. Perhaps here she will find what she had been searching for everywhere.

These brothers and sisters! Why had she tried to put them out of her mind? They came from the same womb, they were raised in the same house, but when a leaf fell from a branch, how far away life blew it. Once she got tired of tossing about she jumped up and grabbed that branch again, but she was out of practice and had to exercise all of her strength; her shoulders ached from the effort. But she found such peace in her mother's lap, it was such a soothing feeling.

What? The whole world was present in her house! In that one family there were some as fair-complexioned as the English, some very dark, a few seemed to carry the tartness of the Mongols, while others were characterised by an Irani sharpness. And all this was the result of the hard work done by four or five women. If Hindustan too needs pure blood like Germany, how much of the native core will remain? As much as the whiteness of a sesame seed, perhaps not even that much. There's a share from the Aryans, the Iranis, then the Afghans, Mongols and Arabs, and what about this fresh English blood which had come home filled in red canisters along with other military wares? Hindustani soil imbibes every seed.

With religious zeal Shamman began working on these brown and yellow relatives. She had never kissed babies before so at first she felt sick and extremely uncomfortable; what kind of saliva- and phlegm-laden, incomplete humans were they? Even dogs were better than them.

Will the demand of an autumn-struck leaf that it hang from the branch again make spring return? If a fallen fruit runs out of a plate and clamours to dangle from the bough again, will it be successful? If these hens try to snuggle under the mother hen's feathers, will they fit there? Her shoulders ached from hanging too long, the tighter she held on to the branch the more she slipped, and soon she realised that you can buy everything with money, you can satisfy your sexual hunger, you can stuff your stomach with food, but motherly love cannot be bought at any cost. To try and adopt someone else's child is as foolish as a crow trying to become a peacock by wearing the peacock's feathers on its tail. An illegitimate child's mother is a mother at least; what would happen if the wild fig tree produces flowers?

First she lovingly took her older sister's daughter under her wing. Once you're a mother you automatically learn how to suffer all kinds of discomforts, but Shamman learned a real lesson by hanging upside-down. '*Teen, teen,*' the baby cried all night and all day. Sometimes she wanted to wring this living radio's neck so that she would be silenced for ever.

Patting a child for hours is also an art. You have to adopt a machine-like pace, swing your head but make sure it doesn't bob suddenly, and at the same time make meaningless, clucking noises with your tongue so that the child can experience both the comforts of sleeping on a spinning wheel and in a human lap. This is how it works; you collect a bit of air in your mouth, then exhale with '*ray*', and then place your tongue against the roof of your mouth, pull out the letter 'q' with a certain degree of tautness, and at the same time continue to pat softly the child's temples. If all these ploys fail to produce the desired effect, then you should solicit the help of as many people as possible and, with their co-operation, shake and rattle all the objects nearby in such a manner that several different types of noises are created which bear upon the child's brain like a hellish clamour. This technique, along with the above-mentioned strategy, should have some effect. If the tapping is regular, synchronising with the scientific principles of time, then, God willing, the child will fall asleep. A child who sleeps with the aid of such a technique will remain mentally asleep even when he is awake.

Shamman was extremely relieved after she returned the baby in one piece. What if, God forbid, the child had contracted some dangerous disease? She wasn't surprised that so many children died in Hindustan. Actually, she herself had experienced the desire a few times to remove the baby's blanket and leave the window open. By morning it would have pneumonia and then by nightfall everything would be over; you could stretch out in peace and sleep. No wonder the mothers, on discovering that there's a new one on the way, start having secretive conferences with the midwives in the neighbourhood. The affliction remains, but they end up with other problems, and when the new one arrives they don't know what to do, but they're mothers after all. Even if they want to get rid of it, they can't.

When the trauma incurred with the first child subsided somewhat, Shamman undertook the patronage of another child, a boy this time. Unfortunately he was rather homely looking, in poor health, and seemed to have a special affinity for filth. She provided him every treatment possible, but all the diseases appeared to have developed a firm hold on him; there was hardly an ailment that hadn't overpowered him at some point. But he didn't seem to be in the mood to die.

Finally, as a last resort, it was Manjhu's daughter whose name was drawn. She was like a Chinese doll. After lengthy preparations, clothes were made for her and Shamman pondered seriously over the question of adopting her. When she was leaving, Manjhu cried as if she was burying the child alive. She had a thousand instructions for Shamman. 'Don't hit her, you have a very bad temper,' she said before she left. Wonder of wonders, this was the same Manjhu *bi* who had taken her from Unna when she was just a baby and raised her. Surely she must have been a hundred times better than Manjhu's spoilt child and perhaps that's why she was able to care for her. This little girl was impossible.

Now came the crows and the peacocks; they poked with their beaks until Shamman was touching her ears with regret. And the girl was like the musk rat in the snake's mouth; it couldn't be spat out and it couldn't be swallowed.

'*Tsk, tsk, tsk*' . . . my, such a little thing and separated from its mother . . . God forgive us!'

'Oh, what's this pampering of someone else's child? This is cruel.' There were as many opinions as there were tongues. Shamman got upset, but thought eventually people would tire of prattling and shut up.

Shamman suffered the taunts because the girl was very pretty, but one night the child soiled her nappy and Shamman made the mistake of washing her with ice-cold water. The next day she developed pneumonia and four days later she was finished.

It seemed as if the girl had died deliberately just to embarrass her. Shamman's grief was overpowered by feelings of shame and anger. She wished those days would return when Manjhu *bi* was raising her. How she had beaten her. If she had known this was going to happen she

266

would have died just to slap Manjhu in the face. Two days later Manjhu arrived weeping and wailing.

Shamman had to hear things she never thought she'd hear even in her wildest imagination. Manjhu blamed her for her daughter's death, stopping short only of having her arrested for murder. If Shamman could help it she would give birth to ten such babies and throw them in Manjhu's face. She didn't think Manjhu would be so mean. To appease her she tried to weep, she donated all the girl's clothes to charity, and arranged the third- and fortieth-day ceremonies with great pomp and show, as if it wasn't a child who had died but a bundle of sins for which atonement was sorely needed.

And to crown it all people proclaimed that without a doubt it was this child that would take Manjhu by the hand and lead her straight to heaven. These innocent children don't just belong in heaven, they are also capable of putting in a good word for you. But everything that Shamman did after the girl's death was entered into Manjhu's account. And still Manjhu bawled and howled.

A stubborn seedling fastened itself to the flat, stony surface of a rock and nurtured hopes of growing, of burgeoning. A thousand waves lapped up to the seedling to wash it away, but instead dashed their heads on the rock and returned. Then one day that seedling too turned into stone.

Professor wrote to her. 'There is such an abundance of girls here that it's useless to marry. If you want to come as a guest (notice the word *guest*), there is room for you here.'

The seedling that has turned to stone is a thousand times better than the shameless thorns of the cactus that are eating away at society's roots like worms. Shamman replied: 'Thank you for your hospitality. If such a time comes, I'll see.'

Time won't drop out of somewhere; you will have to procure it yourself, or else keep in mind that time takes a long while to arrive, but its departure is so hasty that you're left with no option but to chafe your hands regretfully. Be wary of the time when you might have to say:

> *Who cared about shores when the boat was intact?*
> *Now, with a shattered boat, who can long for shores?*

During this period Shamman made an attempt to adopt another child, but she soon realised that her position was like the piece of land on which everyone climbs for sustenance, but which is condemned as barren afterwards and abandoned. Although the child was guileless and simple-minded, he didn't let go of the hem of his mother's mantle; after receiving cheer and nourishment from Shamman, he headed straight for his mother's lap.

'Not mine . . . not mine.' The words rammed into her ears like fiery rods. With one thrust she broke all her shackles. No one is hers, and why does she need anyone? Is she inadequate?

The next day she collected her scattered 'self' and got on a train. Where was she going? She didn't think about her destination. She could travel anywhere in this big wide world. And why shouldn't she? True, she had no fixed destination in mind, and that was just as well. Why should there be a destination? These clouds didn't know where they were going; they soared where they pleased and then poured on a whim, soaking those who were already deluged, or teasing those who were parched as they went on their way. And these storms don't have a destination either as they go hauling rubbish from here to there, sprinting around in isolated caves, screaming, dashing their heads against rocks, tangling with the capricious waves of the ocean, and ascending and plummeting for no apparent reason. There is a certain pleasure in this nomadic life. Perhaps someday she'll find a shore and this lost vessel will ferry across, and what if it doesn't? What's the harm in that? What's wrong with floating like this, without sails, without oars, without a guide?

42

Agra!

She got down here. She wanted to see the Taj Mahal. Perhaps the weight upon her heart will be reduced when she sees this grand symbol of love and romance. How special those people were! What a monument Shah Jahan raised to honour his love for his wife. What a sacred relationship. But why doesn't someone raise a structure like this out of love for the inhabitants of this world? When thousands and thousands of people spend their entire lives on stony footpaths, how can the spirits of the emperor and his queen sleep so peacefully under the marble canopy? The rest of the edifice was inhabited by bats and owls who had a free rein here and never had to pay any taxes.

She had always heard that on moonlit nights the Taj appears as a glimmering diadem on Raja Inder's forehead. But seeing this magnificent corpse during daytime made her hair stand on end. As evening approached, sprightly young men arrived to murmur lovesick pledges in the alcoves and corners of the Taj. There were also 'hoories' bedecked in cheap accessories, their faces, because of a profusion of powder, reminiscent of sweet potatoes buried in hot ashes; they were not even fit to play the role of witches in this lively celebration.

Why do these people enjoy sitting atop a corpse? What is so attractive about these graveyards that you feel impelled to come here and experience life? Perhaps the spirit of vengeance finds some solace here. 'You squeezed the blood of centuries into the foundations of these buildings so that you may be remembered, and we? We do not hesitate to commit any act.' If only revenge could take a straight path and not meander in this fashion.

Lahore!

Her uneasiness grew. If it were up to her, Shalimar Gardens would be developed as a much more interesting place. She had heard a great deal about Nur Jahan's tomb, but when she set eyes on it she burst out laughing. Here too only the donkeys were at peace.

Nur Jahan! One woman's victory makes another woman suspicious. What was so special about Nur Jahan that she was able to overpower Jahangir? And who knows if she loved Sher Afghan more or Jahangir. Or if she loved Sher Afghan first and then fell in love with Jahangir. It's possible she loved both of them at the same time. A woman's heart has so many chambers, a mother's love residing in one, love for her husband in another, for her beloved a third one.

Then Shamman tried to peep into her own heart. What is packed into her chambers? She couldn't see anything except a foggy cloud. If only she could unravel all these cords and make separate balls. The images of lover, beloved and enemy, were all dimmed; if only she could take a pencil and just fill in the necessary details while the rest was erased by time's abrasive movement.

Delhi!

Everything looked unhealthy and unattractive. Dilapidated houses stood cursing their builders, she saw corroding statues that belonged to no one, also hungry dogs, the unfortunate offspring of the streets, still protecting what and at whose bidding, no one knows, and splattered on the walls long lists of cures for revolting diseases that screamed out in honour of the manhood of the city's inhabitants. But its half-sister New Delhi? Clean, tidy, and isolated. It seems as if only bats or spirits live here, an example of the modern Taj Mahal. A great many new masters will arrive, dedicate it to its eternal masters and then proceed to create new shrines.

But the Qutb Minar, so tall and so useless. What is the meaning of this one, lone door? With its hands spread out like some giant, who is it waiting to take into its embrace?

Where? Where? Where should she go? Why can't she find a way out of these mazes? She wanted to tear away the curtain and rush out . . . what could there be in that peaceful emptiness and how much?

Her funds were nearly depleted. It wasn't difficult to return and find a new job. But why? Whom should she ask? Suddenly she thought of Alma. Surely by now she had found the answer to her own 'Why?' She would definitely help her. Shamman left for Bankipur immediately.

She felt envious when she saw Alma. How stable she seemed to be. The earlier signs of perpetual fatigue had disappeared and she looked energetic and alert. What was there to talk about except the lonely and sad moments when time dragged its feet? But Alma was happy. As far as she was concerned, she was existing only as Rolf's widow. In-laws, husband, mother's family – she had received everything from one person, and lost it.

Professor Nathan was still showering his attentions on her. It was his custom to come just as dusk fell, and a hearty chitchat continued late into the night. Shamman was amazed to see how lively this bookworm was. Other professors also accompanied him.

'Shamman, meet Ronnie Taylor,' Alma took her aside one day and said, and Shamman saw that she was shaking hands with an Englishman with small eyes and a round head covered with brownish-yellow hair. With some reluctance she acknowledged the handshake. She didn't like the way Alma had introduced her. Alma was looking at Taylor with such respect and adoration, one would think he was not an ordinary white man, but he was Bhagwan himself who had descended into her home. Shamman hated the Hindustanis who felt elated when they received the slightest attention from these white-skinned people. They don't know that the Englishman only socialises with them so he can return to his country and surprise people by telling them that he has observed and studied the Hindustanis so closely, and that neither did

270

they bite him nor did their dark colour muddy his whiteness. He would show his compatriots their pictures saying, 'Here are the savage monkeys who have been civilised by the English.'

Conversation veered from one topic to another. Shamman was feeling depressed, and although she tried several times to take part in the conversation she kept getting lost in her own entangled thoughts. Finally, she got up and began looking through a bookcase so that the guests might not think she was altogether stupid.

'You must read it . . . it's excellent.'

She turned around to see Taylor pointing to the book in her hand.

'Thanks,' she said drily. She put down the book she was holding and picked up another one.

'By the way,' Taylor tried to secure her attention, 'I'm not English, I'm Irish.'

A man with a white complexion can only be English. This colour strikes such dread into your heart you can't even think clearly. Secondly, they all look the same and she never could tell one from the other.

'That wasn't necessary.'

'Oh, I know very well how sceptical you are of white skin.' He winked at her mischievously. 'It's not your fault.'

'How unfortunate we are,' Shamman said acidly and turned to the books again.

'I have some new books. If you would like . . .' Catching the cynical expression on Shamman's face, he shifted awkwardly. 'Please forgive me if I've insulted you in any way. It's well known that even if you greet a woman she treats it as a profanity. But I thought you were Alma's friend and like her you . . .'

Alma was calling everyone for tea.

'*Array*, Shamman, you haven't talked to Taylor?'

'Yes, we've talked,' Taylor said, making a funny face.

'*Array*, Shamman, he's a journalist. Before the war began he wrote . . . what did you write, Taylor?'

'He worked for a newspaper,' Nathan volunteered.

'He's a very learned man. Come on for tea, we'll be late for the film.' Everyone scrambled when Alma gave orders to move quickly.

The film was not just silly, it was in bad taste. A few white men were exhibiting feats of valour, humanity and generosity in the middle of a jungle. Taylor was some seats away from Shamman, but every now and then she looked in his direction only to find him watching her. The two couldn't hold back their amusement.

271

'And now you can put this down as another blot on my record,' Taylor said with forced meekness when they were together after the film. Shamman burst out laughing.

That night Alma had nothing but the greatest praise for Taylor. Shamman protested. 'You're forgetting what these white-skinned people are. Having suffered persecution at the hands of the rest of the world, they come here, Poles, Jews and who knows who else, and become arrogant and condescending merely on the basis of their white skin. Anyone you meet these days is wearing a lion's skin and pretending to be a lion. Whoever comes here as a guest soon turns into the master.'

'But the fault also lies with us to some extent. Go and see how many beggars, indigents and shopkeepers in the bazaars run after them with shouts of "sahib" and "sarkar".'

'Those unfortunate creatures don't know who they are. They may be just as impoverished as them, but they *look* like sahibs and many of them live in such comfort. Our guests are better off than we are, we're starving, but there isn't a bit of change in our hospitality. When they don't know how to live here graciously, why shouldn't we feel like kicking them out?'

'*Array*, they're oppressed too, oppressed by Hitler.'

'Those oppressed by Hitler are our oppressors. Just think, how can we have any sympathy for them? Where will we go in trying to escape from Hitler? No one will allow us to step on their land.'

Alma was dozing. God knows what was happening to her. The impassioned Alma of the college days was dead, it seemed, and this vanquished Alma was lowering her head in deference to every restriction.

The next morning Alma wasn't feeling very well so she asked Shamman to take the servant with her and get some provisions. A shortage of grain was turning into a real headache. Everywhere else rationing had been set into place, but no one bothered to pay attention to this particular region. Four times of what was spent on ghee was now being expended on wheat alone, and ghee had gone up beyond all expectation.

'Hello.'

She heard a voice behind her and turned to see Taylor trying to look attractive, his small eyes glittering.

'I'm tired of this lazy, lethargic Hindustan and I thought I'd go looking for trouble.' He smiled roguishly, making Shamman break into a smile.

'I'm very disappointed, you know,' he continued.

'Why?'

'Well, I thought you would raise hell. Anyway, that was a good start, so on to another scheme.'

'What's that?'

'That you should come and have tea with me.'

'But I'm here to do some shopping.'

'All right, we'll do the shopping first, and then we'll send off the servant.'

At every shop the shopkeepers saw Taylor and hiked up their prices fourfold. She was having so much trouble she had to get rid of him.

'Why don't you wait in that hotel across the road and I'll join you as soon as I'm done.'

'Why?' He got upset.

'Your presence is interfering with the prices.'

'Oh? And how's that? OK, I won't open my mouth now.'

'You can do what you want. You're from the royal family, you see.'

'Why should I be from the royal family? Don't be silly.'

'All these people here believe anyone who has white skin has to be the king's brother or nephew. We can't help thinking that way, and you know who's been helping us think like that for a hundred years.'

Muttering under his breath, Taylor walked over to the hotel and stood at the door waiting for Shamman to finish. Shamman haggled over prices, bargaining and negotiating to her heart's content, and when she had bought everything she needed she got a taxi and left without giving any thought to Taylor. But as soon as she arrived at Alma's she remembered. Unloading all the provisions, she quickly took the same taxi and was at the gate when another car practically took her taxi into its embrace. Both drivers embarked on a barrage of obscenities and when she leaned out of the window to see what was going on, she saw Taylor. She was immobilised.

'I completely forgot,' she said in a pleading tone. 'There was such a disturbance.'

'I am honoured,' Taylor said sarcastically, bowing. 'I didn't know that you found turmeric, coriander and rice to be more interesting than this living, breathing human being. I tried to waste your time, but I laud your ability to avoid unpleasant tasks with such ease.' He turned to leave.

'But,' Shamman said without thinking. He came back.

'Which car shall we take, yours or the one I brought?' he asked as if nothing had happened.

When the car had gone some distance Taylor started laughing.

'Oh, these women!'

'You're telling yourself that Hindustani girls are uncultured, crude and God knows what else, but . . .'

'But that's not just true of only Hindustani women. Women everywhere are just as unmanageable.' A mischievous smile spread over his face. 'You think that our women run to us as soon as we call them?'

'At least that's the experience of the Hindustanis. As if held on a string, they come all the way here.'

'That's not true at all. The Hindustanis who make such claims haven't been meeting the right girls. The well-educated girls there are very stand-offish, and anyway, these naked, hungry female parasites exist everywhere.'

'Oh, so they have naked, hungry people there as well?' Shamman asked in a biting tone.

'Of course. You think only lords and barons live there? You're lucky to see the handful of Englishmen you see here. As long as there are fiends in the world people will remain hungry as well as naked.'

'To this extent?' Shamman asked, pointing to the shrivelled, mouldering beggars on the roadside.

'No, not to this extent.' Taylor shivered. 'Before I came to Hindustan I had all these ideas . . .'

'That there would be nawabs, rajas, elephants adorned with diamonds . . .'

'Not exactly all this but yes, I had thought that so many years of rule must have resulted in some improvement. Although I read a book or two on Hindustan before coming here, I wasn't ready for what I saw.'

'And after seeing all this you decided it was entirely our fault?'

'Not entirely your fault, but some blame is to be attached. You know, I've noticed that you people seem to pride yourselves in being careless and stubbornly insist on being blameless. After all, you are human, you're not animals.'

'But we're helpless at the hands of animals.'

'As if there are no animals like that in Hindustan.'

'There are. But they're *their* stooges.'

'So what you're saying is that the animals here and the animals there have conspired to bring the country to ruin? But tell me truthfully, have you ever made an attempt to shatter this conspiracy? What sacrifices have you made?'

'Haven't you seen the condition they're in, the ones who did make sacrifices? What they have had to endure?'

The incident was fresh in her mind. One of the largest groups in the country proclaimed open rebellion. They had given an ultimatum that if the British didn't get out of Hindustan they would burn railway tracks, buses and trains. But the white rulers brought this rebellion under control with just batons. The mousetrap opened and the cream disappeared. In a few days the army without a leader was trampled and pulverised into oblivion by the government. Ahimsa was not as harmless as this uprising turned out to be. It seemed as if a few mindless children had decided they wanted the moon. And such children can only be dealt with in two ways. Either give them a moon cut out of tinsel ... but these children are very clever; they recognise the tinsel right away. The other method is to box their ears and say that when Abba comes back from work he'll get them a moon.

'And who knows if Abba, when he comes back from work, will be so tired he won't think the moon is necessary.'

'They don't know the moon should be real and that if it isn't it will be ripped to pieces, brother will fight brother over it and destroy it. We'll keep it in a safe, when you're older you'll get it, they'll be told.'

'But when will we grow up? Only Abba knows when. You might be grown up, but for Amma and Abba you'll always be children. And who knows if Abba will return from the bazaar or not. Hitler is playing games, one blow after another, who knows, maybe the moon will be snatched by him.'

'Yes, and history will always condemn the others for it,' Taylor said seriously.

'But they're the historians. We'll continue to read what we've always been reading, their successes, our follies ... in every era we opened our eyes and started singing our own praises.'

'But there's America this time.'

'America was always there, but only as long as there's the chance of one dollar multiplying to become ten. If it's not a cotton trade, it's a military trade. Now we'll have to sing their praises. Supporting those that are stumbling, helping the defeated to victory, providing strength to the weakened. Our threatened government will also be comforted by America.'

'No, that won't happen. There are many among us who suffered from

275

misconceptions, but now we're becoming aware of the truth. I'm not saying something will definitely happen. There are a few who take an interest in these things, and while many will forget when they return home, there will be some who will perhaps remember.'

'I hope they don't try and remember the way Kipling did. Kipling can't be trusted to establish this new age. You just wait and see, out of this war humanity will arise with a new light. *Array*, where are we going? Driver.'

Deep in conversation, they had travelled farther than planned. The car's driver, astounded at seeing two opposing elements striking each other, had also become deeply engrossed in their conversation. They stopped and ordered tea at a hotel.

'You're the second Hindustani girl I've met after Alma, and I haven't been disappointed. I don't know why people avoid us like this.'

'It's not our fault. It's your girls who consider our boys to be very valuable because they make good husbands. They bring them around to their way of life, and soon we've lost a Hindustani boy.'

'And Hindustani girls can't do that? If they want they can influence European boys to become Hindustani. You don't know this, but a woman has the hidden strength to perform many miracles. If she wished, she could erase this entire conflict involving race and nation.'

'I don't agree. Custom dictates that you should give your daughter away to someone from a higher class than yours, but don't bring a girl from a lower class, because that might prove to be a blot on your reputation.'

'Nonsense! This is all outdated stuff. Perhaps you think like this, but I would happily marry a Hindustani girl.'

'Words are difficult to put into action.'

'But I assure you I can.'

It was getting late, so they both returned. When Shamman got home Alma was waiting for her, a smile mapped across her face.

'So, you're good friends already, eh?'

'Well they're sahibs, you know, they think we've been honoured by all the attention they've given us. We're like particles of dust and they're like the sun!'

'Taylor isn't like that.'

'Look, Alma, they're all minted in the same mill.'

'Why did you go out with him then?'

'Just to show him that we're not as illiterate and uncultured as their

276

traders have made us out to be. Alma, please find me some work, I'm tired of doing nothing.'

'How about the war office?'

'No, I want to stay away from this war business. What interest can I have in fighting someone else's war?'

'What do you mean? Are you going to let the flat-nosed ones come in?'

'Flat-nosed, or chinky-eyed – what do I care?'

'They'll plunder and steal, you'll see – God forgive us!'

'And the ones who are here already aren't stealing and plundering? And secondly, they'll steal from those who have some possessions left. Those who are dying can't be any threat to anyone. No one has ever harmed these hungry, starving farmers until now, and no one can harm them in the future. It's good that the wealthy will be stripped.'

'*Array*, I say, if you steal from the wealthy yourself that's one thing, but where's the cleverness in allowing outsiders to steal from them?'

'If we don't have the strength then let's use the strength of others!'

'*Array*, did you ever hear of a monkey sharing his *jalebis*? Don't you see what outside help has done to us? History is a witness to the fact that whoever was called in for help became the oppressor. Whatever happens now will happen only when we do it ourselves.'

'You didn't bring enough Delhi rice,' Alma suddenly leapt from the political sphere into the domestic arena.

'That was all they had.'

'Lallu didn't take you to the right shop. There's a shopkeeper whom the professor knows well and he'll give you as much as you want. This lumpy rice is just sickening.'

But soon this lumpy rice also began to disappear from the market. A blight spread and secretly consumed the rice, and in no time wheat too was struck by an infestation and it was no ordinary infestation, it was monumental!

'*Array*, get up!' Alma was shaking her shoulder. Usually she let her sleep until later.

'Why?'

'*Array*, your sahib bahadur is here.'

'Which sahib bahadur?'

'*Array*, come on, don't pretend. Taylor, who else?'

'Shut up! Maybe he's *your* sahib bahadur.'

'Do you want to see something?' Alma tried to tease her.

'What?' Shamman sat up.

'Nothing, but get up now.'

'You witch!' Shamman threw a pillow at her.

Professor Nathan was there as well and the four of them started out in the taxi Taylor had come in. They were planning a picnic.

'We usually have picnics near tombs,' Shamman said.

'Good God, why?' Taylor asked in amazement.

'So that we may continue to be blessed.'

'Look, we have some important work in the library, so why don't you and Taylor go.' Professor Nathan and Alma had probably planned something in advance.

'All right, I'll come too,' Shamman said quickly when she saw Professor Nathan maintaining an awkward silence while Alma looked out of the window casually. 'I'll go home, I have a few chores to take care of, there are some clothes that I must see to.'

'Really?' Taylor asked when Alma and the professor had left.

'What?'

'Is it true you have to go home, you have some important chores to take care of?'

'Yes, why, do you have any objections?' Shamman said in a humorous tone.

'Yes, I severely object, because . . .'

'Why?'

'Because I'd like you to have dinner with me.'

'But it's too early for dinner.'

'What a silly thing to say,' he muttered irately.

Shamman laughed. 'Look, in our culture this sort of thing is frowned upon. What will people say when they see me roaming around with you?'

'Who cares about these people? If girls like you continue to be afraid of people, you'll never gain independence.'

'As if roaming around like this is going to guarantee freedom.'

'Of course. All the countries who have no fear of the dread imposed by "these" people are free.'

'Certainly, you can say whatever you want, after all, you are free.'

'Forget this business of freedom, and put aside my colour and my nationality and listen to what I have to say and try to give me a proper response. For just a while forget the hatred that has existed between us for years. Even the soldiers at the front forget everything and mingle with each other like ordinary human beings. Think of me as a visitor away from his country seeking your hospitality.'

'Once we had provided hospitality to your brothers, they came as traders and . . .'

'Tsk, tsk. What a sharp tongue you have.' He laughed good-naturedly.

The taxi stopped in front of the hotel. The fare was six rupees. Taylor gave the driver ten rupees and, when he rummaged through his pockets helplessly for change, Taylor motioned him to keep the change. The driver bowed his head and offered him salaam and responded to Shamman's angry look with a smile as if saying, 'Why, here you are to spoil it for me – you're a native after all. Every day I bring so many white women and none of them cares.'

'This is the ploy that you use to rule this country,' she said, seething.

'Good God! What's happened?'

'You bought his very soul when you gave him the four rupees as a handout.'

'Look here, I didn't think that's what I was doing. I knew he would only return two rupees saying that's all the change he had and he knew I wouldn't be running around looking for change. And I thought, why not four instead of two? What's the use of our money, who do we earn it for anyway?'

'To lead a life of ease and comfort, for which you have been created.'

'Well this *is* our ease and comfort, our money is spent on tongas and taxis,' Taylor said, ignoring the sarcasm in her remark.

Dinner was a melancholy affair. Taylor was quiet and somewhat solemn. Shamman was glad. The wretch had brought her here to flirt with her. He took her home from the hotel.

The next morning Shamman arrived in the drawing room to find Taylor showing Alma his album. He and Shamman exchanged perfunctory greetings. Later, handing Shamman the album, Alma went off to see about tea.

A world seemed to have been shrunk and squeezed into the album.

'Bombs! Bombs!' The words echoed in her head. How much fun it would be if these toys were shattered into a thousand pieces. These bombs could not hurt Hindustan because they'd fall into the softness of the earth and be devoured by it as if they were hot, spicy morsels. But these sky-high buildings, why should they not reverberate with the fear of bombs?

'You're fighting for these buildings, but you are using us for gunpowder,' she said venomously.

'Eh?' Taylor, who had been looking at the pictures with a great deal of interest, said self-consciously. His face fell.

Shamman was embarrassed by her mean-spiritedness.

'What a strange person you are. I'm trying to show you my camera tricks and all you can think about is politics.' He got up sullenly from her side and walked over to stand by the window. 'My friend was right,' he said, turning slowly to face her. 'He said that if the west extends a hand of friendship toward the east, the gesture will be rejected as if it were adultery. Since yesterday I've been trying to ignore your sarcasm and your taunting remarks, but my goodness! Are all Hindustanis the same way? If that's the case then your malady is incurable. Every time you push away the medicine with your own hand and then proceed to shout and scream in protest.'

'We're better off sick than to have to take the medicine offered by Krupp.'

'But where do you see Krupp? What idiot is talking to you about politics? You think you have a deep interest in politics and that is why you talk like this? That's not true at all. You don't understand the first thing about politics. All you can do is constantly accuse others and absolve yourself of blame. Is this fair? True that the Englishman provokes you and makes you fight with each other, but why are you so stupid that you give in and start fighting? I think you'll have to drag the chains of bondage another two hundred years. Only a stupid ruler would grant you independence, he's your enemy, because you're not ready for freedom as yet, you haven't learnt how to protect yourself nor will you ever learn. Turn back the pages of history and give me one example of how you defended yourself against an enemy without any outside help. If the existing rulers leave today, someone else will come in their place, you'll have to stand with outstretched hands all over again.'

'What have you given us that now you threaten to take it away?'

'My dear, if it were in my power I would give everything,' Taylor said playfully, changing the direction the conversation was going in.

'Oh I've seen you, you're all the same. I've also seen the freedom that America has given its black inhabitants.'

'Shall I tell you something? Don't meddle with politics. It's not a game, you can't jump into the arena on the basis of everything you hear. You need extensive study and I can bet that no woman is capable of serious study.'

'And in my opinion there isn't a better politician than a woman; she can not only rule the household, she can also rule the country. You don't attach any importance to the feminine ploys that are used to manipulate a man's income, his personality, indeed his power of imagination?'

'You're wrong, you're absolutely wrong. No woman can take our earnings by force, we spend when and what we want, but I agree that she is the mistress of our imagination, but that just for our own mental relaxation.'

'Such pleasant misconceptions these are. It's just as well that you remain entangled in them. It's amazing how a person is being fooled and continues to think he's very clever.' Having moved away from politics, the conversation now stepped into the circle of romance.

'I told you before, as far as the rule of the heart is concerned, you're the one in charge.' Taylor pointed to Shamman, making her break out in a laugh.

'And the domain of the heart spreads as far as the blanket will allow or is it east and west . . .'

'The domain of the heart isn't restricted by geography, for it the east is as beautiful and bright as the west!' Taylor's eyes shone with a mischievous glint and Shamman realised that his eyes weren't all that small and that his eyebrows were also quite bushy.

Alma came in with tea. She was somewhat restless today. Taylor teased her when he saw her on edge, behaving as if she were waiting for somebody, stiffening every time she heard footsteps.

'What a fool he is,' Taylor said, glancing at his watch.

'Who?' Alma was startled.

'Professor Nathan.'

She blushed. Shamman noted that this feminine blush engulfed her face, making it glow sweetly. As if in expectation of spring, the coarse and dry Alma was blooming. Her defiant eyes, immersed in peace, looked bigger and more alive than before, as though someone had blown away the years of dust that had accumulated on them. A little later the professor walked in briskly. His pale forehead shone like washed crystal.

'We're going to Delhi,' he said animatedly.

'Congratulations!' Taylor shook his hand energetically.

'Eh?' Shamman looked at them foolishly.

Then Alma told her that the professor had finally pulled her out of her dark hole where she had been hiding in terror all this time. His friendly compassion had compelled her to share her burden with him. He was conducting research on early education and he needed an assistant anyway to test his theories, although if someone had said that his personal life would be improved by Alma's presence, no one would have quite believed it. The professor was a strange sort of domestic man; he didn't reveal himself in the work he did. Perhaps he considered Alma to be useful in taking care of the books that he held dearer than his own self. At least this is what Alma believed.

'I've been feeling a need for you for a long time,' was all he kept saying to her. 'And this need will continue to be felt as long it's not fulfilled.'

'I'll sneak some of his contentment and peace for myself and that will be enough to keep me alive,' Alma said.

Alma ignored Shamman's question about her departure.

'You don't want me to go?' Alma asked sulkily.

'No, how can I say you shouldn't go, but . . .'

'So it's all set,' Alma cut her short, 'you'll take care of the house in my absence. Just remember not to let the cook play cards all day, and make sure he doesn't get together the vagabonds from the neighbour-hood. Last time I went away for a day and when I returned the house had turned into a regular gambling den.' Alma considered the whole matter settled.

'But Alma, I do have to go home at some point.' She was afraid Alma might ask her about her destination.

'Oh, so you won't wear out in fifteen or twenty days.'

'And I also have to find a job.'

'Of course, there's time for that. Come help me pack first.'

'Nathan was saying . . .' Alma began while they were putting away her clothes and then stopped.

'Go on, what was he saying? Don't be bashful.'

'No, it's not about me, it's about Taylor.'

'What?' Shamman's curiosity was piqued.

'That . . . that Taylor is a good man. You know, he doesn't seem like an Englishman and sometimes I forget he's English.'

'Yes, he's Irish, but what do you mean he doesn't seem like an Englishman?'

'I mean the way he talks for one thing. You know, Shamman, if we met other such Englishmen we wouldn't hate them.'

'I don't understand what you mean.'

'I mean others like him.'

'Alma, you're a fool.'

'Oh come on, I know you think he's different from other white-skinned people.'

'This difference doesn't affect their real character. There are certain kinds of snakes that won't bite you, they'll just devour you whole, but that doesn't mean they're not snakes.'

'Ah, so he did devour you eventually.' Alma burst out laughing.

'You're crazy. How can he devour me?'

'But you've definitely devoured him. Nathan was saying . . .'

'A curse on Nathan! Why doesn't he say something else?'

'As if you don't know anything. Hunh? You're pretending with me. He wasn't whispering earlier in the drawing room.'

'*Array*, he was just joking.'

'I've known him for three years. He's not accustomed to making such jokes. He's a strange man. Anyway, what's so terrible about the fact that he likes you? It's not a sin.'

'Why should it be a sin? Tell me truthfully, Alma, do you really like him?'

'Taylor? Very much.'

'It's not Taylor that bothers me, it's his white skin that revolts me.'

'What if under that white skin there's a red heart?'

'That may be, but it's very different from our hearts.'

'And he's not white like a monkey. There are Hindustani men who are fairer than he is, but we're not revolted by them. Why?'

'It's all a matter of how we think. Our hearts have transformed the Europeans into ghouls so we can hate them. Come, let me help you with this suitcase, there are too many clothes in it.'

Both of them grappled with the suitcase. Alma was excitedly packing her luggage. Like a free bird, every once in a while she began humming a song under her breath, and then got lost in thought momentarily. Perhaps the past emerged repeatedly to twist a knife in her wounds, but she seemed to be fighting it successfully.

Early the next morning Taylor arrived with a military truck. Working fast like a labourer, he stacked all the luggage in place. When they sat down for tea he mentioned that he was also leaving in two days. He looked somewhat dejected and looked at Shamman to see if she had heard what he had just said.

'Shamman, did you hear that? Taylor is leaving,' Alma announced in a loud voice when she saw Shamman wasn't paying attention.

'Ohho, I'm so sorry to hear that,' Shamman said warmly.

'Alma, please don't torment people like this,' Taylor said sarcastically and a forced smile struggled on Shamman's face.

'I say, let's hurry or we'll be late,' Nathan alerted everyone while taking hurried sips of tea.

'Well, goodbye, I don't think we'll ever meet again.' Taylor extended a hand formally towards Shamman.

'Don't put on a show, Taylor,' Alma said angrily.

'But you were leaving tomorrow.' Shamman looked at the extended hand and innocently presented him with the salt shaker.

'Thanks.' Upset, he stuffed his hands into his pockets.

'*Array*, I thought you were asking for the salt.'

'Salt on the wounds ... very good, very good!' Nathan roared boisterously.

'I think there's some kind of salt deficiency in you. You have very bad taste.' Alma shook his shoulder as she rose to her feet.

After Alma and Nathan left, Taylor drove Shamman back. He seemed to be anxious to take her home quickly, but the traffic was slowing him down.

'Where are you going?'

'Poona,' he said, without turning to look at her.

'Is it nice there?'

'Very, it's like heaven on earth.' Taylor's tone was acid.

'You're very fortunate.'

'Thanks.'

'Are you low on petrol?' Shamman said, trying to get him to speed up and all at once Taylor took off so fast it seemed the car would overturn any minute.

'What is the meaning of this?' Shamman asked, trying to infuse anger into her voice.

'Aren't we human? Are we made of stone? The selfishness and treachery of a few wolves have blackened the faces of an entire nation and to the extent where no amount of effort can erase it.'

'These wolves must have inflicted some special kind of mental anguish that has resulted in all this.'

'I agree, but there's such a thing as common sense.'

'Someone who has been burnt by boiling milk blows even on the buttermilk before drinking it,' Shamman tried to explain in earnest.

'So there's no way the hatred that exists in your heart for me can be erased?' he asked softly.

'I don't hate you,' Shamman spoke as if addressing herself.

'So you only want to torment me?' He was smiling. 'This is enough to make me want to smash this car against a tree.' He slowed down.

'Our hearts are in pain.'

'Especially after the August incident,' Taylor said sympathetically.

'Do you also think that all this disturbance was instigated by Congress?'

'And Congress is to be congratulated.'

Shamman flared up again. 'It seems like a miracle, this impassioned demonstration by such a helpless, happy-go-lucky group. So you don't think this was foolishness on their part?'

'If it's stupid to love freedom, it's stupider to fight for it.'

'But it was foolishness. Is it possible to obtain freedom by shouting and screaming and by dying in anonymity?' Shamman wanted a specific response from him.

'The goddess of freedom wants sacrifice and if she is to be swayed then a thousand such sacrifices will be required. What these impetuous, hot-headed youths enacted does appear to be insignificant because whatever happened was badly organised and chaotic. If this very sacrifice had been conceived in a well-ordered manner, a small part of freedom would definitely have been won over.'

'But how can leaders like Gandhi guide us in the struggle for independence? Ahimsa – hunh, can any country be vanquished by ahimsa?' She began defending her own viewpoint.

'No, even if Genghis Khan had been here at this time and wasn't properly armed, he could have done nothing. Didn't you see, the demonstrators were punished for not doing anything and if they had made the slightest move, they would have been killed.'

'Hunh! They're useless, these leaders. They should all die so new leaders can be born.'

'But leaders don't come out of eggs. Even though your leaders aren't doing much their stubborn silence provides succour to the public. The desire for freedom hasn't perished. Although the leaders lost some of their strength and popularity when they went to jail, a time will come when people will realise their leaders were not useless, they were helpless.'

'Why did they go to jail then? Did they serve the nation this way?' Shamman begged the question like a child.

'Yes, they performed a tremendous service. What they couldn't express verbally, they revealed by their actions.'

'What do you mean?' Shamman asked foolishly.

'The tyrants rarely have any mercy, and the hatred that their actions give rise to among the populace could not be dissipated by any kindness, any concession. And if the government didn't inflict cruelty upon you at this time, you would continue to sing its praises. The dedication to freedom that will inhabit the hearts of future generations will be something that . . . wait a minute! Where are we going? Let me turn around.'

He brought her home and left with the promise that he would return in the evening. There was still quite a bit of sunshine left when the servant came and told her that Taylor had arrived.

'So soon!'

He was wearing lightweight, off-white clothes. His eyes were red, as if he had a fever.

'Do you have a fever?' Shamman asked.

'I always seem to have a fever here. Come on, get ready, we're going to the pictures, and listen, put on that, what do you call it, the dot.'

'Oh, you mean the *bindi*.'

'Yes, yes,' he nodded his head vehemently.

'Why?'

'It looks good.' His tired, red eyes disappeared when he laughed and his teeth sparkled.

Instead of going to the pictures they went to a hotel for coffee. Taylor told her that his fiancée, whom he hated to leave behind, had suddenly forgotten him.

'She's stopped answering my letters,' he said sadly. 'Here, on the battlefield, so far away from home, we spend every waking moment thinking of them, and they don't even care to keep up a pretence. There isn't a moment, a single moment when they're not in our thoughts, but . . . these disloyal pleasure-seekers don't regard us as human.'

Shamman listened silently to his discourse.

'Do you still love her?' she finally asked softly.

'Love is never one-sided. Actually I adore the word "girl".' A mischievous grin appeared on his face. 'And the last few years have made me very unstable . . .'

Hours of trivial conversation made them both feel lighthearted. Later he talked about his childhood, his mother and his sister. He loved his mother very much and he enjoyed scolding and teasing his sister who was very naughty, but lovable. She had a string of boys attached to her and she thought Taylor was a sissy because he was always so reticent.

The following morning Taylor arrived so early that Shamman had to keep him waiting a whole hour while she bathed and got ready. When she came out she found him stretched out on the grass next to the tea tray.

'I've come to say goodbye. I'm leaving tomorrow.'

'Goodbye,' Shamman said.

'Oh, that's all you have to say?' He sat up. 'You haven't even bothered to ask where I'm going . . . you could pretend to be civil.'

'Why should I take this relationship any further?'

'You're right, why?' he said sadly. Turning on his side, he rubbed his forehead on the grass.

'We'll ride our bicycles tonight.'

'Tonight?' Shamman was alarmed. 'Look, I'm scared of riding at night.' He frowned so she quickly added, 'But we can go for a walk in the evening.'

'All right, but listen, tell the cook to make something spicy. The heat has numbed my tongue.'

'You'll eat chillies?'

'Yes,' he said, shaking his head and then he pressed his palms against his eyes.

'Didn't you get enough sleep last night?'

'No,' he said in a brooding tone. 'I don't know what's happening. I admit I like you, but I won't call this feeling love, it's more like some cruel and painful disease.'

'I think you've got heatstroke,' Shamman said with a laugh.

'Do you know of a disease in Hindustan which can turn love into a life-threatening emotion?'

'Yes. Like the heat of the sun there's a heat of love too. But this isn't the season for it, it takes hold during the rainy season, when dark clouds roll in, cuckoos make clamorous noises and nightingales sing.'

'Then I must be suffering from an autumnal disease.'

'Perhaps. It appears to be a dangerous malady.' *Taylor falls in love w/ Shamman*

They both started laughing.

'What if I ask you to marry me?'

'What if? Err . . . look, remember you asked to have spicy food just now. Shall I tell the cook?' She tried to ignore his question.

'I think together we can do a great deal for humanity,' he said seriously.

'But why get married for that?' She was forced to become serious.

'Hmm? I don't know, but we can't just live together, and you don't love me, right?'

'What's the use of lying and anyway, I'm Hindustani and quite accustomed to the heat and I don't have heatstroke either.'

'Shut up. You can't love me because my skin is white.'

'There are men in Hindustan who are fairer than you and we love them and marry them.'

'So if you marry me, can you love me later? I mean can you try?'

'I can't predict the future.'

'Do you have the courage to marry me?'

'I don't know.'

The cook brought *phulkis* and hot chutney. Taylor dipped the *phulkis* in the chutney and ate them greedily. His face turned red like raw meat from the chillies and his eyes began to water profusely.

'Did you get the answer to your question?'

'What?' he said, wiping his nose like a child.

'What do these chillies say?'

'They say . . . they say that you're stupid, Shamsham.' He called her by her name for the first time, distorting it lovingly.

'A gamble!' Shamman's heart sang with unexpected joy. 'The adventure of living lies in taking big risks,' she repeated as if in a dream.

'Do you have the courage?' He bent down to look into her eyes.

'Courage is not such a scarce product. But why do you want to gamble?'

'It's not a gamble for me. I am very attached to Hindustan and it breaks my heart to see it bleed like this. I view it as a limb of the world, the world that is mine.'

'Your view of life is very romantic. You know this is a gamble, but your blood is rushing in fearful anticipation of the results, and there's great pleasure in this fear. But where did you get the taste for this pleasure?' Shamman didn't know where her mind had taken her. The pleasure she had derived in making that blood-stained pledge in an Allahabad camp a long time ago was suddenly fresh in her mind.

'Don't worry about me.'

'I don't have to because you will, you'll regret this later yourself.'

'I will?'

'Yes. You'll go back and think about everything that happened today and you'll be ashamed. This enchantment can't last too long.'

'What enchantment?'

'That of self-deception. You want to do something very unusual. I'm Hindustani and you . . .'

'Just shut up. I don't want to allow geography to stand between us.

288

My only thought is that you and I should come closer. My mother is a wonderful woman and she will like you.' His manner became spirited. 'We'll travel together in Europe, oh it will be just wonderful! This wretched war will be over, I'll resume my education, you can also get a degree, and then we'll both return to Hindustan and . . .'

'*Array!* You travel fast, you're back already.' Shamman laughed boisterously and Taylor joined in.

'Let's go out.' He pulled her up and like two children, laughing, chattering and jabbering away, they walked and talked together a long time.

'Just say yes and we'll begin life in our paradise . . .' A bus drove past at high speed and clouds of dust choked his laugh. His sentence left unfinished, he leaned on Shamman's shoulder and started coughing. The passengers on the bus leaned out from the windows, turning their heads to stare at this strange sight.

'Did you see that?' Shamman asked in a bitter tone.

'I don't care about these dogs, I don't care about anyone,' he said in exasperation.

When she returned to her room the laughter that was earlier blooming in her heart like new buds coming to life, suddenly wilted, as if someone had turned off the light. She sat down quietly on her bed.

'What is this?' a voice asked.

'The very extreme,' she replied.

'Is there any way out?'

'Impossible. Even Khizr has gone astray.'

'The cure?'

'None.'

'Any prayer?'

'Useless!'

She got up swiftly and threw two saris into a suitcase. There must be a train going somewhere, to some part of the world, far from here. The rest of her luggage can follow. And how much luggage do gypsies carry anyway?

What is this foolishness? What is this fear? Stupid. Will he devour you? Tell him in plain words that night and day can't ever coexist with each other.

She tossed away the suitcase. For a long time afterwards she tidied Alma's books, then lay down and went to sleep. It was quite dark when she awoke. The servant came to tell her that Taylor was here. She wrapped on a sari quickly and came out.

'What is it, Ronnie?'

'Come here, come with me.' He looked frightened and anxious. His face was pulled down and ashen. He flicked his cigarette repeatedly to conceal the trembling of his hands.

They walked out to the lawn.

'I think . . . I haven't talked to anyone as yet.'

'About what?'

'You know, about . . .' he floundered nervously.

'Ronnie, why are you so worried? I'm not a child and neither are you. Why were we thinking of marriage? Because both of us can do a lot for the world. Love has nothing to do with it.'

'You'll never love me.'

'I . . . I've never been able to understand what love is and now I've stopped contemplating this question altogether,' she said quietly and Taylor peered at her face closely.

'I'll teach you to love.' He pressed Shamman's hand affectionately.

'You'll teach me?' She burst out laughing. Her voice rang with bitterness and apprehension. 'Love can't be taught. It's a feeling that is born, that grows and . . . anyway, let's drop the subject. So you see, it's foolish to commit such foolishness.'

'Why do you call it foolishness?'

'Do you remember that bus, the one that drove past us? Did you see how the people were staring at us, as if we were monkeys trying audaciously to act like humans?'

'But I don't care about them,' he shouted, grinding his teeth.

'Then you're making a mistake, you're trying to fight nature.'

'But why is this so unthinkable? Hundreds of white girls have lived happily in Hindustan. Why can't you and I be happy?'

'There's a difference between men and women. Once a woman gives everything up to go with a man she makes her home wherever he is, even if it's a place where she has to step down from her earlier life. But a man? He's very temperamental. He'll throw a tantrum at the slightest provocation.'

'But . . .'

'We met and our lives were enriched by a wonderful experience. Listen, you must leave tomorrow. *Array*, I forgot to ask you where you're going.'

'Back to Poona . . .'

'I'll come and see you off at the station. Look, look,' she braced him with her hand as he sighed and held his head in his hands. 'We're friends, our friendship will be very valuable. If everyone is fortunate enough to have a friend like you, Hindustan's future will be a bright one.'

'Will you come in the morning? Will you be at the station?' he pleaded before he left.

'Of course.'

Later she felt as if she had cast off a heavy burden from her shoulders. Once Surdas *ji* took hold of a snake believing it to be a rope and was led to the house of a prostitute. Do such emotions exist that make us blind to this extent?

Feeling as light as a balloon, she fell on her bed; it was as though she had been freed of the responsibilities of life. But sleep evaded her and it seemed that the balloon, cut off from its string, was flying higher and higher. Where was it going? There was no breeze so one couldn't determine its direction.

Suddenly clouds came out of nowhere. There was no thunder, no lightning. The heavy clouds simply poured. The gutters, blocked for years, overflowed. She hid her face in her pillow and sobbed violently. She couldn't remember when she had last wept. Today the stony dam of restraint had burst open with just a tiny jolt. Every fibre of her being was racked by sobs. Hours passed. A lone drowsiness began to stroke her head and slowly her sighs ambled into deep breathing.

The next morning she woke up at eight instead of seven. With a certain uneasy satisfaction she remembered that Taylor was leaving at this very moment. The train was taking him farther and farther away from her. The distance between them was increasing and soon it would grow to such a degree that it would be impossible to measure it.

Scolding the little girl from last night, she got up, took a long hot bath and, clasping her tired shoulders with her hands, she tossed off the last of the lethargy that had enveloped her spirit. She was very hungry. Last night she was too tired to eat. She hoped the orderly hadn't heard the sound of her sobs. After breakfast she sat at the table a long time picking on pine nuts and biscuits left in a basket. Yesterday she and Taylor had eaten from this very basket. How carefree he was. His collar was tight around the neck so he had taken off the top stud and thrown it into the basket. She picked it up and rolled it between her fingers. Then she placed it in a small inside pocket in her handbag.

What was she going to do today? How will this long day pass? She felt as if Hindustan had shrunk, and anyway, what is there in these ruins? So what could she do? She decided a trip to the market would be a good idea.

When she was locking her room the key suddenly fell from her hands. Taylor's ghost, white and still, stood leaning against the wall.

'You lied, you didn't come to the station,' he roared angrily.

'Oh! You didn't go?'

Smiling weakly, he shook his head.

'But . . .'

'To hell with this but and if!' he barked at her.

Later he sat calmly in her room and told her that he was at the station at six in the morning. Shamman's heart softened.

'*Uff*, with all your luggage?'

'No,' he smiled mischievously and shouted when Shamman expressed outrage. 'I know you Hindustanis are deceitful people, I knew you would deceive me so it would have been silly to lug all that luggage . . .' He broke into raucous laughter.

'Look, Ronnie.'

'Be quiet, I'm not looking. You're not a woman, you're a piece of stone. You know I'm so fond of you and yet you . . . yet you persist in giving me lectures. That's enough! And I also want to tell you that I'm never going to Poona again.'

'In that case, I'm leaving tonight.'

'Fine. Which train are we taking?' He spoke excitedly.

'What do you mean "we"? Are you out of your mind?'

'I wouldn't ask for anything more if my mind were all in one piece. Come on, let's eat.'

'Let's go to the dining room then.'

'No, I want to eat right here,' he said, stretching out on her bed.

After they had finished eating he asked, 'Taxi or the same programme as yesterday, or bicycle?'

'Shut up!'

'My head hurts.' Taylor slowly eased his tired head until it was resting against her knee.

'You probably didn't get enough sleep.'

'I didn't get any sleep,' he said, placing his head in her lap.

'Shall I get some Aspro?' She touched his straw-coloured hair tenderly.

'I'll need at least nine pills.' Taylor said, gently put his arm around her waist.

The days passed quietly. Alma was very upset that they did not wait for her.

When they emerged from the Office of Civil Marriage at eleven, the roads were congested with traffic. Taylor couldn't stop smiling. The savage joy that had illuminated his eyes when he signed the forms in the office had dimmed somewhat. His manner was soft and affectionate, and he was making an attempt to retain the sense of victory that had brightened his face earlier. Shamman, stunned, a little apprehensive, was talking hurriedly, trying to shut out the strange voices that were falling like hammers upon her ears.

'Wrong . . . all wrong . . . fire and water . . . can never embrace each other,' someone seemed to be whispering in her ear.

In the small cottage in Simla surrounded by pines, Shamman put on her pale green nightdress and felt as if she had been buried in a mound of snow. Taylor was in the other room writing some important letters. She started putting away her clothes.

The sound of his coughing and the splashing sounds he made while washing indicated he was now in the bathroom. Outside, a brisk breeze whipped about like dry, fluttering sheets. An unknown fear and dread floated in the air. The silence was as quiet as death. It seemed as if the universe had been suddenly silenced after the shock of some terrible occurrence. Two cats chased one another and jumped out of the window. Autumn leaves hung from tree limbs like dead birds.

'Please close the window,' she entreated when Taylor came in.

He muttered something under his breath and latched the window. When he turned around Shamman saw that he was drunk, but his face was ashen, like a piece of paper that's left out in the rain and has been washed of all colour.

43

She was awake, but she remained still, her eyes shut. In the distance the sound of birds chirping was like the jangling of bells rising and falling like a soft melody. She stretched slowly, then relaxed her body, trying to arouse sensations that were languid and unclear. She made an attempt to open her eyes, but it seemed as if the sun had invaded them. Suddenly she remembered something. The thought pricked like a needle and became a spear. Her eyes flew open. The room was empty!

She got up hastily. There was nothing there. A lone, muddy-looking tie swung like a hangman's rope in the place where Taylor's suits had been the night before. The row of shoes she herself had straightened was gone. A dirty sock in one corner seemed to be mocking her.

Silent and wounded, she stared at the dirty sock which appeared to have swelled into a large mud-coloured mound. Blown by a gust of wind, the tie slipped down as if it were a lump of flesh. With both hands she quickly pushed aside the stinging smoke that threatened to blanket her head and walked to the centre of the room.

'Gone! He's gone!' The walls and doors of the room seemed to shriek and howl with laughter.

'So? What now? What will happen now?' she begged for an answer.

'He's gone. You go too. You don't even have a penny on you and when the landlord asks you where he is and why you're still here, he'll think you're one of the prostitutes these white-skinned men bring here for a few pennies and then kick out.'

'So, what should be done then?'

'Run. Run as fast as you can and go to the garden where you stopped last night with him. Remember the pond in which you saw your images to see how this joining of night and day looks? You were frightened by the spiders and the bats there, and it also smells and there are insects in it too, but that's the way. For your broken back there's no other way but that.'

She squatted on the floor, her head held between her hands. She was a day-old bride but there was no bridal fragrance about her, no henna on her hands, there wasn't even a single bangle on her wrist. Her frightened mind shuddered. Is this a wedding or widowhood? Stumbling, she staggered out blindly. In the veranda she was clasped by many arms, no not many, just two, there were just two, but how gentle, and how protective and how healthy and energetic Taylor's ghost looked.

'You're up.' He made her stand by the stairs and, leaping from the veranda, he put his arms around her waist and swung her down. 'I didn't want to waken you. Let me show . . .'

'Ronnie!' She breathed deeply as if she had just emerged from the eye of a storm.

'What happened?' His arms still around her waist, he asked gently as if she were a china doll and might break easily.

'Nothing.' Swallowing her tears, she laughed weakly, an apprehensive, throbbing, artificial laugh.

'Ronnie, where . . . where are your clothes and your shoes?' she asked him hesitatingly during tea.

'Shoes? Clothes? Why do you want to bother your head about these things? I don't want you to get into this bother just yet. Here.' He handed her a piece of toast thick with butter.

'Oh, I was just wondering.'

'What's the matter, Sham?' he asked seriously.

'Er . . .it's nothing . . . I got up and all your things were missing and I thought . . .'

'What did you think?' Taylor became sombre. 'You thought . . .'

'I thought ... we'd had a burglary.' She made up something childishly.

'You're lying. Don't lie to me.' Taylor's face fell. 'I understand.'

'You don't understand anything.'

'If you continue to be so distrustful . . .'

'Be quiet! You think you're so intelligent.'

'Yes, you thought I had left you.'

'You're so clever! If you had so much sense you wouldn't have married me. Now tell me, where are your things?' She turned the subject around and convinced Taylor he was wrong.

'The orderly has taken them away to brush them. Look here, I married you for myself, not for my wretched shoes or clothes. The first thing you do when you wake up is show your concern for the shoes instead of asking me how I'm doing.'

'All right, let's go for a walk.'

'No, I want to lie down here, next to you.' He stretched out close to her on the grass.

A whole month passed in the twinkling of an eye. They laughed, talked, joked and romped. All day long they sat in some isolated corner of the abandoned garden and recited Keats, Byron and Omar Khayyam. Taylor's voice was soft and rich. He sang wild love songs and recited stirring poems to her.

How different he was from what she had imagined him to be. She had thought that Englishmen had filthy minds. And despite all the inventions the west had conceived for keeping teeth clean, she hadn't seen one man with sparkling teeth. The sight of their blackish, yellow teeth always made her recoil. Taylor's teeth were not completely white, but they were even and healthy-looking.

'I don't know what you Hindustanis are made of,' he'd say, admiring her wheat-brown complexion. 'We can't have skins like yours even with the help of creams and medicines. How attractive this colour is, it makes you all honey-eyed.' He'd narrow his eyes. He hated powder and rouge. 'These things cover up the innate softness of the skin.'

'I use them for fragrance.'

'Oh, fragrance! Is there another scent more overpowering than the scent of this skin?'

She wished life would go on like this for ever. She and Taylor sitting under the shade of the pine trees, entangled in Shelley's poetry – she didn't know life could be so beautiful, so tender. Careless laughter, deep sleep, an avid appetite – what more could they want?

Taylor was changing with each passing day. Shamman had thought that it would certainly be difficult, if not impossible, to make this uncultured brute take on a Hindustani hue. But he was being drawn very rapidly to the Hindustani diet and way of life. How easygoing men are. You can give them any life you want. As far as they're concerned, national differences or political leanings do not stand in the way in a situation such as this. They accept acquiescently any lap they find themselves in; now you can do what you want with them.

Dressed in the same clothes day and night, he was like an advertisement for idleness. He'd forget to shave and would have let his beard grow if Shamman hadn't resisted the idea strongly. He didn't like to bathe, ate very hot, spicy food and slept for hours in the afternoon, got up reluctantly in the evening, made a hundred excuses to avoid going out and, if Shamman dragged him by force, he stopped along some isolated, out of the way place and proceeded to sing lengthy praises of the beauty of nature. He extended his leave by secretly applying for two more weeks and when Shamman asked for an explanation he said the extra time was due to him.

Frightened, Shamman realised that he was becoming a mystifying enigma. Most of the time he dozed, and when he awoke he looked terrified and seemed anxious to return to the state of semi-consciousness. He drank quietly late into the night and mumbled answers incoherently when Shamman tried to talk to him.

'I'm learning the art of yoga,' he said jokingly one day.

'The art of yoga?'

'Yes, that's the only way to achieve nirvana.'

'Are you out of your mind?' Shamman got annoyed.

'The world is finite.' The bantering exceeded limits and when Shamman refused to talk to him, he used childish tricks to pacify her, called her silly names which infuriated her further and she left the room. Later she went out for a walk and found him asleep in his chair when she returned.

The way he expressed his love and attention was also changing. There seemed to be an artifice in his passion and the more silent he was the more intense his lovemaking would be. It was as if he was pushing aside some force that threatened to make him unsteady on his feet. An unknown fear and exasperation enervated him and his frenzied love-making left Shamman feeling uneasy.

One day she forcibly dragged him to town. His lethargy disappeared for a short while. Like the Taylor of old he joked and laughed over sips of coffee. But as soon as his laughter subsided, a strange kind of reticence appeared in its place; he behaved as though he wanted to break free of his ropes and escape, as though he was blinded by bright lights. The reason soon became evident. People were silently and smilingly watching this unusual couple. Forgetting his duties, the waiter came to stand next to their table on one pretext or another, and a couple of dried-up old English women were openly hostile.

'I wonder what these people are thinking?' he said with a forced smile.

'What do you think they're thinking?'

'That . . . who is this man . . . and you, oh, well let them think what they want, come.' Seeing colour rise to Shamman's face he tried to be evasive.

'Let's go,' Shamman said curtly.

'Why? Don't be silly.'

'I say, let's leave right now.'

'But . . .' Somewhat flustered, he followed her out of the hotel. Neither of them spoke for a while.

'Are we afraid of them? Are we indebted to them for something?' He trembled with rage. 'Savages! Bastards!' He began swearing excessively. 'Why are people so short-sighted? After all, human beings have all descended from the same seed – big and small, white and black.' But who was going to do the explaining? If only he could put a placard on his back explaining in large, clear letters the hidden purpose of their marriage so that these idiots would not stare at them with these surprised eyes, these eyes that seemed to bore a hole through his back and enter his heart.

297

'It's not their fault. You're always incredulous when you see something out of the ordinary.' Shamman's heart sank.

'But it's none of their business. Why are they so concerned? I know them, they're white on the surface but their hearts are black.'

'Why do they regard me as a woman of loose morals?'

'I'll kill them, the bastards!'

'As if their white dolls are all goddesses.' Shamman said what was in his heart.

And his rage flared. Then he turned on Shamman, as though it was she who had incited all those people.

'Why are you so apologetic?'

'I'm not apologetic.'

'Yes you are, you get anxious and make them bolder.' He wanted to transfer blame from his shoulders to hers. 'But I don't give a damn about their meanness. If they think of me as low, I'll spit on their faces.' He roared so that every word became a reflection of his mental state. Although he shouted angrily, his face was downcast and it was clear that in his heart he knew that these people were not to blame. His heart grieved for Shamman when he saw her looking fearful and he tried to comfort her.

He drowned his mental anguish in alcohol and forced lovemaking, but that only helped him, not Shamman. She was tired of his behaviour. If love only serves to create tension it ends up becoming artificial and worthless. How could she be on the same plane as this intoxicated man when she was fully in control of her senses?

'When will you go to Poona?' she asked gently.

'No, no, I can't leave you and go to work,' he said, attempting to conceal his hidden fears.

'But who's asking you to leave me?' Shamman said, holding back the feeling of degradation she felt at his remark.

'Hmm? But how will I work?'

'Well, what are your plans then? Do you want to erase your being?'

'If I can erase my being while I'm in your lap . . .'

'Shut up, Ronnie! You can't fool me.'

'Fool you? What idiot is trying to fool you?' He avoided looking at her directly.

'You're not only fooling me, you're also deceiving yourself. You . . . you're regretting what you've done.'

'Wrong, you're absolutely wrong! This is a false accusation.' The harsh tone of his voice and his obvious distress confirmed Shamman's statement.

'I can tolerate anything you say, Ronnie, but I don't have the strength to tolerate your lies. If you had openly admitted that you were ashamed to take me with you, I would not have minded so much.'

'I . . . I'll not leave without you, that is certain. And how can you say I feel ashamed of taking you with me?'

'It's not your fault. When people observe this speckled couple and smile and make meaningful gestures, it's natural that you . . .'

'So you've been lying too, because all this time you've acted as though you didn't see anything or understand anything.'

'I do this because . . . because I . . .' She couldn't finish.

'You want to deceive me. You see that my countrymen look at me with disgusted sympathy, as though you're some disease that I've been saddled with because of a mistake I made, and your people think that sitting next to you is not a human being but a vile profanity aimed at their entire nation.'

'People think I'm base.'

'Sham . . . but why are you quarrelling with me? Is any of this my fault? You know I'm ready to do anything for you.'

'Hunh! And your descent into an abyss – is that for me too? You want to go so low that you're on my level. You think I'm so base that in order to be on my level you have to fall, not rise up?'

'This is just a delusion.'

'This is not a delusion. I can see that in order to erase this difference and distance between us you're trying to obliterate your own self.'

'But I'm doing this because of my love for you.' _unhealthy love_

'But what kind of love is this that is slowly sweeping you away? I know what this is. You may or may not love me, but let me tell you that any attempt to lift me up to your level is useless. The world of those who are white is so exalted that you can't take my black existence to that sacred height and insult it, so you're sacrificing your own life to your foolishness instead.'

'Your delusions turn the simplest idea into a monster. This way of thinking . . .'

'Is Hindustani, come on, say it,' she said bitterly.

'What an inferiority complex! You think being Hindustani is an insult. Believe me Shamman, whatever I did, I did unknowingly.'

But it was enough that he 'did' what he did. Why was fate so hostile to every aspect of her life? Bitterness arose and then subsided, but every twist and jab left a mark. Actually they were both tired of the strain; love had become a cheap emotion, they became wary of each other's presence. Even though they were still on their honeymoon, they constantly longed to be away from each other, and these minor skirmishes continued to intensify the hatred that had become rooted in their unconscious and was submerged for the time being.

It seemed as if both of them were stupefied by their mistake. Because contrition might be a blow to their ego, this method of achieving solace was also denied to them. Surely Taylor was in the grip of some peculiar madness or else he would not have enacted this drama so easily. To make matters worse, hot chillies and alcohol were taking their toll.

Both tried to exercise control, but the slightest knock punctured the ripened sore, making it bleed, and they saw only each other's flaws and their own virtues. The very taunts that they saw in the eyes of onlookers they now hurled at each other in the form of words, the very qualities that had proved endearing once now rankled like splinters in their eyes. Taylor's hair looked lifeless and discoloured, his eyes seemed to have disappeared and his skin resembled raw meat. As for Taylor, he began to find Shamman's dark hair and dark eyes frightening.

Finally the troubled period of the honeymoon came to an end and they were forced to leave for Poona. Taylor's fears were revived, leading him to feel as though he were on his way to an unfamiliar and extremely dangerous battlefront. Shamman knew what he was going through and collected all her anger and hatred in her chest where it bubbled like lava, creating havoc in her.

There was no need to exhibit a connection with each other at the station. And if anyone had seen them in the compartment there would have been no indication that they were bound together in any kind of a relationship. Detached from one another, they were too busy trying to establish their aloneness and, even when no one was watching, they remained hostile to each other. They kept a close watch on what was being said just to make sure no one was whispering about them. They had their meals in the dining car like strangers and Taylor's face was flushed when he was paying the bill while Shamman couldn't bring herself to face the waiter's judgemental stare. Two unmatched persons were acutely aware of the awkwardness of their connection.

If, by mistake, they made an interesting comment to each other, they immediately looked around them fearfully to see how surprised people were to see them talking informally. They were forced to camouflage a lawful relationship created with such courage and passion as if it were a sin. When Taylor's head rolled off the pillow while he was sleeping, Shamman didn't have the courage to move it back on the pillow, even though she was afraid he might strain his neck. It was a thought that a couple married for years would still have involuntarily, and these two were newly married. If there had been a white girl instead of her she would be kissing and hugging her coal-black husband in view of everyone, and would probably say proudly, 'Here, look at the power of my silvery charm – I can trap all kinds of animals.' And that dark-skinned man would also address the silvery shower and openly proclaim, 'You think we're dark, but remember Krishna *ji* was also dark and all the milkmaids were crazy about him.' But Shamman? She said nothing.

She wished she could spit on everyone and, bending in view of everybody that very instant, place Taylor's head in a comfortable position and feel the softness of his golden-brown hair with her fingers. If only she could remove the tiny hair that had fallen off from his eyelash and sat on his eyelid like a gold filament; it might get into his eye and irritate it. Already he had been to the bathroom twice to wash out the charcoal particles that were irritating his eyes. How she had wanted to fold a corner of her sari and, blowing into it, warm his eyes with it. But she didn't have the courage to suggest this method of relief to Taylor because she knew he'd rather die than endure this humiliation.

And this was the same Taylor who came to her like a child every day, who stationed himself at her door like a persistent beggar and considered himself the luckiest man in the world because he was near her. This was the same man who clamoured to lie down with his head in her lap and have his hair massaged with oil. When they returned from their walks during which he struggled with the roots of trees, she sat in front of the light in the dry Simla evenings and pulled out the splinters in his palms with a needle. And how naughty he was then. For every splinter she took out he extracted payment, and the following day he deliberately rubbed his hands on dry wooden trees so he could bring her a new batch of splinters. But at this moment, even if she just touched his head, he would die from a feeling of humiliation, and she? She felt sorry for herself too.

She used to think that Englishmen know nothing about love or romance. They're motivated by lust and carnal desire, and have no shame or reticence. How could they keep romance ablaze? How hard and selfish their love must be. But Ronnie was completely different. He understood Hindustani and non-Hindustani banter, and he possessed all those crazy characteristics that she had associated with love and romance in her childhood. He was not crude or rough, and for hours they told each other stories about themselves and laughed. Two people who had lived and grown up in different parts of the world had experienced the same kind of childhood and youth, the same little pranks and punishments, the same innocent interests, and played the same games.

Despite the closeness they had developed, they were distanced, each running from the other's shadow. Instead of seeking closeness when the compartment emptied, they immediately began accusing each other of being craven and unprincipled, and the soft, tender emotions that had been stirring only a short while ago in Shamman's heart, wilted and vanished.

After they arrived in Poona, life became more complicated than before. First the servants had to be dealt with. A shield made of rhinoceros-skin was needed to protect against the arrows flying from the incredulous eyes of the neighbours. Anyone who came did so with the intention of probing. Even the produce-sellers made visits just to sniff around. Taylor's old and new friends and acquaintances, and their friends and acquaintances in turn, arrived wide-eyed to offer felicitations. Their visits only served to aggravate the existing bitterness. Politely and very graciously they demanded to hear all the details of this very strange and unusual event. Their faces were clouded with curiosity and their brains were addled. How in the world did this happen?

There were as many stories as there were tongues. The older, clever Englishmen believed she was a woman of loose morals, the newer arrivals thought she was a rani of some small kingdom, and there were others who couldn't make up their minds about them but who did consider them both to be stupid. The worst of it was when Taylor's superior called him in and tried to explain that his marriage was an undesirable move from a political standpoint, that he had damaged the ancient traditions of his masters. Taylor was not only tired of offering explanations, he also lost faith in himself. And that was not all. The news travelled via mail and reached Taylor's widowed mother. She was not unintelligent or narrow-minded, yet she did ask for a detailed letter. This also infuriated Taylor.

'But why are you so angry?' Shamman rose to the defence of the old woman.

'You're defending her just to rile me. I'll not show her my face. She's a fool if she thinks I'm still a child.'

Taylor's temper was on a short fuse these days. He was fully awake and even alcohol failed to dull his senses. He and Shamman avoided going to meetings and gatherings and, having abandoned the world, they also became weary of each other's company. Most of their time was spent in taunting each other and feeling sorry for themselves. Soon life was no less than a dreadful burden. Even if they did go out to visit someone, conversation eventually veered to the subject of their ill-fated romance.

'Once our uncle married a Red Indian girl,' a friend said spiritedly one day. 'She was very loyal and decent. She used to sing songs in her language and tell stories of her life in the jungles.'

He continued generously. 'The only way to foster friendship with Hindustan is to erase this difference between the natives and the white folk.'

But his generosity bothered Shamman and Taylor. They knew that in reality what this meant was that bringing the east and west together is just as difficult and useless as the desire to turn black into white.

After every meeting the very thought of another meeting made their blood curdle. They felt numb for days afterwards, and finally their feelings erupted in the form of arguments. In the end they formed separate groups of friends so that the questions that arose in people's minds when they were seen together would be diminished, but there was no running away from talk. They made every effort to convince people that they had committed this folly only after suffering defeat at the hands of love and now they were very happy and did not experience a moment's regret, and were ready to take on any opposition. But this persistence to be ready for anything was proof enough that they had surrendered themselves to an interminable struggle.

And about the same time Japanese firecrackers caused a fearful stir in the world. Bombs were falling everywhere and the condition of the people running from them was indeed pathetic. Like sheep who, startled by a mere sound, start running around in all directions and instead of finding a safe haven become a threat themselves, panicked inhabitants of cities began making a dash from one place to the other. Selling all their assets for practically nothing, they besieged the trains. The inhabitants of Bombay were headed for Calcutta and the inhabitants of Calcutta were headed for Bombay. Having moved from one house to another, they thought they would be safe. The accidents resulting from this chaotic move caused more lives to be lost than would have been in one whole year of bombing. A darkness settled not only on streets but also on the minds of people.

But what is this? Coming down a slope they stumbled on a stone and slipped? The lifeless white monster spread his arms from all sides and clasped Hitler's advancing courage within his embrace. Crunched up its very bones. Waves soar wildly, hit their heads against the white rocks, and turn back. On top of this the audacity of the sons of snow – God protect us! Made a sudden turnabout as they were retreating, like a clever wrestler who leads his opponent to a point and then topples him. The failing courage of the world was revived; those who were losing and retreating also steadied themselves and stood their ground. The red star came out, bleeding but still breathing. The patient who had only two months to live received sustenance and became alert.

'We knew we would win in the end,' Taylor said proudly, putting down the newspaper.

'You would win?' Shamman said aggressively. 'In other words, this victory is also yours? And what about the defeats that have left a mark over there, who will get a share of them?'

'What? Well, victory and defeat go hand in hand.'

'Oh, when have you ever lost? You've always said you're winning, retreating bravely is one of your special characteristics. You didn't have it in you to fight a giant like Hitler.'

'You don't understand politics. Accord . . .'

'Yes, as long as there's fear of defeat be a believer in accord, but as soon as you win, dump all accord and run to divide everything up and confiscate shares.'

'That won't happen this time.'

'I say, nothing has changed, human nature hasn't changed. After Germany is destroyed, it will be Russia's turn next. Today they're singing Russia's praises when until yesterday Russia was referred to as humanity's foe. Today China is being embraced lovingly and until yesterday the Chinese were not afforded any other position except that of deceitful pirates. Today those very Chinese are being included in the list of allies. Japan's brutality is being broadcast openly while their own acts are being presented as humanity's safeguard. But remember, there's an extreme point of tyranny at which the tyrant strangles his own throat.'

'I agree, cruelty exists, but sometimes it's all for the best. If you examine the situation closely you'll see that it's not without its merits. Hindustan has improved greatly despite all that it has suffered, and it continues to make progress.'

'The fact that a few million people are speaking English is progress,

304

in your opinion. I wish Hitler had taught you German and converted you into sacred beings.'

'Why are you turning this into a personal battle?' Taylor said irately.

'Because it's connected to our existence.'

'If we want peace we'll have to endure a lot.'

'I'll endure everything, but when I see my country being trampled under the heels of these white-skinned people, my heart will bleed, my heart will weep, and my spirit will cry eternally. Don't think for a moment that because the embers have gone cold there are no sparks left. Some day the wind of change will blow in our direction and then we'll have revenge.'

'But you're already taking your revenge. You'll make me the object of your entire nation's suppressed desire for revenge.' The domestic quarrel became more and more vitriolic.

'And you? After crushing my nation mentally, economically and physically, now you're out to attack its very soul. You have been masters in the political and economic spheres, but now unfortunate women like myself have placed the remaining portion of our wealth at your feet.'

'But who says I'm happy? That was some reward I received. My people spit in my face, I have to suffer the punishment for your presence in the form of their condemnation, they've cut me off as if I were a decomposing finger on their hand.'

'And . . . and me? A prostitute isn't considered as low as my people regard me now. I've placed their proud heads before you to kick, they won't even want my shadow to fall on their respectable women.'

'But how is that my fault? You were not a child, your country's filthy climate and your own brown allure paralysed my mind. I've endured too much, but now I can take no more of this. But I don't see a remedy, I'm lost on this path which prevents me from turning back.'

'You're saying this? You who rubbed your nose on my shoes? I took everything you said to be the truth, I trusted you, I tried to nurse the humanity existing in the depths of your icy self, and now I'm suffering and being punished for that folly. But I know now that you can never be human, you wolves may wear a thousand disguises, but truth will prevail and your secret will be shattered. You brutal animal, you charlatan!'

'Shut up, you impertinent woman!'

'Hunh! It's not impertinent to call a thief a thief and an animal an animal, it's called telling the truth which you plunderers . . .'

'I warn you, don't say anything more or else . . .' Ronnie's words failed him and his eyes reddened with rage. His face became repulsive.

'Ohho, so you think I'll be frightened by your barking? No matter what happens I will unravel the secret of your deception. This is how you dupe . . .' The face that was ablaze like a flame darkened. A large, broad hand came across Shamman's face with full force, crushing her cheek and her temple, pushing her to the floor.

Trembling, shivering, Taylor left the room. Shamman did not make any sound. Lifting herself up slowly, she supported herself against the side of the chair and sat up.

What should she do? What should she do now?

Wait, don't think so much, wait a while. You . . . committed a sin so don't be so afraid to make atonement. Don't expect to break off grapes from a cactus that you have nurtured all this time. Wait. Her head between her hands, she sat on the floor crying for hours. Late at night Taylor returned, totally drunk. She quaked fearfully and, getting to her feet, quickly latched the door. Taylor was asleep, but she lay on her bed with her eyes open all night, staring blankly at the horrifying black night outside her window. Her temples became numb from the pressure of her thoughts, her head ached. But what is she thinking? There was no other sensation alive in her mind except extreme anguish. Her body throbbed like a ripened sore. If only some invisible surgeon's expert hand could ease this throbbing.

The next morning she had tea in bed. After Taylor had left she got up. He took extra care with his clothes this morning and before he left he was whistling joyfully. In the afternoon he telephoned to say he wasn't coming home for lunch and went to the racecourse directly from work. There he lost heavily and returned late in a state of drunken stupor. The servant very nearly received a beating from him. This was something new. Taylor treated servants very differently from the way most white people did. He spoke to them courteously and usually made jokes in their presence. Today he was barking commands at them in a combination of broken English and Urdu.

For two days this hide-and-seek continued. If by accident they saw each other, both turned away their faces hatefully. Taylor presented a very courageous exterior, but Shamman was happy to see that sometimes, his head held between his hands, he would become lost in thought. He also threw things down and lost his temper with the servants. She was unhappy, but Taylor was suffering as well.

Shamman was sitting in a daze, as if she had been running on a solid

306

bridge and had to stop suddenly; the boards were missing in front of her and below her was an immeasurable chasm and intractable rocks. Brown circles had appeared under her eyes because of lack of sleep and her clothes were dirty. But, unmindful of everything, she remained lost in thought. She wanted to suffer alone for whatever she had done. Tired of receiving sympathy, she had not informed any of her friends of what had happened. They too had assumed silence. 'If you're so strong, who are we to help?' they seemed to be saying. Actually they had lost hope a long time ago and nothing could surprise them now. If they were to hear of this outcome they would not be amazed at all, almost as though they had already seen reflections of what was happening now.

She had never cared about money, but today she realised that if she had money life would not appear so stifling. She could easily get a job. Teaching in some faraway, shabby school with uncouth girls and outdated, decaying books, and an eternal loneliness. The spectre of loneliness had terrified her, but this staring into stifling space made her quake. What will happen now? Her head throbbed from all this contemplation, but not even a dim ray of light was forthcoming.

'Sham! Sham!' Ronnie's voice quivered with a combination of anxiety and joy. 'Sham, where are you, darling?' He was running down the gallery. 'Sham!' he screamed from the doorway. 'Look, look, a letter from Mummy, from dearest Mummy.' He came in and sat down on her bed. Shamman turned her feet away from him testily.

'Look . . . read what she's written. "I'm sending my wedding brooch and locket for my dear daughter . . . it has real diamonds, my father loved diamonds" . . . listen . . . "If I could put this on her with my own hands" . . . oh Mum!' He placed his hands in Shamman's lap and burst into loud, happy laughter mixed with sobs.

'Mummy's a gem, Sham, she's a gem!'

And then no one knows how they came together. The broken bridge's boards were repaired and once again the train of life blared forward. Taylor cursed himself, took the blame for everything. He had become a boy, a little Ronnie who couldn't say anything more than 'Sham' and 'Mummy'. That night they saw a crazy Laurel and Hardy film and clapped their hands like children. Despite her protests, he kissed her in front of everyone. He responded to the flabbergasted stares of onlookers with audacious laughter. There were only three people in the world today. Two heartbroken souls and one loving mother who, thousands of miles away in America, held these two in her embrace and kissed them. She probably didn't know how she had drawn her exiled son and her foreign daughter close to her. Their hearts sang with the thought of the white-haired, innocent-looking old woman. They were no longer alone in the world, a third being had stepped into their life. Today they too had a confidante, who, putting aside advice and a lecture on colour and nationalism, had chosen instead to send them loving felicitations. Her daughter-in-law was a woman whom her beloved son had chosen – she didn't think beyond that. And why think further? Her son had never done anything wrong, he always listened to her, and now, a successful young man, he was putting his life in danger for his country. The woman who had loved this stranger from another land, surely she must be worthy of her love. She might be dark, but her soul was undoubtedly white. And that was why she was entrusting her family heirlooms to her care.

Who knows what Ronnie wrote to her? She's a mother after all, her son's stubbornness must have swayed her. The thought made Shamman's heart sink, distrust raised its ugly head. So this mother was also deceitful like her son! *Uff*, this white skin. But when Ronnie was snoring she turned on the bedside lamp and read the letter again. Once, twice. And she couldn't hold back her tears. A lonely mother's letter soaked in tears. There was no mention of any quarrel in it, no mention of any bloody war or national service. She hadn't frightened him with the threat of calamities, she hadn't egged him on; it was as if there was no third thing in the world except a mother and her only son. Yes, there was one more thing. An immutable love, a complete faith in each other, and her new daughter-in-law for whom she had sent a thousand good wishes and prayers in every line. Without ever having seen her she had surrendered the entire store of her love to her. How vast this mother's heart was whom Shamman had imagined to be like one of her haughty old female professors. She was like one of her own – no, she was more than that.

The parcel arrived the following day. If Shamman hadn't stopped him Taylor would have ripped it open at the police station. There was also a picture of his mother in it. Wearing loose-fitting clothes, she was sitting on a chair, holding a newspaper in her hands, but her eyes were raised to look at her two children. Hidden in every wrinkle on her face was the treasure of motherly love and her wet eyes spelled the longing to see her son. She was not from a high-class family. After she was widowed she turned all her attention to her son's upbringing. Her coarse build and the raised bone structure of her face bespoke a life of hardship. Now, in her old age, along with the minor concerns resulting from the war, was the pain of separation from her son. Why did she send her only son to be incinerated in the furnace of war? Was there anything that was dearer to this old woman than the only son for whom she had gambled her entire life savings?

A big tear dropped on the letter and the paper shivered. Separated by thousands of miles, two women embraced each other. Ronnie was turning and tossing in his sleep. His lips were moving and there was a wetness at the corners of his eyes. So there's love and affection hidden in these icy mounds? There are hearts beating in these chests which ache? She had thought that this spirit of sacrifice and compassion was only the eastern woman's tradition; what do these western, waxen puppets know of love, especially love of children? It's said they have very loose morals, they grow old, but their appetites don't diminish, they're like savages, and no matter who the men are, no matter what nationality or race, these women are suspended from their necks like a curse. In the first place they don't want to have children, and if those unfortunate souls do arrive, they treat them worse than dogs.

But where did Shamman see all this? She had never been to their country, nor did the inhabitants living in Hindustan have the right to be regarded as true representatives of their countries. All these stories, all these stories stand between people like steel walls. Is there a flame somewhere that can melt them? Can the blood of millions of brown and white human beings dissolve them?

Mother-in-law! The word made her laugh. She had heard stories about crafty old mothers-in-law. Everything that was rotten or decaying was referred to as 'your mother-in-law's liver'. Not even in her wildest dreams had she thought she would have a mother-in-law who was as guileless as a doll. If only her father-in-law were also living, a man from the novels of Dickens, his head shaking, a pipe between his lips, immersed in gardening.

Who says she's lost? There's a long and straight road ahead, shimmering like gold leaf. On it, two, no three, tiny toy-like people are advancing forward. Ronnie, she and Mummy!

The next morning they read the letter again. A hundred new stories were remembered afresh. Taylor suggested he take a day off, but on Shamman's insistence he left for work, albeit reluctantly. Before he left he instructed her to have a pen and plenty of paper ready for writing the letter to his mother, and he also made a special request for *shami kebabs* and yoghurt for lunch.

In the evening the letter was penned. After the first two words Taylor got lost in thought. 'Dear Mum' . . . No. He threw away the paper. 'My dearest Mum.' And now what? As if there wasn't anything more to say. The whole world had shrunk into these three words. After hours of toil the letter was finally completed. Taylor poured his heart into the letter. More than half of it was about Shamman.

The clouds were dissipated. There was no longer any fear of appearing in public. The mother stood with her umbrella open so that not a single drop of rain could fall on them. Life resumed a happy, swaying course, like a car bouncing along merrily on a bumpy road. Minor disturbances came and went. At every jolt they were separated, but then they collided with each other again, their hearts together once more. Sometimes tears were absorbed by laughter and sometimes laughter was drowned in tears. And the world also gets accustomed to the uncommon, especially when you're stubborn. Now no one turns around to look at them on the streets and if someone does, they're not watching. Soon they were attending meetings and social functions and no one was surprised to see them together any more. People began to feel that east and west had finally met. Their marriage was viewed as exemplary. People made repeated allusions to it.

Taylor's mother was writing frequently to say that they should come and visit her. Shamman wanted to go. Even at this distance she felt the attraction of her mother-in-law's love. She did make plans, but then such a fear set in she lost all sleep. The people here were used to them now, but how will she and Ronnie plough through new mountains and how will they find the strength to beat their foreheads against uneven rocks in order to create straight pathways? How will they listen to the insults of the elderly women in Taylor's family? Not everyone can be like his mother. The nephews and the little children, what will they say? Who will explain everything to them? If she and Taylor are at the zoo the animals there get confused. Won't this heap of rubbish protest? So, how could she go?

After all that had happened she found she had less and less to do. No sooner did the war escalate than time became elusive; it seemed it was constantly slipping from her hands. In addition, when there are two dishes in the same basket they are bound to strike against each other. The cinema was the only place where she and Taylor could spend time together without getting on one another's nerves. Inactivity made Shamman irritable. She had always been busy with reading and teaching, and now time dragged. Taylor came home exhausted and immediately fell asleep while she lay awake next to him. During the day she felt sleepy and took long naps. The interminable nights and the enervating loneliness led to misgivings. Taylor's presence was as good as non-existent. All day he was at work and at night he slept, while Shamman, standing on the fringes of his world, was alone despite the fact that she lived with him, feeling as if she were not his wife but a neighbour with whom he talked only when the need arose.

But conflicts arose even when they were in the cinema. *The Great Dictator* became the basis of a personal argument.

'This is cowardly and shallow ... you can turn everything into a joke.'

Shamman's remark upset Taylor, who had been laughing unreservedly.

'Look, if you read *Mein Kampf* you'll realise what these Nazis are,' he said vehemently. 'They are fiends.'

'There's not much difference between the Nazis and their fellow-brothers. Fiends take many shapes.'

'But no one is like them.'

'Hunh! Why would you say anything about them? After all, you're their compatriot, the protector of royalty.'

'We ... I ... we people are not fighting to protect the British crown.'

'Yes, say that you're fighting to save humanity. Hunh! The sneaky cat is out to protect the *jalebis*! How wonderful.'

'But this time fairness will prevail.'

'Of course! If plunderers don't carry out justice, who will?'

'But look here, I'm not a plunderer.'

'If you side with plunderers you will definitely be viewed as one. You consider yourself to be the protector of humanity. Why don't you regard the Hindustanis as human too?'

'Who says we don't regard them as human?'

'You ran to save France, you beat your chests at Poland's demise, and when Japan stole a few golden birds from Britain's hands you were crestfallen. But what kind of humanity is this that makes you look only at white skin?'

'Why, we're fighting for China as well.'

'Everyone knows how that battle is being fought. You're also helping Russia, aren't you? When is the second front coming into existence? But isn't it strange you can't find the key? We know when the second front will come about. When Germany is crushed and Russia is exhausted.'

'You've gone mad. It's ridiculous to go to the cinema with you.'

It was settled they would no longer see films. But this agreement

311

couldn't be sustained for long. Taylor was the one who suggested a breach. Finally, at Shamman's insistence, they decided they would see an English and a Hindustani film alternately. Taylor could understand simple Hindi easily. But after they had seen one or two stunt films Taylor couldn't restrain himself any longer. One reel into the film and he'd lose his patience.

'Good God, didn't we see this film last week?' he'd ask mulishly.

'How can that be? This film was released this week,' Shamman protested.

'No, no, it's the same. There's that same idiot lover. I recognise him, singing in the jungle, and that flat-chested heroine . . . there she falls again. It's the same. Come on, let's see an English film.'

And Shamman would lose her temper. True that every film was the same — the hero sings songs in the jungle, the heroine falls down and he has to pick her up — but Taylor was deliberately trying to upset her. Even if the film was good, he slept through it and Shamman, her cheeks puffed in anger, continued to sit and stubbornly watch it all the way through. And if they were at an English film she pretended to be tired. In other words, no matter what film it was, neither of them enjoyed it.

'Every character in your films either cries or sings.'

'And what else is there in your films except "*hee hee*!"' she argued.

'They should copy American films.'

'Hunh! American films! What else is there in them except lewdness and obscenity?' She knew, however, that the Hindustani films that were slightly better than most used this very trick as well. But she continued to feign outrage.

'They're excellent. Can't say the same about your films.'

'You're blinded by your narrow views. You don't understand the philosophy that drives our lives. You watch films just to create a turmoil in your emotions.'

'In the first place, our emotions are not bombs so that the slightest jolt will cause them to explode, and secondly what if that is the case?'

The antagonism between them mounted. Arguments veered from ordinary subjects and became focused on topics existing within the four walls of the house. Personal matters became targets, and finally both of them boycotted the cinema. But then the radio took over like a disease. In effect, they both seemed to be looking for an excuse all the time. Taylor couldn't stand Hindi songs and just to rile him Shamman began taking lessons in classical singing. Not only did that provide her with something to pass the time, it also gave her material for battle. She listened to the most intricate classical ragas, trembled at every trill, became ecstatic at every stretching note, drowned herself in every ornate composition. But as soon as Taylor arrived, he transported himself to London in the twinkling of an eye.

'This is real music,' he'd proclaim, shaking his head dreamily.

'Hunh! Like a battered dog howling,' she'd mutter angrily.

'That's why I always say you should learn, you should develop an ear.'

'If you started listening to Hindi music you'd never go back to this din.'

'No one in his right mind can appreciate Hindi music.'

This would lead to further entanglement.

'You want to condemn everything that belongs to me and distance me from my culture.'

'If you live with me you'll have to share my likes and dislikes.'

'Why? If I don't force you to live according to my way of life, why should you try to coerce me?'

'You know that your culture is colourless. Your men are more intelligent than the women. They marry European girls and become cultured and refined. Their entire manner changes, they become more sophisticated.'

'Well, isn't that just wonderful? This is another way of spreading imperialism: use your girls to entrap these idiots. In this way the English way of life will be perpetuated. Dressed in their clothes, speaking their language, sitting in the laps of their women, well, how can they protest? And then they're neither Hindustani nor does their brown skin allow them to become English; they remain suspended in the middle somewhere. Their daughters either walk the streets on the basis of their two-toned skin or lick the shoes of Tommies. There isn't just one way of destroying a people. You can also absorb and destroy.'

'All right, why don't you absorb me in your culture, although it will be difficult getting used to living in this filth?'

'But . . .'

'But the fact of the matter is . . . anyway, let it go.'

'Come on, I'm not a child who will cry at the slightest provocation.'

'Well, that the European way of life is superior to any other and you actually believe that it is good enough to adopt, and for this reason you cannot pull me down with you. In your hearts you people admire European culture.'

'What charming misconceptions!'

313

They bickered endlessly, but secretly Shamman felt remorse. Why was it that despite her staunch opposition to Europe, she was slowly becoming coloured by the European way of life? She sat at a table and used a knife and fork, she slept on a bed with a mattress and also observed other minor English practices. She had never thought about this before and the realisation only helped to sharpen her obstinacy. She began breaking rules deliberately. Pretending to be sick, she had breakfast in bed, instead of a nightdress she wore a *gharara* and *kurta* to bed. But Taylor didn't seem to mind. As a matter of fact, he liked the *gharara* very much, especially because it resembled a skirt.

So anything that reminded him of his own culture was admirable and acceptable. In spite of his liberal attitudes, how narrow-minded he was unconsciously. As far as his conscious self was concerned, he allowed it a broad view, but he had no control over his unconscious. The mildew that had accumulated over a period of centuries could not be scraped off so easily. If those who profess to be liberal are like this, God help those who are narrow-minded. They may try very hard, but they can't rid their minds of the sense of superiority that is deeply instilled there. Humanity proclaims equality. But the prowler hiding in the mind sometimes takes a peep and says, 'All fingers are not the same length, don't cut them and pull them to make them the same, the hand will look misshapen and grotesque. The beauty of the world lies in this unevenness. In this matter open-mindedness is equivalent to self-deception.'

And a strange kind of struggle ensued in their house. It was as if the most famous wrestlers were in each other's grip. Both pull in opposite directions; sometimes one wrestler has the upper hand and flattens the other, sometimes the other lunges in a surprise attack. Along with this a mental tussle also continues to spiral. How will this two-engine boat ever come ashore when both engines are running in opposite directions? Sometimes it flows two inches towards the east and sometimes two inches towards the west. The result is the same. Stagnation, suffocation, distress and, to make matters worse, there's a storm brewing, the gigantic waves are roaring with their jaws open wide, and there's no boatman in sight.

Defeated at the hands of life, Shamman was taking a stroll one day and covered a considerable distance. She had just had a fight with Taylor. The wounds were still fresh. Finding herself in the park, she decided to sit down on a bench and rest for a few minutes. But she felt as if she'd been bitten by a snake. This bench! Why a bench and why not a terrace? Why all these signs and notices in English? She looked around her. Every little bit had been crushed by the oppression of the masters. Dirty, filthy, baggy trousers, grotesque frocks, chairs with broken legs, scratched tables. The murderous claws of these beasts have engraved their imprints everywhere – how will these bruises heal?

She wanted to kick the bench. These imprints of imperialism – if only there was an unseen power that could pick up these blemishes and dump them far away from here, into the ocean perhaps, and also wash away these malignant white stains that had festered into sores due to prolonged exposure to darkness and heat and whose stench had stifled humanity.

'Ohho, *Assalaam alaikum*! What is this I see?' A familiar voice broke into her reverie, startling her.

'*Array*, is it . . . you?' Surprised, she stared at Professor's slovenly appearance, trying to make sure it was him. First she thought she had imagined it to be Professor; there were no signs of the suave, well-dressed man she knew. This man was dressed in loose-fitting *khadar*, looking every inch a dishevelled poet, but obviously an extremely unpoetic man.

'But you left?'

'Yes, and now I'm back. What's so surprising about that? You look like you're seeing a corpse who has jumped out of his shroud to come and stand before you.'

'No, no, actually I hadn't expected to see you like this. But . . .'

'Come on, say what's on your mind.' He smiled good-naturedly.

'Nothing, nothing really. We've met after so long and here we go arguing again. Tell me, are you well?'

'Don't ask, try and figure out for yourself.'

'Now don't blame me afterwards, you're teasing me and if I say the wrong thing you'll get all upset.'

'Test me just once. The luxury of being temperamental has abandoned us.' Professor sighed.

'It seems as if you've fallen in love.'

'It's not your ordinary run-of-the-mill type of love either.'

'Oh, congratulations. But how did this come about?'

'You don't need a plough and oxen to be in love.'

'But, excuse me, this is the guise of a nationalist,' she said, surveying his appearance from top to toe.

'It does seem that way, doesn't it?' Professor said in a whisper.

'But what happened? I didn't expect this of you.'

'Expect what? You mean the masquerade?'

'Yes, this dress, these locks ... you've done wonders! Have you become a communist?'

'Definitely.' Professor was still smiling.

'And that thirteen-hundred-a-month job?'

'I lost it.'

'And the reason? You said ...'

'I couldn't cope, that's why I had to adopt this masquerade.' Professor couldn't conceal the bitterness of sarcasm in his voice.

Shamman stared incredulously at Professor. What was he up to now? She didn't trust him. He could fool you in a minute and you wouldn't know it. But at this moment he was a picture of duplicity himself.

'So, tell me about yourself. Oh yes, I forgot to offer congratulations on your marriage.'

'Yes, I entrapped a worker, after all it is wartime and everything is so expensive.'

'I know, hit me with my own shoe. But I expected this of you. Don't mind my saying this. Actually my advice in the area of marriage has no value. But you didn't happen to get married because you've always been fond of being a little strange and unusual? Listen, don't interrupt – if that had been the reason you wouldn't look so happy and content.'

'I look happy?' She laughed a hollow laugh.

'At least your face and your behaviour seem to say that. Anyway, let's drop the subject. Are you still working or did you give up working altogether?'

'I stopped working a long time ago. What are you doing? Oh, I forgot, you must be "working".'

Professor smiled and said nothing.

'Now you're a government communist, you must be very influential.'

'Of course.'

'The campaign for national warfare also continues?'

'With great speed.'

'I must say, you are so fortunate. There were those communists who used to go around hiding in holes, pursued as if they were mad dogs, and here you are ...'

'Yes we drive around with the viceroy, there's no dearth of cars, horse carriages.' Shamman heard the sarcasm in his voice again. Professor's sunken eyes and his meaningless smile confused her.

'Well, who is your beloved?'

'A Bengali beauty.'

'A Bengali?'

'Yes. Oh, you don't know. I was posted to Bengal and it was there that I was wounded by the arrow of love.'

Shamman moved back nervously. Professor's eyes were narrowed in a frightening manner, a strange and unknown fear floated in them, as if he were recounting a nightmarish dream in a state of half-wakefulness. His body had been reduced to half its original size, his face had aged almost to the extent of disfigurement, and his hair was nearly all grey, giving the impression that he had just come out of a flour mill. She was nonplussed.

'It's getting cold. Would you like to come home with me, or do you think you will be late?'

'Shall I come?' Professor said, as if snapping out of a dream.

'Yes, why not? Taylor will be home later.'

'He won't kick me because I'm a brown native?'

'But you're a government native.'

'That's funny!'

When they got home he roamed around looking at the house. At lunch he started taking large bites, swallowing hurriedly and then stopping suddenly as if he were choking before taking big bites again.

'I've had some problems with digestion from all the rich food I've been eating,' he said, smiling meaningfully again. 'I'll come again. I've seen the house now. The *firni* was delicious.' He didn't make much sense.

After he left Shamman sat quietly for a long time. Russia was advancing, but she wasn't at all impressed. All of them are pretenders. Out to help humanity supposedly. What if they devour what's left of humanity?

He must have come to impress me. I'm not one of those who are easily misled by their antics. He must have embezzled money. The wretch was thrown out and to hide his blackness he cowers under the red banner. These Bengali women aren't much, just have very big eyes, that's all, although these penniless poets are usually crazy about them. But there's a famine in Bengal. And what's so odd about that? Whether there's a famine or whether the crops are flourishing, the widow is always in a pitiful state.

Ronnie had returned from work tired and exhausted and had gone directly to bed. If it had been some other day she would have sought a little retaliation for Bengal's famine by starting an argument with him and making his blood boil. But Professor had somehow succeeded in crushing her spirit.

She was in a very sullen mood when the servant came in to inform her of Professor's arrival. She wanted to give orders to have him kicked out. But she realised that it might be worth her while to let him have a few jabs and twists, so she decided to see him.

She was startled once again when she saw him. Good God! Is the world a magician's sack? You throw in a hen's feather and out comes a baby pigeon!

'You're looking at my hair, no doubt. The stupid barber took off too much. I just asked for a nice trim and he practically scraped off my neck.' He massaged the back of his neck with his hand. 'Here, I've thrown down my weapons,' he seemed to be saying to Shamman, 'come into the arena now.'

'I've come to you for a special purpose. You must get tired of being alone.' Shamman's ears burned and, grasping the situation, he quickly added, 'Don't be so sensitive. All joking aside, listen carefully. First, I ask forgiveness for yesterday's nonsense, that was all in jest. But I discovered you've lost your sense of humour – whatever happened to your powers of perception, or was that all a façade? Here's my story in two words. If you don't believe me that's all right, our relationship shouldn't be affected by personal matters. I was in Calcutta where I got into trouble. I don't believe in spirits, but it seemed as if a spirit had taken possession of me and I had to offer my resignation and run from there. And here I found a shortage of clerks. It's a minor job, just two or three days of supervision, there's no clerical work. Now if you're ready . . .'

'What is this work?'

'I feel like saying . . .' he smiled mischievously.

'Go ahead and say it, come on.'

'Well, there's plenty of time to talk about what I feel. Listen, here's what has to be done. We've opened a few centres where our people go and distribute grain.'

'Oh, grain?' She looked away in embarrassment. She had seen long lines in which people collided with each other like sheep in front of shops where grain was sold.

'It's not very hard work. All you have to do is to keep the women's lines straight and in order and make sure the organisers don't harass them unduly. There are only a few grain centres so the crowds are immense and unruly. Do you think you can help?'

318

'This doesn't sound like too much, but . . .'

'Can you hold back your "but" for a few months? I'm not going to run off. I know there are a thousand questions raising a storm in your head, but this is not the time to ponder over those questions.'

'To do something without full understanding . . .'

'Is foolishness. You're wrong. In the first place, do a little research, take some interest in the news and you'll get all the answers automatically. And anyway, if I start arguing with you I know I'll lose.'

'So you'll work on the basis of hollow foundations. If the foundations are hollow, the whole system will be insubstantial.'

'You see, I've lost already. Look, don't treat this as the work of communists, but as charity. If you want to, that is, I won't force you.'

Professor laid down his arms and adopted the policy of *satyagraha* which maddened Shamman to the point of helplessness. She didn't know how to convince him; the opponent wasn't ready to argue, but if he were, she would destroy him with two words.

'If nothing else it's just something to pass the time. Give me an answer – if you can't help I'll have to make other arrangements.'

'I'll come.'

'Good, so I'll send you the whole week's schedule tomorrow.'

And the next day she left at eight in the morning. It was still two hours before distribution began, but the crowds were milling about as if they were assembled for the worship of a major deity. There was pushing, jostling, scratching and grabbing – they would swallow each other if they could help it. The moment the temple gates opened the crowds spilled over like a storm. 'Move back! Move back!' The police brandished their batons, trying to push back the worshippers. But God forgive us! If the deity's appeal could be weakened by these batons what more could one ask for? These thrashing starving people were capable of ripping off their own skins. Their bodies are like bundles of sticks wrapped in clothing, but their greed equals the greed of ten wrestlers; the minute they see a grain of rice strange monsters suddenly take shape inside their bodies and the same bundles of sticks which, moments earlier, were lifeless, spring to life with an electric swiftness. And their speech, God save us! Because they have no fuel the tongues move so recklessly, but if they came into contact with a few delectable morsels, who knows how far these tongues would travel. And this pandemonium was rampant in the women's lines.

These fidgety worms were being kept in rows with great difficulty. The front lines fell to Shamman's care. A relative calm prevailed here

319

due to proximity to the grain, but the rear portion of the line, despite efforts by three or four women to control it, was in total chaos. The line, at least half a mile long, writhed and thrashed like a deadly snake.

Were these women or hungry bitches? It's very upsetting to see women behaving in this riotous fashion. Shamman tried to organise them several times, but they didn't seem to understand much and began screaming at her in some wild dialect that was incomprehensible to her. The sun was very bright and it seemed a moist ash was falling like rain; it was as though someone was plastering melted ash on your body, and on top of that the foul odour emanating from the bodies of these frenzied women – Shamman's head swam.

The first woman in that line appeared to made from some kind of contentious clay; she had been bickering at the top of her voice with the shopkeeper and wouldn't budge. Sometimes she grasped his feet, then she'd bang her head with the same hand. The police constable's whip swung at her and, whimpering and scowling, she was thrown out of line. Some of the women were grumbling about the quality of the grain. The quota was two kilos in the open market and here it was three yet they couldn't stop complaining. The malady the first woman in line suffered from seemed contagious because whoever came forward got stuck in that position and had to be ejected from there with the aid of batons. After three or four had been forcibly removed the news travelled like wildfire that the merchandise was worm-eaten.

Just then she saw Professor tearing through the crowd, pressing forward with his elbows. His eyes met Shamman's once and then he moved on. Arriving at the front of the shop, he began a tirade with the shopkeeper, wringing his hands as if he were not a learned professor but a comrade of the women standing in line. And his speech was also quite indecipherable, seemingly a garbled mix of Gujarati, Marathi, Urdu and English. As a result of this endeavour the grain distribution was suddenly halted. The snake squirmed angrily and, its tail all curled up, it tried to force its way into the shop. The confusion started at Shamman's end. She turned to Professor for a minute and a mêlée ensued. The boundary collapsed, moans, screams and whimpers spread everywhere, ravenous hands began clawing each other, voices flapped clamorously.

The organisers in the back raced forward. Professor, having dealt with the shopkeeper, arrived at the spot.

'You will all get grain in a little while. These bags are here by mistake. Please be patient, sisters.'

Screaming, he lunged back and forth. But it seemed that patience had also been crushed along with everything else and had turned to dust. Suddenly the moans changed to shrieks. A new stock of grain had arrived. The relief effort swung into motion again.

While helping her into a taxi, Professor looked apologetically at the portion of her fine georgette sari which, having been soaked in the nearby gutter, now looked like a dead rat.

'Today you just came to see the drama, but I'm sure that when you come on Wednesday, you'll have some real fun. You will come? You can rest for a day.'

'I'll try,' she said, leaning her aching shoulders on the back of the seat. The soggy end of the sari crawled against her ankle. She shivered.

44

The work was uninteresting and quite painful, but at least the customary evening silence was broken. Taylor listened enthusiastically to accounts of her work. Every other day a new drama unfolded. Sometimes the human weaknesses she saw enraged her. Why is Hindustan so averse to order? Why is every task characterised by sloppiness?

'It's very difficult to train them to improve,' Taylor said after hearing what she was saying.

'They're illiterate, the poor idiots,' Shamman remarked angrily.

'Yes, and secondly there's also something in their nature.'

'What can one remember when faced with hunger?' Shamman said with forced control.

'But they're constantly getting grain. Actually these people are completely unprincipled.'

'But what are they getting? Mouldy rice and worm-eaten wheat.'

'But we've got new supplies of wheat from the Punjab.'

'You may have got it, but it's not available. Those new supplies of wheat will be brought from the fields when they're all rotting.'

'This is really a problem.'

'Yes, and the government isn't paying any attention.'

'But what can the government do when the crooks are keeping an eye on everything?'

'These crooks are the government's stooges, every year they receive titles in connection with the destruction of human beings.'

'You talk as if I'm the government.'

'You're a supporter of the government.'

'Well, you're a supporter too because now you work for the rationing scheme, which is a governmental agency.'

For a moment Shamman was at a loss for words.

'And what's wrong with that?' Taylor said in a conciliatory tone. 'You talk just like a child.'

'I'd like to stay away from the government's shackles,' she said sadly.

Taylor was bent on pacifying her. 'Be patient, that time will come.'

'What time?'

'The time when you'll be free of these shackles. I don't know why you people are so irresolute. You despair so easily. You've studied the history of our country and still you haven't learned anything. When will your hearts be free of this spirit of defeatism?'

'We should not feel defeat even when we are defeated? This is not fair.'

'If you move forward with renewed vigour after having been defeated, this feeling will automatically be dissipated. If weeping alone could produce results the matter would have been resolved ages ago. How many eyes are there in Hindustan that don't shed dry tears night and day?' Today the lost humanitarian in Taylor was making a comeback. Domestic squabbles had turned them both into savage brutes. Both sides had formed battlefronts and their personal conflicts had reduced for them the effects of the fire that was raging in the world. In the face of their own gashing and bruising, they had lost sight of humanity's bleeding wounds.

She got up on the pretext of getting a drink of water. When she returned she casually placed her fingers in Taylor's golden hair. What a soft feeling that was ... the knot that had formed in her throat began to unravel.

'Ronnie!' She couldn't say anything more and Ronnie didn't let her speak.

When she opened her eyes Ronnie handed her a letter. 'It's Mummy's letter. Just read what the old woman writes. She thinks I'm still that two-foot-tall Ronnie who needs constant care and protection.'

After Ronnie had left she read the letter slowly. Mummy had written about Ronnie's favourite foods and what he disliked the most. 'He loses a lot of handkerchiefs and this can be such a nuisance for a wife. His socks are also always worn, and if he washes his feet before going to bed and has them sprinkled with talcum powder . . .'

The defeated mind, wrapped in slumber, saw dreams filled with fresh green rice shoots. The tiny golden seedlings dropped like tiny bells on the supple bosom of the honey-brown earth. How long could the niggardly earth keep its face turned away? Soon the sun's sharp rays tickled it, stirring up life. Silvery water danced down mirthfully into its heart. In no time lush green shoots were bouncing and swaying like enchanted spirits. Now the struggle will diminish. New rice is here! The slumber of satiated hunger will be deep and peaceful. New rice is here. Now drops of manna will fall into Bengal's starving throat. New rice is here. Now the famine is over. Held within empty fists, this new rice will turn into pieces of gold . . . when she turned, her head fell against Taylor's chest and rested there.

Taylor's dancing whistle echoed in her ears when she opened her eyes. Bent over the mirror, he was scraping his cheek with the safety razor. His eyes were glittering like pure sapphires and suddenly Shamman remembered the glass marbles she and Kaddan had planted in the flower patch when they were children. She smiled.

How silly mothers are! Shamman broke into a quiet laugh. They're all the same. But they're usually right. Shamman hadn't looked at Ronnie's clothes for many days. There are buttons missing and although he has at least fifty pairs of socks, all of them are worn at the heels and the toes. For a long time she sat fingering his clothes.

She wished she could somehow get out of the work at the rationing office. She might be able to do it if she had an argument with Professor. The work was very tiring and she had to go three times a week instead of two because some of the workers had contracted malaria. Also, what was the work but training monkeys! At school she had always taught the more advanced classes so that she never had to deal with naughty, uncouth children. But teaching goats to read was easier than training these women to stay in line. They had no brains; all their energies seemed to be directed towards obtaining grain. Anyway, if it were a matter of a few days, she could do it, but this programme was to go on for months.

An unexpected guest is always a problem, but when she saw Professor walking in she really felt irked. The wretch must be hungry as usual and will try and get both lunch and dinner out of teatime. She had to welcome him.

'No, I don't want any tea. Sheila was the only one left and now she has a fever of a hundred and four. We could take care of everything if it weren't for the women.'

Rubbing his hands together sheepishly, he said, 'You're the only Muslim woman who is taking any interest in this sort of thing. I've heard that many Muslims have dropped purdah, but they're all busy attending meetings and gatherings.'

'But if you do have enough women, why bother with this Hindu–Muslim question?'

'Just like that. I'm narrow-minded. Being a member of this group I sometimes think that . . . anyway, will you come?'

'What do you think? Are you planning to establish Pakistan as part of the rationing scheme?' She poked him with the needle finally.

'Argument again!'

'Don't evade the issue. Tell me, did Lenin or Stalin teach you that if you create divisions you'll get rid of every problem?'

'But . . .'

'You've hit upon this ploy because there are no Hindu–Muslim riots.'

'You think that if Pakistan is given away there will be Hindu–Muslim riots? Listen to me, who is giving Pakistan away? Who has anything to give in the first place?'

'Well, you and others like you are making claims.'

'Right, as if Pakistan is in our pocket so that as soon as anyone asks for it we'll take it out and hand it over.'

'But you accept their claims.'

'What difference does that make? If a group of people demand a certain type of government, what right do we have to refuse? We have a lot of differences of opinion with them, but that is not to say we should deny the concept of Pakistan altogether. Who are we to make this judgement?'

'But using religion . . .'

'I said we have differences, didn't I? They'll be ironed out eventually. Right now only the issue of Pakistan has been raised.'

'And what if the issues of Sikhistan, Budhistan and Isaistan are also raised?'

'Then these issues will be considered. Not to consider any issue that arises is . . .'

'But what is the purpose of wasting time like this?'

'There's only one purpose. Accord.'

'Hunh! What a hackneyed word that is. Has no effect on the ears any more.'

'Yes it's hackneyed, but it hasn't been cut and polished, it's just a crude piece of glass as yet. But, as I said earlier, we'll argue later.'

'This is wonderful. You're afraid of arguments? You make the imagination numb this way.'

'Now how can I go around confronting every non-believer with my arguments? Just think. If I get stuck with two or three other intractable ones like you, I'll spend the rest of my life presenting arguments. And look what a turmoil there is all over, look at Bengal. Do you want us to suffer as they have? If I didn't really need your help I wouldn't waste my precious time like this. Anyway, if you don't have the time . . .'

'Have some tea, that won't take so long,' Shamman said, pouring tea for him.

'Now look, if I didn't care about friendship I wouldn't be sitting here trying to pacify you.' Taking a sip of his tea, Professor smiled. 'We will be friendly, no matter what the price, although it's not easy; we're getting a beating from both sides, but you just wait and see how bullheaded we can be.' He laughed loudly.

'All right, now remember to come early tomorrow morning.' He left hurriedly without eating anything. Shamman saw that like a poet's hair his was growing long on the nape of his neck again, and his clothes looked shabby.

Shamman wasn't interested in dance parties and Taylor professed no interest either. Whether deliberately or reluctantly, he avoided them as much as he could. But this one was being given by the officers and Shamman and Taylor were in charge of the arrangements. Fortunately or unfortunately, Shamman suddenly developed a fever and her problem was solved. For some time now her health hadn't been all that good and now the fever and Taylor's unending involvement with work. Professor no longer visited as often either. He showed up to see her when she had a fever and stayed only a short while. The other girls were feeling better now and he didn't need Shamman desperately any more.

She was in bed, feeling sick and angry. She had already thrown a teacup and two saucers when Taylor, his tie in one hand, walked in taking long strides and looking very cheerful.

'Oh dear, you're having a feast here,' he said smiling and Shamman felt like flinging the tray at him. She hadn't been able to keep anything down since morning and he probably thought she had been nibbling on food all day long.

'I just read Mummy's letter. She's crazy.' He smiled bashfully. 'All that whimpering and mewling, why do women like it so much? Such nonsense.'

Shamman didn't pick up the letter and continued to stir her tea silently. What was he going on about?

'And such an inconvenience – children are so troublesome.'

'Hunh! Isn't it enough one mistake has been made and now another . . .'

'Eh?' He started, abashed.

'What we have sown we should reap, why should we blacken the foreheads of those who are innocent?'

'Mummy, it's her wish . . .' He didn't finish. Colour rushed to his face.

'Mummy is not a child that she won't understand. She will resist this herself.'

'Who? Mummy? No, are you joking? She loves children. She gets together all the children from here and there just to keep them around her.'

'So she can still get together children from here and there.'

'Hmm.' He was silent.

'Half a partridge and the rest a quail,' she said scornfully and Taylor's ears turned red again.

'We've made a grave mistake,' he said in a wooden voice.

'A terrible folly.'

'How will this hell be endured?'

'Why endure it? If you've ingested poison why not vomit it out?'

'What do you mean?'

'I mean instead of surrendering two lives to hell it's better if we go our separate ways.'

'If you were saying this to a Hindustani man he would show you a thing or two,' Taylor said, grinding his teeth in anger.

'Maybe.'

'And you wouldn't have objected either.'

'Maybe.'

'You're so low.' He was foaming at the mouth. 'Such women should be butchered. Oh God! How I hate you!'

'Hunh! As if I'm mad with love for you.'

326

'You . . . you are worse than a whore. Oh, if only someone would strangle you so I could be free.'

'And why shouldn't someone crush you, you who have sucked the blood of this entire nation like a leech. Just look at your sisters and mothers . . . hunh! Such debased and wicked women!'

'Shut up, you wretch! I ignored roses and linked myself instead to a poisonous cactus.'

'And you think you're very handsome? Your bleached, sick-looking skin, your rotting teeth – you monkey!'

'So go and warm the embrace of some common low caste man – if you're such a chaste person, get out of here now!'

'A common low caste man will be a thousand times better than you, you Tommy!' She got up to leave.

Shamman had once jokingly told Taylor that 'Tommy' was a term used by Hindustanis for white illegitimate boys who, it was rumoured, are conscripted in the army to be placed before guns. Hearing this obscenity falling from her mouth stunned Taylor. He sat motionless for a few minutes. He was ashen, as if someone had extracted all the blood from his body. Shamman immediately went to the other room and locked the door. He screamed profanities at her. She had never seen him this angry. He was ranting like a madman, like someone whose control has finally broken its reins and whose anger has exploded, spilling all over his brain. Trembling fearfully, Shamman sat on her bed with her legs dangling. How did things go so far? This is what it has come to?

She heard Taylor pacing all night. He tore about like a wounded tiger. Again and again she heard him opening the cupboard and heard the sound of liquid being poured from a bottle, but not for long because there was only one bottle they kept for visitors. Taylor never drank at home.

Then she heard muffled, stifled sobs. Shamman was shaken to the core of her being. He was crying! Taylor, a stalwart, grown man, was crying because a woman had hurt him. She wanted to get up and . . . but she quaked. Those blue eyes like glass marbles, the red face!

The next day the servant told her that Taylor had packed all his luggage and left for Delhi. There had also been a trunk call, she was told.

A whole week went by and there was no word from Taylor. Shamman's fever persisted and she became quite weak. She tried to call Delhi and find out where he was, but she couldn't get any information.

Perhaps he was on the secret mission he had often mentioned in the past.

Another two weeks passed and still no sign of Taylor. Shamman received his salary cheque from the government.

She had fanned a tiny spark until it ignited into an enormous flame and engulfed everything in its path. If only he'd come back, just once, and then? Then history will not repeat itself . . . if he comes back everything will be reconstructed, everything . . . the remains aren't that dilapidated that they can't be repaired.

'Just once, only once, the last time, the last chance,' she prayed pleadingly, to whom and for what, she did not know.

Time passed. She continued working, but her heart was heavy. She took out all his clothes and had them aired. She was still weak so she sat nearby and gave the servant directions. She brushed everything herself and then packed the clothes with mothballs and put them away. Many times during the day a sense of isolation filled her heart with fear, and she shed silent tears.

More days passed. She has no one in the world. She has lost everything. Gradually she chewed off every cord with her poisonous teeth, but the last string of hope was still intact, although it was fragile and could break at any moment.

She slept fitfully. Everything was topsy turvy. At night she felt as if she had found the way . . . Taylor's car came to a halt, he got out, now he's climbing the stairs, now he's on the landing next to the door, now he's at the door. But suddenly she would find the calculations misleading. How could he get out of the car so quickly? It's one thing to say the words, another for something really to happen. There . . . he shut the car door . . . now . . . he's climbing . . . the stairs . . . she can hear his footsteps clearly. But the footsteps on the stairs did not end, ten or twelve stairs could not be climbed even with a thousand footfalls . . . then she found out that what she thought was the sound of footsteps was actually the '*tip, tip*' of the water dripping from the tap. '*Tip, tip*' – the sound was just like human footsteps. Exasperated, she got up and squeezed the tap tight, strangling it, the wretch!

Her mental anguish grew. She lost her appetite, her tongue became mouldy and everything tasted bitter, stale and musty. She was tired of these dishes, tired of the dining room chairs, the soft-cushioned sofas in the drawing room. She wanted to get rid of everything. Why be embroiled in all of these snarls? Certainly death would be better than this vapid, dull life.

She put a small morsel of *shami kebab* in her mouth and it spread in her mouth like a mountain of filth and stench. With a hand on her mouth so the servant wouldn't see her retching, she quickly got to her feet and ran to her room. Taylor liked these kebabs so much. He used to swallow them dry. Now she'll have them cooked only when Taylor is back, or else they will stick in her throat, making her throw up.

How did a little thing like this become so protracted? She felt like laughing loudly or crying violently. But she could do neither. What would the driver think?

'Hurry, hurry,' she admonished the driver. She wished she could add the beating of her heart to the speed of the car so it would go faster. Today her body seemed bent on becoming light so it could fly away, her eyes filled with tears again and again. How dead and marred her face was, she thought, looking at her image in the rear-view mirror. She didn't care. Beauty and ugliness had merged and were dim in the presence of this new gleam. She was unattractive, but ... but still her heart was suddenly so beautiful, inhabited by this one surprised thought: 'Ronnie ... Ronnie Taylor ... where are you? Ask me to forgive you, you heartless ...' her throat choked with unshed tears.

She will scold Ronnie, just wait and see! She'll place the blame for all her misfortune on him, and Ronnie? He won't have the sense to be angry with her. The brute! Selfish brute! Went away for so long and didn't think for a minute how difficult it is to get patent medicines. Obtaining a calcium injection is like digging a canal of milk. And such carelessness at a time like this? Still, she felt her heart swell with love for him. He was so far away, yet so close to her.

And Mummy? The sweet, silly mother had written: 'Don't worry, I'll knit of all the woollens.'

Shush, the silly woman! She's so excited, she thinks she has such a talent for raising children. Her love will make her over-indulgent, and will she have the energy? Getting up at night isn't easy and what if it's cold and chilly? But how can one think of living when this war goes on? The thought of the whole world splattered with blood made her tremble fearfully. If only this war would stop. May God not allow anyone to be born during these days of hell. Who is safe? And until when? Who knows when flames will rain on them, when they will all be attacked by bombs. She was consumed with the thought of keeping her family together.

And what if she doesn't tell Ronnie anything? Oh, it will be so much fun! He'll be crazy with joy. And if he finds out now he won't let her have one moment of peace. 'Don't do this, don't do that,' he'll fuss. She burst into a laugh suddenly. How giddy she was. But where were the bombs?

When the car entered the compound she felt as if indeed a bomb had fallen. A brown military jeep was standing in the portico. She made a wild dash towards the drawing room.

'Ronnie . . . Ronnie . . .' she shouted, panting as she hurriedly climbed the stairs. Her sari was caught in her feet. Filled with dread, she came to a standstill at the drawing room door.

'Ronnie!' She pushed open the door with all her might. 'Ronnie?'

'Good evening, madam.' A starched soldier saluted her.

'Ronnie.' The word got stuck in her throat.

'Mr Taylor left by air for the front, madam. This is for you.' He handed her a letter, saluted briskly and was gone.

The letter in her hand, she stood motionless, thinking. A thousand whirring planes roared like lions, a thousand bombs blasted, the clamour of war numbed her ears.

'Ronnie, Ronnie.' Her restless spirit moaned as it drowned in the pursuit of a blurry illusion.

Leaving her in charge of all his assets, Ronnie had gone off to fight. She was free! Free like the spirit when it leaves the body, alone and lost.

'You haven't gone, Ronnie, this can't be true, you heartless man, you can't run away like this,' she called as if she could make him hear her, as if she had imprisoned him. 'Listen, Ronnie . . .' but no one heard her. Dark, swirling clouds gathered overhead.

'Wait, wait,' she pleaded with the threatening storm, 'everything will be all right, wait, don't push so hard . . . or else these tightened strings will snap . . . you've gone, Ronnie!' she cried in a stifled, choking voice. But she couldn't scream. Then, all at once, the new life heard her cry. The first shudder of life fluttered like a wave and floated through her body. The forces that were drowning slowly began to re-emerge from the darkness, the strings that had become taut gradually began to slacken.

The pain swelling inside her flowed from her eyes, her sobs turned into laughter and, shedding the terrifying feeling of being attacked, she crawled out from under the squalid rubble . . . alone?

The mother in America, so anxious to knit all the woollens, Ronnie, borne on winged cobras and flying towards the jaws of death . . . and a life closer to her than her own self – was she alone in the midst of this expansive clan? True, they are far away from each other, thousands of miles separate them, but at this moment she felt as though the whole world had shrunk into her own being. Her loneliness was inhabited by such a hustle and bustle today, how well-lit was the isolation of her quarters, how incredulous she was today, but so happy! She had never felt so weak and so courageous, so anxious and so content. And how beautiful the world appeared, how precious life was!

And Ronnie!

Her heart sank. Poor Ronnie, alone and empty-handed! She felt sorry for his impoverishment, just as if she would feel sorry for a wretched beggar shivering in the cold outside her palace window.

'You thief!' she scolded the newly enriched being. 'You also robbed a heartless tyrant.'

Taking short steps, as if she were spellbound, as if there were tiny clusters of silver bells tied to her ankles, she made her way to her bed, sat down, and slowly rested her tired head on the pillow.

Glossary

ahimsa   Indian doctrine of non-violence

alif-bay   first two letters of Urdu alphabet

anar   pomegranate

anchal   section of *dupatta*; also name of wedding ritual involving use of *anchal*

arree/array   informal form of address

arsi-mus'haf   wedding ritual during which bride and groom look at each other's faces in a mirror

banarsi   silk shot with gold thread

Band-e-matram   first words of patriotic song by the Bengali novelist, Bankim Chatterji, popular during the freedom movement

bibi   'miss' or 'madam'; or 'dear girl', 'dear lady', etc

bindi   dot of colour placed in centre of forehead as ornamentation by Hindu women

burka   garment worn by Muslim women to conceal face and body

carom   board game played with round black and white discs and a red disc called the 'Queen'

chat   spicy potpourri made with chick peas, potatoes, tomatoes etc

chausar   game resembling pachisi

choli   small, tight blouse

daal   lentils

dahi baray chat   snack with a yoghurt base

Devdas   eponymous hero of a famous Bengali novel by Sarat Chatterji

devdasi   female worshipper living in the temple

dupatta   long scarf-like garment worn by women

eidi   money given at Eid

faluda   flour noodles eaten with crushed ice and sugar syrup

firni   sweet riceflour and milk dessert

gazak   sweetmeat made of sesame and sugar

gharara   type of garment with flared legs, gathered on the lower section, worn by women

gopis   milkmaids, companions of the young god Krishna

gulab jamuns   fried sweetmeat made from flour and dipped in sugar syrup

Hanuman   Hindu monkey god; see *Lanka*

havan   oblation to the gods; ritual fire sacrifice of Hindus

hoories   celestial nymphs

jalebis   syrupy sweetmeat

jan   life

jhumar   ornament worn on the forehead

ji   title of respect

jim   seventh letter of Urdu alphabet

kameez   tunic-like garment

kachori   spicy snack

khadar   homespun fabric

kheer   sweet rice and milk dessert

khichri   rice cooked with lentils

Khizr   prophet famous for his immortality; also known as spiritual guide

Khuda hafiz   Muslim mode of farewell meaning 'God be with you'

Kok Sastra   medieval treatise on erotica by Koka

kotha   place where dancing girls live and perform

koti   waistcoat-like garment worn over shirt

kumkum   ornamental dot worn on forehead by Hindu women, also called *bindi*

kurta   tunic-like shirt

ladoo   sweetmeat in the shape of small balls

Lanka   kingdom belonging to Ravan, leader of the demons subjugated by Rama in the *Ramayana*. Ravan abducted Rama's wife Sita, and Hanuman, the monkey-god, freed her

lehnga   skirt-like garment extending to the ankles

Madhavi   an actress

Mehmud Ghaznavi   Turko-Afghan king also known as Mahmud of Ghazni, he began raids into India in 997 and formed a dynasty of Ghaznavid kings

mehr   marriage-portion settled on wife before marriage

missi   slivers of fennel stalks used for cleaning teeth

moorah   chair or stool woven from straw

mushaira   gathering of poets in which each poet recites his work and receives praise

Nadir Shah   powerful Persian general, Nadir Quli, who ascended the

Persian throne as Nadir Shah in 1736. In 1739 he invaded Delhi and defeated Mughals

namaz   Muslim prayer ritual

nikah   Muslim marriage ritual

niyat   section of prayer in which intent of prayer is proclaimed

paan-dan   container for *paan* (betel-leaf) and accoutrements for its preparation

Padmini   Rajput queen of Chitor famous for her beauty and bravery

pakori chat   spicy snack

panjtan pak   the five holy persons: the Prophet Muhammad, his daughter Fatima, his son-in-law Ali, his grandsons Husain and Hasan

paranda   special adornment used for braiding hair

parathas   type of flat bread cooked with butter

phulki   spicy snack made from chickpea powder

pulao   rice made with meat and spices

qushka   sectarian mark made by Hindus on the forehead with sandal paste

Raja Inder   Hindu god Indra

Ramchanderji/Rama/Ram   hero of great epic poem *Ramayana*. Husband of Sita. Deified as an incarnation of Hindu god, Vishnu

Rani of Jhansi   Indian warrior queen famous for courage in fighting the British in 1857–8

rasgullas   sweetened round balls made from cheese and dipped in sugar syrup

rewari   crisp, sugary toffee topped with sesame seeds

sajdah   portion of Muslim prayer involving touching forehead to the ground

Sarat, bridge of   considered by Muslims to be an extremely narrow bridge everyone will have to traverse on Judgement Day with only the righteous making it across

sarkar   chief, master, the British–Indian government

satyagraha   struggle for truth – a movement for reform through passive resistance, initiated by Gandhi

sehra   diadem worn by bridegroom/bride

Shab Qadr   the 27th of Ramzan when the Koran is said to have descended from heaven

shalwar   specially cut trousers worn by men and women

shami kebab   special kind of heavily spiced kebabs

shehbala   young man or male child accompanying bridegroom and usually dressed like him *sherwani*   type of knee-length coat worn by men

Sitaji/Sita   wife of Rama, with whom she voluntarily spent fourteen years of exile; exemplary wife

suad   twentieth letter of Urdu alphabet

Sulochana   an actress

Surdas   blind Hindu poet-singer

tasbih   prayer beads, like a rosary

tehsildar   sub-collector of revenue

tika   gold or silver ornament worn in the centre of forehead

ubtan   paste composed of turmeric, oil and perfume rubbed on the body

urad   type of lentil

zuad   twenty-first letter of Urdu alphabet